THE
MUMMY
BLOGGERS

HOLLY WAINWRIGHT

Legend Press Ltd, 107-111 Fleet Street, London, EC4A 2AB
info@legend-paperbooks.co.uk | www.legendpress.co.uk

Contents © Holly Wainright 2017
First published in 2017 by Allen & Unwin, 83 Alexander St, Crows Nest
NSW 2065, Australia | www.allenandunwin.com
The right of the above author to be identified as the author of this work has
been asserted in accordance with the Copyright, Designs and Patents Act
1988. British Library Cataloguing in Publication Data available.

Print ISBN 978-1-78955-0-535
Ebook ISBN 978-1-78955-0-542
Set in Times. Printing managed by Jellyfish Solutions Ltd.
Cover design by Kari Brownlie | www.karibrownlie.co.uk

Holly Wainwright is a writer, editor and broadcaster. Originally from Manchester in the north of England, she's been living in Sydney for more than twenty years and has built a career there in print and digital publishing, most recently as Head of Entertainment at Mamamia Women's Network. Holly also hosts a podcast about family called This Glorious Mess, has two small children, a partner called Brent and wishes there were four more hours in every day.

Follow Holly
@hollycwain

For Brent McKean.
The heart of our family.
His mother's son.

APRIL

CHAPTER ONE

ELLE
The Stylish Mumma

30,167 people know how Elle and Adrian met.

That's how many followers Elle's anonymous blog—Somebody Else's Husband—had at the height of its infamy.

More people than lived in the small brown town where Elle grew up had followed the story of a young personal trainer and the married financier she'd met at the gym.

A sample post:

> Today, Reader [she was twenty-two, after all], I tried to resist A. When he looked at me Like That, I looked away. When he touched my arm Like That (in front of Adam from Zumba!!!) I pulled away. I know what I am doing is wrong. But Reader. How do I stop myself from running towards the only thing that feels right to me???? The only thing that ever has. When I am in his arms, even though I am afraid, I feel safe. It's the strangest thing. I CAN'T FIGHT IT.

That was true—Elle couldn't fight it—because there was nothing to fight. Only a plan to follow through. One night she stayed long after her last class and walked into the deserted men's changing room and right into Adrian's shower cubicle.

Unsurprisingly, that night had inspired the blog's most clicked-on post. Ever.

Elle shut her laptop when she heard footsteps outside the kitchen. Adrian had no idea that that particular blog existed. Not then, not now. But Elle had no intention of unpublishing Somebody Else's Husband. She loved that it lived on, a vivid memento of who she once was. The kind of woman who wrote florid sentences like:

> The smell of my pussy reminds me of A. I think about him the way I used to fantasise about Ryan Gosling. OMG. A and I are living our very own Notebook!

These days Elle blogged under her own name, but about much tamer topics. Her most recent post featured freshly baked beetroot-chocolate brownies, Instagrammed with the hashtag #treatday.

The picture was perfection, of course. A high-angled selfie, it took in Elle biting into a brownie, panning down just enough to show her cropped white gym top and tanned, flat stomach. You could see the edge of the oven behind her, brand name visible, and a glimpse of her new ironbark kitchen benchtop— which, she knew, would generate as many comments as the cakes. Or her abs.

She tipped the brownies into her motion-sensor stainless steel bin, immediately followed by the Organic Annie's packet they'd arrived in. If she left them out, Adrian would be on them in a heartbeat. He couldn't afford that, in her opinion.

Elle had always had a critical eye—possibly, she thought, as the result of growing up in a house where there was much to criticise. She had always felt like she was observing and running commentary on her life from afar. Now, of course, she actually was: she and 154,158 others.

If Somebody Else's Husband had granted her blogging training wheels, The Stylish Mumma was her masterpiece—a tangle of relatable mum-confession and aspirational lifestyle porn. She had changed tack at exactly the moment Instagram had started rewarding aesthetics with armies of followers. And she knew what they wanted.

Her new kitchen, for example. When she and Adrian had begun to renovate their dream glass-and-white box in Melbourne's beachside suburb of Brighton, she'd known that the kitchen would be the heart of her home. Not for her family, but for her followers. It would be the room that made every other woman in Australia feel bad about her kitchen.

And so it was. Sophisticated from every angle, it was a white-on-white masterpiece that barely needed a filter.

Whenever Elle needed a boost, she would open her fridge—the giant, French-doored beast was stacked with shiny, labelled containers. Everything was in its place, so there was no need to rummage around: 'Kale', 'Spinach', 'Rocket', all in identical Tupperware, with lids in primary colours. Then the grains, the proteins, the sliced fruit for the boys.

The fridge was the opposite of the ones in the kitchens of her childhood. From whichever council pick-up those appliances had come, they all had blackened corners and cracked plastic shelves that sagged under the weight of her dad's half-slab. All the kids knew never to take anything from a fridge without a suspicious poke and sniff: discarded apple halves, open yoghurt pots with peeled-back lids, half-eaten cans of beans, hard-edged cheese ends. And always a curdled last-inch of milk.

Elle's own fridge had a compartment just for plucked grapes that had been washed and chilled in the crisper. Her boys—should they grow tall enough or behave well enough to be allowed—could help themselves to crunchy, fresh goodness day and night. And one day, she felt sure, they would.

Her sons wouldn't share her secret fetish for 'poor-people food', as she and her sister had called it: baked beans, packet mac and cheese, two-minute noodles, tinned spaghetti. Salt. Slop. Fat. It tempted and disgusted her in equal measure. Whereas the labelled tub of kimchi on the middle shelf? It made her feel virtuous, in control, beyond temptation. So, the brownies were in the bin.

Elle's kitchen was a reminder of how far she'd come.

'Want me to do anything else before I go?' asked Cate, from the doorway. 'I've laid out the boys' clothes for the next three days in the dressing-room, and we're scheduled through till Tuesday lunchtime.'

Cate never came into the kitchen. Elle hadn't made an explicit rule, but she knew people familiar with the house could sense the force field around her showpiece. Any interloper was bound to put something in the wrong place. Any foot aside from Elle's on the polished concrete floor felt like a child's muddy hand on a fresh white summer dress.

'I think we're good, Cate. How's it looking?'

'Reach is down a little bit, but to be honest recipes aren't going as well as the homes posts at the moment.'

Cate was Elle's social media manager and unofficial au pair. Twenty-one and vibrating with ambition, she had practically stalked Elle, working for free until she was invited to stay. A girl from Sydney's western suburbs who wanted what Elle had—influence and an expensive wardrobe—she tried to style herself on the boss, spending most of each day tapping away at the phone and laptop in her no-name active wear.

What Cate didn't know about social media hadn't been thought of yet, but as an au pair she'd had a lot to learn. Elle had made it clear to Cate that her boys were on a strict daily routine. On Day Two, she'd come home from a photoshoot to find Cate feeding them spaghetti bolognaise in front of *Canimals*. That was nipped in the bud with a printed-out hourly schedule of exactly where Freddie and Teddy should be at any given moment, along with what they should be doing and the foods they should be eating. 'Don't use your initiative when it comes to the boys,' Elle had told Cate firmly. 'Just follow the rules.'

'I'll be home before eleven,' Cate was saying now. 'I think tomorrow's outfit post is going to go gangbusters.'

Elle had recently started a daily post to showcase her sons' outfits.

At two and three, Elle's 'Irish twins' were, she recognised, at the pinnacle of their cuteness, with their overgrown black curls and their mother's green eyes. She could barely keep up with the parcels of free clothes that streamed through the door. Tiny polo shirts and hipster tees, boat shoes and cargo shorts, skinny jeans and drop-crotch leggings, hats and scarves and socks and satchels — all of which would have looked perfectly acceptable on a grown man at a creative agency in Brunswick. The only things missing on her two little #dudes were the beards.

She'd dedicated a whole room to their wardrobe, outfits chosen well in advance and recorded on a polaroid board before posting, to keep track of sponsorships and avoid double-ups. It was almost a full-time job to curate and record the boys' aesthetic — 'It's Prince George meets Harry Styles,' was how Elle and Cate described it to interested PRs.

Elle knew her sons were on the edge of rebellion about the now-weekly shoot. Adrian, too, had his reservations about the boys' photos — after all, he was a 47-year-old man who had, before he'd met Elle, considered fashion to be two things: a suit in the week and a polo shirt on weekends. But the engagement was too good to lose. And anyway, planning the kids' outfits days ahead made her feel calm.

'You know why you're obsessed with order, don't you?' Adrian had said to her on one of their early dates, at that stage in a relationship when the other's neuroses are still charming puzzles to be solved.

That stage in their relationship when he was cheating on his wife.

'It's because you had none when you were growing up. You're obsessed with keeping everything in its place because you think the chaos can't get you then.'

This wasn't news to Elle, a long-time devotee of self-improvement books and life-coaching seminars. And she armchair-analysed Adrian right back — not aloud, of course — quickly diagnosing him with a rescue complex. The more vulnerable she seemed, the more invested he would be.

Elle now felt the same way about her followers. She knew how to keep them interested — she knew that they needed aspiration. They needed to know that their own messy lives were a temporary state, that a broken bird could become a beautiful swan.

Her tribe needed to live and breathe that fairytale so they could believe that one day they too would have a kitchen with a spray tap and a Thermomix, even if they'd grown up with a shitty dad and currently made do with a stick blender.

Elle made sure to reveal just enough of herself, of her story, to attach and keep her followers. She exuded enough success to have them want to see her every day, but she remained vulnerable enough that they didn't completely hate her. She spoke the language of gratitude while appearing to have it all.

As a woman who had already reinvented herself more than once, she'd never felt so well-qualified for anything in her life. After all, her kitchen proved that anything was possible.

'You go, Cate,' she said, when she realised that the girl was still standing there with a fixed smile, unable to leave without permission. 'Have fun! Adrian and I have got the boys.' Actually, iPads had got the boys — a guaranteed way to silence preschoolers.

Cate obviously had a date: she was wearing lipstick and a skirt that could have passed as a belt, and she fairly sprinted out of the house at her boss's wave. Pretty girl, thought Elle, but she could do so much more with herself.

Elle swivelled on her high-backed white leather stool and opened the laptop.

A #grateful day.

Ever had one of those days, Mummas, where you realise that maybe, just maybe, you're doing a good job at this mothering thing after all? One of those days where you can see all of the tiny sacrifices you make for your family paying off?

I feel that way today. The sunlight is coming in through my kitchen window. The washing up is done, the laundry is folded away, the kitchen smells of warm, comforting home cooking. It smells of love. I have just finished baking some #healthytreats for my family that I know will nourish them and make them smile.

It's one of those days when I'm so grateful that I made the choice to stay at home and put my energy into what matters. One of those days when I know that making the effort to prepare healthy meals for my boys was the right decision. It's a day when I'm so happy that I have been the one on the floor playing trains with them.

It's one of those days when I know that everything I have been through, I have been through so I could get to be right here today, in my beautiful home with my three beautiful men. There's nothing like a #grateful day. I hope you're having one, too. And if today's been tough, know that tomorrow can be better #loveandlight

Elle snapped another selfie to go with her post. I am grateful that my new lip filler has settled, she thought, but didn't type. I am grateful that Cate is getting paid to play trains with the boys. I'm grateful for Organic Annie's home-delivery brownies. I'm grateful it's not the day when Adrian's girls come over to sulk at me. I'm grateful I am not Feral Abi.

'Come on, boys, it's bathtime!' Elle called through the kitchen door.

CHAPTER TWO

ABI

The Green Diva

Abi got called a 'dangerous cunt' twenty-five times a day. On average.

She wore it as a badge of honour. She'd had it turned into a meme, a T-shirt and a bumper sticker for the people mover. She was thinking of writing it on her passport form, should she ever leave the country again.

This morning, Abi was looking at her dangerous-cunt self in the tarnished bathroom mirror and wondering if her followers would ever let her get away with botox. She yanked a handful of curls back from her hairline with full force.

'Gracey, is there such a thing as organic botox?' Abi shouted through the open bathroom door.

'Yes. Babe, it's called "acceptance".'

'Fuck that.' Abi had a camera crew arriving soon for an *interview on An Evening Affair*, and every time she saw her head looming large on TV she felt like kicking the screen in. Who *was* that old bag, anyway?

'You're just freaking out because rent-a-quote are on their

way,' said Grace, coming into the bathroom barefoot and sticking a kiss on Abi's bare shoulder. To Abi, Grace smelt, like she looked, of sunshine and oatmeal and all things golden and good. 'Don't worry about it. They're not looking at your face, they're listening to your words.'

'Now, even you know that's bullshit.' Abi turned to Grace and kissed her lips.

'*MUUUUUUUUUUUUM!*'

Suddenly Otto was between them—he always was, it seemed. Grace's younger son, he was a tangle of seven-year-old neediness, wild hair, bare feet and knock-knees too big for his spindly legs.

'Sol's bashing Arden, and Alex is drawing anime on the kitchen wall. And I can't find my shoooooooooooooooes.'

Abi sighed into Grace's smile and they separated, Grace taking Otto's hand and walking him out of the bathroom, onto the bare boards of the bedroom, and down the squeaking staircase to where the mayhem of the morning routine was in full swing. Theirs was a household that ran mostly on chaos theory, where the kids had as much say as the adults, but some things still needed to be achieved each day.

This year, Otto had decided to start going to school, instead of being home-schooled like his brother and stepsisters. He now needed shoes every morning, and someone to get in the van and take him into Daylesford. It had been a shock to the household's system. But hey, sometimes Abi understood exactly why the poor kid needed windows of escape from the madhouse—she certainly did.

Still staring into the bathroom mirror, she muttered to herself, 'Maybe I'll ask the people.'

In the bedroom, she rummaged around in the unmade sheets to find her phone under the pillow. She snapped a selfie and tapped out a caption.

> Too wrinkly for TV? Any ideas for a botox substitute that doesnt fill my frontal lobes with poison?????

She added a skull and crossbones emoji for good measure, hit Post and threw her phone back on the bed, then started to dig through the piles on the floor for something to wear. She knew that when she picked up her phone again in a few minutes, there would already be a stream of validation.

No KWEEN, your PERFECT. #keepitreal

There isn't a wrinkle on your wise head, honey. For reals.

Laughter lines are LIFE, sister. Never become one of those blank Instagram bitches. You're so much better than that.

YOU DO YOU, darling.

And, of course:

Neck yourself now and save the money, you Dangerous Cunt.

Abi liked to think of all this as her Greek chorus of support and affirmation and shit-kicking awfulness. It was hard to imagine life without it.

An Evening Affair wanted her opinion on the Melbourne woman who'd been thrown out of a cafe for breastfeeding her four-year-old daughter. The woman in question had gone to ground, but a helpful bystander had captured the whole thing: the child standing beside her mother and suckling, the cafe manager charging over, hands waving, the woman tearily gathering her kid and her bags and practically sprinting out of the place. Now that matter was all over the internet and the breakfast shows, face pixelated, being called a 'pervert' and a 'sicko' and an 'incestuous bitch'.

Abi was more than happy to pull on her armour and go to

war with the Parenting Police for a like-minded sister. The *AEA* producer had known exactly what he was going to get—that was why he'd called her, why he always called her for stories like this. 'Just be you, Abi. Tell us why we're wrong.'

Even before doing the interview, Abi knew that the very next shot after her soundbite— 'It's not that poor woman who's sick, it's the society that thinks there's something sexual about a mother feeding her child. If that's what you see here, ask yourself what's wrong with *you*? Are *YOU* the real pervert?'—would be of a reasonable-looking paediatrician in a frock making a point about there being no *need* to breastfeed your children past one, or even at all.

But Abi didn't give a fuck.

In the past two years, she'd realised that the only way to get anyone to listen to you was to keep it simple and shout the loudest. Clouding your argument with nuance was the road to oblivion, in Abi's book, and she was very clear on what she stood for.

Ironically, it was her treacherous suit of an ex-husband who had taught her all about brands. And now she was one.

Suck on that, Adrian, she thought, as she yanked a blue top that she knew worked for the cameras from the pile on the floor, sniffed it and pulled it on. All she needed now was one of her signature chunky bead necklaces and a dab of matte red lipstick, and she'd be ready to battle with the tabloid masses.

Reinvention was the only thing she had in common with Adrian's replacement wife.

'Hardly the *only* thing,' she could almost hear Grace correct her.

Okay, okay. Some children. A blog. Possibly some crossover audience. A few secrets.

Abi laughed, as she always did when she let herself think about what was going on in that sterile modern box in the city. Whenever Arden and Alex came home from the (very) rare weekends at Dad's, she pumped them for information.

But really, she didn't need to. She followed Elle's posts with interest—from a fake account, obviously. She'd seen the new kitchen. She'd clocked the new boobs. She knew replacement wife wasn't worried about the poison in botox.

But Abi hadn't seen—and loved to imagine—Elle's face when her tween and teen turned up with their unbrushed hair and their henna tatts and their steampunk-meets-the-littlest-hobo outfits, stomping their big boots on her white fluffy rugs and smearing their sticky fingers across her all-glass everything.

Speaking of which, Abi could hear the monsters downstairs, still fighting despite Grace's insistence that it was time to calm down and think about what lessons they wanted to learn today. She really ought to weigh in.

But first, a quick post for the people. Back to the phone and some furious finger-typing.

TODAY'S WAR CRY:
Today, my Green Divas, I am calling to arms and heading into battle with the culture, yet again.
Today, I continue to fight to keep us out of that subservient place where THEY want us—doing everything by the new rule-book that none of us helped write.

Whatever shape your day takes today, remember this: There's a reason you're not one of the sheep. There's a reason you're reading this blog right now.

There's a reason the goddess gave you your own mind.

When the world is telling you your child doesn't fit in and you need to fix him, tell them where to go.

When they're trying to sell you all that processed food that kills you slowly, tell them you nourish yourself and your family with authenticity and you wouldn't spread that crap on your garden.

When they're telling you that you love too hard

and too loud, tell them one day they might realise their little lives are just a pale imitation of yours.

You are POWERFUL, never forget it. Your choices are powerful. Parent fiercely. Love loudly. Hit life with all the gusto you can summon from the earth.

Today's a big day. Live large.

PS: You can see me on An Evening Affair, 6.30 tonight, Channel 8. xx

Oh, and:
A quick message to my GD Becca, who messaged me to say her kid's teacher had been complaining about her boy's beautiful hair: Remember, cutting and combing against his will does not make you a 'good mother', it makes you a violator of his personal space and free will. Tell that teacher to do their job and stop imposing their bullshit rules on a little person who's more than capable of setting their own compass. We're with you. #divapower #fighttheman

A yell from downstairs yanked Abi off the bed. She guessed it was up to her to take Otto into town today. She'd make it back in time for the film crew.

CHAPTER THREE

LEISEL
The Working Mum

If one more of Leisel's colleagues told her how exhausted they were, she might just pull their hair.

In the lift this morning, she'd been sandwiched between two millennials in sunglasses, complaining over their takeaway coffee cups. The young women were tired because they'd worked back the night before, then gone drinking at that ironic new '80s pop-up bar. It *was* exhausting, eating ironic $22 Jatz and French onion dip and sipping ironic tequila sunrises until midnight, and then getting up at seven to make it to Barre Body before you could collapse into your chair and consume your first oversized cold-drip.

Leisel was tired because she was forty-three and had a baby, a toddler and a child in kindergarten. She was also the managing editor of a group of women's magazines. Once upon a time, she had been managing editor of *one* women's magazine—a feisty feminist glossy called *HER*—but in the new media world order, she was now responsible for five ever-sunnier titles.

Most mornings, like this one, when she was smiling along to Snapchat stories in the office kitchen, the only thing staving off exhausted sobs was the prospect of the kettle boiling and delivering her a caffeinated beverage that she could drink all the way to the bottom.

Last night, she'd made it home just in time to kiss The Toddler—Rich—and feed The Baby—Harriet—before their bedtime. Then she'd done home readers with The Kindy Kid—Maggie.

Then came an hour of what she labelled The Returns: walking small children back to their beds, over and over, until they stuck. She did a solid session of 'shush and pat' with The Baby, and finally, finally, she was able to back out of the big bedroom the kids all shared, picking up bottles and onesies and teeny-tiny plastic toys as she went.

It was 8.30 p.m. She took off her shoes and her work clothes and turned to her husband, Mark—who, after a solid day of kid duty, had handed over to her as soon as she got home. While she'd been doing the bedtime dance, he'd been sitting on the lounge, watching the news, putting in a cameo only when Baby Harri demanded it. It occurred to Leisel as she got into her pyjamas, her work make-up only a smeared memory, that she and Mark hadn't looked at each other once since she'd got home.

There he was. Crumpled, tired around the eyes, wearing his decidedly non-office uniform: a faded White Stripes T-shirt, baggy dark shorts, bare feet. He hadn't shaved in three days. This is what a stay-at-home dad looks like in 2017, she thought. Like an ageing rocker with nowhere to be.

She asked Mark about his day. His eyes still on the screen, he told her about Harri's tooth and what the teacher had said at pick-up. He told her that a local furniture-maker had offered him a couple of jobs for the coming week, so they should ask Wendy from next door to pick the kids up one afternoon, she'd generally do it on her day off...

Leisel's internal to-do list began to spool. She had to keep reminding herself to listen to her husband.

'Your sister called me,' Mark was saying. 'She said you're not answering your phone. She's coming to Sydney with Abi soon. Wants to see you. That won't be awkward at all.'

Shit, that was right. Leisel's little sister was her favourite person, but ever since Leisel's blog had broken fifty thousand followers, things had been complicated. Abi seemed to consider her sister-in-law competition, rarely missing an opportunity to take a dig at blogs like Leisel's, whose fans she labelled 'Corporate Slaves'.

'I'll call Grace tomorrow,' Leisel told Mark. When Abi isn't home, she added in her head.

Apparently she and Mark were talked out. Dinner was a wordless affair in front of a recorded *Australian Story*. Then Leisel took care of a tedious line-up of household must-dos and work emails before bed, where Mark read for his obligatory, pre-sleep five minutes and she opened her laptop, clicked her blog's Facebook page and wrote:

> I think The Baby likes Wonder Dad better than me. In fact, I know it. When I came in tonight she was almost down. I went to give her a bed-time bottle and she squirmed out of my arms, reaching for him.
>
> Part of me was hurt, but part of me was relieved. WD had to take over and, you know what? I was just happy to let go of a job, to scratch one thing off The List. After all, I still had to read to The Toddler and try to squeeze in homework with The Kindy Kid.
>
> Am I the worst mother in the world for quietly loving the fact that TB only likes WD to give her the bed-time bottle??? Anyone else?

Then Leisel rolled over to sleep next to a gently snoring Mark, knowing that if she was lucky, she probably had two hours ahead of her.

As she slept, the responses rolled in from night-moving mothers all over the country.

> Oh, darling, you're putting on a brave face. Of course The Baby loves his mummy. Chin up! #mumknowsbest

> I love it when the kids ask for their Daddy in the night! Not an ounce of mum guilt here. #freedom

> I wish my two would even ask for their dad. He's hardly ever here, he'd have to be reminded of their names! #allmen

Harriet woke at midnight, as she always did, and Leisel remembered the promise she and Mark made themselves every night: Harri would NOT be getting a midnight bottle. Of course, by 12.12 Leisel was at the microwave, pushing buttons, warming the formula.

The beeping woke Rich, as it always did, and he whined his way out of the kids' room and into sleeping next to Daddy in 'the big bed'. Leisel lay on the floor beside Harri's cot, patting her through the bars as she finished her bottle and finally went back to sleep.

A shiver of cold and a sharp pain in Leisel's shoulder woke her up. She was on the floor next to Harri's cot, again. She went to the marital bedroom only to find both Rich and Maggie snoring next to Mark. Back in the kids' room, she tried to squeeze her considerable self into the bottom of their IKEA bunk. Every night, every time, she cursed her and Mark's misguided decision not to buy the king single beds that all her friends had bought for their kids. What an indulgence, she'd thought at the time, not knowing that it would be her feet dangling off the end of those cheap bunk beds.

Then she was up again at 4 a.m. when Harriet pulled herself to her feet in her cot and screamed her little red head off. Remembering the last passive-aggressive note from their neighbours, Leisel headed back to the microwave for another bottle. She turned around to find Rich staring at her: 'I want to sleep with you, Mummy.' It was such a rare request that Leisel couldn't refuse, returning to the kids' room with the toddler under one arm and the bottle in the other. She settled Harri, lay next to her son and willed herself another hour's rest.

But Rich wanted to talk. Guilt prevented her from shutting down his commentary on what had happened at preschool because, hell, it wasn't like she'd been around to see or hear any of it.

'That's lovely, Richie, go to sleep darling,' she whispered as a list of grievances against every other kid in the centre was recounted.

'And then Sookie pushed me over, and Savannah stole my Lego, and then Little Archie called me a bad name, and DO YOU KNOW WHAT MISS EMMA DID?'

'No, Rich, but could you go back to sleep now? You'll be tired, darling.'

'Nothing. She did *nothing*, Mummy. My heart was broken.'

Leisel's was too, by that point.

Then she heard the bleat of her iPhone alarm and tipped herself out of the narrow bed in a commando roll, sprinting down the hall to get to it before it woke Maggie and Mark. Too late. Now everyone was up but Harri, who was, miraculously, asleep again. Mark was filthy at being disturbed so early, and it was clear that Leisel's planned hour of pre-breakfast writing had just been scrubbed from the schedule.

Instead, Leisel defused three fights before she left the house for work — including one between herself and Mark — and wiped three shitty bottoms, packed two lunches and made five breakfasts (everyone wanted something different, obviously).

As she walked out the door with Maggie and Rich and their assortment of unfeasibly heavy bags, Mark — with Harri on his hip — asked, 'What time will you be home? Not late, right? I've got a Meeting tonight.' And Leisel felt that familiar twist of acid in her stomach: she would have to find a way to tell Zac—her 27-year-old boss—that she couldn't stay for deadline. Again.

'Of course not, babe. I'll see you later.' She bumped the door closed with her bum.

***

After Leisel managed not to cry in front of the millennials in the office kitchen, she took her hot tea back to her desk. Before she got to her 128 unread emails, she tapped out a status update.

> Not for the first time, guys, I find myself asking: How did I get here? Tell me, how did you get there? Doing everything. For everyone. All. The. Time. Failing. Stressed. Exhausted. Is this just 'one of those days'? or is every day just one of those days????? full blog post tonight. Chins up ladies.

And then turned to TweetDeck:

> Full blog post coming tonight, WMs, if you can send me enough energy to get that far. Firing last of mine your way #runningonempty

That should tide them over, she thought. Leisel's intensely loyal army of followers were as exhausted as she was. She thought of them—and the flood of correspondence proved her right—as slumped over their phones at night, clutching their glasses of wine like lifelines, taking a break from the work-mails and the washing mountain to find a little solace in a life every bit as chaotic as their own.

Until a couple of her blog posts had gone viral, Leisel had had no idea there were quite so many frazzled women in need of a place to vent every night. None of them knew exactly how they had got there, but in Leisel (aka The Working Mum) they found someone whose life experiences mirrored their own: after a million seemingly insignificant decisions, they had become parents at just the moment when their bodies wanted to lie down, but they still needed to lean in.

Leisel clicked on her untackled inbox. At the top was an email from her boss.

Leisel—I need to talk to you just as soon as you have a moment. Zac xxxx

That 'xxxx' seemed like one big F-you. Whatever he wanted to see her about, it wouldn't end in understanding hugs and air kisses.

She steeled herself, stood up and walked to Zac's nook— he didn't have an office, no one had an office. 'You wanted to see me?'

'Leisel.' Zac pushed his chair back, looking into her face but not quite meeting her eyes. He wore an almost-black T-shirt that was faded and lightly frayed at the neck, skinny white jeans and hi-tops that Leisel knew cost $350—they'd been in the men's pages of the latest *BUY THIS,* one of her titles. He was so young and so white, almost transparent. Leisel suppressed an urge to ask him if he ever went outside, the way that young people should. She looked at the four types of screens he had within a finger's reach and thought better of it.

'Zac. How's things?'

'Things are alright, you know. Alright.' He always struggled to make eye contact. Was it because he was always on the brink of delivering bad news, or was he just one of those young people she'd read about who found face-to-face interaction impossible? 'This is awkward, Leisel, but it's about your hours.'

'My hours?' Here we go, she thought.

'You know how much we value you around here. Your experience, your commitment.'

Uh-huh.

'But it's been brought to my attention that some of the other, um, other staff feel that you are not pulling your weight as part of the team.' Zac lifted his giant plastic smoothie cup and took a long sip from the straw. He looks like my preschooler, thought Leisel. This conversation must be causing him so much pain—confrontation is, like, the worst.

'You leave...' He stopped. Looked up at Leisel again. His eyes seemed almost pleading. He wanted her to put him out of his misery.

'I leave... ?' Leisel looked back. Eye contact, for almost seconds. 'Okay. I leave at five-thirty. Zac, you know I have to leave. I have three kids. I have to see them sometimes.'

'Oh, I know, Leisel, but you can see how that's not really my—'

'Problem. Not really your problem, I know.' Change tack, Leisel, she told herself. Think of the mortgage. 'Well, Zac, look. I always make a point of keeping one eye on emails and any changing status of production from home. What if I agree to always log back on at a certain time every night to check everything's off and running with the printers? I mean, I wasn't aware there was a problem, but if there's a problem, I want to fix it.'

Zac looked relieved. He wanted to give her a reprieve, she could tell. He didn't want to be the guy who fired The Mum. 'Well, that would be great. Let's say 8 p.m.? Just always check back in at 8 p.m.?'

'Sure, Zac. Eight p.m.' As if any of these office kids was still here at 8 p.m.

Leisel fleetingly wondered how she would manage to check in every night, smack-bang in the middle of The Returns, but she'd just have to talk to Mark.

'Is that it?' she asked Zac.

'Sure. Have a good day, Leisel. Lots to do!'

Yes. There was. Leisel went back to her desk. She could feel her emails shouting at her.

Can Juicy Tubes have the cover mount? They'll be two days past the deadline but PLEEEEEEASE?

She sat down and gulped a mouthful of lukewarm tea. She knew exactly what tonight's post would be. She also knew if Zac ever read it, he'd be horrified, but the unlikelihood of him ever reading a 'mummy blog' certainly worked in her favour. Leisel just needed to make it home to write it.

To Every Woman Who Has To Leave Early.
I hear you. I hear you making your excuses.
'I'm sorry. I'm so sorry.
Is it okay? I'll make it up. I didn't take a lunch break.
Yes, of course I'll log back on. Yes, of course I'll do five days' work in four. Yes. Of course, I understand my pay will reflect that I won't always make it in for the 9 a.m. meeting.'
To every woman who has a boss who doesn't understand that sometimes, sometimes, there are more important things in life than deadlines and reports.
There are children with fevers, and schoolkids who need to learn to read. There are babies who need feeding and there are teenagers who are online chatting to... who knows who.
To every woman who has ever felt bad for the people she's leaving behind at work and the people she's leaving behind at home.
To every woman who didn't get that promotion, wasn't considered for that pay rise, wasn't offered that new project... I know, you weren't 'front of mind'

because it's been six months since you went for after-work drinks.

To every woman whose boss is a man who has a wife at home and has no idea what 'she does all day'.

To every woman whose boss is a woman who hasn't had kids yet but knows when she does, she'll magically do a much better job than you're doing.

To every woman who's read every article on the internet about work–life balance and still can't find time to empty the school bag:

There are some things we all have that they don't, you know. Perspective. And each other.

You can make me feel small at work, Boss. But at home, the only people who can make me feel small are much, much tinier than you and they need me more.

Share this with someone who needs to be heard today. I did. And I'm lucky, because I have all of you to listen.

L—The Working Mum x

CHAPTER FOUR

ELLE

Tell me again how new mothers aren't interested in
having sex with their husbands.

Elle had written this line under a photo of a still-dripping
pregnancy test to announce she was expecting her second
baby when her first was only four months old.

That post was passed around by her then-modest following
of about two thousand, before it was picked up by a parenting
site that used it to hook a think-piece:

WOMEN WHO ARE SAYING YES TO SEX AFTER BABY

The commenters weren't kind—sample line: *SLUTS like
you should be thinking about your babies, not your sex
life*—but the story was followed by a rash of posts about
post-natal sex drive and the perfect age-gap between siblings,
and by the time a staffer at the *Daily Trail* had raided Elle's
Instagram account, she was on her way to going viral.

The *Trail* couldn't have been more delighted by what they
found—an opinionated young woman in various stages of
undress—and The Stylish Mumma became a goldmine for

them as Elle followed that post with a content series, 'Pregnant In Heels': a blow-by-blow account of the next eight months.

It's time to prove, once and for all, that the modern mumma does not do shapeless floral smocks and use Baby as an excuse for sensible shoes and letting her greys grow in. After all, when is there a more important time to present yourself with confidence and grace than when you're about to guide a little human into the world? Start as you mean to go on. Who's with me?

Lots of people. Elle's followers doubled, tripled and doubled again, as young women posted photo after photo to her blog. Always accompanying their selfies with modest captions about weight gain and 'out of control boobs', a slew of women showed their stomachs in swimwear—#bikinibumpshot—and pledged to stay 'hot' during pregnancy.

'What the hell are you going to write about now?' Elle's sister Zoe asked after she'd finished live-blogging Freddie's birth—the first 'gentle caesarean' to be reported by an Australian site, complete with a clear barrier sheet, vaginal swabbing and an Ed Sheeran playlist piped through the otherwise ordered-to-be-silent theatre.

'Don't worry about that,' said Elle. 'There's always something.'

And there was. The 'body bounce-back', obviously. That filled days and weeks and months with a training regime and ever-more flattering progress pictures. Endless Instagrams of salad bowls and breastmilk-encouraging protein shakes. Like, Like, Like.

Now, Cate was telling Elle that The Stylish Mumma had been nominated for Best Parenting Blog of 2017 at the Blog-ahhs, as part of a major tech-publishing conference sponsored by Silicon Valley firm ATGT. It was the first time the Blog-ahhs had been held in Australia—and it was, Cate insisted with phone-waving enthusiasm, a *very* big deal. The winner would score major investment, both in a hefty cash prize and in introductions to venture capitalists who could help Elle develop her blog into a full-scale business.

Cate also told her who the other two contenders were: Feral Abi (of course, and *as if*) and that whingeing working mum from Sydney, whom Elle had never met and never really read.

Elle wasn't worried. She could picture her name on that award. She could feel its weight in her hands. She was already counting the sponsorship money that would come pouring in as a result of this nomination—for starters, the Abbott's Smoothies contract that was up for grabs. They were looking to invest heavily in an influencer, and she knew she was it.

Last month, Elle had filled in the questionnaire from the Blog-ahh organisers:

DESCRIBE YOUR BLOG IN ONE WORD:
Inspirational.

WHY DID YOU START BLOGGING?
I see sharing as a gift. We are all going through the same things. We are all trying to make our lives that little bit better, more beautiful, more meaningful. I knew I had something to say to all those dedicated mums out there who are always trying to make themselves, their homes, their marriages, even their children, that little bit better. I am one of those women, and I knew I could help.

WHO ARE YOUR READERS?
They're women who really care about doing a great job of motherhood. They show their love to their families by cooking beautiful meals and making them a wonderful home, and by taking pride in themselves, too. We don't do baked beans on toast for dinner or school drop-off in our pyjamas at TSM!

WHAT ARE YOUR MOST POPULAR POSTS?

My work-out and kids' fashion posts are going very well at the moment, and my stories about my beginnings have also really resonated with my readers. Even my life wasn't always so great. It's important to acknowledge that. I have worked very hard to live my best life.

WHAT ADVICE WOULD YOU GIVE TO ASPIRING BLOGGERS?

Decide your aesthetic early. Don't be shouty. Keep yourself nice!

HOW DO YOU DEAL WITH TROLLS?

Four words: jealousy is a curse.

IF YOU WIN BLOGGER OF THE YEAR, WHAT'S YOUR BIG IDEA TO DEVELOP WITH ATGT?

We are working on a calorie-counting app for mums on the go. You can snap a photo of whatever you are going to eat or feed your kids, and the app will calculate the nutritional value of whatever it is you are about to put in your mouth! It's a complete game-changer.

The nomination was validation, Elle was certain, that she was doing everything right. Hiring Cate had been the perfect choice, she knew, even if it had come at a cost. TSM was on its way to the next level.

When the babies were small, Elle's sister had been around to help with social media promotion, but after she had thrown Zoe out of her house, it was clear she was going to have to hire an actual professional to work with her.

Until that day, Zoe had been the only member of her family Elle still spoke to at all.

***

Elle had called Zoe down from the country when she was pregnant with Freddie. At the time, Elle and her growing family were living in a Hampton townhouse while their Brighton glass box was finished. Elle invited Zoe to live with them.

'Like, serious?' asked Zoe, who had never been invited into Elle's new life before. 'You're going to pay for the flight?'

'Yesssss. Please, darling, I need you to help me. I promised Adrian this would be perfect, and it's not... perfect. Not yet.'

For Elle, kids had always seemed like something that needed to be ticked off a list — like eating your vegetables. You didn't want to be one of those women who didn't do it. You didn't want to be all alone when you were old. There were only two types of grown-up women: mothers and the pitied. And Elle did not do pity.

What she had done was give up working at the gym, encourage Adrian to sell the family home to buy the glass box, and stop taking her Pill.

When Elle told Adrian she was expecting their first child, he had only been out of a house ruled by children for less than a year. As she held up that dripping pee-stick, Adrian's eyes almost gave away his shock. Almost. Not quite.

Elle watched his smile struggle to reach his eyes — his status as a midlife cliché must have dawned on him then, if it hadn't already. He was swapping one tightly controlled life for another. One wife for another. One family for another. Expanding his set of responsibilities, rather than freeing himself from them, as it must have felt that evening in the shower at the gym.

'I'll be buying a fucking sports car next,' he mumbled in a weak moment, four Scotches into a solo Friday-night session.

'You already have one of those,' Elle muttered, before assuring him that everything, *everything* would be different this time — their children would not run their lives, they wouldn't fuck up her figure, they wouldn't sit above him on her pecking order. 'Just keep telling yourself: Elle's not Abi. Elle's not Abi.'

But as the months crept on, it was exhausting, even for Elle, to maintain this part of the bargain. Discipline is one thing: resistance to biology turned out to be quite another.

She banned Adrian from Teddy's birth, insisting she didn't want him to see her 'like that'. Then she blogged about this decision, of course.

> The last thing I want my husband to see me as is needy, sweaty and out-of-control. He doesn't need to bear witness to me howling or swearing or looking like a bedraggled mess. There's a REASON why men used to wait in the corridor with cigars, ladies. It was to keep them from the trauma of seeing the person they love most in the world at their most vulnerable... and yes, unattractive. There's no way A will be visiting me until bubba's had the goop cleaned off him and I've had access to a comb and some lipgloss. #keepitclassy.

She went through that labour without cheerleaders, other than ones who got paid.

With the help of a baby nurse and a downloaded regimen, Elle settled Teddy into a routine at four weeks, and she never wavered from it. Never. The only way she could deal with the chaotic horror of pregnancy, birth and raising a baby was to impose order on it all. She was holding on for dear life. And, as always, she was succeeding.

Elle was determined to show Adrian that she could handle everything: wrangling an active one-year-old (with a little hired help, of course), being the country's most glamorous new mother, keeping their home beautiful, planning their new one, running her blog.

Those parents she saw all around her, the ones whose lives were beholden to their kids' every whimper? She knew the truth about them: they were weak, plagued with guilt and fear.

The reason they couldn't get their lives in order was that they were terrified of getting it wrong—all the time. She was not.

She was getting it so right that she was pregnant again. And the news of the 'Irish twins' was a point of difference that could only help her blog, so she posted the pee-stick picture. After it went viral and she pledged to her growing social media 'army' that she would detail every step of this pregnancy, she realised she needed some more help. Someone she could trust. So... Zoe.

'Like, serious?'

Zoe was nineteen then. The youngest of Elle's four siblings. Her only sister. Just a tiny baby when their mother had died in a car accident on a high-speed country highway, Zoe had never known a life that wasn't Plan B. She had never known what it was like not to feel ripped off.

After their mother was gone, the five siblings hadn't grown closer. They'd retreated into their own survival modes.

Elle's oldest brother, Liam, had been MIA from an early age. Ten years old when he lost his mum, he had retreated, figuratively and literally—rarely around, always 'out bush'. Their dad tried for a while to keep tabs on him, but it proved too hard, too soon. Elle's few memories of Liam were of him appearing unannounced, wild-eyed and incoherent, on futile missions to scrounge for cash or something to sell. Those appearances stopped suddenly when Elle was fifteen. If she allowed herself to think about it, she imagined he was most likely in jail or dead, but she didn't allow herself to think about it very much.

Bobby and Kai were tougher. Solid little thugs in a small town. They'd run with the kids Elle imagined their mother would never have let them near, and by the time they were teens, they were mostly drunk, fighting and fucking. They visited dramatic scenes on the front yards of the family's rental houses: weeping women with bruised arms, or tattooed men yelling about their cars. But 'the boys', as her dad called them, were tight—they had each other. They were still living in the town, as far as Elle knew, working on-and-off on surrounding properties, drinking in the same pubs they'd snuck into when they were fifteen, fighting with the same blokes. The thought of it made her itch.

They surely didn't know she was Facebook famous. They didn't do social media.

Zoe had got out. Sort of. She'd been working on properties since she was twelve and, like Elle, she possessed a discipline that had seen her hide that money hard and save up for a crappy car. At sixteen, she drove it out of town, stopped to pick up a hitcher—and promptly moved in with him and his parents. She'd made it a hundred k's to the next town along, slightly bigger, slightly less full of people who hated her brothers. The hitcher was feckless, and Zoe took jobs in pubs and cafes, and presumably also worked hard at not getting pregnant, until she finally gathered the nerve to leave him.

Elle thought of all this as Zoe's *Escape, Interrupted* and was thankful that back when it was her turn, she had got the bus.

***

When Elle called, Zoe was deciding which fork in the road to take next. Literally. She had parked her battered Gemini at the highway turn-off and was sitting behind the steering wheel, chain-smoking, listening to the Dixie Chicks and wondering what would be worse—driving back to wherever Dad was, or starting again. Again.

Then the phone rang.

'You'll love the city, you'll love Teddy,' her big sister said. 'Adrian's hardly ever around. And you can have your own room.'

Of course, Zoe knew all about Elle's world, because: Instagram. Zoe had been stalking her sister online for years. When Elle had told her that she was marrying an older man who worked in finance (no family invited, obviously), this had made complete sense to Zoe. Of course, that was exactly who Elle would be marrying.

Elle—christened Ellen—was not a nurturing big sister, but she was an inspiration. She too had left their town at sixteen and never returned.

Their father, by that time, was resigned to the fact that his elder daughter had never considered herself at home in that dusty, dying place. Zoe knew her dad could feel Elle's judgement, her disdain at his decision—or rather, indecision—to stay put after he lost his wife. Elle had never understood why he didn't pack up his broken family and move on, but Zoe knew he just didn't have it in him. He couldn't leave the place where his wife had lived, where he could still see her in every streetscape, catch a glimpse of her out of every car window. And anyway, where would he go?

So when his first daughter told him she was leaving, he didn't raise any objections, not that any would have been listened to. Elle bought a bus ticket with money she'd got from god-knew-where, looked up her mother's cousin who'd moved to Melbourne in the '90s, and took off. That was that.

From where Zoe sat—ten years old in a crumbling fibro rental house with three erratic men—Elle's move was brave, selfish and absolutely typical of her.

Elle had been in touch now and then, but Zoe didn't see her again until two days after her phone call, outside Tullamarine Airport.

That night, Zoe disembarked from the first plane she'd ever taken and made her way to the pick-up area, where Elle stepped down from her white Range Rover and gave her a big smile. For a split second, their hug threatened to devolve into a clutch, and Elle's smile looked like it might become tears—but then it didn't.

She pulled away and stood back, staring. Zoe felt her sister's eyes on her, taking in the flesh that pushed against the front of her pale skinny jeans, then the NYC T-shirt and bejewelled jelly-thongs. 'Wow,' said Elle. 'Thank god you're here. You need me more than I need you.'

Fuck you, thought Zoe. But what she said was, 'You can take me shopping.'

Elle's face was recognisable from the internet, but not from Zoe's childhood or the few printed, curling photos that Dad had taped on the fridge. That person had hair the colour of weak tea and a wide pink-and-freckled face. This Elle had glossy black hair that curled around her shoulders to her elbows. She was syrupy brown, everywhere. Everything about her was tiny and tight, including the curve of her very-pregnant belly. Her nails were long and as white and shiny as her car. Her lashes were unfeasibly thick—like a cow's, thought Zoe—and her boobs seemed enormous. She wore a tight white dress, a creamy, fluffy grey jacket and extremely high-heeled ankle boots.

One thing the two Elles had in common? They didn't smile much.

'Yep, we'll go shopping at the Emporium,' said Elle. 'Get in.'

At first, everything worked beautifully between Elle and Zoe. Elle played the role of the benefactor, taking her little sister shopping, getting her hair done, confiscating fizzy drinks and hot chips. Zoe loved Teddy, just as Elle had promised, and as soon as Elle deemed that she looked presentable enough, she took over from his nanny, taking him to the playground and Nursery Rhyme Time and Baby Bangs drum club, pushing him all over Hampton in his beige-and-black Bugaboo.

'Don't bother Adrian too much, he's pretty stressed at work,' Elle told Zoe, so she tried to stay out of his way, smiling when she passed him in the hall, staying quiet at the rare sit-down dinners when he and Elle would talk business and property.

She would visit the site of the Brighton house with Elle and watch on as her sister—this tiny person who had grown up in a place where women were looked at and never listened to—calmly ordered all these men around, telling the architect he'd got it wrong, the kitchen bench was going to need to be bigger, *bigger*. Then barked at the workmen about footprints in 'her' poured concrete floor. The men all gave each other a certain sideways look, but they did what she said.

In the evenings, after Teddy's strict six-thirty bedtime, Elle showed Zoe the secrets of her now-booming blog and all its 'platforms'. Zoe had always been good at English—it was the only subject she'd enjoyed—and Elle taught her how to write in her 'voice'. They plotted the coverage of Freddie's birth, pre-preparing the graphics that would announce his arrival—Elle had found a sepia shot of a tiny hand on a cashmere blanket that was perfect, she'd already typed in the name and date, all that Zoe would need to add was his weight—and Zoe took what seemed like hundreds of shots of Elle in her 'going to the hospital' outfit to get an approved one of her climbing into the Range Rover to be posted on the day. Elle really did like to be organised.

Adrian was often working or playing squash or having dinner with his daughters in town—Elle didn't like Alex and Arden to visit the 'small' townhouse—but he would loom in a doorway to take Elle to bed at ten most evenings, and she would make a big deal about being pulled away from her phone and her laptop and her sister. But really, Zoe could tell, she loved that he wanted her. Zoe would put her headphones on and watch TV, wondering how the hell it was possible for such a very pregnant woman to still have such loud sex every night. Still, she knew her sister well enough to suspect that some of the noise was for her benefit.

Zoe was happy. She was with her sister. She had something to do every day and people depending on her. She had family.

***

But, for Elle, the sheen began to come off her sister's visit shortly after Freddie's birth. Yes, she'd done a good job of the blog. At Freddie's birth, she had booked the hair and make-up people to come at exactly the right time for the 'after' shot and Adrian's first visit. In fact, Elle's sister had the makings of an excellent PA—if only she could work on her voice and lose a bit more weight.

But with Zoe around, the neat lines that bordered Elle's life had begun to smudge.

Zoe had insisted on phoning their dad on the day Freddie was born. Next thing he'd be suggesting a visit, something that was never going to happen. And Zoe had called Elle 'Ellen' more than once in front of Adrian and his friends when they'd come to see the baby. She had also expressed too many opinions about the colour scheme in the new house: 'So much white? Wouldn't you like to forget being in hospital?' And she was interfering with the baby nurse, insisting on holding Freddie when it was time for his put-down, overstimulating him by waving toys around when it was specifically wind-down time, and cuddling him constantly.

And Elle had seen her smoking when she walked the pram down to the playground.

'How long do I need to have her here?' Elle asked Adrian, six weeks in. 'It would be way less stressful to have a professional help with the blog. And Freddie will get in his routine faster if she's not always in his face.'

'I'm more than happy for her to piss off.' Adrian had his head in the fridge, probably looking for something calorific. 'She's nice enough, but she's always in the way, and it's not like we'll miss her sparkling conversation.'

It was time for Zoe to go.

There wasn't, of course, a trace of Zoe on The Stylish Mumma. Nor was there a mention of the baby nurse, the nannies who had come and gone, or any hint that anyone looked after Elle's boys or home other than herself. One of the most frequent comments from new followers was, 'How the hell do you find time for everything?' and Elle would stay smugly silent or occasionally throw back a comment about her organisational skills, her Type A personality and her octopus-like ability to multitask. 'Super Mumma indeed!' her fans would reply, with many cats-with-love-heart-eyes emojis.

So, almost exactly six weeks after her sister had got off the plane in her skinny jeans and her jelly-thongs, Elle changed all The Stylish Mumma's passwords and packed Zoe's bag. She let her keep all the new clothes—too big for Elle, anyway—and put a few hundred bucks in an envelope at the top of her duffel bag. Then she waited for Zoe to come back from her morning playground trip with Teddy and the double-buggy, and met her at the door.

'Zo, it's time for you to go,' she said, taking the handle of the pram. 'It's been great, but I have to think of my family now. And having you here is not the best thing for us. You're a bit of a bad influence, to be honest.'

Zoe looked about twelve as she stared up into Elle's face. 'Bad influence? But, I... I've been doing everything around here.'

'That's the problem, Zo. You're trying to take over. And this isn't your life. I know it's tough when you see someone else having something you want, but what you've been doing is just a bit... creepy, to be honest.'

Elle had never had any problem with confrontation—in fact, she didn't understand anyone who did. Why not tell people what you think, or what you want them to think? Don't they know, she often wondered, how freeing it is just to say whatever the hell you want?

'Where will I go?' asked Zoe, whose voice wasn't quite steady. 'It's not like I can stay with Auntie Liane, not after you...'

'You can go wherever,' Elle said quickly. 'I've put some money in your case. And I think you've learnt a lot here. It would be a shame for you to go back to Dad's, but if you have to, you have to.' As she spoke, Elle was busying herself getting Teddy out of the pram. When he toddled towards Zoe, Elle pulled his little hand back, hard. He started to cry. 'I think it would be best, though, if you left right now. You're starting to upset the kids. And... Zo, I saw you smoking.'

Zoe looked as if she'd been stepped on—honestly, she was still such a sensitive child. 'I'm not... upsetting the kids,' she whined. 'I fucking love those kids.'

'As I said, it's been great,' Elle said calmly. 'See you online.'

Zoe, bag in hand, stepped back into the laneway, and Elle stepped forward and shut the door with a bang.

Both babies let out enormous wails.

Job done, thought Elle.

Two nannies later, Elle hired Cate, who set about managing the babies and the blog with professionalism unusual for her years. And once she'd learnt to follow the rules, Elle had what she wanted: no messy edges.

When the Brighton house was finished, Cate moved in too.

And in all that time, Elle didn't hear from Zoe.

CHAPTER FIVE

ABI

Abi hated being in Melbourne now. To think I used to fucking live here, she thought, as she waited outside the cinema, watching all the well-dressed sheep go by. To think I used to care what everyone here cares about: parking spaces and lunch reservations and getting into the best schools and house prices—and house prices.

In front of her, a four-wheel drive stopped in traffic. A woman was at the wheel, two girls in the back with private school straw hats on, tidy bows at the necks of their chequered dresses, neat plaits swinging. The woman's hair was an expensive streaky blonde. She was talking to her girls in the rear-view mirror, her forehead furrowed with stress. The girls were eye-rolling, looking at their phones.

To Abi, it was like seeing her past self in the street. The years she'd spent in traffic on the school run, the months she'd wasted chatting to other women with the same haircut at the school gate—talking about that teacher whose English barely seemed good enough for him to be leading the science department, and have you seen what Rose and Greg have done to their deck, and are we going to the snow this winter?

For years, Abi had never felt good enough in those circles, and yet she'd wanted to be in them so badly. What the hell had she been thinking? She and Adrian, just a couple of '90s grunge kids when they'd met, coming over all suburban and aspirational, falling into step with every cliché they had ever ridiculed.

Abi was starting to worry about getting everything done before the traffic back to the farm went from annoying to unfeasible. Why was this guy so late? She ran her hand through her hair, fighting the urge to post her irritation away.

The woman in the four-wheel drive was wearing Breton stripes, and Abi knew she'd also be in three-quarter pants and ballet flats—the uniform Abi had once worn. These days she sported a uniform of a different sort: cotton sundresses, ugly shoes and chunky beads. She was letting her greys grow in, letting her curls unfurl after decades of straightening. A bold matte lip. Colourful statement earrings. Of course, she was sending a message with her new uniform, just as she had been with her old one. But her followers needed signals, and this look suited her so much better. She'd always been fucking dieting to look any good in those three-quarter pants. The ballet shoes had given her no arch support. She looked shit in stripes.

She just wanted to go inside the theatre, but the guy still wasn't in sight. It had been a three-act drama to get out of the house that morning, but she had promised to meet him about the film and now she was so annoyed by his lateness that she'd forgotten why this was so very important. She angrily tapped on her phone.

> FACT: Men are later than women. Is it their excessive white privilege that makes them quite so comfortable keeping women waiting?????? 😠

Responses pinged instantly.

Hells yes!

Just fucking walk, QGD!

Maybe they can't see their clocks for their giant cocks.

And then a text message from the guy.
So soooooorry! Trouble parking, be there in 2!!!!
Hmm. So busy parking you saw my tweet, thought Abi.

One of the things she loved most about her 'new' life was that she hardly had to deal with men and their bullshit at all anymore. Grace's gorgeous boys, yes. Her brothers and some school-friend dads, sure. But generally, she worked for herself, she lived with a woman she adored, she watched her beautiful girls grow like weeds. It was a woman's world, and she had no idea what had taken her so long to get there.

Fucking Adrian. Why had she wasted all those good years—the sap-rising years—on a man who'd turned out to be such a clichéd disappointment?

They'd met at uni party (of course they had). She had been a doctor's daughter who'd never even smoked a joint, and he'd been a handsome stoner who was going to change the world. He was *always* a cliché, she saw now, he just changed sides.

On the night they met, he was trying to explain the lyrics to something by Soundgarden, and she thought he was deep. She also thought he had kind eyes and strong hands, and those were two things she believed a man should have. But she should also have noticed that he had *no* sense of humour.

The two of them were always grunge-lite, really. A lot of middle-class kids at Melbourne Uni in the '90s were trying to emulate their heroes by shooting up and dropping out, but Abi and Adrian stayed on the respectable fringes and finished their degrees—she in Literature, he with a Masters in Commerce (he was going to change the world one ethical investment at a time). Then they went backpacking together, living in the obligatory London share house in Kilburn, where they broke up for a while. Abi went to Pamplona and had her first sexual encounter with a woman—Daphne, a South African with a dirty laugh—while Adrian went to Gallipoli with Stella from Sweden. He returned to Kilburn chastened and declaring his love for Abi, begging her to take him back.

It seemed to Abi, at the time, like destiny. She believed in fate in those days, in written-in-the-stars and everything-happens-for-a-reason and the-universe-will-provide. She decided that the universe was telling her that the Daphnes of the world were a frivolous distraction—her real purpose was to be by Adrian's side as he fulfilled his mission to change the way the world made money.

They moved out of the Kilburn house, where half-conscious bodies littered the floor and beer bottles served as the second toilet, and into a tiny flat by the river in Hammersmith, just the two of them. Abi worked for a publishing house, Adrian at an ethical investment consultancy. They were happy, she was sure of it—then.

In the year 2000, full of optimism, they moved back to Melbourne. She was going to write, Adrian was going to form an ethical trading company that would consult to big banks. They were going to live in an inner-city loft and never have children. And they would never, ever become their parents.

Fast-forward ten years, and they were living in leafy suburban Balwyn with two fair-haired daughters. Adrian worked as a corporate investment specialist for a major finance firm. Every day, Abi—who'd quit her job when Arden was born—sat in traffic in her giant suburban tank, taking her pigtailed girls to and from their private school.

Her parents had been delighted, of course. This was exactly what they'd imagined for their only daughter. Their life, only more so. A big house. The right school. Lunch every Sunday. Summers at the family beach house.

The traffic restarted. Old Abi moved off in her four-wheel drive. And the guy that New Abi had been waiting for finally turned up.

She immediately regretted her 'white privilege' tweet. Stephen was brown, and young, and panting. 'I am sooooo sorry,' he gasped. 'Traffic was a killer.'

Abi wondered what an ecowarrior like Stephen—leader of the Keen Clean Green action group—was doing driving a car in the inner city. Then she remembered her people mover, which was stashed at the train station car park, and said nothing.

Stephen wanted her to be the guest speaker at the official premiere of a movie called *Spiked*. She had met him here today to watch it and decide if she should take it on. A preview copy couldn't be sent to her, Stephen had explained over a long chain of emails, because it was so controversial they couldn't risk it falling into the wrong hands online. Instead, this small arthouse cinema near the city had agreed to host this pre-screening for Abi, Stephen and a handful of other potential supporters. The owner was sympathetic, apparently.

Abi had a feeling she would like *Spiked*. A documentary made by one of her most passionate GDs—the Green Divas, who followed her religiously—it was about 'spiking' the lies of 'Big Pharma', one of Abi's most popular blog topics.

Until she'd embraced The Cause, Abi's blog had languished in a three-digit following. She'd been so enjoying writing again that she didn't really care that she was just another divorced mum posting about starting over. She and Adrian—and yes, even Elle—had made a promise not to talk publicly about the circumstances of their split for the sake of Alex and Arden. And as much as her fingers itched with temptation, Abi kept that side of the bargain.

She didn't write about the afternoon she had been driving to school pick-up when she got a phone call from a woman who said she was sleeping with Adrian. 'You need to know.

He wants to tell you, but he's not strong enough. What's between us is too powerful to ignore. We are in love.'

Abi didn't write about the next call either—the one she made to ask Adrian if this was a sick joke, only to be met by a hesitation that told her it wasn't.

And she didn't write about the third call. To Grace. The one when Abi said, 'It's done.'

She didn't write about what happened that night, when she sat on the upstairs landing of her beautiful home, listening to her daughters sleep-breathe while she systematically shredded her own clothes with the sharpest scissors she could find. Slicing up her bullshit life, one tasteful tee at a time.

She didn't write about the worst moment of it all, the one when she and Adrian sat Alex and Arden down at the kitchen table and watched them flush with confusion as their parents told them that everything about their safe little lives was about to change.

Or the second worst moment, when she had to sit in front of her own parents, the Doctor and his loyal wife, married for forty years, and tell them the same. The look on her father's face. His insistence this would blow over. Surely.

There was so much from that time that Abi never wrote about. Instead, she wrote about moving to the country, and buying chickens, and letting her new garden grow wild.

Gradually, as she felt more and more relieved about what had happened to her life, she realised that if she wanted a true reinvention, she needed a cause.

Now, The Green Diva had just been nominated for a fucking award, if you could believe it. And the sweetest part? Abi was up against the lovely Elle. Abi hadn't had even a moment's doubt that her passionate following would trounce Elle's powdered poseurs, and her confidence had oozed onto the questionnaire she'd filled out for the organisers:

DESCRIBE YOUR BLOG IN ONE WORD:
REVOLUTIONARY.

WHY DID YOU START BLOGGING?
There wasn't any truth on the internet. Only bullshit. Women have a good bullshit detector. I wanted to cut through the crap and actually be useful, not just ornamental.

WHO ARE YOUR READERS?
They are the Green Divas (GDs). They know most of what they're being fed out there, by Big Pharma, Big Food, Big Data, is DANGEROUS RUBBISH. They are looking for the Truth and they find it with us. Don't fuck with the Divas.

WHAT ARE YOUR MOST POPULAR POSTS?
Anything that tells my Divas what they can do to drop the crap and live a real life. A healthy life. A truthful life. My girls want to be in the kind of form where they can conquer the world.

WHAT ADVICE WOULD YOU GIVE TO ASPIRING BLOGGERS?
BE REAL. GET REAL. Don't worry about your abs. Seriously. Who gives a fuck about abs?

HOW DO YOU DEAL WITH THE TROLLS?
Sister, I AM a troll. The scariest of them all. Bring it.

IF YOU WIN BLOGGER OF THE YEAR, WHAT'S YOUR BIG IDEA TO DEVELOP WITH ATGT?
A 'dating' app for Green Divas. Wherever you are in the world, you can find a like-minded mum to offer advice about the best naturopath in the neighbourhood, the closest place to get raw milk, someone to hang out with who isn't going to be pushing all their corporate BS on you. It's the ANTI-SHEEP TINDER for mums who know their shit. It will organise and mobilise and change the fucking world.

In the art-house cinema, distraught parents of 'vaccine-injured' kids flickered across the screen. Mountains of cheeseburgers represented the decline of children's natural immunity. A measles party looked like the most fun ever. Stylised hipster fonts and hand-drawn graphs climbed ever higher, showing the 'terrifying levels' of toxins being pumped into tiny babies, all over the world, every day.

When the credits rolled, the tiny crowd erupted in cheers. The woman next to Abi was crying.

Abi was the Doctor's daughter. She knew every bit of this was bullshit. But she also knew that this was the stony path to the next level for her blog. Where controversy went, numbers followed.

She was going to win this thing.

CHAPTER SIX

GRACE

'I have no idea where you get this calm Earth Mother thing from,' Leisel was saying to Grace. 'Every time I speak to you, I feel like I've taken a Valium.'

'That's what I'm here for.' Grace was in the garden, phone tucked into her shoulder, fingers in the dirt. 'You just need to get out of the city, breathe a little.'

'I don't know how to do that.' Leisel laughed. 'Tell me something relaxing.'

'Abi and I are going to build a teepee over by the barn.'

'That's not relaxing—that's just hysterical.'

'The kids will love it. It will give the girls somewhere to go away from the noise of the little ones, and it'll be a great family project.' Grace pulled something yellow up by the roots and squinted at it. 'I think I just killed something edible.'

'Well, lucky you can still get to Coles.'

'Haha.'

'You'd better get back to building your sweat lodge.'

'Teepee.'

'Whatever. Quick, the teenagers need somewhere to smoke bongs.'

'Stop being so cynical, Lee, no wonder you're stressed out. So much negativity.'

'Ha. Says the partner of the woman who's telling us we're all toxic.'

'*So* not getting into that with you. Congratulations, by the way.'

'On what?'

'Getting nominated for that award. You, and Abi and Elle. You couldn't make that stuff up, could you?'

Grace could hear Leisel's sigh as loudly as if her sister was squatting in the dirt beside her. 'You're telling me,' she said. 'I think we all know who's going to win that one. I'm practising my gracious loser face. I hope Abi is, too.'

'As if.' Grace laughed, stood up and took the phone in her hand, stretched out her back, took off her sunhat for a moment. 'Abi is gearing up. You guys had better bring it. Anyway...'

Whenever Grace and Leisel talked about Abi, there was always a moment when Grace felt like she was being disloyal. It was probably the same the other way around. Best to move on. 'How are my gorgeous nieces and nephew? I miss them.'

'They are breaking me, but they're fantastic. Harriet's trying to get the phone off me right now. She's obsessed with Candy Crush. Harri!'

'Leisel, I'm going to pretend I didn't hear that. You know how bad screen time is for infants. All the studies show...'

'I'm shitting you, Gracey! Harri can't play Candy Crush, she's not even one. She's still on Words with Friends. You'd better get back to your abacus there.'

'Very funny. Very funny. Okay. Tell Mum I'll call her soon. We'll be up there for the awards. I can't wait to see you. Love you.'

'Love you, sis. Give the kids a squeeze for me?'

'Even the bong-smoking teenagers?'

'Especially them, they'll appreciate it.'

Grace hung up, dropped the phone in her apron pocket and got back to the garden. It was usually the place she felt most calm, with her hands in the earth. But as she eased out some more (non-edible) weeds, she worried about Leisel. Her sister hid behind humour, but she sounded on edge — like she was only just managing to keep things together.

***

Leisel and Grace were the only children of an absent father and a mother who wouldn't leave her suburb. They were each other's family. Family who lived a thousand kilometres apart.

The last time Grace had seen her mum, she'd invited her down to stay at the farm for a holiday. 'It's beautiful, Mum, you have no idea. You won't know yourself.'

'Why would I do that, darling?' Anne had asked. 'I don't think you and Abi need any more mouths to feed, do you?'

A dig, obviously, but also an excuse. Her mum was comfortable doing what she'd been doing for decades — working part-time at a local builders' office, playing lawn bowls with her friends at the Gordon Club, and moaning about how many 'Chinese' were moving into her street. Grace and Abi's world was way too confronting for her.

Anne had never quite forgiven Grace for two things: being gay and moving to Melbourne. Despite her mother's instinctive conservatism, Grace wasn't really convinced that she felt more strongly about one than the other.

Anne was welded to the chip on her shoulder. After being left by the man who was supposed to provide for her, she'd always felt ashamed. Ashamed that she lived in a unit block amid leafy streets and detached brick homes. Ashamed that she wasn't as educated as the doctors' wives she met at bowls. She'd always kept things nice — hair done, clothes clean and pressed — but she felt marked with the bruise of rejection.

And she was sad. An enduring memory for both girls — from an early age — was coming home from school or netball to a darkened flat, the only light the glowing end of Anne's cigarette as she sat there listening to Air Supply. No one ever said anything about it.

Grace had worked out she was gay when she realised that the other girls at school weren't looking at the popstars and actresses in the same way that she did. White-bread Gordon in the '90s wasn't ready for gay schoolgirls, but there they were, coming ready or not, as Grace and her girlfriends used to say. Teen romance was conducted in strict secrecy, and although Anne must have known—especially after she walked in on Grace and Josephine from two doors down—no one ever said anything about that either.

After Leisel sprinted off to a Newtown share house, Grace and Anne were alone. The silence suffocated Grace, who, even then, was drawn to colour and movement and the chaos of little children. She had to leave, but Anne never really forgave her for this. 'Family meant something, once,' she would say, darkly, after a rare port.

Grace moved to Melbourne to train as a teacher in 1998, the same year that Abi graduated from uni and headed to London. Grace liked to imagine them both in airport taxis at the same time—she leaving the Tullamarine domestic terminal to start her new life, Abi and Adrian arriving at departures to fly off to their own. Imagine if those cars had passed each other, and they'd made eye contact.

But that wasn't meant to be.

Grace did her training, but she hated classrooms and their rules. She wanted to travel, and applied for temporary roles all over Australia, then taught English in Europe and South America. Wherever she was, she sought out the most colourful people—the ones who rejected the suburban attitudes that had shamed a thirty-something single mother in Gordon. Grace spent her mid-twenties temping in Aboriginal communities and joining permaculture groups and training as a doula, happily falling in and out of relationships with intense women. Then she met Edie at a Territory school and soon found herself back in Melbourne, living with a headmistress and trying on a suburban life for size.

Grace was a romantic. She knew this about herself. She believed that a higher power had sent her to knock at Abi's door in the summer of 2011 when Arden needed extra help with reading and maths—the summer when Abi was questioning everything.

Grace had loved Arden before she loved Abi. If you asked Grace, the dreamy, creative eight-year-old was trapped at a school that didn't fit her. And Abi did eventually ask Grace for her opinion on this, over tea in the kitchen (something that had become a post-tutoring session ritual between them).

'You need to get her into a new school, or get her out of school entirely,' Grace said to Abi, stirring a teaspoon of honey into her tea. 'She just needs the space to learn the way she needs to learn.'

Abi didn't listen. But she did hear. Grace was aware that Abi heard everything she said, and that she was watching her mouth closely when she said it. It wasn't the first time that Grace had been the object of an older, married woman's interest. Her partner Edie told her it happened because she was non-threatening, feminine—beautiful even—and open. She seemed like a safe canvas onto which these suburban wives could project the fantasies they pretended they weren't having.

But Grace could sense that more was going on in that Balwyn kitchen than a crush. As they talked and talked over cooling teas, Otto entertained by the girls in the next room, she got the sense that Abi was playing a role in which she was miscast. She even looked like she was wearing the wrong costume, constrained by the stylish wardrobe demanded of the school-gate mums.

Later—much later, when Grace and Edie had wrung each other out with goodbyes, and Adrian and Abi were done—Grace witnessed Abi's metamorphosis into a different woman in her bed. As each of Abi's sweat-drenched curls sprang back, as her huge, generous smile filled her bare, freckled face, as she cried out in a guttural voice, Grace thought she was watching a woman become her true self. It was intoxicating. It was binding.

And they had four children between them.

**

Otto and Sol were running towards her through the veggie patch, wanting to show her something. 'Abi's back from town, Mum, and she bought us Creme Eggs!'

Jesus, Abi. Online she was the Green Diva, all organic and gluten-free, but she spoiled these kids with too much crap—if you asked Grace, who would no more eat a Creme Egg than shoot heroin.

'Don't eat those, boys. They're full of chemicals. I don't think they're even real food.' Grace put her hand out for her sons to hand over the sugar.

'But Muuuuum, that's why they're so good,' Sol said, laughing, but he did as he'd been told. Grace had trained her boys well: that was why they'd brought her the contraband in the first place. 'Can we have them at Easter?'

'I doubt it.' Grace put the chocolate in her apron pocket and looked over the boys' heads to see if Abi was visible behind them, up at the house.

There she was, waving out of a window and calling, 'Hey, you! I'm hooooome!'

Grace put a soily hand up to her eyes and squinted into the sun to see her better.

'Oh my *god*!' Abi shouted. 'I just saw a movie that you would LOVE!'

'I would? Well then, you're going to need to tell the world about it, babe.'

'I'm coming down!'

Grace smiled to herself.

***

Grace's friends had often asked her: Why Abi? Why Abi when she and Edie had gone through so much together to have their gorgeous boys? Sperm donors and counselling and IUI and family meetings and legals and then the beauty of the babies inside her and becoming what she had always felt born to be—a mother, part of a family. So, why Abi?

When people asked, she always said the same thing: 'If you've ever been in love, you already know.' Yes, it was an infuriating, patronising answer. But it was her only answer.

To Grace, the big things in life were best guided by instinct. By gut. But having her babies with Edie hadn't been about that. She and Edie were so different—Grace had talked herself into that relationship, she could see that now. Edie was deeply ambitious for a respectable middle-class life that would have seen them living in Abbotsford forever and working in education and being 'accepted' by the straight neighbours and having Friday night dinners with them in the family-friendly beer garden. But Grace had never wanted to be like everyone else.

And then came a moment in that Balwyn house when Grace caught a glimpse of who Abi could be, who she really was.

After a tutoring session with Grace in the living room, Arden told her mum that she wanted to show her something. She sat on an armchair, lowered her little blonde pigtailed head and read a whole book to Abi. Even Otto, who usually staggered around banging things, was quiet, perhaps sensing the weight of the moment. Abi—who had been quiet herself recently, thin-skinned around the eyes with the look of someone who wasn't sleeping well—sat next to Arden and listened, hands crossed in her lap.

When her daughter had finished, Abi leapt from the tasteful, neutral lounge and began to whoop. She scooped Arden up, all eight skinny years of her, and danced her around the living room. Her energy was so infectious that soon Alex and Otto were dancing too. And Grace was laughing and laughing from the sidelines, until Abi passed her on a turn, grabbed her by the waist and pulled her in tight, kissing her cheek hard: 'Thank you, thank you, thank you!' And they all danced.

And that Abi, the Abi with her head shaking and her feet stomping, whooping and laughing and wearing her joy on the outside, she felt like someone Grace knew. And they felt like family.

That evening, she went home and told Edie that she thought she was leaving.

Not for Abi. Not yet. Abi was married. But that glimpse of the family she wanted had changed everything for Grace.

***

Abi was down in the veggie patch with her. For a beat or two they just stood there, smiling at each other.

'I had a good day in the city, as it turns out,' Abi said. 'Fucking nightmare place not so fucking nightmarish today.'

Grace kissed her, twirling a piece of curly hair around her dirty finger. 'That's good. Got to love a day that doesn't turn out how you'd expect.'

'And Gracey. I tell you. *Spiked.* I'm going to push it. It's going to help. It's going to be big. We're going to be biiiiiiiiiiiiigg...' And Abi was kind of stomp-dancing around the veggie patch, and the boys were back around her waist, and Grace was laughing.

It was just like that moment from the living room in Balwyn. Grace had been right—she'd glimpsed a scene from the future.

'You are going to be big, baby,' she said with a laugh. 'As big as you deserve.'

CHAPTER SEVEN

LEISEL

The problem with blogging was that some days, nothing happened.

Some days, there was so much to say, you were itching to get to your keyboard where the words poured like hot tea. But other days, well, they were just... the same as the last one.

Especially, Leisel thought, when you're working every hour god sends, and dealing with children's myriad needs in the other, less god-sent hours.

Meanwhile, Abi and Elle seemed to have all the time in the world to sit around arranging pomegranates in white china bowls or recording interviews with Mothers Who Matter. Their blogs were their jobs.

Leisel knew, through the small details her sister had let slip, that money wasn't a big concern for Abi and Grace. Abi's divorce settlement, the sale of the Balwyn house and the inheritance Abi had received from her old-money grandparents meant that their modest lifestyle was pretty much taken care of.

How nice for them, Leisel had to stop herself from thinking.

She never used to be envious of others' lives. Their

decisions to marry 'up', their high-flying corporate jobs with the annual bonus that dictated whether or not they could holiday somewhere cold this summer? Not her scene. She was a gen Xer, and they were not a materialistic people.

BUT. But, but.

Leisel now knew that money could buy something that was definitely worth having—time.

That was something that she didn't have. As she stared at the cursor blinking on a blank blog page, she wondered what she could write about when life was simultaneously frantic and boring.

She'd been surprised to make the Blog-ahhs shortlist.

Compared to the seductive slickness of The Stylish Mumma and Abi's activism over at The Green Diva, Leisel's blog was small fry. But the organisers had told her they liked The Working Mum's authenticity, and that her audience, though smaller, was remarkably engaged. They were keen, their email read, to see what she could do in the next few months with a little more focus.

A little more focus.

Leisel had summoned all the confidence she could and filled out their questionnaire.

DESCRIBE YOUR BLOG IN ONE WORD:
Relatable.

WHY DID YOU START BLOGGING?
I had my first baby at 38. Life just hadn't got it together for me before then, but once I was pregnant, I had so much to say and I found there were women all around me who were exactly the same—not the youngest parents, maybe with not-great support, who needed a place to share and vent. It's been an extraordinary experience.

WHO ARE YOUR READERS?
Working mothers who aren't ashamed.

WHAT ARE YOUR MOST POPULAR POSTS?
The ones I write at night before I go to sleep about all the things I have to do the next day. I think they alternately freak people out or inspire them. Perhaps both.

HOW DO YOU DEAL WITH TROLLS?
I wonder what it would be like to have so much hatred in your heart for someone you've never met. I try to have some empathy, and I'm attempting to grow a thick skin.

WHAT ADVICE WOULD YOU GIVE TO ASPIRING BLOGGERS?
Only consider this a profession if: you have an independent source of income! No, seriously, you need to do it because you love it, not because you think it will set you free.

IF YOU WIN BLOGGER OF THE YEAR, WHAT'S YOUR BIG IDEA TO DEVELOP WITH ATGT?
I keep imagining a Work Wife network where women can share nannies, food, recipes, ideas and car pool. Like Uber, but for women with way too much on their plates. And I'll have a holiday. A long one.

It was all true. She did blog for the connection. She did blog to help women feel a little less alone. And now, she also blogged because she was addicted.

The idea of taking a holiday actually made her laugh because, in fact, the last time they'd tried to have a peaceful family break, Leisel had spent much of it infuriating Mark by chasing wi-fi around the campground.

On the third morning, he emerged from their cabin, rumpled and shirtless, to ask if she wanted to come back to bed—his cousin had taken the big kids to the beach and the baby was asleep. But Leisel had found a spot at the back of the property where, if you sat on the second branch of a tree, you'd get a strong-enough signal to check if your scheduled

Facebook posts had gone out, and what mentions had come back in.

'I'm sorry, Mark!' she called. 'I'll be there in a moment. I'm just...'

'This *is* the moment, Leisel. They'll all be back soon. Are you kidding me about this? You'd rather be in the tree with your phone, than with me in a bed you didn't have to make?'

Leisel considered this question. Immediately, a post came to mind:

When holiday sex just isn't sexy anymore

Before she answered Mark, she quickly tapped the title into her Notes app.

'Fuck you, Leisel. Seriously, fuck you.' The cabin door slammed as hard as a plywood door could. I'll deal with that later, thought Leisel, rearranging herself on the branch.

Leisel was addicted to the Likes, to seeing her modest followers growing, to watching engagement creep up. She was addicted to the emails from other working mums, but also from PRs wanting her to feature their products, to write about their family-fair days and BPA-free lunchboxes. She was beginning to see the potential in all of this.

But some days, nothing much happened worth mentioning. Like today. It was 10 p.m., the flat was quiet, this was her window. She started typing.

Groundhog Day
When you're out of bed on auto-pilot and it's breakfast and lunchboxes and three-times 'Brush your teeth!'. When it's baby-food production and double-drop-off and stumble into the office just in time. When it's meetings and lunch-time calls to the schoolmums about who's picking up who for what tomorrow and that doctor's appointment you should have made last week. Groundhog Day when it's the

bus and car to pick-up and home-time and two kinds
of dinner. Homework and books and bath and three-
times 'Brush your teeth!' and then it's stories and
cuddles and 'Are they asleep yet?' And it's clean-up
and washing-folding and talk-to-your-spouse time.
Then it's work emails and 'are-the-uniforms-clean?'
and washing out the lunchboxes you were going to do
three hours ago. Then it's collapse and considering
sex for five seconds before deciding sleep is better
than sex, has been for six years, and then it's down
and out before you're ready to do it all again...

I'm not going to win the award with this, thought Leisel.

The only blog-worthy thing to have happened that day was
the one thing she didn't want to write about.

Leisel had been called over to Zac's nook for the second
time in a week—but this time, it wasn't about her hours.

It was about her troll.

***

When Leisel was a kid, a troll was a monster who lived
under a bridge. Her father told her that the one under the
Sydney Harbour Bridge was an enormous, many-tentacled sea
creature that only came out at night. He convinced her that
the New Year's Eve Harbour fireworks had been invented as
a warning ceremony to scare the monster away for another
year. She believed him. She believed most things her father
told her—he was a serious guy with a powerful imagination.
Of course, the true curses of that story were that she'd been
deadset terrified of crossing the Bridge for years and now she
thought of her father every time she did. The fucker.

In her adult life, the trolls were real. They lived in her
computer, on her phone—and occasionally in her mailbox.
That was why Zac had summoned her to his nook.

'So... your blog,' he said. He wasn't getting any better

at the eye contact. 'It's good that you have a hobby, but you've received a parcel, Leisel, and it's... not a good one.' He pushed a brown cardboard box across the desk.

Leisel looked at it, her hands folded in her lap.

'Open it, Leisel,' said Zac.

It was a cake box, she realised. A plain brown cake box. She lifted the edge with her index finger and peered inside.

'Cupcakes?' she asked. Sometimes PRs sent them to the magazine staff. Zac had called her in for cupcakes?

'Look at them.'

She lifted the lid right up. Thirteen cupcakes. And they were iced with letters that spelled out DIE WORKING MUM.

'Oh.' She'd received death threats before from trolls—but never on baked goods.

'I wouldn't eat those, if I were you,' Zac said unnecessarily. 'They were delivered to the front desk by a woman. All we know about her is that she's short, around five feet, and was wearing a hooded jacket and sunglasses. She didn't say anything to the receptionist.'

Leisel's stomach lurched. 'Well, of course... I mean...'

Zac closed the lid. 'Now, obviously, Leisel, what you do in your spare time is up to you.' He said 'spare time' with an accusatory edge that wasn't lost on her, even though she hadn't actually had any 'spare time' for five years. 'But when the hatred that this little blog inspires spills over into your workplace—again—it becomes our business.'

Leisel could tell that moments before she'd entered the nook, Zac had been on the phone to HR. There was no way that Millennial Man was prepped to have this kind of adult conversation without a script.

'We will support and back you in any way we can, of course—' definitely HR '—but your job here has nothing to do with what you write online, and it's unfortunate that these... people... have decided that it does. We can defend you from work-related harassment, which we all have to endure in this business to a point—' Leisel almost rolled her eyes, because

67

Zac, as a man, actually had very little experience of that ' —
but this goes beyond that. And those phone calls were very
disruptive to everyone who works here.'

He was referring to the day a couple of months ago when
the receptionist's phone had rung every five minutes until they
blocked the number, a woman's voice demanding, 'Where is
The Working Mum?' every time. The calls had come from an
old-fashioned pay phone. At the time, Zac had said, 'Leisel,
surely these people shouldn't know where you work.'

But it was too late for her to hide her identity: The Working
Mum had never been an anonymous blog. Leisel hadn't
considered, when she'd made that decision, that it would have
any effect on her job — actually, she'd thought it would be a nice
break from what she was used to dealing with. In her work life,
she and many of her female colleagues were frequently insulted
by angry readers, but back when she'd started blogging, she
hadn't considered her posts controversial or provocative enough
to encourage trolls. Oh, to be so innocent.

Leisel got to her feet and picked up the cake box. 'Yes,
Zac, I am the subject of harassment. Again. It is not my fault.
Nor is it yours, and I know it's unfortunate that you have to
deal with this at all — but, to be perfectly honest, you've never
experienced what lots of women have to deal with online on
a daily basis.' Sometimes, the best way to handle her young
boss was to be very, very grown-up. 'I've faced threats before
and I am not going to stop writing because of some pathetic
keyboard warriors. Hopefully this is the end of it, but if the
harassment escalates, I will report it to the police. And I want
to emphasise that the blog does not affect my work here — it's
very much an out-of-hours project.'

She could see on Zac's face that he thought she shouldn't
have enough out-of-hours time to work on anything, but he
managed something like a smile. 'Of course, Leisel, I know
this must be hard for you. Good luck.'

Leisel got back to her desk, opened the box and studied the
cupcakes. She picked one up and broke off a piece. Inside, they

were red. Blood red. Even Leisel, a woman of non-existent baking skills, could see that it would have taken a lot of time, effort and discipline to get all of the cakes the exact same size, not overspilling from their pretty daisy-print cases. The icing was a cheery pink and yellow. The letters that willed her to die were glossy and black. Her troll knew their way around an icing bag, clearly.

Leisel lifted her phone, took a picture and wrote:

A monster sent me these today.

Then she hesitated.

She was almost sure of the troll's online identity — her most persistent and vicious abuse came from an account called The Contented Mum.

This person, who, let's face it, was probably a woman, had been trolling Leisel's comments section for about a year, and lately she could be relied upon to provide the first post on anything Leisel wrote. It had begun to feel as if she was lying in wait.

On a recent status update of Leisel's about bringing home takeaway after a long day, The Contented Mum had written:

How lazy do you have to be not to stir a few healthy ingredients together for your own children at the end of the day? You are neglecting those kids and don't deserve their love.

On a photo of several overflowing baskets of washing, waiting to be folded on a Sunday night, she'd said:

Someone should take those kids away from you, give them to a mother who loves them enough not to complain about having to look after them, you ungrateful bitch.

And on a long post about how increased paid maternity leave might encourage women to stay in the workplace, she'd written:

> You disgust me. You shouldn't need to be paid to stay at home with your baby. It should be the first and last priority in your life. Your children would be better off without you.

Leisel pictured The Contented Mum as a crazed 1950s-style housewife, complete with apron and lipstick. Baking her hatred for Leisel and all working mothers into cupcakes way beyond their domestic skill-set seemed perfect for her.

Whatever Leisel wrote about the cupcakes, this troll and any others would read it and revel in the reaction. She didn't want to give them the satisfaction. She put her phone away.

***

That night, the cakes were still on Leisel's mind. Ordinarily, she didn't tell Mark about the abuse she copped online — she knew it only irritated him. But tonight, she needed to vent. Leaning against the kitchen bench while he dug around in a drawer for the kids' dinner forks, she told him, 'The troll's back. They sent me some death-wish cupcakes at work today.'

Mark looked up. 'They sent you what?'

'A box of cupcakes, telling me to die.' She decided not to mention the blood-red filling.

'That's fucked up, Leisel. You've got to tell the police.'

'What will they do? I don't think it's illegal to send baked goods.'

'It's illegal to send death threats.'

'Oh, come on, it wasn't quite a threat, more of a wish...' Her attempt at humour fell flat, judging by Mark's expression. 'Look, this kind of thing comes with the territory. And can you imagine the response I'd get from the police? I'd be laughed out of the station.'

'What if the cakes were full of rat poison?'

'I didn't eat them, I just chucked them out! No one would have been mad enough to eat them. It would have been pointless to put poison in them. Anyway—' she smiled, trying to keep it light '—the troll's probably got it out of their system now.'

'I don't even understand what you've done to upset them. It's not like you're vicious online.'

'No, but they think I complain too much. Parenthood's a breeze, remember?'

'Oh, that's right.' Mark smiled back at her, the evidence of a day spent with a non-verbal baby written in the wrinkles around his eyes. 'Easy-peasy.'

And they went out to feed the kids together.

Now, sitting at her laptop, Leisel chose not to write about that part of her day. She'd tried engaging with the people who abused her online. She'd tried blocking and ignoring them. She'd asked other bloggers what they did, and everyone's answer was a variation on 'grow a thick skin'. She was working on it.

So tonight, 'Groundhog Day' it was. She pushed publish.

CHAPTER EIGHT

ABI

Abi was deeply shitty about the fact that the kombucha hadn't brewed in time.

> How hard is it to get your shit together in time for a visit from the neo-peasant high-priestess? #kombuchafail #kids #peasantlife

As each finger whacked the iPhone screen, there was a tiny, satisfying thud.

She hadn't tagged in today's famous guest—that would just alert her to the mess of disorganisation she was walking into. But Abi was pretty sure that Shannon Smart followed her anyway. Oh well.

'Muuuum! You're STOMPING,' yelled Arden from her and Alex's room. 'Stop it. I'm trying to read in here.'

'Shannon Smart's on her way to the farm, Arden,' Abi yelled back. 'The kombucha didn't ferment. And the cupboards are bare. How fucking self-sufficient is that, do you think?'

'Go to the FUCKING shops, Mum,' came the high-volume

reply from her fourteen-year-old. 'Shannon Smart doesn't give a SHIT about your kombucha.'

That was probably true, Abi had to admit. Shannon bottled almost a million-dollars-worth of her own kombucha a year. It might have been more appropriate to have a few bottles of that on hand.

Where the hell was Grace? Didn't she know how important today was? Abi leant out of the window, looking around. It was a 'school' day, so Grace was probably off somewhere with Sol, lecturing him about bugs or wombats or some shit.

Even through her stress, the view from the house never failed to delight Abi. Coming outside every morning and sitting on the deck with a big mug of tea made her feel calm in a way that she didn't remember from her old life. The tree-change had been, hands-down, the best of all the big decisions made during the great family crash of 2012.

Such a huge one at the time. And there had been so many questions. Did the girls need any more upheaval? Would changing schools be the worst thing for them? What about their friends in the city?

But one weekend in the middle of all the drama, Abi and Grace and the kids had driven up to Daylesford (they'd had to take two cars in those days). As they wound their way through the beautiful scenery, it had seemed to Abi that if change was in the air, maybe it was better—as her English grandmother would have said—to be hung for a sheep as a lamb. In other words, if you're going to change everything, change *everything*.

'GRAAAACE!' Abi wailed out of the window. 'Graaaaaaaaaacey! I need you.'

'This isn't *Little House on the Prairie*, Mum,' Arden yelled. 'Ring her fucking phone.'

Too true, you little smart-arse, thought Abi. But Grace's phone rang out. Abi would just have to deal with the catering issues herself. She had ninety minutes before Shannon Smart was meant to arrive. Town was fifteen minutes away.

Once upon a time, Shannon had been a TV presenter, working for a national network on one of those inane morning shows. She was on the cover of *Woman's Say* every second week: PREGNANT! DIVORCED! ENGAGED! PREGNANT AGAIN! She spent almost twenty years interviewing celebrities and hosting the Logies red carpet and laughing at her co-host's jokes, wearing unfeasibly tight day dresses while balancing, knees-together, on the edge of a white couch. She never was pregnant.

And then, one day, Shannon blew it all up. She vanished in a flurry of BREAKDOWN! headlines and rumours of struggles with booze, drugs, even Scientology. But it was much more confusing than that. Shannon, when she reappeared on *Sunday Evening* two years later, had gone off the grid—she had gone 'crunchy'.

Shannon wrote a book, *Quitting the Toxic World*, and espoused her new-found enviro-evangelism everywhere that would have her. The new Shannon didn't eat gluten, sugar, wheat or dairy and considered coffee and alcohol to be the devil's work. More shockingly for her daytime TV audience, she also swore off cosmetics, deodorants, perfumes, leather and possessions in general. Oh, and mainstream medicine. The once smooth-faced, painted and primped celebrity now arrived at interviews on a pushbike with a backpack, wearing hemp. And she was forty-seven.

Abi was in awe of how Shannon had turned all this into a business. You could buy Shannon Smart-branded moon-cups, quilted menstrual pads and 'family paper' (toilet 'un-paper' to the uninitiated: recycled material to wipe with and wash). You could buy Shannon Smart natural facial oils that doubled as hair oils that doubled as salad dressings. You could buy Shannon Smart charcoal mascara. And yes, you could buy Shannon Smart kombucha, coconut oil and something called ShannonKraut—a mason jar of fermented vegetables that would set you back $28.

Shannon was a freaking genius and an alt-culture goddess. And she was coming to the farm shed to appear on Abi's podcast—a coup that would help no end with the Blog-ahhs. This, Abi knew, was going to be a meeting of like minds.

Arden and Alex had been the ones to tell Abi that she needed a podcast: 'Everyone's got one, Mum.' And so, *The Green Diva's Shed* was born. The shed itself was one of the things that had made Abi want to buy the farm. After that family trip to Daylesford, she and Grace had begun to plot. If Adrian was so keen to sell the big Balwyn house, why not take her share somewhere her new family could start a completely different kind of life?

As soon as she and Grace had seen Halcyon, they'd known it was the right place. It was a fixer-upper with good bones, according to the real estate agent—but, for Abi and Grace, it was perfect as it was. Fifteen minutes' drive out of Daylesford, the main building was a stone farmhouse with a low, wraparound veranda. It looked out onto fields that were burnt-gold in summer and crisp, frosted white in winter.

The two of them hadn't had—and still didn't have—any fucking idea what to do with a farm. Really, the twelve acres' productivity was limited to Grace's ever-growing veggie patch, the fortified chicken coups and, yes, kombucha production. But the farm had also brought forth Abi's incarnation as The Green Diva.

She'd spent a fortune getting a router installed to make sure the property had an unshakable internet connection, and then she'd gone about picking and choosing the bits of alt-culture dogma that suited her needs. Grace, as always, was her muse. Artistic Arden was her designer and teenage social media expert. It had been a family project to create a little soundproof podcast cave in the shed—which was really a converted barn—then a sound engineer's job to hook it up. The girls added fairy lights and cacti, and Abi's podshed was born. Once a week she dropped a show, usually a rambling affair in which she offloaded her thoughts and lessons from the week. She'd found that the more popular shows were her interviews with prominent people in the 'crunchy' world.

That TV chef who had gone paleo. The mum of five

who hadn't bought anything new in a year. The actress who had Snapchatted her homebirth. The woman who was still breastfeeding her five-year-old.

And today, Shannon Smart. Abi was running to the people mover, ready to head to the co-op for kale chips and ShannonKraut, when Grace finally appeared.

'What's the matter?' She had Sol trailing after her, stick in hand. His halo of wild blond hair was blowing out all around him, and she was wearing a cheesecloth dress that billowed around her legs, clearly visible through the translucent fabric. God, Grace was beautiful—and out here, with the sun on her face and kids trailing and chickens clucking, she was like Mother fucking Earth.

'Babe. Shannon Smart is going to be here in an hour, and we've got nothing in the house to offer her. Well, nothing we *can* offer her.' Abi thought about the secret packets of Twisties that the girls had stashed at the back of the pantry, behind the zoodle-maker.

Grace was unfazed, as Abi could have predicted. Very little fazed Grace, and especially not anything to do with websites, podcasts, celebrities and appearances. 'Sol and I will go pick some pears from next door's orchard. We have water, don't we? What does Shannon Smart want?'

'Not fruit. Fruit is NOT approved of. Fructose.'

'Alright. I guess I'm getting in the car then. So green. Thanks, Shannon. C'mon, Sol.'

'You're a lifesaver,' barked Abi. Then, 'WAIT!'

She grabbed her phone and bashed out:

If Shannon Smart was coming to your house for lunch, what would you serve her? #divaproblems

Within seconds:

Cauliflower popcorn. She's got the recipe #shannonisgod

Jeeeeeerky, baby! #paleoalltheway

Kale chips and pumpkin hommus. Homemade, obvs.

My cock. #dangerouscunt

'Get some kale chips. And some hommus, please, Gracey.'

Grace, who'd been standing there watching Abi hammer her phone, rolled her eyes and got in the people mover. 'Good to see you can make your own decisions, babe. C'mon, Sol. Let's go save Abi's face. AGAIN.' And she blew Abi a kiss as they trundled off.

What had she done to deserve that woman? It was a question that Abi asked herself daily.

***

Back in her Balwyn days, Abi—like every middle-class parent she knew—had been successfully suckered into an ever-escalating anxiety spiral about her children's academic performance. She feared that Arden was in serious danger of screwing up NAPLAN, the national schools' test, and she could not deal with the idea of having to tell her social circle that her daughter was single-handedly responsible for dragging down house prices in the district by getting a less-than-stellar mark.

It was the talk of the school gate pick-up line: 'A three per cent drop across Year Five can literally wipe fifty thousand dollars off your resale value,' one parent would say, then another would add, 'But if the school lifts just a couple of points, we can justify putting the pressure on for that second Gifted and Talented group. Would be *so* good for intake.'

Arden was a great kid. A creative kid. A friendly, happy kid. A kid who had, despite the ever-more exorbitant cost of her education, consistently got Cs on her reports. Lovely platitudes—'tries hard', 'a pleasure to teach'—but Cs all the same.

'We can't have an average daughter,' Abi said to Adrian one night, over a giant glass of wine. 'We just can't.'

'There's nothing average about Arden,' Adrian replied. 'There are just a lot of smart kids at that school. She'll be fine. She's EIGHT.'

But Abi had still taken the path of many a middle-class parent and found Arden a tutor. Grace came recommended by one of the mum-friends Abi could trust. After all, you didn't want just anyone knowing you were getting your kids tutored. Some thought it was cheating. Some thought it was a weakness. Everyone was secretly doing it.

Grace arrived at the Balwyn house with one-year-old Otto swathed in a paisley sling across her body, his chubby legs wrapped around her waist. 'I'm feeding on demand,' she explained. And, sure enough, ten minutes into Arden's finger-walk through the reader she should have cleared the year before, Otto undid Grace's shirt and started suckling. Grace stroked his little golden head and kept right on reading with Arden.

From the minute she'd opened the door to Grace, Abi had felt her presence. To put it another way, as she later would, she was 'profoundly attracted to her energy'. Abi's life seemed like a chaotic whirl of 'never doing enough', and Grace was a calm centre. Abi had embraced parental anxiety so hard, she marvelled at how any mother could focus on an actual, out-of-the-house job and still do it. Grace just seemed to get things done. She didn't say much to Abi at first, but she always gave off an air of a raised eyebrow. When Abi poured out her concerns about NAPLAN and the house prices and whether average could ever be enough, Grace just smiled, put a hand on her arm and said, 'Arden is fine.'

Slowly, Abi and Grace became friends, sharing cups of tea after Arden's sessions since Grace never seemed in a hurry to leave. Soon, Tuesdays at 4 p.m. became Abi's favourite time of the week. She would leave Grace's teacup on the bench long after she and Otto had gone, wanting the evidence of her presence to hang in the air a little longer.

These days, Abi looked back at that time as the calm before the storm. But if she was honest with herself, the storm had already been gathering. There were her longings for women, which could no longer be batted away as fantasy. Adrian's increasing absence. The girls' rising anxiety. Pressure was building in the Balwyn house, threatening to blow its tasteful period windows from their frames.

Abi had felt her old self stirring. And despite her fury at Adrian for shattering their family life with his affair, she'd come to realise that his old self had been stirring too. Why? Had they repeated the same tiny rituals — Abi cutting the crusts off sandwiches on the same board with the same knife every morning, Adrian turning his car out of the driveway at 7.20 a.m. every day — one time too many?

***

Shannon Smart had arrived, and not on a pushbike. She stepped out of her chauffeured Prius and into the glaring sun of spa country in a whirl of colour and movement. Several years into her second act, her eco-epiphany seemed to have melded with her glamorous TV aesthetic, Abi noted. She was a picture of ethical chic, wrapped in African print and wooden beads, and her smile as big as her canvas tote bag — which contained many, many bottles of kombucha. And ShannonKraut.

'Wow, your place is gorgeous!' Shannon said, thrusting the bag at Abi. 'A little gift.'

Abi knew for a fact that Shannon's place — a purpose-built eco lodge fifty k's away — was much more gorgeous, but she still appreciated the compliment.

'Where's your tribe? I've heard so much about them.'

Shannon *did* follow her, thought Abi smugly, battling an

almost overwhelming urge to grab her phone and tell the world.

'Oh, they're... everywhere.' She gestured towards the farmhouse, then towards the woods and the creek behind. 'Running wild, as ever.'

Actually, the girls were in their room on their computers, probably watching YouTube tutorials on excessive eyeliner application. Grace and Sol were in the kitchen, throwing away the containers that Shannon Smart's homemade lunch had arrived in.

'Grace is just making us something to eat. I thought that...'

'Oh, darling, I haven't really got time for that. Crazy schedule. Shall we just get down to it?' Shannon was already starting towards the podshed. Her driver was climbing back into the Prius.

'You can go and wait in the house,' Abi said to him, through the wound-up window. 'Grace will make you some tea...' But the driver just raised a single hand to silence her, the hum of the air-con audible over her words.

'Tell me, who listens to your show?' Shannon's stride was fast. Abi found herself scurrying to keep up. 'How tuned-in are they? How basic do I have to be? And how far does it go?'

'It's an intimate audience. But my women are pretty switched on. There are a lot of wannabes, gasping to be inspired. Great audience for you, lots of potential.'

Shannon nodded. She was looking around the podshed with an expression that Abi couldn't quite read. Was she impressed? Amused?

'So this is where the magic happens,' she said, smiling. 'Bit different from Studio 18.'

Abi assumed this was a reference to where Shannon had filmed her TV show for years. 'Yes, it is. I bet you didn't have a problem with possums chewing through wires there.'

Shannon's laugh was high-pitched and tinkly. Her eyes, fixed on Abi, were famously blue, her forehead still suspiciously unlined. I bet she knows the secret to eco-botox, thought Abi, reflexively touching her own wrinkles.

In actual fact, the shed's rustic look was deliberate: it had polished made-to-seem-original floorboards and faux-brick walls, a bathroom, a mini-kitchen, and, of course, the soundproof cave. This was hardly roughing it. Although, it was true about the possums.

Grace appeared with cold water, taking Shannon's gifts away with a knowing look at Abi and flicking on the recording equipment. 'Your wife is gorgeous,' Shannon remarked, as Grace headed back to the house.

'Unfortunately, Grace is not my wife.' As Shannon knew. 'One day, when this country gets its fucking act together—'

'Yes, of course,' Shannon said quickly, smile still in place. 'You know, I met your husband's new wife. She asked me to do a sponsored content post for her blog. We got chai together. She's... lovely. How strange, that your ex should marry two bloggers.'

Abi had the lurching sensation that her dream meeting of minds was going wrong. 'Well,' she replied, 'I wasn't a blogger when we were married. You could say I found my voice after we separated.'

Abi thought about the phone conversation she'd had with Adrian just yesterday. They were meant to be working out where Alex and Arden would spend the July school holidays, when Adrian suddenly started talking about Elle.

This was something he never did—not anymore. Five years ago, they had sprayed the walls of the Balwyn house with insults and blame as they fought their way through the confusion of their split. For a long time after that, communication was limited to logistics: child exchange, legals, finance. Now, they'd grown comfortable enough to be at the same birthday dinners, to be the one the other called when they were worried about their girls. But they never, ever talked about Elle.

'Abi, there's something Elle and I want to discuss with you.'

'Um. Really?'

'It's about the award.' Another surprise. Adrian never mentioned the blog either—too close to home.

'The Blog-ahhs? Are you going to go? Because the girls can stay with my parents.'

'It's just...' Adrian almost sounded nervous. 'Well, look, Elle has really big plans for The Stylish Mumma. Actually, *we* have *really* big plans for it. You know, after the awards.'

The name of Elle's blog sounded ridiculous coming out of Adrian's mouth. 'What kind of plans?'

'Business plans. Big business plans. I've been laying the groundwork for it to take us in a really different direction, and the award would be a great springboard for that.' Adrian was talking quickly, as if he needed to get this over with. Had Elle asked him to have this conversation?

'Okay, Adrian. Well, yes, we're all hoping that the award's investment will help us change things...'

'Abi?'

'What? Spit it out, Adrian.'

'Alex and Arden deserve the best education that we can give them. I know right now your thoughts on that are... unusual, but as we head towards university—well, I hope that will change. And when it comes to travel, when it comes to where they'll live one day... The plans and investments we're making mean that Elle and I could really set the girls up. The success of her brand could change everything about their future.'

Suddenly Abi got it. No matter how tolerant Adrian was—had to be, really—about the choices she and the girls were making, he was never going to get over the idea that his job in life was to smooth the path ahead of them with money. The sun would rise, the sun would set, and Adrian would pay for a top-notch university.

'Are you asking me to pull out of the Blog-ahhs, Adrian? For the girls? Because that seems... counterintuitive.'

'I don't want to fight about it, Abi, so don't get offended—'

'I'm not fucking offended, Adrian. I'm surprised. I thought you'd want the girls to see their mother do well. You know, see their primary role model achieving her dreams and all that inspirational meme stuff that Elle goes in for—'

'Abi. I get it. I do. But if you were looking at this pragmatically, like I am—'

'You are?'

'Yes, I am. Elle has really big plans. This could be the beginning. Apps and licensing and books and... I know you're imagining the same things, but you just aren't set up for that, Abi. With all the good will in the world, you're not. And we are. With this extra kick, we are. And the girls would benefit enormously. I really believe that. I'm just asking you to think about it, realistically. About what it could mean for our family...'

While Adrian talked and talked, Abi stared out her bedroom window into the veggie garden. Arden was there with Grace. They were picking sprigs of some herb, filling up a cracked enamel bowl with little bits of green, deep in conversation. Could it really be a school lesson? What exactly was her daughter learning out there?

Adrian's words were obviously niggling at something. Abi shook her head. 'Adrian. I understand what you're trying to tell me—of course I do. But seriously, I am not going to... what? Pull out of the award? Throw the award?'

'Well, "throw" is a strong word...'

'The girls are fine. They will continue to be fine, whatever the outcome of the Blog-ahhs. Their opportunities are not going to be decided by this one award. If you and Elle are enjoying planning your empire, you just keep on doing that. Sounds like you're looking for an escape plan, am I right? From working with the Partners?'

Adrian sighed. 'Abi. I have a lot of responsibilities. I have four children.'

'You don't need to tell *me* that.'

'Well, then, you know I can't just walk out on the Partners. I don't want any battles here, especially not with you, but I am under... pressure.'

'These are not my problems, Adrian.' Abi kept her voice as calm as she could. 'These are *your* problems. And maybe your wife's problems. Look, I appreciate the thought, but we'll just keep going as we are, thanks.'

They never did get around to discussing the school holidays.

The call was still bothering her: she wasn't used to hearing Adrian unsettled like that. But she just wanted to forget about it and enjoy her Shannon Smart coup. She decided to move on from Shannon's dig—had it been a dig?—and focus on the interview.

She pulled on her headphones, gestured for Shannon to do the same, and started the interview, as she always did, by asking about what a 'typical day' looked like for a powerhouse like Shannon, and how she balanced her personal wellness with the wellness business.

'I like to start with meditation. It's crucial to set your intention for every day before it begins.'

For breakfast: 'Always, always, water with bee pollen. Then maybe a cheeky chia bowl. Or an activated almond and kale smoothie. Or a turmeric and egg scramble... I'm pretty low maintenance.'

Work routine: 'My staff work from everywhere but we all come together on a Hangout at nine to go through some yoga moves and set our group intention. I trust them to be on top of what they need to be on top of, but I'm also a control freak, so I might pop up at any time on their computers to see what they're up to. Trust issues! Working on that!'

Shannon took Abi through how she made business trips everywhere in the world with just a tiny Kanken backpack for company. 'Stuff, Abi. Stuff is the enemy. It weighs you down—spiritually, mentally, environmentally. I used to have a beautiful home, full of shiny things. Now I basically live in a yurt.'

'Well, it's not quite a yurt...' Abi couldn't help herself, thinking of the sprawling estate down the road.

'It's the same concept, Abi. It's a simple structure in a beautiful place. And I just have the basics of what I need to get by. Wi-fi...'

'A Thermomix?'

'Oh, exactly.'

Finally, Abi and her idol were in a rhythm. They were gelling just as Abi had imagined they would.

'So, Shannon. Have you seen the film *Spiked*? One of my followers has made this documentary that I just think is so fucking important. It's about medicine, and Big Food—'

'About time,' snapped Shannon. 'The biggest challenge facing us today is everyone's blind allegiance to traditional medicine and Big Pharma. If only they knew the truth! If only they would wake up to the fact that the reason there's so much cancer in our world is because of the rubbish they're feeding themselves and their children. Sugar! Sunscreen, fluoride, dairy.' Shannon leant into the mic and said, 'If you are feeding your family sugary breakfast cereal, ham sandwiches, chicken nuggets and SlurpShakes, you are neglecting your children. You are signing their early death certificates. Honestly, I think some parents should be arrested for the way they're feeding their families.'

'Arrested? Well, I agree with you, but that sounds—'

'People are so *stupid*, Abi. You're not, of course, you have seen the light, but I swear, the day I started being present to the real dangers that are all around us was the day the scales fell from my eyes. Shoot little children full of poison so they don't get sick? Douse your home in toxic chemicals so you can call it clean? Put a ready-meal in the microwave to feed your fat kids in front of the TV? Drink milk from a cow, a completely different species from us, and be surprised that it doesn't work with your gut? *Stupid, stupid, stupid*. Honestly, some people deserve to die.'

In person, Shannon's insane rant was glorious to behold. Her voice didn't rise an octave or quiver with uncertainty. She never broke eye contact with Abi.

She drew breath, then dropped a dazzling smile. 'Don't you agree?'

Abi drew her own breath. She thought of her father, the Doctor. She thought of her fully vaccinated daughters' Twisties at the back of the pantry. She thought of the people mover and the three wide-screen TVs in the house.

Then she thought of the Blog-ahhs. And that conversation with Adrian.

'Well, yes, Shannon. I guess I do agree. You could call it natural selection.'

Shannon beamed. 'That's right, Abi. Natural selection.'

**

After their meeting of minds, the two women emerged from the shed, bonded. Shannon's driver was asleep in the front seat of the Prius, air-con still running. Grace and Sol were in the veggie patch, digging up some dinner.

Abi felt elated. That podcast was going to be HUGE, she knew it. It would get picked up by everyone. Her engagement scores would go through the roof.

Shannon hugged her. She smelt of green tea, lavender oil and... cigarettes? 'I didn't do the deal with your husband's wife, by the way,' she said to Abi. 'Such a phoney. I have a few products we could push your way, though—I think we could definitely work together. I'll start talking to some people about you.'

Things were falling into place. What a day. Shannon climbed into the back of the Prius, waving vaguely towards Grace and Sol and the veggie patch.

Dust rose from the car's wheels as it pulled off down the driveway.

What a day.

CHAPTER NINE

ELLE

Sports bras are the new ball gowns.

Elle was working on her 'Helpful Wednesday' post:

How to Take the Best Gym Selfie

Gals—Not everyone can take a great photo at the gym. But a great workout shot is a must-have for motivation.

The last thing you want to be putting out there is some bird's-nest hair, sweaty-pits shocker with a greying bra strap showing. No, no, hell no. Always take your gym selfie BEFORE you start your workout. The only exception to this, ladies, is if you are trying to accentuate your muscle definition—THEN, you need to do an after shot, when you're nice and pumped. So always have an extra pair of tights and a sports bra in your bag to change into for a post-shower pic.

Let's start with some rules:

1. Always check the mirror. Once, I was busy posting pics of my new Lulu ute belt and I noticed that the guy reflected behind me had something dangling from his shorts. Euuuuuw. NOT the look I was going for, believe me.

2. Grey marle. Just don't. Not ever. One word, five letters: S-W-E-A-T.

3. Butt selfies are always best taken at an angle of about 45 degrees. Pop your hip and arch your back. Remember, hand on hip = skinny arm.

4. Cool kicks. If you're posting regularly from the gym—while you're trying to slay your baby weight, let's say—don't always have the same boring trainers. I have 11 pairs on rotation at the moment, and I really let my mood decide the style, but you could have them on a timetable...

Elle's people loved her 'helpful' posts. She had wanted to call them 'Be Like Me', but Cate had suggested, on her second week in, that Elle might want a little more inclusivity in the name. 'Make it about THEM,' she'd said.

Along with her home-tips, the boys' fashion posts and her weekly marriage hacks—sample: *Do not fall into the trap of leaving sex for the weekends. Jump him with a random 'It's Tuesday And The Kids Are In Bed' treat*—Elle's regular weekly posts were building a huge following. And attracting more and more sponsorship dollars.

Today, Elle had been leaving the gym when she got a text that made her want to pash the screen.

Abbott's Farm are in for $150,000.

It was Adrian. He'd been doing a bit of moonlighting to help boost the blog's commercial side. Sponsored posts and paid-for mentions had been rolling along on The Stylish Mumma for a year, but this was their first 'big' client, and competition had been fierce. Feral Abi missing out just made it all the sweeter.

Elle's signature colour was white ('That's not even a colour,' Zoe had told her) and Abbott's Farm was launching a range of white smoothies for mothers and toddlers to share. Thanks to Elle's suggestion of turning her blog bright blue for a week to let all the Abbott's display advertising and product posts stand out, they were about to launch The Stylish Mumma's first big commercial partnership.

As part of their bid, Elle and Cate had shot a sample video for Abbott's—the only problem being that Teddy and Freddie hated the almond-milk-and-chia-seed smoothies they were meant to be sipping, dressed in cobalt blue in Elle's all-white kitchen.

'*Muuuuuum*, this is *grooooooosssss*,' three-year-old Teddy kept saying, every time the iPhone was pointed at him. Two-year-old Freddie just kept spitting it onto the benchtop.

Cate had come up with the genius plan of replacing the smoothies with McDonald's vanilla thick shakes. No one would know. As far as Elle was aware, her boys had never tasted anything from Maccas, but Cate disappeared in the Range Rover and returned to a rapturous reception. 'I LOVE those!' exclaimed Freddie. Elle looked sideways at Cate. We'll be talking about this later, she thought.

At least Cate's plan had worked—she'd been so useful that day.

When Elle got the text message from Adrian, Abbott's had obviously just said yes, and she was tempted to run all the way home in delight, despite the fact she had just done the kind of butt-workout that makes big men cry.

***

Back when she was staying at her Auntie Liane's house in Dandenong, Elle had started doing an online personal training course. She'd also found her first proper job.

Liane wasn't really her aunt, but her mother's favourite cousin. She had two adult sons by the time Elle turned up on her doorstep—one who'd joined the army and was on tour in

Afghanistan, one who was in prison out at Beechworth — and two empty rooms.

Liane was never going to send her cousin's tear-streaked seventeen-year-old daughter away, but she was also determined not to let her lie around clogging up her empty nest. 'You can stay,' she'd told Elle, 'but you have to get out of here every day. Get a job. Get busy.' Lessons had been learnt in Liane's house.

At first, Elle would jump on the train to the city, talk her way through the barriers and just walk around Melbourne all day. She had spent her whole childhood imagining this place. She'd been told it was dangerous and soulless, hostile and expensive, but everywhere she looked, she saw possibility. She loved how people marched with pace and purpose.

Sometimes she'd find a crowd — heading to the footy, or the train station at peak hour — and follow it, just enjoying the sensation of being carried along. She dodged the approaches of the men who hung around stations with an eye for teenage girls with nothing to fill their days.

After a few weeks, Elle started walking into shops and asking for jobs. What was the worst that could happen? What happened was, eventually, Sportsgirl said yes. And four weeks after getting on a Greyhound out of her hometown, Elle had a bed and a job and an auntie who fed her. And she had started her personal training. She began to see herself as full of possibility, too.

***

Adrian. I love you, Elle typed back to his Abbott's text. *I love you I love you I love you. Definitely dessert tonight!*

Oh, Abi would be *spitting*. This was fabulous. And it was bound to help with the Blog-ahhs. Abi could be a threat in the 'organic space', as the marketers called it, but seriously, she and her whingeing sister-in-law couldn't touch Elle and Adrian as a team. She had persuaded Adrian to put the pressure on Abi to bow out, but since it hadn't worked, beating her was the best revenge.

Abbott's wanted the boys to be in the campaign, of course—who wouldn't? But there was a gap between Teddy and Freddie's photogenic appeal and their willingness to cooperate. 'They're little boys, after all,' Adrian would often remind Elle. 'They should be outside, playing with balls,' he'd say, as Elle and Cate squeezed one of Freddie's chubby toddler legs into another pair of skinny-rough-hem jeans.

'Come on, Adrian,' Elle would argue, 'boys don't need to be sporty at this age. And don't be so narrow-minded. Boys can love fashion and photography, you know. Look at Romeo Beckham!'

'Maybe. But not when they're two.'

The other sore point was their hair. Elle loved the aesthetic of long, shaggy black curls, but Adrian thought it should be cut.

'I wouldn't even know who they were with short hair,' Elle argued.

'Then we have more of a problem than I thought.'

Elle knew she would win these arguments because, ultimately, Adrian wanted what she wanted: for her to be happy. To have a successful business. And to win. That, Elle was convinced, was what set the two of them apart. Shared goals. Teamwork. Determination.

***

At Sportsgirl, Elle had made a friend. Tina was trying to get work as a promotional model and through her, Elle came to understand that if you were young and pretty and could string a few sentences together, you could get paid to spend Saturday nights going around bars talking people into trying a burrito or an energy drink. Or you could spend your weekend mornings down at St Kilda giving out samples of a new coffee, cold cans of cola, a gym membership, a phone plan. She and Tina helped each other with headshots, with applications, with fending off the sleazy men who ran the agencies—and, soon enough, Elle was a weekend 'promo girl'.

The only drawback was the endless flirting: her with the guys, the guys with her. It involved routine harassment and the occasional groping. The odd idiot who decided that she and him were meant to be and wouldn't take no for an answer.

Some of the other girls wanted to meet a footballer—access to them was a perk of the job. But Elle had grown up with big, brash men who behaved like angry toddlers when they were drunk. She knew exactly what they were capable of. She had no interest in men like that. She liked the Suits. The meek ones, the older ones, the ones who couldn't quite believe you were talking to them. Those guys were Elle's sweet spot, even then.

By her twenty-first birthday, Sportsgirl was history and so was Auntie Liane's. Elle was living in a South Yarra apartment with Tina and two other models, and making enough money for rent and her personal training course. The job she really wanted had nothing to do with convincing tipsy meatheads to try an American hotdog. On the back of her bedroom door she had taped a picture of who she wanted to be.

It was Tracy Anderson, trainer to the stars, self-created goddess, Gwyneth Paltrow's bestie. The woman whose mantra was 'No Excuses'.

Elle's first real taste of 'community' came from the suburban gym she joined when she was training for her PT course. She didn't count her hometown—there was nothing particularly supportive about that, unless you counted the women who would periodically swarm her father, armed with port and pies. He was a young widow and not a known psychopath, so he was a catch. But five shitbag kids wasn't a drawcard, it turned out, especially since the women had a few brats of their own trailing behind them.

But at the gym, Elle found people who wanted to help one another, to make one another stronger, literally. They were obsessive about a common goal — self-improvement — and that was a drive that Elle understood. While at the gym, she started her first-ever blog: a training diary, mostly, a dry repetition of what she'd lifted and squatted and sprinted, with photos documenting her changing body. She liked to lie in bed and feel her stomach, let her fingers walk across her tightening abs, find her hipbones. She was getting harder every day. This proved to her what she genuinely believed to be true — you could change anything if you tried hard enough: what you looked like, how you spoke, how you thought, who you were. What had happened to you.

You could actually create your own reality.

Not that snippets of ugly realism didn't impinge on Elle's life in those years. One morning, before a pre-dawn PT session, a hulking roid-head tried to rape her in the changing room. She was 'saved' from that moment by the arrival of three weight-training sisters. Years later, she still fingered the places on her wrist and neck where the bruises had been.

She'd had to leave Auntie Liane's because of her cousin Kane. He got out of prison, found her living in his mum's house and called her a 'gold-digging piece of shit' to her face, sparking an eruption that meant she was no longer welcome with that side of the family. Although the notion there was any gold to be dug was hilarious, it had stung because she knew he must have talked to her brothers before he picked those words.

There were friendships with women that burned bright and hard for a short time, but always fizzled out. Elle suspected — her self-help books backed her up — that losing her mother so young had bruised her ability to trust in other women entirely. There was always something performative in the way she behaved around girlfriends, however much she actively liked them. Elle was not, by nature, a pack animal.

By the time she had started writing her anonymous blog about falling in love with a married man, she was working at the gym full-time, only doing promo shifts on fitness-related jobs—no more meatheads in bars—and planning the next stage.

And the next stage was Security.

***

Adrian, Elle knew, was worried about money. The Brighton house renovation had gone over budget, not least because of her need for the interior to be picture-perfect from every angle. 'It's an investment,' she'd told him. 'This is our set. Our backdrop.'

'I thought it was our home.'

'Well, that too. But really, it's win-win. We live somewhere beautiful, and we don't need to hire location houses or studios. It's everything.'

Having two preschoolers in a show home had its drawbacks, of course. Freddie had banged his head on the raised Italian-slate edge of the fireplace more than once. Teddy had drawn on the white silk lounge and then endured three days of mum-silence. Elle had begrudgingly—and expensively—needed to glass off her floating staircase after it became clear that it was a deathtrap for toddlers.

'Not sure that's the best idea when you've got little kids around,' the architect had told a then-pregnant Elle when they were planning the stairs. 'You can't put a safety gate on that.'

'They won't be little forever,' Elle had replied. 'It raises the bar.'

But after Freddie had almost toppled through them for the second time, she'd realised it might be a bad look. Of course, she'd made sure to let Instagram know how she was sacrificing style for safety.

> Can't believe my architect didn't warn me about the dangers of my #floatingstairs My beautiful boys' safety comes before everything else, and the end result looks pretty special, too. #mummabear

94

Her perfectionism was paying off, Elle could feel it. She had Abbott's smoothies. Next she'd win the Blog-ahhs, and Adrian's money worries would be over for good.

5. The most important tip, my stylish friends, is not to be self-conscious about taking your gym selfie. If you try to sneak your phone out and snap a pic from a bad angle, you will get a bad picture. Be out, be proud. Mediocre efforts get mediocre results. Wear your tightest and brightest, pop that bum, push those girls out. You only get one chance to show off the best you. Do not apologise. And remember: No Excuses.

CHAPTER TEN

LEISEL

I waited so long to be a mother. And now I'm here, some days I can't stand it.

For decades I imagined I had tiny hands in mine as I walked down the street. Now I have that. In fact, I don't have enough hands to guide all the little people who need me.

So why do I so often wish my children would get away from me? Stop needing me so much? Why am I so quick to anger at them when they are just loving their mum?

I spent so long imagining having all these people to love, why do I sit here some days feeling as if I hate what they've done to my life?

Today's was the kind of post that Leisel's followers loved the most. It was also the kind of post that really, really pissed off her troll.

Well, her trolls.

Her many posts about motherhood angst and regret had ignited a small, committed band of mum-warriors who were triggered into a keyboard-bashing and cupcake-baking rage by any hint of negativity about the holy business of mothering.

The Contented Mum set the tone:

> Some of us feel blessed every moment that we are lucky enough to spend with our children. And then there's you, who barely even sees her kids, and when she does, only moans about how demanding they are. It's women like you, Working Mum, who should never have had kids in the first place. You are a disgrace.

Grateful for Gifts wrote:

> We have fought so hard to have our babies, given up so much for the privilege of calling ourselves 'mothers', it's very hard to hear someone like you shit all over it.

Of course, things escalated quickly. This was the internet. Soon almost every post she wrote attracted a smattering of abuse.

From BlessedMumOfFour:

> I hope something terrible happens to your children, you shitty excuse for a mother. #notsorry

And from AngelMama76:

> Why women like you have children, I'll never know, you ungrateful turd. #sewitup

Women like her.

Five years ago, Leisel hadn't had any idea that there were other women like her. She hadn't seen them anywhere. The women all around her had seemed to be bounding through life, baby on hip, briefcase in hand, handsome husband at the barbecue.

When Leisel looked back on this now, it seemed so ridiculous, so naive, but she had truly thought that she was the only one wondering why parenthood wasn't as perfect as it looked in the brochure.

She'd never been the only one, of course. And she'd learnt that by blogging. The solace she'd found there had been the start of her addiction. It had become the reason why she was searching for stories to share every day.

***

Leisel was thirty-eight when she and Mark had Maggie. She'd read the magazines. Hell, she'd written some of the magazines. She knew how unlikely it was that she and her middle-aged boyfriend—who had spent a portion of his adulthood filling his body with addictive poison—had successfully created a life. If she'd been a TV star, she would have been wearing white and beaming from a magazine cover with MY MIRACLE BABY across her chest. Instead, she was a tired and bloated daily commuter, secretly delighted that her script had been rewritten.

Leisel had spent all of her thirties being pitied and patronised. She was one of the many women of her generation who didn't settle down early that no one seemed to know what to do with. This was the era post-Bridget Jones, mid-RSVP, pre-Tinder. She had travelled. She had a 'good' job. She had her own apartment in one of the more desirable parts of Sydney, one of the world's more desirable cities.

She was happy, mostly, and known for telling her friends—three wines in—that she'd never been that maternal anyway. Weekends were spin class and brunch and dinners, dinners, dinners. She'd survived that early thirties stage where every Saturday afternoon was spent at someone's beachside wedding, dodging the singles' table and the cries of 'You next!' She'd got through all those Sunday morning baby showers, with their Bellinis and macarons and humiliating games involving toilet paper and tape measures. She went on improving solo holidays and girls' weekends to the Hunter, and she wondered what her forties would look like. Some days, she felt hopeful about unchartered waters. Other days, she felt certain she would drown.

And then, one day, she woke up and everything had changed. Overnight, she had been replaced by a pulsing sack of hormonal longing. She wanted a baby. Her guts wanted a baby. Her *hair* wanted a baby.

Before, she had handled her friends' newborns nervously with a polite disinterest. Now, she had to stop herself from inhaling them.

Worst of all, Leisel knew she had become a walking cliché. She had spent years arguing over the very existence of the 'biological clock'. And here it was, clanging so loudly that she couldn't hear anything else.

And that was when she looked up Mark on Facebook. It wasn't—she assured her followers much later—as premeditated as it sounded. She was having a low moment, she was thinking about her past. She was wondering why she had spent so much of her twenties only interested in men with (to use a polite word) 'issues'. Mark was one of those guys. She was twenty-four when they got together, twenty-six when they broke up, and the things she'd learnt in between were useful in choosing her next boyfriend. She'd learnt that the words 'drug habit' were entirely inadequate. Picking your nose was a habit. What Mark was compelled to do on those frequent falls off the wagon was more like the Terminator's kamikaze mission—pre-programmed, irreversible.

She'd learnt that drug addicts lie. Even soft-souled, considerate, poetic, beautiful ones. Ones who knew all your secrets, ones whose secrets you knew (or at least thought you knew). They could look you in the eye and say that they hadn't taken that twenty dollars from your wallet. They could look you in the eye and say that they hadn't taken that fifty dollars from your mum's wallet. They could look you in the eye and say that they hadn't gone around to their ex-girlfriend's place, slept with her and taken a hundred dollars from her wallet, even though she was now screaming blue murder on your doorstep.

Leisel had certainly been in love with Mark. But, ultimately, she had never been interested in a life Like That. During their time together, he was always getting clean and holding it together for weeks or days. Then he would disappear. Or reappear, with a certain look in his eye, a certain way of holding his shoulders that signalled he was using.

They'd been crashing in his travelling friend's studio in Surry Hills. When Mark had sold his mate's CDs, TV and even his rag rug, Leisel knew it was time to go. He was demonstratively broken-hearted—for a day. 'You could be the only one who can save me from myself,' he actually said, with a straight face. Then, he vanished.

Leisel moved home to her mum's on the north shore until she found a share house with a friend and shook off what she quickly came to view as a sordid chapter in her otherwise pretty standard twenty-something story.

But there she was, ten years later, looking for Mark online. And she was surprised to find him. She'd assumed he was the kind of guy who thought social media was tacky and held himself apart from it.

But there he was. In photos, a little older, a little softer around the edges. He was living in Milton, a small coastal town a few hours south of Sydney, framing pictures for a living. His posts were sparse. Some political stuff about refugees. Some pictures of his work. Some words about wood and the pleasures of working with recycled native timber.

She messaged him.

It's been a long time. How are you?

He messaged back.

I am ashamed of how I treated you. I am ashamed
of a lot of things.

Maybe it was nostalgia, maybe it was the whole pulsing-sack-of-hormonal-longing thing, but Leisel kept writing to Mark. And he kept writing back. He'd been clean for five years. It was still a struggle. He felt like he'd had to rebuild his personality from the ground up. Sometimes days without using still seemed unbearably long, but mostly he was doing well. He was enjoying a quieter life.

He came to the city to see his new nephew. He and Leisel met up for a coffee—not a drink.

And it was a revelation. Leisel found herself just saying things that were true. 'I'm tired of being alone. I'm ready for my life to change. I'm ready to stop messing around.'

And Mark looked at her, and he said, 'Me too.'

The sex had always been great. It still was.

It seemed like only days passed between coffee and Mark moving back to town and in with her, but it must have been months, surely? And then it seemed like only months between that and their wedding—not on a Saturday at a beach, but on a Friday afternoon in a city park they'd always loved. Just a few people. Her mother, glowering. His parents, beaming. Friends and all their babies. Babies everywhere. A quick dinner at the local pub. All over by 9 p.m. The two of them in bed in her little flat, looking at each other, laughing about how such old people could feel so young and hopeful again.

And so: the 'miracle' of Maggie.

Motherhood, as Leisel would later write in her blog, smacked her across the face with a wet nappy.

Everything changed. Mark, it seemed, was a natural. He was instinctive in the way he could hold and comfort and cradle his baby girl. But Leisel reverted to being the single girl who held babies at arm's-length. She adored Maggie instantly in a way she didn't fully understand, but she had no idea what to do with her.

Maggie cried a lot. She didn't feed well. She had reflux, apparently, although no one could really tell Leisel what that was. Nobody slept. The flat felt smaller and smaller.

Leisel went back to work after six months because her savings ran out and Mark didn't have any. He took what work he could get as a carpenter for friends, but he didn't have his papers. So he looked after Maggie, and Leisel headed to the office.

Those first few months were a brutal blur of stumbling, sleepless days, of pretending she knew what she was doing in meetings, what she was meant to say—when really, her tongue was thick in her mouth and her brain couldn't hold a thought.

Everything was changing at work, in magazines. Cuts, everywhere. As the teams shrank, Leisel took on more work.

In the middle of this craziness, when Maggie was less than one, Leisel got pregnant again. 'Who knew?' she said to Mark. 'Who knew that after all these years of spinsterdom, I'm the most fertile old woman on the planet?'

At ten weeks, she miscarried. She'd had no idea what that was going to feel like. A baby that wasn't planned, early in the pregnancy. It felt like the end of the world.

She wrote about it and had the piece published on a parenting site.

You don't have to pay for the ultrasound when your baby is dead. The woman hands you the tissues and says how very sorry she is. She gives you a moment. You look back at the screen, where there's meant to be a small, white, beating spot. There isn't. There's only smudge.

You pull up your jeans. You find a bin. And you walk out to the waiting room where no one asks you for your credit card. The women who are waiting, who are desperately hoping they are not you, they try not to make eye contact. You try not to make eye contact.

Because you will cry.

And when you go outside, you do. And you can't stop.

It was Leisel's first taste of online sharing. And it changed everything. The response from the women who had been through the same thing was enormous. And it helped.

So much grief and guilt and pain. How were there so many women walking around with all of this? Why was no one talking about it?

So Leisel started to write about motherhood. It began as a way to make sense of her feelings about where she was: completely overwhelmed by the responsibility of one child but unreasonably desperate to have another.

And then Rich happened. A beautiful boy.

This time, while life was every bit as chaotic as before, Leisel had an outlet. She wrote and wrote—late at night, as dawn broke, on the bus, quietly at her desk. Her followers grew, slowly, solidly. Women who also couldn't understand how there was room in their heads and hearts for all these battling emotions. Or how the hell they got through every day. The feeling of community made the odd negative sledge seem worth it.

And then, completely unexpectedly, came a pregnancy classified as 'geriatric': Harriet. The over-forty pregnancy diary had been good for the blog.

Now there were five in Leisel's family. And they still lived in the flat she had bought when there was one of her.

And here she was, after a difficult day, pouring her last remaining energy into writing about her love and her rage, and attracting the fury of a few angry women.

Leisel closed her laptop. She tiptoed into the adult bedroom, where Mark was snoring, and lay down next to him, curled into his back. Mark. She hadn't asked him how he was. She realised that she hadn't asked him for days. Guilt.

Her phone chirped quietly. She knew she shouldn't look. It was late, and Harri would be crying soon. She looked.

It was a Facebook message.

It was from The Contented Mum.

I'm at your front door.

MAY

CHAPTER ELEVEN

ELLE

To those of you who've missed my boys these past few days, thank you for your messages. We're all just reeling from some family news and need some time to regroup. Stay tuned. I'll need all your support soon. #loveandlight

Elle had not posted on social media for two whole days. This was not normal. Not normal at all. At the very least, Elle's followers expected their morning update on what the boys were wearing.

Her inbox was full of messages:

Where are you, girl? #MIA

Are the boys okay? #missmygorgeousbabies

Elle was fine. The boys were fine. Right now, Cate was upstairs shooting them in distressed 'My Dad's My

Hero' T-shirts for this week's announcement. They were complaining, loudly.

Elle was in her kitchen/office, working on the post. Building anticipation was crucial. Her followers would be talking among themselves right now about what that family news could be. Another baby? A divorce?

'Maybe she broke a nail,' someone would be sniping.

Adrian was sitting at the kitchen table, spinning his phone in his hands. Every minute or so he nervously poked at the screen to lock and unlock. He was quiet. He'd been looking anxious ever since Elle had convened their war room about the Leisel Situation.

It was Cate who had first seen the messages about what had happened to Leisel Adams. Two words started spiking all over the Facebook groups that she monitored as a matter of course:

Troll attack.

'This is a disaster,' Cate said, taking the unusual step of crossing the kitchen threshold, iPad in hand.

Elle glanced up from the juicing ingredients she'd been laying out on the wooden benchtop for an Instagram post for PulpPump Juicers. Uneven celery sticks were frustrating her aesthetic.

'What now, Cate?' she asked, irritated by the intrusion. Then she looked at the iPad. She looked at Cate. 'Fuck,' was all she said.

The Blog-ahhs nominations announcement had made the conditions clear: each blogger had three months to build maximum exposure. And simple numbers of Likes were not enough. How did the audience engage with your brand? How much time did they spend with you daily? What was the number of meaningful interactions? Did you peak and trough? Could you hold their attention? Were your numbers growing in a sustainable way? Were your followers commenting and sharing, or just passively reading your posts, bitching to their friends about you and then getting on with their day? Crucially, were you bringing your 'partners' a return on their investment?

All those millions of people—in the coffee queue, on the tram, mindlessly scrolling through their feeds all day, every day—had no idea. They didn't understand that where they hovered and paused, where they watched and clicked, where they swiped and tapped, where their thumb stopped while they turned to yell at their toddler, all of that had major implications for a brand like Elle's. It could make or break you.

Cate understood all of this very well. She had studied digital media at uni. Social media was the primary language she'd spoken since she was twelve. Cate had told Elle that she, like all her friends, spent about ten hours a day on Facebook, Instagram and Snapchat, but hers was a professional passion: she knew how to decode the analytics, how to chase engagement, how to beat the shifts in algorithms that the Californian overlords twisted and tweaked to keep you on your toes. In the battle for the Blog-ahhs, Cate was Elle's secret weapon.

But even Cate couldn't compete with this shit.

Elle didn't know Leisel. They had never met, and Elle had never taken her seriously. All she knew was that Leisel's sister was Feral Abi's girlfriend, and that Leisel was an amateur, a whiner. The way that the Leisels of the world saw blogging, like some kind of helpline for sad women feeling guilty about their depressing lives? Pathetic.

But Elle's instincts were sharp. She knew that two things would follow this news about the troll attack: first, an outpouring of sympathy and support for Leisel as the victim of a terrible crime. And then scrutiny of all three nominated bloggers and their work. A moment in the mainstream spotlight. An opportunity.

And like a politician gearing up to campaign, Elle knew that what The Stylish Mumma needed to stand out was a talking point. Something to change the conversation.

Elle looked over at Adrian again. There he was, the man who was going to change the conversation. The man who was going to keep those numbers coming for Abbott's and the other clients who would follow.

Men like Adrian, in Elle's experience, headed into middle age by either relaxing into a beer gut and succumbing to every footy pie they'd ever met, or buying a bike and training for a triathlon. Adrian, of course, fell into the latter category. When Elle had met him, at the gym, he was what the trainers called a 'MAMIL'—a Middle-Aged Man in Lycra. It was as though he'd woken up to realise that he wasn't twenty-seven or even thirty-seven anymore, and that turning out at the last minute for a weekend footy game wasn't as easy as it had always been.

Rowing, squash, a Saturday morning kick of the footy: Adrian was a private school boy used to sport punctuating his week and being a way to keep up with old mates. But in those middle Abi years, life overtook him—and, Elle knew, he looked down at his gut in the shower one day and panicked. This was not who he was.

Adrian wasn't the first married man Elle had 'dated'. He was the second. But the first time, she reasoned, didn't count because she hadn't known. Well, not at first.

***

Lachy was a client at the gym. In those years, her whole life was the gym. After her move from the suburbs, she worked out of one near her shared apartment in South Yarra. Lots of Pilates.

The staff were encouraged to be friendly to the clients—to make them feel like they were part of the 'family' and that they were all in this together. It bred intimacy and demolished boundaries. 'We want the civilians to feel like they could be trainers, if only they were prepared to give up the nine-to-five,' was how the head trainer put it. The staff would giggle:

they knew that wasn't possible. Three spin classes a week did not a professional make.

Lachy turned up at the gym most evenings, definitely one of the wannabes. Handsome, polite, respectful—at least compared to the meatheads who tried to grab Elle as she walked past—he asked her out for a post-work smoothie at least once a week. Used to saying no, Elle surprised herself when, one evening, she didn't. It had been a long time, she reasoned, and she wanted to feel something.

But it only took one visit to his place for her to realise that the flatmate he'd mentioned was a lot more than that. A pink toothbrush in the mug. A woman's razor and sponge hanging by the shower. Tampons, pads and lube in the bathroom cabinet. A collection of deep-conditioning shampoos that Lachy definitely wasn't using on his crew cut.

A few evenings later, Elle watched on from the front desk with all the curiosity of David Attenborough observing a chimp-mating ritual when a young woman, throbbing with indignation, marched into the gym and berated Lachy as he was powering away at the pec-deck. 'What did you do, you fucker? *WHO IS SHE?!*' she screamed, before breaking down. 'Why did we ever get married? I told you, you could go.'

What a waste, thought Elle. What a waste of a good woman, crying over a man too foolish to check the bathroom for booby-traps. On her final visit to the loft, just last night, Elle had planted a hair-tie—a garish, fluoro-pink one at that—under the soap by the sink. She'd followed up with a spare bra in the washing basket.

Silly, silly man. Caught out by two women. As Lachy glanced at her, panicked, Elle just smiled at him, a little too brightly, and got on with the next day's schedule.

One more week and she transferred to a city gym. She was finished with screwing around. The next man in her life was going to be her husband.

Adrian, Elle knew, hated his job at the Partners. No longer a MAMIL, he was still a strong man in his prime. Having her at his side made him feel powerful and wanted. Now, they had to use that confidence to push them where they wanted to go.

Where Elle wanted to go, Adrian wanted to go — it was for his own good, after all.

Watching him fiddle with his phone, probably deciding what to say to Alex and Arden, Elle knew that Adrian's desire to change his life was bigger than his fear of a lie. Although her husband thought of himself as a decent man, a family man, a man of honourable intentions, the real Adrian was competitive and insecure, and looking at fifty with a deep-seated fear that he wasn't living up to his promise. At the moment in his life when he'd met Elle, he'd been looking for what came next — his Second Act.

She just hoped that during their war room chat, she had convinced him that this was the step to take to make it count.

'But I look perfectly healthy!' had been his first response, when Elle had suggested the idea. 'No one will believe it.'

'They don't need to see you,' she'd told him. 'Your face never appears on the blog anyway. We won't change that. The only people who'll need to be convinced are the ones who know us, the ones who know you're married to me.'

'Yes, our family and friends. The people who know me best — the people who might care that I'm dying.'

'Not *dying*, babe. Don't be dramatic. Sick. Struggling. In treatment.'

'And what about work?'

'Well, plenty of people work through treatment.'

Elle did this thing whenever she wanted to talk Adrian into something. Like getting married. Like building the glass house. Like pretending he had cancer.

She lowered her voice, the voice she'd worked so hard on, and she put a really firm hand on his arm. She leant in close, so he could smell her. 'And the Partners could give you some time off, you know, if things get bad.'

'If things get bad?'

'You know, if we need to turn it up a bit.'

How many people make up a conspiracy? Elle and Adrian at the kitchen bench. Cate outside the door waiting for the green light. The kids asleep upstairs.

'We're building something, Adrian. Something that can change all of our lives. We've got clients who want to spend more, we've got the awards coming up. We just need a big story. This is it. This is our story.'

'But what about the girls? What about Abi?'

'A lot of people's dads get sick, babe. You're not going to die, that's the important part. To be honest, being worried about you might not be a bad thing for those girls. They could appreciate you more.'

He was giving her that 'Who *are* you?' look, and Elle realised she'd gone too far. 'I'm joking, Adrian.' She squeezed his arm tighter. 'They're teenagers. They'll be a bit worried, then everything will be okay. No big deal. Don't you want to give them the very best of everything? As for Abi...' What to say about Feral Abi? 'She'll just send you some organic soup and think you're cured.' Elle forced a laugh.

Adrian didn't look convinced. 'I don't want people feeling sorry for me,' he said. '"Victim" isn't an image I'm interested in cultivating.'

'What about "hero"? Fighting this is about strength, not weakness.'

Already, 'this' was sounding real.

'So,' said Adrian, 'what do we do?'

It was done, Elle realised. The next wave of The Stylish Mumma would be about grace under pressure. It was going to be huge.

She left Adrian in the kitchen and went to tell Cate the news.

'He's in.' Elle smiled. 'Now, we need to tell some people

before the post. Clients, first up. I'll talk to Abbott's, you take PulpPump. Adrian's telling the girls, but not until the post is ready. We don't want them going all emo on Instagram before we get the word out.'

'Wow, Elle.' Cate trailed after her, two steps to Elle's every one. 'I didn't think he'd go for it. *Why* would he do that?'

'I told you,' Elle said shortly, starting up the stairs to the boys and their wardrobes — what they were going to wear for the announcement was crucial. 'Adrian and I are a team. He believes in what we're doing.'

He can see the dollar signs, she added in her head. She was also silently praising him for making sure that Cate signed a non-disclosure agreement when she started working for them — she wouldn't have thought of it. Adrian could be so useful.

'He completes me,' she said aloud. 'He really does.'

***

How had Elle known that Adrian was the right husband?

At the city gym, the clientele were different. Not so much Pilates and not as many tattoos. The men came in distinct groups: the MAMILs, the Gorgeous Gays and the Masters of the Universe. The Masters were young, intense, driven. They wanted intimidating pecs under their Tom Ford shirts, and they chased results the way they chased business — with complete focus and zero humour.

Elle saw potential in them, but she also saw trouble. She saw men who would never be satisfied, who would always be more focused on their success than her own, whose future held many Elles.

This is what people get wrong when they wonder why young women go for older men, Elle thought. They think it's a compromise for money and status, but it's a strategic move not to have to spend the next twenty years looking over your shoulder.

Since Elle had decided that a husband was what she wanted, she'd been studying the men around her, dividing them into groups and weighing up their pros and cons. But while she watched the men, she mostly trained the women — ambitious young women whose goals were focused, like those of the Masters, on specific body parts: lifting their butt, pumping up their calves, shredding their arms. Elle respected this objectivity. 'You are,' she would tell them, 'a work in progress. You will never be finished, but along the way you'll get close to perfection.'

She sometimes took on an older woman, but their self-deprecation infuriated her. They would apologise their way through the weigh-in, refuse to own their goals — 'I just need to be able to run around with my kids' — and never let themselves celebrate milestones — 'Yes, but I really need to lose another five.'

From where she sat now, Elle knew she'd learnt a lot about her blog audience from those days at the gym. But back then, she was watching the men.

Adrian came in every weekday. Sometimes at 6 a.m. Sometimes during a break in afternoon meetings. Sometimes after the office and before some evening function.

Elle noticed him immediately, because of his eyes. Adrian was handsome but not troublingly so. He was tall but not imposing, his body was good but not perfect. His eyes, though, were kind, and warm, and seemed to really focus on things — like Elle, when she entered his awareness — with intensity. He was forty-two, almost twice Elle's age in the year that they met.

So she began to watch him. While she was training one of her girls, or clearing up or getting her paperwork straight, or working out herself, she took note of when he'd be there. She started to take some of the classes he took. She asked around.

He was married, although he never mentioned his wife. He worked in finance (they all worked in finance, as far as Elle could tell) and she could see that the other MAMILs and

Masters treated him with some deference when they chatted by the machines, denoting his status. He seemed confident but not arrogant. He was polite to trainers and staff, and he didn't ogle. He didn't grab.

Elle googled him. Corporate page from his firm. Facebook page he hadn't updated in over a year. Old Boys' rowing club.

Married adds a layer of difficulty, she had written in her diary, the precursor to Somebody Else's Husband. But really, she thought, who isn't married at forty-two? The Bad Guys, that's who.

It was time to talk to him. So one night, as Adrian crunched in front of a mirror in the floor room, Elle walked in with an armful of boxing gloves and said, 'You're here every day. I hope your wife appreciates the progress you're making.'

Adrian stopped, looked up and smiled. 'I don't think she's noticed,' he said, reaching for his water. 'But that's fine. I'm not doing it for her. I just want the second half of my life to be better than the first.'

He would tell her later that he had no idea why he'd said that. Why he'd offered up something so personal to a strange young woman with boxing gloves.

But what she'd thought at the time was: bingo.

***

At the kitchen table, Adrian stopped fiddling with his phone and called the girls. With Elle listening in closely, he played down the situation exactly as he would have done if he really did have lymphoma.

'You don't need to worry,' he told them. 'It's all going to look a bit scary for a while, but I'll be fine.'

Alex and Arden didn't wail or sob. They didn't promise to leap on the next train to the city. They were silent. And then Arden asked a few questions: 'Are you going to die, Dad?' and 'Will you lose your hair?' and 'Do you think it's because you guys use a microwave?'

Fucking home-schooling, Elle thought. Fucking Grace and Abi.

Adrian assured them no, no and no. He got off the phone, promising he would call their mother later. Then he gave Elle the nod. And she pushed publish on her blog, and Cate did the same on four different social media platforms at once.

Hello ladies. There's something I need to tell you. In the past few days, I've had to face the possibility of losing my true north, the centre of my family, the reason why every day I try to be the very best version of myself that I can: My beloved A.

Three days ago, I sat beside him in a doctors' office and heard the words that we all dread hearing more than any others, words that I know many of you have had to hear, too: 'It's cancer.'

For us, 'cancer' means Non-Hodgkin Lymphoma. It's been attacking A from the inside for months, even as he's been providing for us as he always does, being a loving father and husband and friend as he always is, playing his beloved sport, riding his beloved bike.

Life can change in a moment for any of us, and ours has in these past few days. We've taken a little while to decide how we want, as a family, to face this, and I don't think many of you will be surprised to hear we have decided to face it with style. With a smile. With a united front and an unshakable resolve that NO, it's not going to break us. We won't be weeping in corners. We won't be staying in our pyjamas all day.

We will share this journey with you, my fellow SMs, because we need to feel your support. But we will also be going on as usual, trying to brighten every life we can, in any way we can, because, after all, what else is there? What is more important?

Please send us your support and prayers. A needs all the love he can get—but, in the meantime, know that we will not be lying down, and that he has his army around him, led by these two little guys who think Daddy hung the moon. #screwcancer #astylishfight #hospitalfashion #dontrainonmyparade #coolcottonkidz

The photo was perfection: Teddy and Freddie in their rock'n'roll 'My Dad's My Hero' tees, with shaggy hair across their sad eyes (Cate had threatened them with removing their iPad privileges), fists shaking at the camera.

It had only been up for fifty seconds and there were already 250 Likes.

CHAPTER TWELVE

ABI

'You can't drop that, Abi, you just CAN'T!' Grace was waving a phone in Abi's face and shouting.

It seemed too early for this kind of drama. Abi was trying to eat her paleo granola. 'Gracey, calm the fuck down.'

'Calm the fuck down? *Really*?'

The kids had made themselves scarce. Otto was the last one disappearing out the door. 'If you two are going to fight, I'm going to hitch a ride to school,' he'd muttered. Even this hadn't distracted Grace.

'My sister has just been attacked by a crazy person for saying that motherhood can be hard sometimes, and you are about to release a podcast telling parents that they are killing their kids if they feed them sugar.' Grace's voice dropped from a yell to a whisper. 'Does that seem sensible to you? Does that seem safe?'

Abi stopped eating her granola. It was very unusual for Grace to get so worked up about anything, but then again, this awful Leisel thing had really knocked her—she'd just got back from a visit to her sister in Sydney, and she wasn't her usual sunshine-and-oatmeal self. 'Grace. Babe. Please.' Abi reached out and grabbed Grace's hand, pulling her into one of the mismatched chairs at their wooden kitchen table. 'I know this will make you crazy, but... I think you're overreacting.'

Grace tugged her hand away from Abi's, folded her arms on the table and put her head on them. 'Am I? Am I really?' She sighed. 'Maybe. But it feels provocative to me. People are threatening to picket *Spiked*, you know. I can't stop thinking about what happened to Lee in her own home. I feel like someone's turning up the heat under the pan.'

Abi looked at the top of Grace's tangled head and put her hand on it. 'Babe. If you're not pissing anyone off, you're not doing it right. These are dangerous ideas because they're worth hearing.'

'But...' Grace raised her head. 'Are they really even your ideas, Abi? I mean, your girls are vaccinated. You go to the doctor. How can you complain about Big Pharma when you pop a Naprogesic every time you get a cramp?'

'Shhh, Grace.' Abi was irritated. This was not how her morning was supposed to start. She'd been looking forward to today—now they knew that Leisel was okay, she wanted to get back to business. She'd planned to release the podcast this morning, and the blog post she'd written to go with it, and then she was going to sip tea while watching the Twitter fight explode, jumping in and swinging chairs whenever she needed to: it was the only kind of sport she could get behind.

'You know life's more complicated than that, Gracey.' She crunched a mouthful of granola, her voice muffled when she said, 'Anyway, I do NOT. I always try that fucking cinnamon tea first.'

'Gaaaaah.' Grace got up, leaving her phone on the table, and went to the kettle. 'Okay. So what's your plan? What are you going to do when the *Daily Trail* picks up that you and Shannon Smart are calling most Australian parents negligent? Saying that they deserve to die?'

'We didn't say that. Come on.'

'Abi, you said the words "natural selection".'

Abi couldn't help chuckling. 'I am allowed an opinion,

Grace. And if the *Trail* calls, I will tell them that their readers could do with a dose of reality. That it's a relief to see them care about something other than the shape of a soap star's arse.'

'Well.' Grace turned around, leaning against the stove, and looked at Abi. 'I'm sure that will help a lot.'

'Grace, here's the thing.' Spoon down. 'We are up against the big guns here. Adrian's idiot wife and her endless duck-face selfies are getting more followers by the minute. I lost Abbott's smoothies, you know—that should have been mine, it should have been The Green Diva's first big contract. Fucking chia seeds! And, I'm sorry to say this, but now your sister, well, she's all over the headlines...'

'For being *stabbed*, Abi.'

'Yes, I know. And I'm not a monster, Gracey, I'm as horrified by that as anyone, of course. But the fact is, I need to get a look-in. We need to make some noise or we're just going to be the also-rans, the country mice.'

'Abi, I don't think that calling parents "killers" is going to attract the big bucks. Brands will run a mile.'

'The wrong brands, Gracey, the wrong brands. We are the real deal here—we're having important conversations. Engagement is going to be through the roof. I know plenty of companies with integrity who want to talk to the people who are listening to us. And so does Shannon.'

Grace sighed.

Seeing that she was softening, Abi went over and put her arms around her. 'I know it's a risk. But it's a calculated risk. And believe me, it's not a risk to us and our family. There aren't that many nutters in the world. Leisel was unlucky to meet one.' She pulled Grace into a bear hug. 'People will understand we're not being literal, babe. It's just a conversation.'

'I wish I had that much faith in people,' Grace said into Abi's neck. 'Okay. Okay. I'd better go and find Otto. He could be halfway to the highway by now.'

'Go on.' Abi kissed Grace's lips. They smiled. Crisis averted. 'I'll see you in a bit.'

As Grace headed out to the car, Abi went back to her granola. Got to get some of the shine back on this day, she thought. It's going to be a glorious battle.

Grace was right about *Spiked*. A week before its release, campaigns to stop it from screening were popping up everywhere. More than one change.org petition was asking cinemas to refuse to show it, while many Facebook groups had been set up to debunk every detail that it expressed. The cinemas who had agreed to host it were getting hate-mail by the bucketload. As was Abi. But that was nothing new.

> You are aiding and abetting the spread of dangerous lies. You will have the blood of babies on your hands. #spiked #howdoyousleep

> You and your woo-woo mates need to sit down and shut up. You are anti-science, anti-common-sense, anti-child. #spiked #dangerouscunt

> The link between vaccines and autism has been so thoroughly debunked you might as well talk about the link between breathing and autism. Shut up, you idiot #spiked

The truth was, Abi had no trouble sleeping. The way she saw it, there would always be people who disagreed with the status quo, and it was healthy to give them a voice.

It was an argument that she knew didn't fly with her father. The Doctor was another one to add to the list of people who were angry with her right now.

***

Three nights ago, Abi and the girls had been at her parents' place in Armadale. 'There are no sides in this debate, Abi,' her father told her over dinner. 'There is scientific fact. And there are lies.'

'So those parents who are convinced their children became ill after getting their vaccines, are they all lying?' Abi asked him.

'They are misguided.' Graham, now seventy-four, could say 'misguided' in a tone that made it interchangeable with 'stupid'. 'They are looking for simple answers to complex problems. It's understandable.'

It was remarkable how you could be a 41-year-old woman and still feel like a foolish girl in the presence of your father.

Luckily for Abi and the way this conversation was going, he did not follow The Green Diva. Her mother would sneakily turn to the commercial channels when Abi was on *AEA* or *The Process*, but she knew her father only watched the ABC and listened to the World Service, blissfully unaware of the full extent of her medical treachery.

Even her mother didn't always quite get the gist of Abi's lifestyle change. 'I worry about you living up there with all those hippies,' Sarah said, passing the potatoes.

'HA!' Arden laughed out loud so hard that Abi almost jumped. Her dad certainly did. 'Mum *is* a hippie, Gran! She's one of the biggest hippies around.'

'Arden...' Abi shot her eldest daughter a very serious look.

'We don't even go to school anymore, she's such a hippie,' said Alex helpfully. 'We haven't been all year. Grace teaches us now.'

The good doctor generally tuned out any dinner conversation that didn't involve him holding forth with his own particular expertise, but now he was listening again. 'What's that? You're not going to school?'

Sigh. Internally, Abi prepared for battle. 'They *are* going to school, Dad. Just at home. Grace used to be a teacher, you know.'

Abi had always had a good relationship with her parents — as in, they didn't argue, they were polite. She had never gone to therapy, but if she did, she had a suspicion the therapist might tell her that her current combative career choice—if you could call it that—had something to do with her formative years of saying nothing and smiling.

When Abi was little, she hadn't considered her parents conservative. The dinner table had often been a place of 'enlightening discussion'. But now she understood that her father liked his children to expand their minds as long as they snapped straight back into line after any debate. From where she sat, she could see that Graham and Sarah were as conservative as retired, white, middle-class Australians come.

Graham had been a GP, eventually heading his own practice, and he had always told Abi that he was energised by the different people and their stories coming in and out of his office—but clearly he preferred the 'characters' to stay at work. Sarah had never worked outside the home: she was a diligent mother and a conscientious volunteer. Abi and her brothers had spent much of their childhood hiding under tables at fundraisers and bake sales and CWA meetings and hospital committees.

When Graham had retired ten years ago, he and Sarah had sold the family home and bought a classic double-fronted cottage just down the road. It was tasteful to the point of suffocation.

Dinner visits were a semi-formal occasion at the cottage, with a dry sherry at six and soup at six-thirty. Arden and Alex's presence at her parents' long, formal dining table seemed so strange to Abi—they were like parakeets at a dove convention. She knew the very sight of them made her parents uncomfortable, but when she thought about the fact that this kind of family meal would never be 'normal' to her girls, it gave her a twinge of satisfaction.

'Home-schooling?' Graham's voice suddenly boomed. 'Abi, have you lost your mind? Why is this the first we have heard about it?'

Abi didn't get down to Armadale so much since her

divorce: this was quite possibly the reason. She left a lot of the grandparent-pleasing duties to her brothers, who lived nearby and were still following the script: Toorak. Blonde wives. Private schools. Range Rovers.

Alex seemed alarmed by Graham's questions, but Arden was smiling, shifting her roast around on her plate. Little trouble-maker.

'Darling, we can help you with the school fees if that's the problem,' offered Sarah.

Graham shot her a sharp look.

'That is not the problem.' Abi summoned all of her GD confidence. Oh, how she missed her phone at these dinners— with her phone in her pocket, she had an army at her side. Of course, it was out of the question at the cottage table. 'It's a considered decision that Grace and I have made. It's what's best for the girls right now.'

'*How* could it possibly be better for them than Fintona?' Graham boomed back.

'Or Melbourne Girls'?' added Sarah.

'We don't live here anymore,' Abi said firmly. 'And we have decided on a different kind of life for our family.'

'*Our* family.' Graham snorted. 'As if there's such a thing.'

At this, Abi felt her daughters' eyes on her. Arden had stopped smiling.

'Dad,' Abi said, putting down her fork, 'you might be right about vaccination. In fact, I am certain that you are. But you are *not* right about everything. And on the matter of how Grace and I are raising our family...'

'This is not *her* family...'

'About how we're raising *our* family, Dad, you are not right. In fact, you do not even have a right to an expressed opinion about that. Come on, girls.' Abi pushed back her chair.

'Abi...' Sarah started.

'No, Mum. I can feel what Dad wants to say. I can feel it underneath my skin. And I won't have it. Not in front of my girls. *You*—' she looked straight at Graham '—have a choice.

You accept that my family doesn't look like it used to, or you're no longer welcome to be a part of it. Your call.'

She stood up and grabbed her bag. Alex and Arden, wide-eyed, uncharacteristically speechless, stood with her.

'Abigail. Sit down,' her father said. His voice was tired. 'If I have offended you, I apologise. But you have to admit,' he added, his hands spread wide, 'it's a lot of change in a few short years. For some of us.'

'Embrace it, Dad. Change keeps you young.'

Abi tried not to storm out of the cottage, but she walked quickly, the girls right behind her.

'Mum,' Alex said, when they were standing outside in the cold air, Abi scraping around for her car keys in her enormous carpet bag. 'It's a two-hour drive.'

'She's standing on her principles,' said Arden. 'Can't sleep at the enemy's house, can you, Mum?'

Abi found her keys and kissed Arden on the head before she could squirm away.

'Who wanted to stay there anyway?' she asked. 'It's soooooo boring. Let's get home to Grace and the boys and the chickens.'

'They did have cake, though,' Alex said, as they climbed into the people mover.

***

The irony was, Abi thought, as she made her way out to the podshed, she knew that her ex-mother-in-law gave Adrian just as hard a time about his new life. These poor teenage girls and their black-sheep parents — rebelling was going to be very complicated for them.

Abi sat down at the computer and opened the software that would upload the Shannon Smart podcast to the world.

She really was pissed off about the Abbott's deal going to Elle. The word had been out that they were wanting to pair with an influencer for their smoothie campaign. Why wasn't it her? Her following wasn't as big as Elle's, granted, but it was more passionate, more engaged. If she told them to buy something, they'd buy it. If she sent them to war, they'd go.

She'd been having some small success with 'crunchy' brands—like the eco-period people, like the cloth nappy company who picked up your kids' shitty pants. But, as she had moaned to Grace, she'd like some money from a brand that wasn't about bodily fluids: 'Is it something about me? Do people look at me and think "blood and piss"?'

But she knew she could never carry a big mainstream brand, because the Divas wouldn't deal. Last year, she'd been approached by a major food company that made—among other things—toddler formula. 'Temptation is knocking,' she'd told Grace, who'd taken one look at their offer, laughed and said, 'No way in hell.'

See, Grace really did believe that formula was poison. Abi didn't have the heart to tell her that both her girls had been bottle-fed after three months. Her supply had been shit-house.

Grace was a counterculture true believer. Abi's eco-muse. So it was interesting that she felt this Shannon Smart podcast was going too far.

Fuck it. Abi pressed publish, sipped her tea and settled back to watch the fallout.

At that moment, Arden put her head around the door. She was pale under her pale make-up. Serious face.

'It's Dad,' she said. 'He's dying.'

CHAPTER THIRTEEN

ADRIAN

Nobody wanted to talk about cancer.

This worked to Adrian's advantage. All he had to do was allude to 'the diagnosis' and people would make sympathetic faces and change the subject.

If I actually had cancer, Adrian wondered, would this infuriate me, or would it be a blessed relief?

He'd had to tell his boss. That was a difficult day—he'd known Dean for more than twenty years. But they were men of a certain age: 'cancer' was in their world. It didn't have to mean that everything changed.

That was what Adrian had told Dean, sitting in his office after a meeting, in the moment when they would usually have been talking about the Magpies.

'Mate, remember when Ben had chemo and he only missed three days' work? That'll be me, mate. It's going to be fine.'

Yes, Adrian thought, I just used my sick friend Ben's name in a lie.

Adrian told Dean that he didn't want to tell his staff. 'They don't need to know, mate. Really. I'll tell Jenny, because she deals with my appointments and everything, but really, the whole bloody company doesn't need to know. I'll run my own race.'

'You're kidding yourself, mate,' said Dean, putting a big hand on Adrian's back. 'They all read your wife's website. They probably know more than you do.'

That was true. The women on his team were all a little bit obsessed with Elle. When she came into the office, a jolt of excitement shot down the aisles, as if a celebrity was walking among them. Adrian didn't hate it, if he was honest, although it was a bit weird when someone whose name he didn't know would say, 'Oh, is Teddy's cold better?'

Dean went back around to the seat at his desk. 'Mate, if there's anything you need, anything at all—I'm here, mate. We'll work it out.'

Dean. Done. *Tick.*

***

Five years ago, if anyone had told Adrian that he would lie to his own mother about having cancer, he wouldn't have just laughed, he might have punched them. Apparently, there can be quite a gap between who you thought you were and who you are.

His mother had not been all that sympathetic, as it turned out.

'Look at those beautiful boys.'

Bonnie was standing at the bay window of the house she'd lived in with Adrian's father until his death six years ago. The boys were meant to be playing in the backyard, but since unstructured play was foreign to Teddy and Freddie, they were just standing around, probably wondering whether to pick up a stick.

'You go through all this trouble to make them, and then you go and get sick. Honestly.'

'Mum...'

'You should never have left Abi. Then you'd have a doctor

in the family, and you might not have had to face leaving four children fatherless, instead of two.'

'I have a doctor, Mum. And it's going to be fine. Non-Hodgkin is treatable.'

We're all clichés in the end, Adrian thought. There he was with his young wife and his second family. Here his mother was, a well-to-do Malvern widow with her book club and her volunteering and her barely supressed anger.

'Come on, boys, let's go!' he yelled out the window.

'Please.' There was a little desperation in Bonnie's voice, and a stab of guilt made Adrian flinch and turn around. 'Please can you ask Elle to cut the boys' hair? It's getting ridiculous.'

'Bye, Mum. We'll see you next week.'

***

Abi hadn't been so easy to escape. When his phone flashed her name an hour after he'd told the girls, Adrian felt actual fear.

While they were together, he had never considered his wife intimidating. But Abi 2.0 was terrifying. She spoke her mind, and her mind was clear: everyone was a dickhead, especially him.

'Adrian. What the fuck's going on?' There she was. 'You're sick?'

'Abi, I've spoken to the girls. I really don't want to keep talking about this.'

'Oh, you don't?' He heard the kids' screeches in the background, and maybe a cockerel crowing. She was living in a madhouse. 'Well, you're going to talk to me. What happened? How long has this been going on? What does the doctor say? Have you spoken to my dad? The girls are upset. We need some answers.'

'Abi.' Inexplicably, given the circumstances, Adrian found himself getting angry. 'You don't get to control this. This isn't about you.'

Perhaps, he thought. Perhaps, when Elle and I are done

with all this, my girls will stop being so entranced by Grace and Abi and that feral farm. They'll see the lives they could have—travel, a place of their own in the city, the best education money can buy. Food that doesn't grow in the front garden.

But as infuriating as Abi was, of all the people left in the world, she knew him best. When Elle had first brought up this idea, one of his first thoughts had been: I'll never be able to fool Abi. She would look at him once and know this was bullshit.

So his plan was to make sure he and Abi were not in the same room together until all this was over.

She had always been able to read him. They were just kids when they met, but what he remembered most about those early days was her looking at him like he was a puzzle to solve. It was seductive.

Before then, Adrian had never felt intriguing or mysterious. He came from a solid middle-class family. He had gone to a blue-ribbon school. His friends were the rowing club. They were all going into finance. At the moment he met Abi, he was staging a mini-rebellion: smoking pot, ranting about politics, threatening to drop out.

She got him. Abi was from his world, but there was a strength about her that he was drawn to. That, and her amazing breasts.

Even then, Adrian had doubted that he could detour from the script handed to him at birth, but Abi was a believer, and he loved her for it. She had dreams for them, even then. She wanted to go to London—so as soon as she graduated, they went. He hated the cold, the low skies and the sleeping on floors, but Abi was adamant there wasn't a person worth knowing who hadn't travelled, and he wanted to be a person worth knowing, for her.

Sometimes he imagined himself back at twenty-eight, on a windy walk on some godforsaken frosty common in West London. He could feel the excitement in his stomach when he'd looked at Abi. She had wild curly hair and was wearing one of those silky nightie dresses that all the girls wore back then, with Doc Marten boots and a hefty granny cardigan. He saw the way she looked at him—like he was interesting, like he was going to make her life interesting.

He could conjure up that feeling of infinite possibility.

And then he'd fucked some Swedish girl. I was a cliché then, too, he thought.

He could have kept moving, following young and beautiful women around the backpacker trails of Europe and South America. Instead, he went back to London and asked Abi to forgive him. If he was a woman, he would call that his 'sliding doors' moment.

He now knew enough about himself to know that even if he'd gone in the other direction, he probably would have ended up in the same place: working in finance in Melbourne. It was what he'd been schooled for. It was what he'd been bred to do. And ultimately, he knew, he was the one who had allowed himself and Abi to be pulled back to the script.

Of course, it would be different for his boys: the money and the education, yes, but also the drive and ambition to take those advantages anywhere they chose. There would be no script for them.

***

Adrian had been exercising in secret. Tonight, he was running in the dark. Elle had ordered him to lose weight, but no one could see him do it. Ridiculous but necessary.

His face had never appeared on Elle's blog. All you ever saw of him was a hand, a forearm, perhaps the back of his head. He had wanted it that way: he had clients, and teenage daughters, and serious people to sit down with and talk to about serious things.

'You're so old-fashioned,' Elle had said. But she was comfortable with his decision. A little too comfortable, Adrian suspected. Her followers probably thought he was much younger and more handsome than he was—but that was good for the brand, of course.

Still, she was paranoid about him being seen looking healthy in public. 'You never know who's out there,' she would say when he insisted he wouldn't get recognised. 'Look at Leisel Adams.' As though this was meant to make him feel better about running in the dark: the fact that crazed stalkers could be loitering outside.

Elle's preferred option for his weight loss was strict dieting. He was on severe food rations at home. The boys were eating more than he was. And at work he couldn't be seen to be wolfing down Big Macs. So he was constantly hungry—it was giving him a headache. Fittingly, for a man pretending to be seriously ill, he felt pretty awful.

Now he ran into a convenience store, pulled his bank card out of his sock and bought a pie in a plastic wrapper. He ran to the park on the corner of his street, sank onto a bench and devoured it. 'Don't tell my wife' were the words running through his head as he did.

It was funny—when he thought of his wife, he still thought of Abi. Even though she was a lesbian now, and he had two sons with his 27-year-old wife.

A lesbian now. How had he not seen that coming? But he knew the answer—he hadn't been looking at Abi for years. Not really. He turned up, he made noises, he took the girls to netball, he took Abi out to dinner with their friends. They played the happy couple at crowded tables of other happy couples. The blokes talked to the blokes. The women talked to the women. That was how it was. Not how it started, but how it became.

Adrian looked around the park, fringed by so many houses just like his own: white and glass, all newness, all shine. He wondered, How many of the families living in these houses are just like mine? How many of these houses were built from the money of some rich old guy to impress a young wife? How many homes across Melbourne did each middle-class family take up these days? Two each? Three each?

***

Ever since he'd met Elle, ever since she'd decided he was going to be hers—he was under no illusions about that—he had been moving slowly towards this lie.

He had fucked other women before Elle. But they had been one-night things: some woman at a conference in Perth, another in Kuala Lumpur. He had never been interested in an 'Affair'. When his mates would tell him—usually out of necessity in a moment of crisis, that's how men friends were—about the woman whose rent they'd been paying for years, or about the marketing exec they'd been stringing along for months, or about (shudder) the nanny, the dance teacher, the babysitter, Adrian always judged them: they were gutless or stupid. For years he'd been saying, 'Mate, if you're over it, just leave.'

Of course, as time ticked on, he knew it wasn't that simple. Do you blow up your life, your children's lives, your financial future, for a fuck? No. But still, all the more reason to keep it as simple as possible.

But then Adrian looked down at himself in the shower one day, and he couldn't breathe. Perhaps it was a panic attack. Perhaps it was a moment of clarity. But that day, with the water pummelling him, he really couldn't breathe. He grabbed at his stomach and looked at the folds, then the brown spots on the back of his hands. He thought about going to his office that day. And he cried. In the shower, he sank to his knees and he cried and he cried and he cried.

Abi knocked on the ensuite door and asked him, 'Are you okay?' She sounded worried, but he heard an edge of disgust: why was this grown man sobbing in the shower? Then she would have thought of his father—it was only six months after

his heart attack. She would have decided that this was grief.
'Adrian, are you okay?'

'Yes, fine,' he managed, although he could hardly speak. He sat there for a few more minutes, breathing deeply, letting the water pour on him.

So this is a midlife crisis, he thought. I get why they call it a crisis.

In the shower that day, Adrian decided to dig up the man on the common in London. The one with all the possibility.

He would get strong. He would push through all the bullshit at work and get to a position where he could go it alone, run his own race. He had let go of the dream of 'Making a difference', but he'd never replaced it with another. He'd just allowed his career to happen to him: moving up, taking on more clients, but not pushing through. That was going to change.

For Adrian, everything changed that day. But as far as he could see, Abi didn't notice.

'Adrian's always at the gym these days,' she would complain to their friends at those interminable dinners. But she said it in the same way that she'd complained in the past about him always being at work or always being at conferences. His absence was expected—a reversal of that would have confused everyone.

When he looked at his daughters now, he realised he had no idea who they were. Not because of the eyeliner and the rags and the boots, but because he never had. Arden and Alex had always been Abi's domain.

***

Adrian screwed up the pie wrapper in his hand, making it disappear. Then he stood and leant over the back of the bench, stuck his fingers down his throat and threw the pie back up. His mouth tasted like cheap meat for the second time. Disgusting. He took a big glug of water from his running bottle and spat it out over the bench.

This wasn't quite what he'd had in mind when he'd had that vision of reinvention. He had imagined something more honest, more real.

But he'd also seen what had come of going with the flow. He admired Elle's refusal to be limited by anyone else's vision: she was whoever she said she was. Sometimes, that was terrifying. Sometimes, she seemed so focused that he didn't think she could see him at all. But then, when her attention was on him, he was invincible.

At his bucks night, four years before, a drunk Dean had asked him, 'How can you be sure she's really into it, Ade? How do you know it's not just the nice house and the cars?'

Adrian knew this was what every one of his friends had thought when they'd found out about the divorce, about the engagement, about the wedding: What a sucker.

But what they didn't get was how it didn't matter. What mattered was how Elle made him feel full of possibility again. With her, he felt like he could do anything, be anything—and that she was going to will him into it.

So no, this was not what he'd imagined, exactly, eating and purging a Four'N Twenty on a bench in the dark.

But he knew that soon—when Elle's blog was the biggest in the country and she walked away with the award, and when the investment money met his and they began to rebuild—everything would be different.

CHAPTER FOURTEEN

LEISEL

The *After Breakfast!* studio was freezing.

'It stops your make-up running,' the wardrobe assistant noted cheerfully, dusting Leisel's nose for the fourteenth time.

The set of the morning show was tiny—a couple of lurid couches in the corner of a cavernous aircraft hangar. A miniature world within a world. Right next to it, just a few steps away, was the much more complex set-up of *Breakfast!* where the celebrity cast were finishing up, delivering their goodbyes to camera, signalling for the soundmen to unhook them so they could get off to Pilates or squash or whatever it was that famous people did when their workday finished at 9 a.m.

Leisel's arm throbbed but it was no contest for her nerves, which were actually clanging in her ears. What the fuck was she doing? Why had she let Claire talk her into this? And where the hell was Claire?

She hadn't seen her friend since Claire had deposited her, beaming, into the make-up chair at some ungodly hour. How long did it take to make a forty-something mother-of-three look acceptable for a national television audience?

Forty-five minutes, evidently, with the full attention of two professionals who'd applied layer after layer of ever-so-slightly different shades of nude foundation to her face with as many teeny-tiny brushes. When they'd finished, one of the make-up artists had sighed a small sigh and said, 'You look great. So natural.' Yup, natural.

Claire and Leisel were both once keen young journos on a weekly 'human interest' magazine, *Let's Talk*. Together, they'd tracked down mothers who had slept with their sons-in-law, Australia's heaviest housewife and the woman who'd married her cat. Theirs was a friendship forged through long hours, after-work drinks and interminable road-trips out to places like the TINY TOWN THAT WON LOTTO—HOW THEY BLEW IT ALL.

These days, Claire was the executive producer on *After Breakfast!* A big job, one way above shepherding guests in and out of make-up chairs and holding their nervous hands, but it was only because of Claire that Leisel had agreed to go on the show.

***

After the attack, Mark had confiscated Leisel's phone. He took it off her in the hospital, as she tried to type out a status update with her still-good hand, mind addled with painkillers, tears still flowing. 'For fuck's sake, Leisel. *Stop.*'

'I need to let them know I'm okay...' she said.

'Who? *Who* do you need to let know you're okay? Your mum? She's on her way. Your sister? I just spoke to her, she's flying up. Our kids? They're with Wendy. They're fine. No one else needs to know. Not right now.'

'But they'll know...'

'Who gives a fuck, Leisel? This is your real life, you know. Your *real life*.' She had rarely seen Mark so emotional. She handed over her phone.

But they did know, Leisel's followers. They knew because

the attacker posted on The Working Mum's Facebook page that night.

> I hope I killed you. Or at least made you realise what it is to be in pain. The world will be a better place without you in it. You don't deserve that family. You don't deserve anything.

It sent Leisel's friends and followers into a frenzy of calling and mailing and checking. Poor Mark had to deal with it all.

***

Claire reappeared, trailed by two young women with clipboards. Everyone was edgy, checking their Apple watches—they looked at Leisel, looked at her arm, looked worried.

'You ready, darl?' Claire smiled at her, arm outstretched. She looked exactly the same as she had back in those mag days, if a little smoother.

'Sure.' Leisel offered a weak smile. 'Sure I am.'

The two young women helped Leisel out of her chair and over to the set, where the shiny-haired hosts sat side-by-side, engrossed in their phones, waiting for the signal to smile and go Live again. Leisel shrugged the girls' hands off, politely. She could walk. She was *fine*. 'You owe me,' she hissed to Claire.

Claire hugged her, gingerly. 'Are you fucking kidding? This is going to be *great* for you. Great for both of us. You are going to be amazing.'

***

When Leisel had got her phone back, after four whole days, it would have been impossible to look at every message, every mention, every notification, every text.

Her boss, Zac, had sent her maybe fifteen texts, all along the lines of: *We're all thinking of you, darling Leisel. And when you're ready,* WL, AWD *and* JFH *are standing by to tell your side of the story. xxx*

I bet they are, thought Leisel. *Woman's Life*, *Australian Women's Daily* and *Just for Her*. All magazines in the stable. All magazines for which she was managing editor. Yeah, she knew Zac's sympathies were deeply genuine.

The police had caught The Contented Mum within hours. Not exactly a master criminal, she had posted about the attack from her own home computer, and when they knocked on her door, she answered it in her dressing-gown. The knife was back in the kitchen drawer. She was arrested. Her real name, it turned out, was Kristen Worther.

Leisel posted to her followers on Day Five:

> Working Mums, thank you so much for giving so much of a shit that I am safe. I know you have a lot of other things to worry about. I am. I am fine. My family is safe. The person who attacked me is in custody. Let's get on with things, hey? #survivor

There was an eruption. The blog had never had so much traffic. Her Facebook followers tripled. Twitter was melting down.

> We thought we'd lost you, WM. Thank the Goddess you're safe. #survivor

> Trolls will never beat us. #survivor

> That crazy bitch should rot in jail. #survivor

The story, whether Leisel was telling it or not, spread everywhere. *The Daily Trail* was running almost hourly updates. Everyone who knew her was being called for comment. Every time she picked up her phone, more think-pieces about trolls had sprung up like mushrooms.

'Sure,' she told Zac on Day Seven. 'I'll tell the story, let's get this over with.' And then she called Claire.

***

Leisel took her seat on the couch next to the *After Breakfast!* hosts. The show had once been hosted by Shannon Smart and, in all honesty, Leisel had struggled to keep up with who'd been in and out of the seats since then, despite them appearing on her magazines almost weekly. But here they were—the very shiny Diane and Darryl—and they gave her three beats to sit down before turning to the autocue:

'The world of mummy blogging isn't all dinnertime tips and feeding schedules. It can get pretty fiery out there on the internet—right, Diane?'

'Absolutely, Darryl, and no one knows that better than our next guest, Leisel Adams. The whole nation has been rooting for Leisel, who blogs as The Working Mum, since she was brutally attacked by a crazed critic just ten days ago. She survived the horrific knife attack and today is here to talk about it publicly for the very first time. Hello, Leisel...'

'Hi, Diane.' Leisel remembered Claire's advice: Pretend it's just you and them. Look them in the eyes. Just tell it like it is.

'First, I'm sure I speak for the whole country when I say, "We're so glad you're okay." Are you okay?'

'Yes, Diane, I am. I'm fine.'

'We are so happy to hear that, aren't we, Darryl? Can I ask you to take us through what happened that day? Are you okay to do that?'

Leisel blinked, swallowed. Breathe. 'Well, Diane, I had just got my kids off to bed and I was getting ready to go to sleep myself—'

'You have three kids, right?'

'Yes. Yes, I have a six-year-old, a three-year-old and my baby, who's almost one—'

'So your hands are full!' Tinkling laugh.

'Very.' Harriet's face popped into Leisel's head. Big, blinking eyes. Smile.

'Leisel? Are you okay? So, you've put the kids to bed...'

'Yes. Sorry, I...' Blink, breathe. Leisel shook her head ever so slightly. Harri disappeared. 'The kids were asleep, and my husband, he was asleep, and I went to lie down too, and my phone beeped. And there was a message. You know, a Facebook message. I'm not sure why I looked at it, really. I get a lot of Facebook messages. I can't always read them all, and I—'

Mark had moved a little in bed, kind of juddered, when she'd grabbed her phone.

'It said, "I'm at the front door." And it was from... well, I can't tell you who it was from, but a name I recognised as someone who has sent me some not very nice messages.'

'Do you get a lot of those, Leisel?' asked Darryl, leaning in.

Leisel shifted on the couch, adjusting the sling on her arm. 'Darryl, all bloggers, especially women bloggers, we get a lot of people disagreeing with us. Some of them get pretty upset. You have to get used to it, and I guess I had.'

'But this person, they had bothered you before?'

'The name was familiar from other messages. But I had no reason to think—well, I don't know...'

The cupcakes. Really, Leisel? You had no reason to think that the person who sent you death-threat cupcakes might have a screw loose?

'So,' said Diane, a little too brightly, 'you get this message that they're at your front door. And so, you just go and answer it? You weren't worried?'

'It was late, I was tired. I remember really that what I felt was irritated. I mean, I'm at home, my kids are there, my husband's there. This is my house. No one is supposed to know where I live. I'm not famous or anything.'

Except, she thought, now you're on national TV.

'And I felt annoyed. Like, it could have been a joke, and

they could not have been there, but I was a bit like... I'm going to tell them off.'

'Did you wake up your husband?'

'No. He sleeps soundly. He'd had a big day.'

But she had shaken him awake: 'Mark, Mark... I think someone's at the front door.' He'd said: 'Shhhhh, Lee, go back to sleep, it's late. Put your fucking phone down.'

'So, another message popped up. It said, "I'm not going away until you talk to me." And I was just like, frustrated. So I got up.'

'And you opened the door?'

'Just a little bit. I looked around it. We don't have one of those chains, but it was like I had one of those chains, you know. I looked around it and I said, "What do you want?"'

Remember, she told herself, the police told you not to provide many details.

'And there was this face. This wo... person I didn't recognise. And she kind of smiled at me and said she wanted to talk, and then suddenly I—' Leisel felt sweat forming on her forehead. A few minutes ago, she'd been freezing. Was it the lights? She glanced up. They were really, really strong lights.

'Leisel, I'm sorry, I know this must be hard for you.' Diane put her hand on Leisel's. 'Can you tell us what happened after that?'

'Well, sort of.' A *bang*. 'I was tired. I thought, Oh, she wants to talk. And then, I guess she... they just shoved the door, really hard, because I was knocked over and then they were on me.'

That smell—her attacker had smelt like vanilla, like baking.

'And I put my arm up over my face and I guess she...' Leisel's left hand went to her right arm, touching the sling. 'I guess they had a knife and—'

'Leisel. This is truly an awful story. I know all our viewers will be thinking the same thing. How terrifying, and with your family in the house, too. But how did you get away from her? What happened?'

Mark. Mark had happened.

'It must have been only a few seconds. We were tussling on the floor, and I didn't realise at first that I was hurt, but I could see the... metal. And the first door from the front door, down the hall, that's where my kids sleep, and all I can remember thinking was, She mustn't get there.'

She mustn't get there.

'But was she saying anything to make you think that your children were in danger?'

Leisel stared at Darryl. 'She had a knife and she was trying to kill me, so I had no reason NOT to think my children were in danger.'

'Of course. Sorry about that. So, how did you get her to stop?'

'Well, my husband came out of our room.'

Mark. Naked. In the doorway. Leisel could see him somehow, in her peripheral vision.

'And he yelled. And she looked up, and I pushed her, hard. And she scrambled up and just ran away.'

'And did you run after her?'

'I couldn't really run anywhere, Diane.' Leisel gestured to her bandaged arm. 'And it was all very confusing. And my husband came to see if I was okay.' Mark had been crying. 'And I asked him to check on the kids. He called an ambulance, and then our next-door neighbour was there, and then... I don't remember much else.'

'Leisel, we are all so proud of you for reliving that awful experience for us,' said Darryl. 'We know how hard it was for you. Is it—do you think—a cautionary tale about the dangers of living your life online?'

Leisel glanced up, past Darryl, towards where she knew her old friend Claire was sitting in the control room. Her stomach was churning again, but now it wasn't nerves. It was anger. 'No, Darryl, I don't think that's what it is. I don't think it's a cautionary tale. I don't think it was my fault.'

He frowned as if he didn't understand. 'Of course not,

Leisel. So, why are you sharing your story here today? What message would you like people watching this to take away with them?'

'Lots of people are mentally ill, Darryl. The vast majority of those people aren't dangerous. And some mentally ill people could use a bit more help from society than they're already getting.'

'And would you say that the internet is a dangerous place for those people, Leisel? Are there some, perhaps, who shouldn't be online?'

'That's a silly idea, Darryl.' Leisel looked directly at his earpiece and then up to the control room again. 'You can't block people from the internet just because they're mentally ill.'

'No, of course not, but maybe we should all be a little more careful. Don't you think so, Diane? Anyway, that's about all we have time for today. I want to thank you again—'

Leisel took a deep breath and lifted her good hand. 'There is one more thing I'd like to say, Diane, Darryl, if I can. We should all remember that we can use technology to help bring us together, or we can use it to push us further apart. And we all need to know that, actually, when we see someone's life online and it looks perfect, and they look so perfect, and we're all saying, "Why isn't my life like that?" Well, their life isn't like that either.'

'Are you saying that mummy bloggers are fakes, Leisel?'

'Well, no, Diane. Some of us are just here to say, "Hey, it's alright, I'm not perfect either." But if you're looking at something, day in and day out—whether it's me or whether it's The Stylish Mumma, or whatever—if something is making you feel bad, or unsafe, or envious... Just stop. Just look away. It's your choice.'

Darryl chuckled. 'Then you'd be out of a job, though— right, Leisel?'

'This is not my job, Darryl. I have a job. But thanks, sure, I don't want to make money at the expense of other people hurting. So, fine.'

'Leisel Adams, everyone.' Diane gave a little clap. 'Thank you so much for sharing, and I think we can all say, "Get well soon."'

Leisel nodded. She felt breathless. Her arm throbbed.

'Next,' said Darryl, 'we meet the man who says you've been cutting vegetables wrong your whole life. And he has just the gadget to fix it...'

One of the clipboard women was up and at Leisel's side, guiding her off set. Darryl and Diane were back looking at their phones.

'Can I see Claire before I go?' Leisel asked, as she collected her bag and headed for the little door in the wall of the huge studio, back towards the real world. 'I know it's the middle of the show...'

The assistant nodded. As Leisel waited for the message to go up to Claire, she overheard one of the clipboard women hissing to another: 'She could have done *60 Minutes*. WHY would you come on *After Breakfast!*? With Darryl?'

Claire was waving to Leisel from the door in the wall. 'Shhh, darling, come here. That was AMAZING! Socials are going crazy. Your phone will be blowing up.'

Leisel's phone was on silent, but she'd been feeling it vibrate for the past ten minutes.

'Claire,' she said, 'a "cautionary tale"? Really? Is that what I am?'

'Oh come on, darl.' Claire pushed the fringe of her short, bleached hair out of her eyes. 'You know how all this works. Darryl's a bit of a dick, but it was all good. You did so well.'

'I hope I just got you a bonus, Claire,' Leisel said, her good hand trembling. Why was she so upset? 'Because really, that was bullshit.'

She walked away from her old friend, who called after her, 'I'll give you a buzz, yeah? When you've calmed down. We'll have dinner.'

Leisel walked through reception, out to the car park. She

leant against the Subaru, still shaking. Mark had been right—
it had been too soon to do this. What had she been thinking?

She climbed into her car. The coffee cups, the familiar
smell of rotting apple cores, the baby seat, the booster: it was
like a little cocoon of home. That place she didn't feel so
safe anymore. Yes, they had the attacker, Kristen Worther, in
custody, but she was still very much at large for Leisel—who
had, like any good internet stalker, been doing her research
on The Contented Mum.

Kristen was twenty-eight. She lived two bus rides away
from Leisel, and she didn't have a car. She had two young
kids who lived with their father.

And she had just lost a baby.

CHAPTER FIFTEEN

ELLE

'White is a good chemo colour, don't you think?' Elle called out of her closet to Cate.

'Sure. But you need a bright heel.'

Elle was pulling clothes from her dressing-room and laying them on the king-sized bed. She had some important posts to shoot today and the outfits needed to be perfect.

In the three weeks since Adrian's cancer announcement, traffic to the blog had been insane. The Facebook page had doubled its followers, while Instagram and Snapchat weren't far behind. Her people were devouring every post about her and Adrian's 'struggle', every inspirational quote, every cancer-fighting recipe, every thoughtful selfie of Elle trying to 'cheer up' the kids. The house was full of flowers—including extravagant arrangements from the Blog-ahhs, Abbott's and PulpPump.

Today, fictional chemo began. Elle and Cate had been prepping posts all week about the turmeric and ginger icy poles Elle had made (laid out against a pleasing red-and-white check tablecloth) for Adrian's potential imaginary mouth ulcers, the reading material she was taking with them to his first session—*My A can't go without a copy of #malehealth and the latest Dan Brown!*—and now, of course, the outfit she would be wearing: a cheery white Carla Zampatti sundress, sky-high red heels and a neutral neck scarf.

Elle had even gone to the extent of making Adrian take the afternoon off so they could stage the outing. 'You never know,' she told Cate, 'when someone is looking.'

The social was all prepped and ready, of course. Adrian's face was still absent from the blog, but she'd staged a shot of his arm, sleeve rolled up, fist clenched, ready for the needle later in the day. Some cropping and a grainy filter made it work beautifully.

***

Elle had coined a hashtag—#cancerwife—that was getting a lot of traction. It had started quite the trend on Twitter and Instagram, as followers posted their own photos and stories on how to survive having a sick spouse—an actual sick spouse, presumably.

It was all going exactly as Elle had hoped. She was bringing a particular Stylish Mumma take on this whole depressing topic.

Six Things I Know For Sure About Being A #Cancerwife

1. Grooming is so, so important. There's nothing uplifting about me moping about the house in trackie pants with a sour face. Adrian needs me to lift his spirits when he comes through that door. His day at work or at the hospital is so much worse than whatever I'm dealing with. So I'm making a little extra effort to always have a bright lip, to be wearing one of his favourite dresses, to be the wife he loves. I want to give him everything to live for.

2. Home-cooked meals are more important than ever. I've really upped the whole family's intake of cruciferous vegetables, which are proven to have cancer-fighting properties. Cruciferous are those leafy veggies you didn't like when you were a kid. So it's roasted cauliflower and steamed broccoli with our fatty, life-giving fish. Lucky for me, my kids have always loved raw cruciferous. What can I say, I am #blessed

3. Fear is my enemy. Yes, I am afraid. But every day is a battle to keep smiling and to force my mind to stay positive. Going to the dark place, where my A doesn't triumph, that's not helping anyone. I will not be fearful. And no one in my home is allowed to bring any negativity through that door. If you are not smiling, you are not welcome in this home of hope.

4. It's my turn to sacrifice. You know I recommend Me Time to be the best wife and mumma you can be, but right now it's all about A. Do I sometimes have to go without my usual 5am yoga class, so A can rest and not have to worry about getting up with the boys? Of course.

5. My job is to protect my boys. I wrestle with this one. I have never wanted to hide anything from Freddie and Teddy, because I believe that honesty between parent and child is absolutely crucial. But my boys are so little, and despite my dark nights of the soul, their Daddy is going to be fine, right? So now, I am trying to keep life just as normal for them as it can be, right down to their reassuring routine. Mumma's got this, boys.

6. I am a warrior wife. Yes. I am. And so are you, all of you out there who are dealing with things you never dreamed you'd have to deal with. This is how you find your strength, am I right? I will fight by my man's side for as long as he needs me to. I will never give up. He will always be First for me. #warriorwife #cancerwife #astylishfight

Cate was the one who watched that the blog didn't get too 'cancer-y'. Her content schedule meant that Elle's beloved regular posts were still appearing like clockwork: the boys and their fashions, the home-tips, the recipes.

The blog's upbeat tone was crucial for clients, and they couldn't be happier. PulpPump loved that Elle had included juices with 'cancer-fighting properties' in their regular posts—shares were through the roof. And the video series with the boys and Elle for Abbott's had been shot with extra poignancy: 'It's never been more important for me and my boys to share moments that matter. Moments like drinking a delicious banana and pecan smoothie from Abbott's together.'

The Daily Trail were following every cancer-related post with interest—sample headline: STUNNING MUMMY BLOGGER FLAUNTS THE SEXY BODY THAT DISTRACTS HER MAN FROM CANCER which was one of the reasons that Elle was obsessed with Adrian looking the part and staging the odd photo opportunity. You never knew when they might send a pap.

And the media requests were coming in. One glossy magazine had expressed interest in an at-home feature, and more than one current affairs show wanted an exclusive interview—some were offering cash. But there was a problem: the media wanted Adrian by her side. They wanted to meet 'the man behind the woman behind the man,' as one press department had put it to her.

Adrian had flatly refused. 'It's where I draw the line, it absolutely is.' He was peering into the ensuite's mirror at his ageing, thinning face. She wasn't sure if the weight loss made him look younger or older. 'We agreed, Elle. You can talk about me on the blog, but I am not sitting next to you, holding your hand, and telling lies on national TV. It's just a step too far.'

'But, babe...' Elle was at the other side of the his-and-hers bathroom sinks. She leant over to do her arm-squeezing trick on Adrian, but he shook her off, this time to examine his hairline. 'There's more interest in this than I thought. The fact that you're *not* on the site makes you more interesting to the media. This could take the story to the next level. It could be worth a lot to us. It's smart.'

'I don't *want* this story to go to the next level, Elle.' He turned to look at her. 'This was meant to give you a content play—something new to write about. Something to boost traffic and help us win the Blog-ahh. It's working. After three months of treatment, I'll be "better"—' Adrian wiggled his fingers in air quotes '—and we'll launch the business. It's a success story. So I am not becoming known as a professional victim on TV. I *can't* do that. We're talking about your brand, but I have one, too.'

At that, Elle let out a little snort.

'What was that?' He looked at her again, quickly.

'Nothing, babe, nothing.' She left the ensuite and went over to the giant white bed. 'It's just...'

'What?'

'What's the use of a job half done, Adrian? We didn't come here for that, did we?'

He was in the doorway. Elle saw herself through his eyes. She wore a white silk robe. She was lying back on the bed, her arms over her head. This was generally a time when she could get him to agree to anything.

But something wasn't right. Adrian just looked her over and went back into the ensuite. 'NO, Elle. Just. No. I have a reputation to protect. Having the nation pity me on TV is not going to help me do that. Besides, I feel like shit.'

Elle snapped back up. 'Thanks for the support,' she said. She went into her dressing-room and started shuffling coathangers with noticeable force.

He didn't follow her.

So now Elle knew she had to go easy on the invisible star of the show. As tempted as she'd been that morning to throw a full-scale tantrum and bring on the tears, she also knew that she needed to be careful with Adrian. She needed his buy-in, and she couldn't push him too far. Not yet.

Elle knew he was getting a hard time from Abi and the girls — she just didn't know why he cared. Abi was constantly calling, offering the names of all kinds of shamans and nature-healers who specialised in non-Hodgkin. The girls had asked if they could come and stay more often, and Elle had told Adrian no: it would only to add to the pressure and complicate their lives. At least he'd seen sense with that one.

She and Cate were busy strategising some alternate media plans that didn't involve Adrian. The one they were pitching to the big guns at *Sunday Evening* was particularly high-risk. But, as Elle kept telling herself, you've got to leave it all out on the field.

***

Elle heard Adrian's car keys go in the bowl by the door. 'Is that you, babe?' she called down the stairs as she walked out of her bedroom.

'Yes.' He looked up at her and smiled. 'Nice outfit.'

'Well, only the best for spirit-lifting chemo day,' Elle said.

'Far out. I think you're beginning to forget this isn't real.'

Looking at Adrian, you could be forgiven for forgetting. His face was drawn and grey. His Van Noten shirt was hanging open a little at the collar, his suit a little looser at the shoulders than usual.

'Adrian.' Elle came down the stairs. 'It's alright, you know. You do know, don't you?'

'Sure. I'm missing an important acquisitions meeting so that we can pretend we're going to the hospital, just in case anyone is stalking us. Things are great.'

'Yes, but you get to spend the afternoon with me. Bonus?' Elle kissed him. Adrian seemed unmoved. 'Besides, those stalkers at your work will see the posts.'

'Where are the boys?'

'Preschool. Cate will pick them up at three — we'll take the Range Rover.'

'Do we have to do this every time?'

'Nope,' said Elle. 'It's just to get us started on the right foot, babe.' She yelled up the floating staircase. 'Cate! We're going. You've got that chemo post scheduled for 4 p.m., right?'

'Got it. Good luck!' she yelled back.

Elle could tell from Adrian's face that he believed everyone was losing it. But also that he wouldn't make a fuss. Good boy, she thought.

'Hold on.' There was one more optic to fix: a cashmere zip-up bomber for Adrian. She went to get it from the cloakroom. 'You'd want to be comfy-cosy at chemo.'

'You are the worst person in the world,' he said. But he was smiling.

Elle had a plan to make him smile some more. They were driving to the Peter MacPherson's Cancer Centre—the home of Melbourne's best oncologists—and she'd scouted it. They would park and go in the front door, then out the back and straight around the corner to where a boutique hotel room awaited them, complete with a bucket of Bollinger on ice.

'I think you're going to like this afternoon,' she said, pushing him through the door.

And so would the pap out the front of the cancer centre— she'd got Cate to call him, giving him an ETA. There would be a shot of her and Adrian getting out of the car and heading into the centre. And after it had appeared on the *Trail*, she would post it to her Instagram and ask for privacy at this difficult time.

It was all coming together beautifully.

CHAPTER SIXTEEN

ABI

'Hashtag cancerwife! Give me a fucking break.'

Abi was melting down at her local wholefoods co-op.

She was on the phone to her friend Marg, who in a past life did PR for a major tech company but since moving to the country just did a bit of consulting work for a few low-key clients. Abi had started using her to help with the Blog-ahhs after the whole Shannon Smart thing.

Stressed-out people yelling into their phones were frowned upon at the co-op, where you were meant to be scooping quinoa in bulk and sourcing the perfect matcha for your gut health — but these days Abi was finding it harder to locate her zen.

'I know, love,' Marg was saying. 'She's painful, but I have to tell you it's working. Engagement on her page is up 150 per cent on pre-Adrian levels.'

'I can't believe it.' Abi's voice was wrestling something between a giggle and a sob. 'He was my dickhead husband, and he was no use to me whatsoever. Now he's sleeping with the fucking enemy, he's elevating her to greatness.'

'Watch it, Abi,' Marg cautioned, a touch of sarcasm in her

voice. 'Anyone would think you were jealous of someone having cancer.'

'Well, obviously not. *Obviously* not.' Abi stopped in the aisle near the raw almond mountain. 'I just... I just can't believe all this shit is happening. Poor fucking Leisel's going great guns now she's a survivor, and Duckface is exploiting the father of my children for clicks. Meanwhile, I'm being crucified for having an opinion. It's just—' Abi was *this* close to kicking the almond bucket and watching the mountain topple. '—frustrating.'

'Abi. I think we have to consider our options here. You don't sound like you're in a good headspace right now to talk about it, but we need to think about going into damage control. Maybe I can come 'round later, talk to you and Grace?'

'Sure, sure. We'll both be home about five. Come then. If the kids haven't nicked the SCOBY again, we'll have a fresh batch of kombucha.'

'Why would the kids nick...?' Abi could hear Marg picturing the white, flabby starter disc of bacteria that spawned fermentation in the sour, fizzy tea.

'They play frisbee with it—they're fucking monsters. Come over at five. The way things are going, we might have some wine, too.'

'I'll see you then,' said Marg. 'Hold off on the wine. So much negativity.'

***

Abi's problems had begun not on the day she found out about Adrian—although that had hit her harder than she'd expected—but the next, when she got a call from Shannon Smart.

'Darling Abi,' the woman started, and Abi immediately sensed impending doom.

Within hours of the podcast's release and the accompanying story, the interview's more forthright moments had been picked up by every media outlet, exactly as Abi had anticipated.

GREEN GODDESS SHANNON SMART SAYS UNHEALTHY PEOPLE DESERVE TO DIE was a typical headline. THESE DANGEROUS WOMEN NEED TO BE SILENCED screamed another.

Podcast downloads had never been bigger, and the Twitter war was the best entertainment Abi had had for weeks.

@shannonsmarter speaks the truth when no one else will #greendivashed #spiked

Anti-science propaganda shouldn't be allowed to spread unchecked. Get these witches off the air #greendivashed #spiked

Can't understand why this truth-teller isn't on my TV every morning anymore. We need more like @shannonsmarter #greendivashed #spiked

Couldn't vaccinations and sugar have taken out @thegreendiva and @shannonsmarter before they became insufferable zealots? #hoping

Abi's phone was buzzing non-stop with requests for comment and TV soundbites. She was digging up her favourite blue top for back-to-back studio segments when Shannon called. 'Darling Abi. We have a problem.'

'Oh no, Shannon, I hope everything's okay. What's up?'

'Well, darling, it's the podcast. I'm going to need to ask a little favour.'

'Of course, what is it?' Abi was now rummaging in the back of the wardrobe for her favourite flower crown. She'd had to hide it from the girls.

'I need you to take it down.'

Abi stopped. 'What? But it's getting such a big response!'

'I know, but Abi, darling, I had no idea it would get this kind of attention. A candid chat in the country, all over the mainstream media—'

'Well, Shannon, that's kind of what we wanted, right? Spreading the word?'

'Abi. You need to understand. It's not me, you know, but my... *people*, they are very protective of my brand. It's millions of dollars, you know. And maybe that day I was a little unguarded and went a little further than I might if I'd had my publicist with me. You know...'

'I don't know, Shannon. But I'm trying to understand.'

Silence for a moment. Abi remembered something Adrian had told her. 'In any negotiation, the most powerful person is the one who says the least.' Saying the least was not Abi's strong suit.

'Shannon, I can't take it down. I'm on my way to Melbourne to do *The Process...*'

'I know, darling. They called me, too. Everyone's calling. And I'm afraid that we've started telling them...'

'Telling them what?' Abi's stomach lurched.

'That you edited me. That you misquoted me. That you took what I said out of context to make me look bad.'

'But Shannon, you SAID it!' What the fuck was happening?

'Abi, darling, it's up to you. If you take the podcast down, it will just fade away —'

'I am *NOT* taking it down.' Abi was furious now.

'Then I'm afraid my people will just keep saying you're misrepresenting me.'

'How can I misrepresent you? Those words actually came out of your mouth.'

'Well, I don't know, darling.' Shannon's voice was so calm, so steady. 'People these days, they can do all kinds of things with technology. Chop things up, filter and alter them. I'm not saying you did —'

'Because I didn't and you know I didn't.'

'But I'm not going to say you didn't. Basically, you won't have my backing and that conversation will always have a question mark over it. That's it, really. Think about it, darling.'

'Shannon, I —'

'And I think it would be better if we spoke through my agent now, don't you? Just to clear up any confusion. You have Marvin's number, don't you, darling? Good. You have a think. Bye.' And Shannon Smart hung up.

Abi starcd at her phone, stunned.

***

In the wholefoods co-op, Abi set off in search of Otto and Alex, who were off somewhere in the gluten-free aisle.

Alex didn't like to be away from her at the moment— Adrian's cancer had really shaken her. Last night, she'd come into Abi and Grace's bed, something she hadn't done since everything was topsy-turvy right after the divorce. She hadn't said much, but Abi sensed her younger daughtcr wanted to make sure that at least one of her parents was right where she could see them.

Adrian was holding the girls at arm's length. They had only been to see him once in the past three weeks, and he had made it clear to Abi that she was not welcome.

'Put them on the bus,' he'd said on the phone. 'I'll meet them at Southern Cross.'

'Adrian, it's a bus and a train. There's no way I'm letting them do that change on their own.'

'Then drive them to Woodend and put them on there. Seriously, Abi, I can't do a big scene right now. I just can't.'

'Who said anything about a big sccne, Adrian? I just want to put our daughters in your hands. They're shaken up.'

'Come on, Abi. It won't be any better for them to have to see us together.'

A compromise had been reached. Abi had driven all the way in to Brighton and dropped the girls off at the glass-and-white box. She'd waited in the car as Elle came to the door, looking nothing at all like a stressed #cancerwife, smiling at the girls and waving to Abi. And then closing the door.

It was too weird, even for Abi, hearing about her

ex-husband's health problems through a series of sparkly Instagram posts and smoothie recipes. Abi and Grace were keeping the girls offline as much as they could, but she knew they were seeing all this too. The chemo post had been a bit much, really—Elle was going too far. Abi couldn't help it, she felt furiously protective of her girls. And even, she surprised herself in admitting, of Adrian.

'Alex? Otto? Where are you guys?'

She found them looking at the labels on Super-Greens powder packets. 'What are you doing?'

'This one says it can alleviate cancer treatment side-effects, Mum. Can we get some for Dad?'

Abi pulled her daughter into a hug. 'Of course, darling. Throw it in the basket.'

Quietly, Abi had been texting Adrian with advice on how he should really be dealing with his cancer diagnosis. Her father knew many of the best oncologists in Melbourne, and a couple of calls from the Doctor could put Adrian near the top of their lists.

Abi—Elle and I are dealing with it. Thank you, was all that had come back.

'Let's go, kids. Gracey's waiting.'

***

Abi hadn't taken the podcast down. And Shannon Smart had been true to her word—she'd backed away from the comments and made a statement so infuriating in its ambiguity that Abi couldn't believe it worked.

Shannon Smart would like to apologise to anyone who was offended by the views she appeared to express on the niche podcast The Green Diva's Shed. The interview has been heavily edited, and Shannon's comments have been taken out of context.

Ms Smart would like to make it particularly clear

that she does not support calling any child 'fat' and she only advises that any parents who are considering the implications of vaccinating their child speak to their preferred medical professional.

But it did work. The tone of the raging media storm turned from attacking irresponsible Shannon Smart to eviscerating irresponsible social media 'celebrities' like Abi Black.

'They'd rather go you than one of their own,' Marg had explained to Abi on their first call. 'Shannon has some serious status, and they need her to sell their shows and magazines. You, on the other hand, are fair game.'

'Great.'

Abi didn't usually shy away from a social media dust-up. She had built her brand on being the mainstream voice of alt-culture, and was more than used to the barrage of shockingly personal insults and death threats that followed an appearance. But there was something so *unjust* in taking the fall for Shannon Smart that made this onslaught worse.

Also, it was relentless. Wave after wave of abusive tweets, comments, messages. Even for Abi, this was too much. It was like being at war.

'Take it down,' Grace had ordered.

But Marg agreed with Abi. 'It won't make any difference now. It's out there. Taking it down won't change that. They'll move on eventually.'

And they would. But not before Abi had to steel herself every time she glanced at her phone. Not before an all-out screen ban was finally imposed on the house by Grace.

Holding her tongue had been the hardest part for Abi, but it had also been Marg's sternest advice. 'Do not hit back. Do not attack Shannon Smart. Lie low. And stop answering all those requests for comment. Put my number on your voice message.'

Abi did those things. But she kept looking. It was impossible not to.

'I've been upgraded,' Abi had told Grace, after one parenting site ran a story titled, IS THIS THE MOST DANGEROUS WOMAN IN AUSTRALIA? 'I used to be a dangerous cunt, now I'm the most dangerous cunt of all. Here, look.'

Abi Black thinks that children dying of obesity-related diseases is a product of 'natural selection', she's against vaccination, thinks calcium-rich dairy is poison and that feeding your children a ham sandwich is like 'signing their death certificate'...

'You're not supposed to be looking at that. It's banned, remember?'

'I didn't even say that stuff! Shannon said that stuff. Now they're just straight up putting her words in my mouth.'

'Put it *down*.' Grace grabbed the phone from Abi's hands. 'I'm burying this thing for twenty-four hours.'

'Come on,' Abi said. 'Imagine this: you know that everyone in town is talking about you—everyone, not just a few people—and you can hear what they're saying. Would you want to know? Of course you would want to know.'

'I would not want to know.' Grace folded her hands in front of her.

'Bullshit.'

Grace rolled her eyes.

'Okay. Well then, that's the difference between you and me. How could you *not* listen? And then, how could you *not* tell them they're wrong about you, that they have the wrong end of the stick, that they're twisting things?'

'Abi.' Grace took her hand. 'You need to wait for this storm to die down. For the wave to crash over. For the circus to move on. Whichever cliché you would like to choose, pick it, live it. Sit it out. You can't reason with unreasonable people. And anyway—'

'Anyway, what? Are you going to say, "I told you so"? I know you've been dying to say, "I told you so."'

'No, babe. I wasn't going to say that. I was just going to say that I'm worried about real hurt being inflicted on real people, like Leisel. And also, this time these commenters kind of have a point.'

***

Abi took the kids home. Driving up to the farmhouse had always given her peace, a smug pinch of sunshine in her belly. Not at the moment. Everything irritated her, everything felt itchy. Her stomach was constantly unsettled, and there was an immoveable lump in her throat.

As Abi unloaded the shopping and the kids from the people mover, Grace came out of the house, eyeing her carefully. 'How you going? How was town?'

'Fine.'

None of this was Grace's fault, but Abi was shitty. She was shitty with everyone who didn't understand what it felt like to be muzzled. What it felt like to watch your hard-won Facebook Likes drop off a cliff. What it felt like to be ridiculed publicly everywhere you turned. She was shitty with the media who were siding with the wrong person.

And she was shitty with Elle. In fact, she was mighty shitty with Elle for locking her out of her daughters' father's life — and printing money while doing it.

Fuck you all, Abi thought over and over, as she pulled the hessian bags up to the kitchen.

She was still thinking this when Marg turned up, three kids in tow, at 5 p.m. Alex and Arden took all the kids upstairs, and Marg, Grace and Abi sat around the kitchen table, glasses of fermented bubbling goodness in hand. Abi was barely concealing her annoyance. Marg looked serious. Grace ran her hands through her hair.

'What's up, Marg?' she asked. 'When are we all just getting back to normal?'

'Well...' Marg looked at her glass. 'Define normal.'

'Me back online,' Abi snapped. 'That would be a start.'

'Darling...' Grace reached out her hand. Abi moved hers away.

'I have to tell you two things,' said Marg. 'A protest against *Spiked* got out of hand in Sydney. Nothing serious, but a young protester got pushed over by people going to see the film and now he's suing.'

'What's that got to do with me?' Abi really, really wished she'd gone with the wine.

'The woman who pushed the boy is one of your followers — she was wearing a #dangerouscunt T-shirt and has posted her side of the story on your site.'

'Well, we can take that down,' said Grace. 'Surely.'

Marg shook her head. 'That's not so easy. It's been up for a while, so the media have all the screenshots they need.'

'Great,' said Abi. 'What's the other thing?'

'Not finished the first thing, yet. Cinemas have got cold feet about liability and pulled the movie, nationwide.'

'Well, that sucks, but not for us, right?'

'You've gone out on a limb defending it, and the filmmaker quotes you as inspiration, so...'

Abi pushed back her chair, scraping the tiles. She went into the pantry.

'*What* are you doing, babe?' Grace asked.

'Looking for wine.' Every now and then someone would bring a bottle for dinner and it would get stashed away.

'Abi. Come on...'

'I have a feeling that Marg's about to drop the other shoe. I want to be prepared.' She came out waving a dusty bottle of organic chardonnay. Bingo.

Marg pushed on. 'So, the second thing.'

Abi slammed three mugs down on the table with the bottle. 'Who's with me?'

'No, thanks, Abi,' said Marg. 'So... We've had an email from the Blog-ahhs. They are concerned by the negative attention that the blog has been getting. They're reviewing your eligibility for the award.'

'Fuck. Them.' Abi filled her mug to the brim, took a big swig. 'Ahhh. I remember that.'

Grace picked up the bottle and poured herself an inch— Abi appreciated this show of solidarity. 'Well, that's okay. I feel like we need to pull back from everything anyway. Let's just shift focus to real life, Abi. You know, all this hoo-ha, it only matters if we let it.'

'If we let it? Grace. I am not getting thrown out of that competition. Can you imagine Elle's crowing? The humiliation?'

'Who cares, Abi? All that matters is here under our roof, right now.'

Marg looked at Grace, looked at Abi. 'It's true, Abi. This doesn't have to be a big deal if we just back away. Bow out of the award. Leave the blog for a while. Let things die down.'

Abi took another mouthful of wine. 'Nope. You know what you're both forgetting?'

'What?' Grace tried to take the mug from Abi's hand, but she pulled it back.

'I have an army. A fucking army. We are focusing on the negatives here, on all the people who are pissed off with me. But thousands of people love what we stand for and will defend my right to say it: the Green Divas. I am not going to abandon them. I am going to fucking mobilise them. We are not backing down. We are digging in.'

For the first time in two weeks, Abi's stomach didn't feel queasy. Her throat felt clear. Her head was swimming—sure, from the first drop of booze that had passed her lips in a year— but through the warm haze, she could see a plan forming. It was suddenly clear that no one else knew what was best for her and her people.

'If we are in trouble, I am going on the attack.' Abi stood, picked up the wine bottle and her mug, and walked to the kitchen door.

Behind her, Grace said, 'Jesus, Abi. Sometimes...'

As she opened the door, she heard Marg whisper, 'What do you do with this?'

'Nothing, absolutely nothing. Just let her go.'

Abi went to her shed, sat down at the big desktop computer, and fired it up. She took a gulp of the warm white wine, launched her Facebook page and wrote:

Hey GDs.

Missed me? Oh, how I have missed you. People have been telling me that the best way to deal with being attacked is to lie low and take cover. I listened. And I have been miserable. I need to speak.

Some of the shit that people have thrown at me in the last few weeks is fair enough. But, come on. I do not believe it is 'natural selection' that kids who eat ham should die. OF COURSE I don't think that.

Ham is full of carcinogens, and the bread ought to be sprouted, but I digress...

Do I stand here to speak the truth about all of the unhealthy bullshit we are all too comfortable swallowing? Yes, I do. I truly do.

We should all be able to challenge the epic Group Think that's all around us without fear.

You know it. I know it. But I am not a monster.

There are some enemies worth fighting and they don't all come with ugly words and threats.

Enemies like this woman—The Stylish Mumma. She does not speak the truth, GDs. She represents a life you can never live up to. She is constantly trying to sell you shit that you don't need. Your marriage will not be perfect if you buy a $250 juicer. Your husband's cancer will not be cured because you are wearing $380 shoes while they shove a chemo needle into his arm. Your kids will not love and respect you because you dress them up in designer clothes and make them pose like tiny supermodels.

None of this shit is important.

Go to her page now. Tell her what you think of the materialistic bullshit that is being forced down your throat every day.

Let's show the world that women, and mothers, are smarter than that.

We stand for authenticity, for a raw life that matters. And we will not be silenced.

So if you are with me: Like, Share, Comment. Let's build this baby back up, and tear down the bullshit while we're at it.

I'm at your side, GDs—are you at mine?

Onwards. Your QGD xx

Abi hit publish. She refilled the mug. She left the barn and walked back into the kitchen.

Grace and Marg were still at the table, talking in hushed voices. One of Marg's little tousle-headed kids was curled up on her knee. Otto was loitering near the stove.

Grace looked up at Abi. 'What did you do?'

'I fought back,' said Abi. 'And I did not attack Shannon Smart. Look at your phones.'

CHAPTER SEVENTEEN

LEISEL

'You're not part of this, are you?' Leisel's boss, Zac, put an iPad in front of her face as she came out of a meeting room.

Mummy Bloggers At War! yelled the headline on the homepage.

Leisel shuddered. 'No. Of course not. I'm not a "mummy blogger"—what a patronising term.'

Leisel kept walking. Zac kept walking with her. 'But that's what you are, right? That TV show you were on, the stories we've been running...'

'I'm a woman who writes about parenthood online, Zac.'

'Yes. A mummy blogger.'

'Jesus.' Leisel was not so afraid to talk back to her patronising boss these days: her stock was up. 'If you say so.'

'So, what's going on here? Do you know these people?'

It was a complicated question. Although Abi was a member of her family, Leisel wouldn't say she *knew* her. Elle, of course, she'd never met.

But in just a few weeks, that was supposed to change. They were all meant to be on *Breakfast!* together before the

Blog-ahhs. Given the way that things were going, the idea made her itch.

'I don't know, Zac. Really, it has nothing to do with me. Listen, I need to talk to you about *Just for Her*'s cover. It's not working, Jayne wants to push the deadline and—'

'You women have been taking up a lot of oxygen lately,' Zac said, still looking at the iPad.

You women?

'It's like you're the new soap stars or something.'

The squabble between Abi and Elle had captured the tabloid imagination. Abi had 'sent her followers' to attack Elle, and Elle had posted about how it felt to be stung by a swarm of 'hairy, hemp-wearing, feminist wasps'. An internet feud was born.

What amazed Leisel—and, if she was honest, made her a bit sad about the current state of tabloid reporting—was that no one had yet dug up the common thread between these two women: Adrian. Tabloid reporters never left Facebook, obviously.

'Everyone's just desperate for content, Zac, you know that,' Leisel said, and picked up her pace to her desk.

The worst things that can happen to you are the ones people online like the best, Leisel now knew first-hand. She was proof that your lowest moments could translate into something that looked like success—if you were willing to share it.

As her arm had healed and the story of the 'troll attack' spread, The Working Mum had been receiving more traffic than ever. She was talking commercial offers with brands that wanted to 'connect with the busy, working woman'. A mentoring organisation had asked her to give a talk on resilience to a group of young women who'd survived violence. And she had clocked over a hundred thousand Facebook followers. She was interviewing interns—which made her laugh out loud—and the site was being redesigned in Vietnam into a slick, hipster dream for less than she paid in childcare each week.

She'd even been about to ask Zac if she could cut back to four days a week in the office.

Maybe not today.

***

When Leisel had come back from *After Breakfast!* that day, shaking, Mark had been home with Harri.

He met her at the door, looked at her once and folded her into a hug. He helped her to bed. He tucked her in and lay down beside her, stroking her head, saying nothing.

Finally, Leisel said, 'She lost a baby.'

Mark didn't ask who.

After what seemed like a really long time, he said, 'I don't care.'

Leisel looked at him. 'How can you say that?'

'There are a finite number of things I can care about, Leisel.'

She stayed in bed for the next two days. Mark wrangled the kids, keeping them away when she needed peace and bringing them close when she needed to feel them. He brought her food she didn't eat, changed her dressing. He dealt with her phone, and her work, and her mother.

And on the third day, she rolled out of bed, picked up her laptop and saw thousands of messages blinking at her—messages of support and healing. People she'd never met wished her a speedy recovery, praising her bravery. Media offers overflowed from her inbox.

Leisel wrote something:

> Friends—I know I told you before that I was 'back'.
>
> I was wrong. I was still in the middle of trying to understand what had just happened. I still am. I might not be 'back' for a while. But I am here now. And being here now is just fine.
>
> Now, I need to tell you about someone.
>
> I write about Wonder Dad on this blog all the time.

Often, I write about him to complain that he's not doing a good enough job. Or that he's doing too good a job. Sometimes, I suggest my life would be better if I was with some other sort of man. Less of a Wonder Dad, perhaps. More of a Super Man.

Today I need to write to tell you that the man I call WD is really called Mark. And that he has saved my life.

Literally, yes, but that's not the half of it. He saves me in a million different ways, every day. He saves me from disappearing into a mess of chaos and confusion and self-loathing. He saves me from being eaten alive by mother guilt, because every ball I drop, he catches before it concusses anyone on the way to the floor. He saves me from poisoning our children with my terrible cooking. He saves me from being the most boring, baby-obsessed woman on the planet. He saves me from loneliness. From boredom. From thinking that there are 'no good men'.

So yes, he did save my life, but not only once, and not only from a troubled woman with a knife.

He kind of saves it every day.

If you are very lucky, as I am very lucky, there might be someone like that in your life.

Someone who makes the shitty things bearable. Who you often don't notice, except to criticise, but without whom you would be completely at sea.

Without you even realising it, this is the person who helps to reconstruct your frazzled pieces at the end of every day. And you are the one who helps them see that their broken bits are beautiful.

Mark is my partner in chaos.

And if you are lucky enough to have one of those, please look at them today and say Thank you. Thank you. I love you. I'm sorry I don't say that every day.

I'm on my way back.

L x

And she did something that she had never done before: she posted a photo of Mark and the kids.

The post had a thousand shares while she was in the shower. A thousand more while she was getting dressed. Women were tagging their partners and friends in the comments. They were telling Leisel how happy they were that she was back and safe and happy. They were talking about how much they wished they had a Mark, or pining for the Marks they'd loved and lost.

Leisel found herself literally basking in the love—lying on her bed, laptop on her tummy, watching the Shares and Likes and complimentary comments roll in. There was no feeling like it. It was like millions of tiny warm hands all over her. Like she was lighting up with energy from her toes to her tummy.

Suddenly, Leisel was starving.

And then Mark walked into the bedroom with his own old, battered iPhone in his hand. 'I want that down, now,' he told her.

'But Mark, I wrote it for you! And people LOVE it!'

'I know you're not feeling yourself right now, but you must have a head injury as well as a fucked arm if you think now is a good time to start sharing personal information and *pictures of our children* online, Leisel.'

She opened her mouth to disagree.

'A crazy woman came to our *door*, Lee.'

'Okay, okay.' Leisel took the photo off the post. She removed Mark's name. She went back to the WD initials. 'A lot of people are interested in the blog right now,' she snapped.

'You mean since it almost got you *killed*?'

Leisel brooded at him. Incredible, she thought, how your feelings for your significant other can go from adoration to fury in a matter of minutes.

That was the end of the conversation.

***

Mark's reaction had presented Leisel with the problem she was now wrestling with at her cubicle while her colleagues worked silently, headphones in, around her. The *Women's Daily* had asked her to do a survivor's shoot—with the family. A brand of children's clothes was launching a range for 'feisty girls', and they had asked her if she and Maggie would like to front it. She was hyper-aware of the Likes Elle got on every post that featured her boys. Leisel wasn't proud of it, but she thought: My kids are cuter than that.

Some bloggers were happy to share pictures of their children, some weren't. Some had a 'no faces' policy, posting the backs of heads or artfully blurred motion shots. Some used old baby pictures, even if their kids were now teens. Leisel had never done it, aside from that once. She and Mark hadn't even discussed it—she knew he would think it was the most crass invasion of their privacy. And her first instincts were to agree with him.

But now, she saw that something wonderful could come out of the awful, violent thing that had happened to her family. She could harness the positive energy that surrounded her in cyberspace and build something that she—and the Blog-ahhs—could be proud of.

But could she do all that without sharing more of herself and her family? The messages flooding her inboxes were from women overcoming their own traumas—and they were so personal, they were difficult to read. These people felt like they knew her, along with her kids and Mark, even though she only wrote about them with initials.

Imagine, she let herself think, if we really could make a living out of TWM. Mark could go back to work slowly, maybe start his own picture-framing business like he'd been talking about since they got back together. She could write. Maybe they could move out of town. Life could be less stressful. There might be some room to breathe.

Some days it was difficult to be at home, where they had all once felt so safe. Some days it was difficult to answer the children's questions about what had happened to Mummy. That night had been terrifying for all of them.

At her desk, Leisel put her head in her hands. That's it, she thought, I'm going to make sure none of this is in vain. Let Abi and Elle roll around in the shit. I'll go high. I'll go high—and I'm going to change our lives.

Leisel googled 'survivors of violence charity' and clicked around for a few moments before opening her email and typing:

> Hello—My name is Leisel Adams, and I am the survivor of a vicious, violent attack on my family. You can read about it here [she inserted the link to one of the many stories about her attack]. I am also an editor, blogger and writer with a substantial social media profile.
>
> Would you be interested in me representing The Jasmine Foundation and helping you to do some fundraising? I have some media opportunities coming up that I think we could do some very interesting things with.
>
> Let me know—Leisel Adams—The Working Mum.

She hit send and got back to work, willing the hours to pass until she could be home with her family, where she would tell Mark about her plan to make it all okay.

CHAPTER EIGHTEEN

ELLE

'Babe, we need to decide how your treatment's going.' Elle was packing a bag on the big white bed.

Adrian was in the ensuite, staring at himself in the mirror again. He looked convincing, and he'd told Elle that he felt like shit. He had orange-brown smudges under his eyes, he'd cropped his hair close to his head—'You might do that if you thought you were about to lose it,' Elle had suggested—and he was probably thinner than he'd been since puberty.

'By the looks of me,' he said, 'it's going terribly.'

'No, darling, by the looks of you, it's working.' Elle came into the ensuite and kissed him on his bare shoulder. 'You are doing so much for us. I am so proud of you.'

Adrian grunted. Elle picked up her toothbrush and went back to her bag. She was packing for a journey that she couldn't believe she was taking—back to her hometown. And she was meeting a film crew there.

The Sunday Evening team were doing an episode about successful bloggers. They had wanted to sit down with Elle and Adrian for an interview about his cancer, but he hadn't changed his mind. So Elle and Cate had offered them something just as exciting: a bittersweet rags-to-riches tale that would air before the Blog-ahhs. They'd cooked it up over a work-out session on the deck, and the producers at *SE* had needed little convincing.

Everything looks perfect in Elle Campbell's world. Her home, her beautiful boys, the success of her glamorous lifestyle blog. But privately, she's helping her husband take on the fight of his life. Now her story is inspiring others who face losing a loved one. Was it her true-blue upbringing—as one of five children raised by a widower in an outback town— that gave her the grit to become #cancerwife?

The *SE* crew had already spent a day filming at the glass-and-white house. They'd captured Elle feeding her stylish boys organic kale at the kitchen bench while they sipped their Abbott's smoothies. Elle walking up the floating staircase with Freddie in her arms. Elle in her dressing-room, showing off her shoe collection. Elle doing her drills in the lap-pool on the deck. Elle at her crystal-cased laptop, typing away, serious face.

That had been a stressful couple of days. She and Cate had hired professional stylists to touch up the house—an oversized vase of peonies here, a bold throw cushion there— and an army of cleaners to polish it within an inch of its life. She had made the boys wear socks on their hands until the film crew arrived, just a little game to keep their sticky paws from smudging shiny surfaces.

But that had only been the 'after' shoot: now she was heading back to her own hellhole for the 'before'.

So she was packing, Adrian was moping, and the nanny she'd called to help him with the boys hadn't turned up yet.

'I can just call the girls,' Adrian said. 'They'd come and help.'

'On their own with you for three nights? No way. You'd let something slip.'

Seriously, sometimes Elle got sick of being the one who thought of everything.

She was nervous about going 'home', of course, but not as nervous as she would have been had she not transferred half of an agreed fee into her dad's bank account. The other half would drop post-filming, when no one had said anything too humiliating on camera.

***

At first, her dad hadn't liked the idea. 'What the hell are you worried I'm going to say, Ellie?' he wheezed over the phone. 'I haven't seen you for ten years. I just wanna look at you.'

'That, Dad. Don't say that.'

'You mean—'

'I mean, don't act like you haven't seen me for ten years. At least, not if the film crew is around. That's one of the conditions.'

Not only had Elle not seen her father for a decade, but she'd also barely spoken to him. When Zoe had been around, she'd been forced into a couple of polite conversations—since her sister called the old bugger daily—but otherwise Elle had successfully avoided him. She just hadn't seen the point in dredging all that stuff up.

Until now.

'So what will they ask me?' he asked. Elle heard the flick of the cigarette lighter, the sharp intake of breath. A cough.

'Well, Dad.' Elle paused for a moment, bracing herself to say two words she never said. 'They will probably ask you about my mum.'

Silence except for the pull of breath on a smoke.

'You know, what it was like being left with all the kids. How you managed.'

'You've never even asked me that,' her dad said.

'Well, maybe this is the moment.'

'I don't need money to do that.'

'The money's not a payment for you, Dad. I just know it will be a bit of trouble for you on the day—and anyway, I was thinking you could give it to Bobby and Kai... to, you know, help them to be somewhere else.'

'You want your brothers to be somewhere else.' It wasn't a question.

'The thing about TV, Dad, is it's confusing if there are too many characters. The crew just want me to take them around town and then visit you at home and have a chat there.'

'Hmmmm. What about your sister?'

'Zoe?' Elle hadn't factored her in. The last time she'd seen Zoe, on Instagram, she had been in Mildura, working for a river boat company. She was managing their marketing and social media pages, among other things. Elle liked to think she could take credit for that.

'You got another sister?'

I wish, thought Elle. 'I'll talk to Zoe,' was what she said.

'Hmmmm.' Just the smoking breath again.

There was one more thing.

'Dad, where are you living now?'

'At Pam's. Out of town.'

'Who's Pam?'

'Well, you'd know if you ever called me, wouldn't you, Ellen?'

'Dad. Please don't say things like that either.'

'She's my girlfriend. Four years now. Good woman. You'd like her.'

Elle doubted it. 'What's... Pam's house like?'

'Nice enough. It does us. No kids at home these days, you know.'

Elle was going to head into town a day early, to scout out where the crew could shoot. It wouldn't play well for The Stylish Mumma if her old dad was sleeping in squalor while she lived in a Brighton mansion.

'Dad, I'll be up on Tuesday. The crew will up on Thursday morning. We can do a lot of talking before they come, smooth all this out.'

'We've got a spare room for you,' he said. 'Pam'll just clear the dogs out.'

Elle almost laughed at the idea of her staying with her dad and his girlfriend in the dogs' room. 'I'll stay at the motel, Dad. It's fine.'

'Hmmmmmm.'

***

Cate had never been to the country. She'd rarely left the western suburbs of Sydney before moving to Melbourne to work with Elle.

'Glamorous, isn't it?' Elle said to her on the small plane. 'Swan Hill's not even the end of the line. We've got quite the drive after that.'

'Are there snakes?' Cate asked. Elle had noticed that she'd packed her sturdiest boots.

But when Elle stepped out of the airport, she couldn't help grabbing Cate's arm for support, overcome by a wave of intense familiarity. Ten years evaporated as the sky stretching ahead of her, the tight chill in the air and the smell—the smell of the ocean being thousands of kilometres away—all hit her at once.

They picked up a hire car, a hulking Toyota, and began the drive. Cate's eyes were glued out the window to the nothingness that began at Swan Hill's city limits. 'What did you *do* out here? How did you end up out here? Why does anyone live out here?'

Elle hoped her silence told Cate that she wasn't in the mood for questions.

The signpost for Thalwyn North popped up before any indication of life. Then a property in the centre of sprawling fields. A house. A little group of houses. A small school.

Eventually, a main street. A row of shops with a pub at each end. An IGA. A motel.

'Why are these things even here?'

'Can you stop asking questions?' Elle snapped. 'You're here to document and work. I'm going to set you up at the motel. And don't talk to anyone, okay?'

Cate nodded and bit her lip.

'Anyway,' Elle added, a few minutes later, 'there are farms out here. There's sheep. And a lot of work comes from sheep. There's more going on than you can see. Well, a little bit more.'

They pulled up at the front of the fake-Tudor Thalwyn Inn, and Elle climbed out. She thought she had dressed down for this trip, but at the airport she'd realised that even in jeans, a white Puffa jacket and Timberlands, she was going to stick out like a peacock in a chicken coop. It wouldn't be long before word got around. Oh well, let them look, she thought, as she headed to reception and the back of the woman who ran the place.

Elle just kept thinking: *I can't fucking believe I'm here*.

This motel had been in town since she could remember, but she'd never been inside. It was scrupulously clean but surely hadn't been redecorated in thirty years. A fat ginger cat slept on the green floral lounge. A spinning rack of leaflets of the local 'attractions' stood near the window, all of them at least an hour's drive away.

Please don't recognise me, Mrs Gleason, Elle thought. She genuinely wished she was invisible, an unfamiliar sensation. Oh, the conversations she did not want to have. It was dawning on her that this visit would be more complicated than she'd imagined.

'You must be what the film crew's about.' Mrs Gleason looked up from her thick paper ledger. 'We've got a booking from some TV people on Thursday. Is that you?'

'Sort of.' Don't look at me, don't look at me.

'Two rooms, three nights.' Mrs Gleason went back to her book. And then... 'Oh! You're not Ellen Wright, are you?'

It wasn't like Elle to avoid an uncomfortable situation. She reminded herself of that and swallowed and smiled. *Own it*, she told herself.

'I used to be, Mrs Gleason, yes. Elle Campbell now.'

'Ohhhh!' The older woman's face cracked into an excited smile. 'You look so different! I remember you when you were so tiny. Oh! My Deb's going to be so excited.'

Mrs Gleason didn't know Elle, big or small, from a bar of soap. Not really. Yes, Thalwyn was tiny, but the locals had always been grumpy at the Gleasons because they hired traveller labour to clean their toilets and make their beds— 'Rather than pay a local,' Elle could hear her dad moaning. 'Those kids will work for next to nothing.'

Those Gleasons are smart, little Elle used to think.

'I've heard some things about you from my Deb,' Mrs Gleason was saying now. 'That you're famous on the internet or something, but I didn't know it was you with the television people. Gosh, Deb is going to be so excited. And—' She stopped mid sentence, and her eyes went straight to Elle's hand.

Of course, her engagement ring. She hadn't even thought of it.

'Would you look at that!' Mrs Gleason took Elle's hand, turning it left and right as if the hefty diamond solitaire was a rock of Liz Taylor proportions. 'Would you just *look* at that.' And then, 'I'd be a bit careful around here, you know. People aren't doing so well.'

Good point, Mrs Gleason.

The idea of this *Sunday Evening* piece was not for the film crew to capture a vain prodigal daughter, lording it over her country cousins. No, they were going to see a woman in touch with her roots—someone who 'knew where she came from'. Ordinary Australians liked that. Elle made a mental note to take the ring off before filming.

'There's another one coming today, right, luv?' Mrs Gleason headed back around the counter.

'Yes—Cate, she's in the car. We have two rooms.' Elle started filling in her paperwork.

'No, another one from the TV company, I mean. A producer, I think they said.'

'Really?' Elle tried to keep her voice flat, unalarmed. 'Not here yet?'

'No, but there's another flight in this evening. I suppose she's doing some research. A lot more goes into these TV shows than you think, doesn't it?'

***

When Elle and Cate got up to their rooms, they looked around at the chintz bedspreads and the windows that didn't open in abject horror.

Elle took charge. 'You get all set up in here. If there's no wi-fi, tether to your phone.'

Cate glanced dubiously at the few bars of reception.

'Get onto today's posts, prep some of those travelling pics for when it's time,' Elle said. 'I'm going to see what sort of a state my dad's in. Don't leave the hotel. Seriously.'

Cate looked at the TV, probably wondering if it had Netflix. Elle didn't tell her that the chances were slim to none. 'But, dinner?'

'I'll be back by seven, we can eat at the pub. Unless some excellent sushi place has sprung up since I left...'

'And what about the researcher?'

'I'll see what my dad's heard.' Elle was taking off her ring. 'And if she gets here this evening, it's a fair bet she'll be having dinner in the pub, too.'

'How will we know it's her?'

'Believe me, Cate, we'll know it's her.'

***

Elle drove down the wide main street out of town. Looking around, she wanted to be able to say that nothing had changed, but some things had. Three or four of the main-street shops were boarded up, empty. There was a moneylender next to the supermarket. There were some non-Anglo faces in the street, unheard of when Elle was growing up: they must be the 'migrant farm workers' she'd heard about on the news. She couldn't imagine what kind of a welcome they got in Andy's Butchers.

On the drive to Pam's, Elle played 'Where I used to live'. The town only had a few hundred houses, but she felt like she'd lived in half of them. There was no family pile to show the cameras, just weatherboard rentals with too many cars in their front yards.

Something was bothering Elle.

As she'd promised her dad, she had called her sister before she'd left the city. 'Where are you, Zoe?'

'I'm at home, Elle. And I'm fine, thanks for asking.'

Such a baby. 'Where's home?'

'With Dad.'

Shit. 'I thought you were in Mildura.'

'I was. I am. I'm visiting.'

'Oh.' Well, that wasn't too bad.

'I saw about Adrian. I'm sorry. Is he okay?'

'Yes, he's... in treatment. It's alright.'

'What about the boys? I... miss them.'

'They're fine. They don't really know what's going on, so, you know...'

Awkward silence.

'I know there's something you want to ask me, Ellen. I spoke to Dad. And you wouldn't be calling if...'

Elle spoke quickly. 'Are you going to be there when I come with the film crew?'

'Because you'd rather I wasn't? Wouldn't it be a nice story for you, if I told the Sunday show how you taught me everything I know?'

'Zoe, it's not you. It's just confusing. It's best to keep a simple narrative. That's all.'

'*Narrative*? I don't think the narrative is going to be as simple as you think,' Zoe said. Her voice was clouded, like she'd been crying.

'What do you mean by that, Zo? Come on. I know we didn't end things well after Freddie. But, you know, that was two years ago. Let's just go back to being—'

'Estranged?'

'Whatever you want to call it.' Elle was already sick of this conversation. This was why she didn't call her family. 'I've got to go. I just wanted to check about next week.'

'Sure, whatever.' Elle was about to hang up, but Zoe rushed to say, 'Look, even if it's for some bullshit TV show, I think it's good you're coming to see Dad.'

Elle was struck by a thought. 'But why are *you* visiting Dad? Why would you go back there?'

'Because I'm his daughter, Ellen. He brought us up, remember?'

That time, Elle really did hang up.

But it bothered her. And as she found Pam's house— another weatherboard bungalow behind a rusting metal fence around a random quarter-acre space—she thought about it. Why hadn't she asked Zoe about Pam? Or their brothers?

Two big utes and an old Ford were parked outside. Elle pulled the Toyota up behind them and looked in her rear-view mirror at herself before she got out. Nerves, she thought. What bullshit. She found herself wishing she had brought Adrian.

She climbed out of the giant car, and headed for the house. A woman came flying out of the red front door. She was fiftyish, round, dressed in a sparkly pink T-shirt that said 'Bad Girls Go Everywhere', tight pale jeans and uggs. She looked genuinely pleased to see Elle.

'Ellen!' she called. 'Ellen! So wonderful to meet you.'

Elle looked at her dad's girlfriend cautiously. Did she

know Pam from somewhere? This was a small town, after all, and women had been circling Dad for years.

Pam seemed to read her mind. 'We've never met, love. I've only been in town six years.' She grabbed Elle in a hug and enveloped her in a cloud of body spray and cigarette smoke. 'I hadn't met any of you for years. And then you all come at once. Like buses!'

So Pam is cheerful, thought Elle. I suppose that's a good thing—Dad can be such a miserable bastard. Elle smiled, said hello, and kept moving towards the house.

'Ellen, Ellen.' Pam tugged her arm. 'Don't go in there yet. I need to talk to you. Woman to woman.'

'Look, I...' Elle was surprised by the words that came out of her mouth to this woman she'd never met. 'I just want to see my dad.' It was true.

'I know, of course you do, he's so excited.' Pam kept hold of Elle's arm. Looked back to the house and then again at Elle. 'But I need to prepare you.'

Elle's stomach dropped. 'For what?'

'Your dad. He was just so excited to see you, to have you here, he didn't want to say anything that might... I don't know.'

'What? *What?*' Elle shook off Pam's pink-fingernailed hand.

'He's not well, love,' Pam said. 'He's not well at all.' Her hand went to the pocket of her tight jeans, fought their way in for a mangled tissue. 'Your dad has cancer. The doctor is saying it's a matter of months, maybe weeks.'

JUNE

CHAPTER NINETEEN

MARK

Being the only man at mothers' group had never bothered Mark.

In fact, back when Maggie was a baby, he'd quite liked it. At first, the mums had treated him as an oddity, rushing to help him with simple tasks he'd long ago mastered. When he asked the barista for a cup of hot water to warm a bottle, he was met with cries of, 'You are *so* clever. My husband would never think of that.' 'I wish my Nick was so good with the baby.' 'Got to love a man who knows his way around a baby bottle!'

Being a male primary carer gave him rock-star status in a female world. 'Your wife is a lucky woman,' was the common refrain from complete strangers whenever he picked the kids up, dropped the kids off, or accomplished a complex task like a doctor's visit or a swimming lesson.

Early on, Mark discovered that the bar set for fathers was disturbingly low.

'If I manage to get through coffee without dropping Maggie on her head, I'm a hero,' he'd reported back to Leisel that first week. 'It's incredible. I need to tell other men that this is where you go to get an instant status upgrade.'

'Jesus, I wish it was like that for women,' Leisel had said, taking a deep reunion sniff of Maggie's head. 'We can't do anything right.'

That was obviously still the case, Mark thought as he sat at playgroup, scrolling through Leisel's blog on his phone. It was the comments that depressed him. All these unhappy women. All this guilt, all this exhaustion, all this fear of failure.

Something was familiar about the cone of confession that women had created on *The Working Mum*. It reminded Mark of recovery—of his Narcotics Anonymous Meetings: the declarations of 'no judgement', the raw honesty, the rush to support and reassure, the understanding that sharing these stories was a gift to those who were struggling.

It was kind of beautiful.

Still. Mark fucking hated it.

He put a steadying hand out to Harri, who was pulling herself up on the side of the sandpit where her brother was constructing a complex tunnel system.

Mark hated that Leisel wouldn't leave this thing alone. Looking through the comments, he was trying to understand why she refused to block a portal that, to him, was just a pipeline chugging angst and negativity into their home.

***

Mark kept flashing back to the night when Kristen Worther had come to their door. He'd talked about it in therapy and at his Meetings. He'd been urging Leisel to find the same kind of support—but she wouldn't listen. Mark sensed she saw it as weakness to be struggling, and he was trying not to feel judged about that.

'I can't make her talk about it,' he'd said on the phone to his brother, Dan, the night before. 'She seems to think it's a problem that can be solved.'

'Says Therapy Guy,' said Dan. 'That's actually how most of us think. We don't like to make a fuss, we think things will go away if we just get on with it. It's only guys like you who know that's not true.'

'Whatever. We have kids who can't sleep because of what happened to their mum. I think it's time she asked for some help.'

'Isn't that what you're there for?'

'Only a guy who has never been to therapy could ask that question.'

Dan shifted topics. 'I keep seeing Leisel on TV — she looks great. She was on *The Nightly* the other day, talking about trolls.'

'Yeah. She's doing better than the rest of us. On the outside, at least.' Mark tried to keep his voice neutral. 'She's very focused on these blogging awards.'

'Okay,' Dan said. Mark knew he wanted to say more.

The brothers were two years apart, and Dan was Mark's closest friend. Years of messing people around as an unreliable drug addict had whittled his circle down to those who had no choice but to stick around: family.

'Shut up, brother,' Mark said.

'I didn't say a thing.'

***

When Mark heard a wail, he looked up from scrolling to see Rich banging another kid over the head with his spade. Harri was laughing delightedly from the sidelines.

He stood to intervene — but before he got there, the little boy's mother swooped in and gathered him up, glaring at Mark. 'Keep an eye on your boy,' she hissed.

The dad-halo was slipping.

'Time to go, Rich,' he called over, picking up Harri and brushing the sand off her.

Being the lone dad at playgroup was enlightening. Women

saw him as a safe space—they told him things about their husbands that they wouldn't say to a 'normal' man. Mostly, they complained. Since having children, their previously equal relationships had shifted: the women were in a constant state of physical and emotional stress, while their husband's lives had barely changed.

Mark made tolerant noises. His most-often used line was, 'Maybe he doesn't feel like he knows what to do. You should talk to him.'

'But it's not like you and Leisel,' the women would say. 'You guys *share* parenting. It's beautiful.'

Yes, but also not strictly true. Mark did the majority of the grunt work. He was the one who knew the names of the kids in Maggie's class. He was the one who knew that on Rich's day-care days he needed the *green* water bottle or there would be a meltdown of epic proportions. He was the one who could soothe Harri to sleep. 'Maternal instinct' was a matter of proximity and practice, in Mark's experience.

On Leisel's blog, his alias was Wonder Dad, and he found it—as with most things about the blog—irritating. Would a woman doing what he did be Wonder Mum? Silly question.

He had more in common with the women complaining to him than with their oblivious husbands.

But the truth was—as he suspected it was for some of the mothers at playgroup—it suited him to be the one at home. He was good at it. He enjoyed having his day carved into the manageable chunks of gentle parenting rhythms. He appreciated the structure. His work as a carpenter was flexible, more off than on at the moment. And it suited his temperament to focus so completely on the one job in hand: child-wrangling.

And then there were his kids. He was a grown man who could well up at the thought of his children's faces. Maggie was a funny, sensitive girl. Rich was a loud, dramatic ball of energy. Harri was all kamikaze confidence and giggles.

Mark marvelled at the fact that he'd lived almost forty

years without these people. And now they were all here, he didn't need anything else. Nothing at all. They could all live in a dark cave in a hostile forest, and he would have everything he needed right there.

But he knew that Leisel did not feel the same way.

***

These days, Mark liked to say that he'd always known Leisel would come back into his life.

She had been his last girlfriend before his addiction had swallowed him whole. The way he remembered it, when he and Leisel were lovers, he was still dabbling, dancing around the edges of the darkness that was coming for him. He knew she did not remember it so romantically.

He had been enchanted by Leisel, by her intelligence and her independence. She didn't seem to need him. But when they were alone, she opened up to him completely. She wrote poems and let him read them. He remembered every story she ever told him about her missing father and her devastated mother, and about escaping the suburbs for a different life. And then, later, he remembered the look on her face every time he let her down.

After Leisel packed up and left the little Surry Hills studio, he had an excuse to lose himself completely. His disapproving girlfriend had been a tether to normality—once that was severed, he let himself float free. Now, he considered himself lucky that ten years passed before she saw him again. There was no way she would happily let him care for their children if she'd ever met that empty-eyed junkie.

It was his brother, really, who'd pulled him back: who hadn't stopped dragging him out of shitty, enabling share houses and dangerous relationships, who had got him into rehab and then another rehab, who had sold his own car and talked their parents out of a large chunk of their savings to fix this grown man.

They say rehab can need a few attempts to 'take', and that was true for Mark. He was so roundly sick of himself, so desperate to change this terrible, sad-arsed script, that he knew Dan's couch wasn't the answer this time. That couch was too easy to fall off, to wander from. He had to get away.

Mark moved to Milton, a small coastal town where the winters were cold and the summers brought a tide of tourists. He returned to something that he had loved way before he hadn't loved anything except heroin: working with wood. He made picture frames from recycled native timber for the local craft shops and markets, out of a studio that he shared with an old woodworker in exchange for stories and smokes. He lived alone in two rooms above a cafe, working a few shifts a week downstairs for rent.

Slowly, slowly, Mark built himself back up into an actual person. He felt like he had missed his twenties altogether. Sometimes he felt like he'd slept through his youth in fitful bad dreams and emerged in middle-age — worn, tired, in need of comfort and closure.

In rehab, in therapy, in group, there were many opportunities to explore why things had gone the way they had. Why he'd made those choices. Like the one to let Leisel walk out of that Surry Hills studio. The answers weren't satisfying to him or his despairing, guilt-ridden parents, but he believed it came down to biology, a missing internal brake.

So as a person living in recovery, he had been wary of any extremes. Everything had to be measured: there could be no obsessive plunges. Dan checked on him monthly. Mark made safe, sober friends. He stayed away from the city. He was religious about his Meetings — that was why he'd found a flat in town, he didn't yet have a car and he was in walking distance of the village hall. He lived a small life.

And then came Leisel's message.

As soon as he saw it, he realised it was the only reason he'd asked the waitress downstairs to help him set up a Facebook page. Social media was an unknown world to him, a world that had emerged during those missing years. He saw it as an enticing danger, a possible plunge, and treated it with suspicion. Until Leisel.

Moving back to Sydney to be with her had been the most dangerous thing Mark could have done. But it also felt like the only thing that he could do, that he was meant to do.

Everything he remembered about Leisel was still there— her wit, her humour, her warmth, her curtain of thick, sweet-smelling hair. Her honesty. She was so clear about telling him what she wanted, so honest about telling him what she would not tolerate. Her openness attracted him, her insistence made him feel safe.

In return, he was honest with Leisel. She would never set eyes on the man he'd been, but he painted her the pictures. In the early days of their reunion, they would lie in bed for hours (oh, how impossible to imagine now) and talk about the years that separated them. Leisel told him about a life full of work and friends and travel and words, and he told her about his world of dope and desperation and sickness and deceit. She listened, without speaking. He expected her to recoil from him, to change her mind. She didn't.

He knew that being in a relationship with a recovering junkie was no garden party. Darkness was beneath the surface, a life that the other person could never completely understand, along with a whole lot of tedious self-flagellation. There was temptation and the constant worry of relapse, even after six years. Even after twelve.

But it had been twelve. Twelve years, and Mark was as proud of that as he was of his marriage and his family.

**

As an addict, Mark hadn't known that he was capable of being this person, the man who right now was standing in the kitchen of their flat, cutting up an orange for his baby daughter. He never knew that he could live a boring, beautiful life.

He was the parent planning Harri's first birthday party for next week, the one the teachers called when Maggie was sick. Of course, this domestic grind wasn't perfect—the days could be long, tempers could be short. Small people could be more infuriating and unreasonable and single-minded than jonesing drug addicts. But what peace they brought him.

That peace had been shattered by the woman at the door.

Years of therapy had taught Mark that regret was useless. But he was reliving that night over and over, sometimes hourly. He was reliving it even as he stood at the bench, slicing the apple.

He'd gone to bed early. He always did. He savoured the peace that came when the kids were down, when he and Leisel would eat together, talk about their days. She liked to sit up and write. He had read Franzen for five minutes and was out. He knew not to underestimate sleep.

He was dreaming about the ocean when he felt Leisel kicking him gently.

'I think there's someone at the door,' she whispered.

Why didn't he get up? Because he was half asleep. Because he was still half in his dream, wrestling tentacles in the dark. Because he was tired. Because, clearly, he was more concerned with his sleep than his wife's safety. 'Shhh, Lee, ignore it, go back to sleep,' and he rolled over.

Of course, Leisel had been going through her own nightly ritual—his least favourite thing—of scrolling through her phone. Putting all these strangers and their problems in her head before she went to sleep. He would never understand that.

The next thing he remembered was shouting. Strange noises penetrating his dream. He stretched out a leg, and Leisel wasn't there. That made him open his eyes, and it took another few seconds for him to get out of bed. Those few seconds were the ones when Leisel had a knife pushed into her flesh.

He should have just fucking got up. Fucking lazy useless junkie.

When he did stumble out of the bedroom door, naked, confused, he saw Leisel on the floor. There was something on top of her—a strange, dark shape. In those muddled moments, it looked like a child. Nothing was making sense. And there was something else, something dark on the ground beneath Leisel.

It probably took him a split second to understand what he was looking at, but it felt like minutes. Then he lunged, shouting at the dark shape, and it sprang up.

The shape was a woman. A tiny woman wearing a hooded jacket and holding a large knife. She was breathing heavily, panting like a small dog. She smelt sweet. For another endless split second he was holding her by the shoulders, looking into her face. Her features were close together, and she had big, round eyes that didn't focus on him. Thin blonde wisps escaped from her hood. Before he even realised he had her, the tiny woman just wriggled free and ran. Right through the open door.

Later, the police asked him about his 'decision' not to chase her. About 'choosing' to stay with Leisel. But it hadn't been a choice—he didn't even think about chasing the woman. He only thought about Leisel, about getting to her.

Blood was spilling from Leisel's arm, though at the time he had no idea where it was coming from. He lay down next to her and looked into her eyes. She was staring at him. She looked like she was trying to smile. He was crying.

This was their life together. Their second chance. What was happening to it?

Leisel had to tell him, 'Call an ambulance. Please.'

And as he jumped up and ran to find the phone, he suddenly thought to be quiet—the children. They were right behind that door. They had been only metres from the woman with the knife.

Now, looking back, he had so many critical questions about what he'd done that night. Why hadn't he thought of his children before that moment? Why hadn't he already called for help? Why had his injured wife needed to tell him to do it?

He'd called the ambulance, yelling into the phone. The door was still open, and people began to emerge from their apartments. Wendy, the next-door neighbour in her dressing-gown, hair in a frizzy halo, crouched next to Leisel and pushed down hard on her arm.

So that's where it is, he thought.

Leisel didn't scream. Her eyes were on the kids' door — like Mark, she could probably sense the movement behind it. She started calling out quietly, 'Mummy's okay, Mummy's okay.' And then there was the sound of Rich crying from his bed, and then Harri. So much noise. So much awful noise. Mark asked Wendy to leave Leisel and go to sit with the kids.

So many minutes passed before the ambulance arrived. Wendy behind the kids' door. Mark with Leisel. The sound of Harri wailing. So many things he didn't do when the moment came. At least he'd finally remembered to pull on some pants.

Now, at the kitchen bench, Mark set down the knife. He put the slices of orange into two brightly coloured plastic bowls.

The next day, when Leisel had still been in hospital and the kids had been with Dan and his mum, Mark had gone to a Meeting. He couldn't talk about what happened yet, but he could sit there and begin to process it.

All he had been doing since was processing it. And he realised that he blamed her.

He blamed Leisel. He couldn't help it.

Why had she invited that hatred into their house? Why hadn't she asked for help when she needed it most, after they lost their baby? Why was she now running from this trauma, back into the arms of the faceless hordes who didn't know her, didn't care, saw her life as a sideshow? Why did she push away his attempts to get her to invest more in her real life, the one that wasn't inside a machine?

Why couldn't all these women stop picking at their scabs? Why wasn't this life enough for his wife?

CHAPTER TWENTY

ABI

'Going into battle is just so *invigorating*. I feel ten years younger. I just feel so positive about the world.'

Conflict suited Abi. She would have made an excellent wartime general. Perhaps she was one in a former life—she should ask Rosa, the local psychic.

'You know you sound crazy, right?' Grace was asking her.

'I *am* crazy, Graccy, and I don't give a fuck.'

They were getting ready for Otto's parent–teacher night, and Grace was in a state of high anxiety. For her, Otto's decision to stop being home-educated and head to the local public school had been a personal rejection. Abi knew that Grace couldn't decide if she wanted the teacher to say things were terrible or excellent.

'Flower crown?' Abi asked, holding her most extravagant favourite next to her head.

'No, Abi. No flower crown. This evening is not about you—it's about Otto.'

'Darling, I don't know what you think a parent–teacher meeting is like, but believe me, we will be in and out of there in minutes. Don't get your hopes up. These are busy people.'

'That's exactly what worries me. Otto's well-being is just one thing on their very long list of priorities. And it's probably not near the top.'

'Oh, shush.' Abi wrapped her arms around Grace and kissed her. 'You need to relax. Want to relax?' She started pulling Grace towards the bed.

'Abi. We don't have time for that.' Grace pushed her away. 'You are so fucking weird at the moment.'

'What's weird about being madly in love with you?' Abi persisted, reaching for Grace as she twirled away.

'Oh, stop it. How can you be in such a good mood with all the shit that's going on?'

That was a good question. It was mostly down to a meeting she'd had that afternoon.

***

After Abi's call to arms, her followers had attacked the fakery of The Stylish Mumma with gusto. They'd left a million messages on Elle's Facebook page and relentlessly trolled her Instagram and Twitter. A particularly ingenious Green Diva had hacked Elle's blog, and for one glorious hour every image was replaced by one of a lipstick-wearing pig. It wasn't subtle — but fuck, it made Abi laugh.

It also made her feel extraordinarily powerful, even as she knew that Elle's fans would retaliate.

By the time Abi called off her swarm, The Stylish Mumma crowd had flooded her socials with thousands of variations on 'ugly/old/dangerous cunt'. They'd even pulled off a hack of their own, translating Abi's site into Mandarin for twenty-four hours. Clever, Mummas, clever.

Abi thought it was fun. But it irritated the Blog-ahh people no end. She received a stern call from their PR spokeswoman, who explained that they couldn't be seen to reward bullying behaviour. The woman assured Abi that Elle had received a call too. It was too late to disqualify two out of three contestants, but any further infractions would affect how the awards were judged.

'I'm so sorry,' Abi told the woman. 'Of course, I can't be held responsible for the crazy actions of some of my followers, but I will certainly be more cautious about anything that could be seen as encouraging them into negative behaviour.'

She hung up smiling.

The ensuing publicity calmed the storm about the Shannon Smart comments, and Abi's Facebook following got a healthy boost from the curious and the newly converted.

This week's podcast was an interview with a fruitarian mother of four: she fed her whole family only on fruit that fell from trees of its own free will. The podcast was going gangbusters—and since Abi hadn't suggested that her listeners follow the diet, so far the 'You crazy bitch' comments were aimed at the guest, not the host, which was a refreshing change.

She was back on track.

***

The persistent blackspot had been Adrian. He was still refusing to return her calls or messages, and was still pushing Alex and Arden away. She'd caught sight of him on a Facetime chat with Alex, and he looked like shit.

Arden, in particular, was acting out. A few days ago she had disappeared, and after several hours of frantic searching and calling, Abi had found her trying to hitch a ride on the highway. She'd said she wanted to go to Melbourne, but her dad wouldn't let her. 'I'm going anyway! Fuck what he wants, what about what I want?' she'd yelled at her mother, all flashing eyes and adolescent fury. Then she'd collapsed onto Abi, crying, and Abi had driven her home via a highly against-the-rules ice-cream shop.

That had worked out okay. Next time, who knew?

Abi had been composing an email to Adrian that night about how they needed to come together—as a 'modern family'—to deal with this, when a message popped into her box from a name she didn't recognise but with a subject line that made her click instantly.

I am Elle Campbell's sister. And I want to help you.

Abi liked that the email was short and to the point:

Abi—You don't know me. I don't know you. But there's someone in common in our lives—Elle Campbell.

I know you are up against Elle in the Blog-ahh awards. Right now, she is certainly going to win. I know how to help you compete. I know all the workings of Elle's site and all her social media tricks. I am very happy to come and help you elevate your site to a place where you could make sure Elle doesn't get that award.

Why would I do that? Because my sister is not who she says she is. Things in her home are not how they seem. And she has just done something so despicable to my family that I don't think I can ever forgive her.

Are you interested in meeting me?

Zoe Wright

Abi's response was instant:

Are you kidding me? YES.

Abi hadn't told Grace about the email. She hadn't told Grace about the meeting. But earlier today, Abi had said that she had a sit-down with a potential tourism advertiser before jumping in the people mover to drive the hour or so to Bendigo.

This is like a scene from a spy film, Abi had thought as she walked into the agreed coffee shop at the agreed time. She was thrilled by the very idea. And then it occurred to her: given what had happened to Leisel Adams, should she be worried? Oh well, too late.

The cafe was busy. Friends with prams catching up for coffee, a few office workers finishing up their salads. Abi walked through to the courtyard at the back, and instantly recognised Zoe Wright. The young woman looked like a 'before' photo of Elle. Before the gym obsession, before the boob job. Before the botox. Lovely, and very young.

And from the way she was sucking down that cigarette, she seemed really, *really* pissed off.

She looked up at Abi. 'Hope you don't mind sitting outside,' she said.

'Not at all.' Abi smiled. She sat down. 'So, I was surprised to hear from you. You sounded upset in your email. Are you... alright?'

'I'd like some cake,' said Zoe, in the tone of a sulking teen. 'Something really gooey and sweet. It might make me feel better about my shitty family.'

'Well, sugar is a good defence against shitty families,' Abi said, feeling maternal towards this young woman. 'That and wine, and cheese, and girlfriends.'

'Cake will do me.' Zoe stubbed out her cigarette. 'Elle says comfort-eating is really self-harm.'

'Fuck that.' Abi grabbed the menu. 'Most of the time I have to live on kale and activated nuts and sprouted seeds — and I can tell you, it really does nothing for my mood.'

Zoe looked like she was trying not to laugh. 'What the fuck is an activated nut?'

'Oh, to be so innocent.' Abi did laugh. 'Let's both have cake. And hot chocolate.'

And that was how two women with a common enemy

came to be sitting in a cafe in rural Victoria hatching a plan over giant slices of gateaux.

Abi found out that Zoe knew about her and Elle's shared history.

'Of course I do,' said Zoe. 'I lived with them for a while, after Freddie was born. I met your girls. Nice girls.'

'Ha! Nice? You mustn't have known them very well!'

'They didn't stay. It was before they moved to the big house. Elle always said there wasn't enough room for the girls there. But they came by a couple of times.'

Abi tried to quash her rising fury at the idea of there not being room for her daughters in their own father's house. Breathe, Abi, she told herself. Not the time.

'Talk to me about what you want to do, Zoe,' she said instead.

'I want you to give me a job on your blog,' Zoe said, almost too quickly. 'Just for a little while. I had to leave Melbourne because Elle even stuffed up my relationship with my family there. And then I had a good job in Mildura, but I had to quit to go home and see my dad, who's... Well, it's a long story. I don't want to go there now. At the moment, there are two things I need to do: earn a bit of money and piss off my sister.'

Zoe told Abi how she never thought she'd have a proper job, coming from where she did, and how the whole drama with Elle had ended up boosting her confidence — she'd done an online course in social media marketing, moved around a bit, got work here and there. 'I'm good at it. I can see some really simple things we can do to push up The Green Diva's engagement score. Have you ever had a professional consult with you about that?'

No, Abi hadn't. She was impressed by the resilience of this young woman who was bouncing from place to place alone, trying to make a life.

Hearing Zoe talk about her family background in such a matter-of-fact way also changed how she saw Elle. It took guts to get anywhere on your own, Abi had to admit that. She thought about her own middle-class childhood, about how hard she'd tried to shake off her family's weighty expectations. It would be far worse, she knew, for no one to expect anything from you at all.

***

Abi and Grace were driving back to the farm from parent–teacher night, which had been blessedly short, as Abi predicted. Now it was dark and getting cold. Otto was in the back seat with a rug on his skinny knees. Grace was trying to talk to him, her eyes on the rear-view mirror. 'So what did you think about what Mrs Patel says. How did it make you feel?'

Otto shrugged. 'I like her, whatever.'

'You like being taught by her, better than by Mummy?'

'Grace! *Shut up*.' Abi laughed. 'You can't ask that. Seriously, babe, who's crazy now?'

Otto laughed, too. '*Muuuum*. It's not like that. It's school. I like being with the other kids. I like not being at home all the time. Okay?'

'Okay?' Abi mimicked, from the driver's seat.

They pulled up the long driveway to the farm. 'Speaking of people being at home... there's something I need to talk to you about,' Abi said.

'What's that?'

'I need some help, with the blog.'

'Really? Okay. I can let Arden do it as part of her tech courses.'

'No, babe, I mean, professional help.'

'Oh. *Really*?'

They parked outside the farmhouse. Otto flung his door open and ran to the house, where the lights were on and teen-punk was pounding out of the windows.

Grace looked at Abi. 'What?'

'So, I met this girl...'

'This gets stranger and stranger,' said Grace. 'I can tell you're plotting something. Just hit me with it.'

'Okay.' So Abi told Grace about Zoe. About how she was Elle's younger sister. About how they were estranged. About how Zoe wanted to help Abi win the Blog-ahhs, and how Abi knew she could help make that happen.

'Zoe can move into the barn for a few weeks. Help me set a lot of stuff up. She would move on after the awards.'

Grace just stared at her. 'Abi, do you know what you're doing?'

'What?'

'You are obsessing over Elle. If I didn't know better, I'd say you were trying to settle a score with her.' Grace's famous composure was slipping. 'You and Adrian have been apart for *five years*, Abi. And this is our family. Is there something I'm missing here? Are you not *happy*?'

Abi grabbed Grace's hand. 'Grace. Seriously, I'm so fucking happy. You need to believe me that this has nothing to do with that. NOTHING. It's more complicated than that and anyway...'

'Anyway, what?'

Abi had planned not to, but she would have to tell Grace about the last part of the conversation she'd had with Zoe that afternoon. The bit that really changed everything.

Abi had been telling Zoe about her frustration at how Elle was blocking her and the girls from helping Adrian deal with his cancer. How it was the thing keeping her up at night—the thing fuelling her current fury at Elle.

'I don't know, maybe I'm fucking overreacting about it. It's just... He's their father. And he's really sick, and I just can't seem to get him to connect with them about it.'

Zoe's eyes dropped to her lap, where her fingers were fiddling with her small white lighter. She looked a little broken. And then she said, 'Look, I wasn't going to say this, because false hope or whatever...' She reached for a cigarette.

'What? You can't just say that and stop, Zoe!'

'I don't think your husband has cancer.'

Zoe looked up as she said it, looked straight at Abi. And as soon as Abi heard those words, she registered the truth in them.

It was like she'd been scratching a hundred tiny mosquito bites, and suddenly they all stopped itching at once. A calm came. And then a smile. 'Can you prove it?'

'No. But I think we could, with a bit of work. Don't you?'

Back in the car, in the dark driveway of the farm, lit only by the old house's windows, Grace's mouth was hanging open.

'Holy fuck,' was all she could say.

CHAPTER TWENTY-ONE

LEISEL

'I know you're shitty with me, Leisel, but this is going to be important television. Really important.'

It was Claire—Leisel's old journo friend had caught wind of her plan and wanted a part of it.

'I know that, Claire, and that's why I can't do it on *After Breakfast!*'

'I'm just going to pretend you didn't say that to an old mate, Leese.'

'Come on, Claire, you know exactly what I mean. I live and learn.'

'Okay, what if I come with you to wherever you take it, as a guest producer? If you're shopping this kind of story, you can probably have whoever you want.'

'Claire?'

'What?'

'When did you get so desperate?'

Leisel already knew the answer. Five years ago, as a single woman approaching forty in the 'man's world' of TV, Claire had begun to question what the next twenty years were going to look like. She'd decided she needed to get serious, to 'play the game', but found herself cock-blocked at every turn by the old school tie.

'That's just fucking rude, Leese. I'm not desperate for anything other than a promotion and a favour from an old friend.'

'You've had your favour, Claire. Remember *Darryl*?'

Leisel's plan had nothing to do with TV ratings. She was motivated by two things: to do something good in the world, and to win the Blog-ahhs.

She was going to sit down with Kristen Worther, the troll who'd attacked her. And she was going to stream the whole thing live. If you wanted to watch it, you'd have to come to The Working Mum.

***

Mark, of course, thought that this time she really had lost her fucking mind.

'You have lost your fucking mind,' he'd said, a forkful of spaghetti halfway to his lips.

Leisel had made the wise decision of arranging the holy grail for busy parents—Date Night—and using the occasion to raise a big, ugly bugbear from its fitful slumber.

Uncle Dan was babysitting the kids, and she'd booked a restaurant that wasn't so flash it made Mark feel uncomfortable but more special than family dinner at the local bowlo. Food was served on slates. Wine—sparkling water for Mark—came as an inch in the bottom of a giant balloon-glass. Date Night was *on*.

And then, somewhere between the starter and the main, Leisel had decided to tell Mark about her plan.

'I have spoken to the police and the social workers. They think she'll go for it. It's a public service—it will help her at sentencing.'

'As I said, you have lost your fucking mind.'

'We won't talk about the specifics of the crime. She's

going to discuss trolling. Why people do it. How it makes them feel. This is a big issue right now, Mark. It could help a lot of people.'

He took a gulp of his fizzy water, glanced around the room and ran his hands through his thick hair, making it stand on end. 'Is that why you're doing it, Lee? To help people?'

'Yes, sure. Look, online bullying is an issue that everyone has to grapple with. It's going to be huge for our kids—'

'Bullshit.'

'What's bullshit?'

'You're talking bullshit. And it's my job to call you on your bullshit. It's what we've always agreed to, right?'

Hissing at each other over uneaten octopus was not how Leisel had pictured Date Night. But that was exactly where it was going.

'Great, Mark, that's just great. So why don't you tell me why I'm doing it, since you know so much?'

'You are doing it to win that award.'

Leisel sat back in her chair. It was true. Partly true. 'What if that's a product of doing something worthwhile? Why is that so awful?'

'Because you are chasing something, Lee. This blog— talking about your family, unpicking all the shitty little bits of your life—it's become an addiction for you.'

'Well, you'd know.' Leisel didn't usually fight mean. She felt mean, though. She felt cornered.

Mark winced. But he kept going. 'How do you think it makes your family feel to know that instead of actually dealing with what's hurting you, you'd rather be slagging us off on the internet?'

'That is not fair, Mark. That is not fair.' Leisel leant across the table. Her and Mark's faces were inches apart now. 'But if we're talking about feelings, how do you think it feels to be the one who has to earn all the money? How do you think it feels to be the one who's carrying everything all the time? I want our lives to change, Mark. I want to be able to breathe.

And I think there's a chance of that happening now. It's been a shitty time for all of us, I know, but this is the silver lining. We have a chance to make a success out of this.'

'And what does that look like for you? I seriously want to know. Because all I see here is downside—more attention means more harassment means more attention... I don't get it.'

'Of course you don't get it. You don't get it because you don't have any ambition. You would be happy with us doing exactly what we're doing for ever.'

'What's so wrong with that? My ambition is to have a happy family. What the fuck's wrong with that?'

People were looking.

'I want *more!*' Leisel said. 'It's okay to want more, Mark. I want to stop working so hard all the time. I want to not always be running, being behind, feeling guilty. You have one job, and it's the kids, but I feel like I have a million jobs. And it's exhausting. What you don't understand about the women on my blog is that they all feel like that too. And the support we give each other is something precious. If I can make my life more about that, and less about being in an office ten hours a day working for a teenager, then that's what *I* want.'

'But, Lee.' Mark seemed to have stopped being angry. He took her hand across the table. She took a mouthful of octopus. 'You could do that in other ways. Talk to someone. Get another job. The cost of this is too high. Look at what happened. Look at what came into *our home*.'

'Don't you dare try to blame me for that, Mark. Don't you dare. I didn't provoke that woman. She's ill.'

'Well then, if she's ill, getting her in front of a camera to talk about it seems like a really, really dumb idea.'

Date Night. Always so fun.

The words she'd thrown at Mark had left bruises, she could tell. Since Date Night, they'd been tiptoeing around each other. He had made some noises about taking on more carpentry work. She'd said there was no need. She hadn't mentioned the interview again, but she was making plans, whether he liked it or not.

He made one last attempt before they stopped discussing it. 'Leisel, I know you feel like you're over this, but sitting down with the woman who attacked you could be very triggering for you. I'm not worried about her mental health—I'm worried about *your* mental health.'

Sometimes, having a husband who had done so much therapy was infuriating.

***

Leisel didn't take up Claire's offer. She was putting together a production team of her own: a video crew that she'd worked with at the magazines, a writer from *Woman's Daily* who would do a print follow-up, two psychologists and a police liaison officer.

But she still hadn't met Kristen Worther. Leisel had word through her social worker that the woman was happy to do the interview, but that was all she knew.

Two days before the agreed date, Leisel wrote a post:

> On Thursday, on The Working Mum, something extraordinary is going to happen.
>
> It's a very important day for me.
>
> I am going to sit down with the woman who attacked me in my home. I am going to talk to her about how anyone could get to such a dark place. About what drives anyone to hate someone they have never even met.
>
> How we can all use social media for good is an important discussion to be having in 2017. But beyond that, I want us to think about how it feels to forgive.
>
> This woman—and she is not alone—trolled me for months before she stepped over the line that

separates the digital and physical worlds and invaded the only space in the world where we all expect to feel safe, our own homes.

But demonising the woman who was hurting enough to take such drastic action is not the answer.

After learning about the woman who attacked me, I have decided that I will not aggressively pursue charges against her. I have decided that we will all be best served by helping this woman, and other people like her, rather than trying to lock her up.

This decision has not been an easy one. There are people very close to me who think it's the worst idea I've ever had. To them, I respectfully say, this is my decision to make.

During the interview on Thursday, I'm going to ask you to do a few things: Donate to the anti-violence, anti-bullying women's charity The Jasmine Foundation. Like and Share and tell your friends that the event is happening.

And bring an open mind.

With love—Leisel.

The response was instantaneous.

What an idiot. You are not a judge, you don't get to decide who's safe to be on the streets and who's not. #dangerousbitch

I am in awe of your spirit. I'll be watching #sobrave

God complex. Fucking mummy bloggers #ugh

What an important conversation to start. So proud of you. #sobrave

The Blog-ahh people called her: 'This ties in so well with our anti-bullying platform. We couldn't be more excited!'

Grace called her: 'I don't know what's happening but it seems like all of my people are going crazy at the same time. Are you absolutely sure about this?'

Her mother called her: 'Darling, Emily from the club tells me her daughter saw on the internet that you are going to drop the charges against that woman who stabbed you. Surely that's not right?'

Zac, meanwhile, was furious: 'Why would you do that on your own, rather than on one of our channels? I'm seriously beginning to doubt your loyalty to this company!'

And Mark—Mark called her, too. She missed his call, but he left a voicemail.

'Hey, Lee, it's me. I'm struggling a bit with all this. I'll go to Dan's for a few nights, clear my head, do some Meetings. I'll take Harri. Wendy is picking up Rich and Mags today. I'll call you soon.'

CHAPTER TWENTY-TWO

ELLE

Elle had never been so happy to see her Thermomix, her KitchenAid and her Vitamix.

It was nice to see the boys, too, of course, but when she walked back into her oasis of a kitchen after three nights in Thalwyn, Elle could have kissed the French doors of her giant fridge.

'Seriously, Adrian. I used to live there and I don't know how anyone does.'

'Or *why* anyone does,' Cate added, heading upstairs with her bag.

'Some people like peace and quiet,' Adrian offered, as he peeled a weeping Freddie off Elle's leg.

'Well, they won't get it there,' said Elle. 'The sound of an Australian small town is a revving engine and a pub band who still think it's 1990.'

'Harsh, Elle.' He hugged her. 'How the hell did you manage?'

'You have *no idea*.'

Adrian really didn't have any idea. She hadn't told him

everything that had happened at Pam's house. She hadn't told him about Dad. She hadn't told him about the rogue researcher.

Teddy and Freddie were standing in front of Elle, eerily quiet. They were waiting for presents, she realised. Of course, whenever Adrian went away for work, he brought them something back.

'Oh, darlings, there really wasn't anything I could bring back for you...' Maybe a souvenir tea towel or an STI from the pub toilet seat, she thought.

Freddie started to cry.

'Oh, baby.' Elle picked him up, gave him a squeeze. 'Caaate!' she called through the house. 'Can you come and take Freddie, please? I'm sure he's missed you. Maybe you could take them both to the playground.' She ushered the boys out of the kitchen and turned to Adrian. 'You look well. Tell me you weren't eating healthily while I was gone.' Elle had seen sick up-close now. It had shifted her perspective.

'I promise. I survived on a cheeseburger and three cans of V a day, as prescribed.' Adrian smiled — he seemed happy to see her.

'While I was gone, I had some good ideas about what else we can do to keep things real.' Elle put her arms around Adrian's neck and kissed his sunken cheek. 'There was a bit of inspiration in Thalwyn, as it turns out.'

'How so?'

Her father's face popped into her head, and she flicked it away. 'I have a lot to tell you,' she said. 'No more Abi attacks that I can see, at least.'

'She seems to have calmed down, thank god.'

'She's just a sore loser, babe. And she knows she's going to lose.'

Adrian said nothing.

Cate appeared in the hallway with coats for the boys. 'I'm taking them to the playground, guys. I'm sure you two have a lot to catch up on.'

Cate's new habit of making Elle's instructions sound like

her own ideas was beginning to grate. 'I think you'll find I asked you to do that, Cate. When you get back, we've got a lot of outfit planning to do.'

'That girl might need some time off,' Adrian said as Cate and the boys left the house. 'I'm sure Thalwyn was no picnic, and it's been kind of 24-7, hasn't it?'

'Oh, don't feel too sorry for her. She spent most of the time sitting in her motel room watching Austar.'

'Well, then I definitely feel sorry for her.' Adrian's attempt at a joke fell flat with Elle, preoccupied as she was with restoring order to her fridge. 'Look, I've got to get back to work, Elle. What do you have to tell me?'

***

Three days ago, on that patchy front lawn, it had taken Elle a few moments to be able to say anything to Pam.

She heard a lazy winter fly buzzing near her ear. She looked at the older woman's face, creased with genuine concern. She flashed to her latest #cancerwife post—*Keeping the house full of fresh flowers does wonders for Adrian's spirits. And mine!! #peonies @alphaflorist*—and she felt a gentle thud in her stomach.

'How do you know?' she asked Pam.

'What... what do you mean?'

'How do you know about the months or weeks?'

Pam looked back at the house. 'He'll want to talk to you about it himself, love.'

'Just let me... give me a minute.'

'The hospital says. It took him a long time to get around to going with his cough, and he'd been losing weight and... Well, it was pretty far along.'

Elle glanced at the utes in the front yard. 'Are my brothers here?'

Pam nodded. 'They've been around a lot lately.' She pushed her tissue back into her pocket. 'Understandable.'

Elle knew that as soon as she walked into the house, she would lose all of her power. In that living room—which she could picture perfectly, down to the faded wallpaper and the giant television—she would be twelve years old again. Five minutes in there, and she'd probably be fetching the boys a beer from the fridge and emptying the ashtrays.

'Pam. I can't come in.'

'But, love, your dad's so looking forward to seeing you.' Pam held Elle's arm. 'Really, it's not my place, but you need to see him. It'll be good for everyone.'

'I know.' She did know. 'But this whole thing has... shocked me. I need to go away and think about it. I'll be back in the morning, I promise. Can you tell Dad that? And also, I know that this sounds bad, Pam, but I would really like to see him on my own. Not with Kai and Bobby around. You know, the first time.'

God knows what she thinks of me, Elle thought as she walked back to her car.

She surprised herself for considering this—the thought must have been prompted by the utterly confused expression on Pam's face as Elle walked away.

'I shouldn't have told you, love, should I?' Pam called after her, following a few steps behind. 'Was a bit much, wasn't it?'

'No, I'm glad you did.' Then Elle remembered something. 'If anyone else comes here to see Dad, keep them away from him until I've been back, hey?'

Pam looked worried. 'Like who else?'

'Oh, I'm just talking about the TV people. We need to work out how to play this before we talk to them.' Elle got into the car.

'Play this?' Pam asked, as Elle shut the Toyota's door and started the engine.

Then, as she started to drive away, she saw Kai come out the front door, shouting over to Pam, pointing at Elle's car. He looked big, heavy, older. She put her foot down.

Back at the motel, Elle felt more rattled than she could

remember ever being. Her father had called her mobile. Mrs Gleason wanted to chat. Elle went straight to her room, lay down on the seashell bed cover and put her hands over her face.

My mum, she thought. I'm going to be an orphan. This is it.

Elle had some well-tried tactics for gathering her armour. Positive self-talk was one. Wardrobe was another. But perhaps the best defence of all was scrolling through her Instagram feed.

She reached for her giant bejewelled phone and looked at the most recent post. It was of Elle with Teddy—she wore a white crop-top and leggings, while Teddy was in a navy jersey 'Daddy's Secret Weapon' T-shirt that a Melbourne designer, Ingrid K, had made specially and sent over. Elle was holding Teddy's waist and smiling at him, but keeping him just far enough away to display her body. Her tan, her abs. Teeth and hair. In the corner of the frame was a glimpse of the white-washed wooden back deck and aqua pool.

> This little guy can put a smile on my face on the toughest of days. #teddy #cancerwife #mumlife #ingridk

Perfection.
It had 25,000 Likes. Elle flicked through some comments:

> When I have kids I need them to be exactly this cute. #mumgoals

> I know your husband will be just fine with such a gorgeous support crew #loveandlight

> Who does your hair? #todiefor

> Abs for days #killme #goddess

'Come on, Elle,' she said aloud, throwing her phone back on the bed. 'You can deal with this. You can deal with anything. Just another bump in the road. You're made of stronger stuff. Self-pity is for losers.'

And she got up and went into the bathroom to have a shower and put herself back together.

***

'You are joking?' Adrian asked.

Elle wasn't sure she'd ever seen someone's jaw actually drop before, but his just had.

'No, not joking.'

'What are you even doing here, Elle? Shouldn't you be there? What did you tell the *Sunday Evening* crew? What the fuck?' Adrian picked up his jaw and paced the kitchen.

At the double sink, Elle was rearranging the organic dish soap and handwash, making the labels face the right way. 'I'll get to all that, babe.' She wiped down the spray mixer tap, putting it back in its holder. 'But seriously, calm down. You have never even met my father and you've known me for five years. Wouldn't it be a bit hypocritical of me to be wailing by his bedside? I'll leave that to Zoe.'

'Far out, Elle.'

She didn't turn around, but she was pretty sure he was staring at her.

Her brother Bobby had stared at her when he'd found her and Cate having dinner in the pub that first night in Thalwyn. Tall, wide, paunchy, with cropped hair, a broken nose and tattoos that snaked from the neck of his Bonds T-shirt, Bobby was clearly not the kind of man that Cate was comfortable around—she recoiled as he approached their table.

'What the fuck are you doing here?' he asked Elle, standing a foot away from where she and Cate were heroically avoiding carbs with their schnitzel and salad.

'Hi, Bobby.' Elle's armour was in back in place, but she

was aware that the TV researcher could walk into the pub at any moment, and she didn't want to be in a screaming match with her hooligan brother if that happened. Still, she had known there was a good chance one of her brothers would turn up here tonight—actually, it was part of the plan she had hatched on the seashell bedspread. She just had to keep things civil.

'Don't give me that shit.' Bobby squared his shoulders and puffed out his chest, but Elle saw his eyes slide to the neon-lit bar.

'Sit down, have a drink with us. We're just having dinner. This is my friend, Cate.'

'I said, what the fuck are you doing here? You need to be over at Dad's.'

Elle reached for her purse. 'Cate, can you go and get Bobby a drink? This is my little brother, by the way. I think he'll have a VB—right, Bobby?'

'Bundy.'

Of course, thought Elle, someone else is paying. Some things really don't change.

'Just ask the barman for a Bundy and cola,' she told a terrified-looking Cate, who hopped down from her stool and took Elle's purse in the direction of the bar.

'Sit down, Bobby, please.' Elle knew her brother was taking in what she was wearing, her hair, her tan, her boobs—to him, she surely looked like one of those girls in the magazines. He seemed confused.

He sat at the table. 'I'm going to ask you again,' he said, closer to her face. 'Why are you here, having a fucken schnitty with your girlfriend, when your dad's wondering why the hell you didn't even come in to see if he's okay?'

'Is he okay?'

'No, he's fucken *not* okay, Ellen. And you know that, Pam told me.'

'I'm going to see him in the morning, Bobby. Seriously, I am. I was really freaked out today. It's been a long time.'

'You're fucken telling me.'

'And I knew you and Kai were in there, and I couldn't face you all at once.' Elle looked down at her soda water, cast her eyes low. 'I know I've got a lot of talking to do.'

Cate came back with Bobby's drink, and slid up onto her stool. Still looking terrified, she said nothing.

'We know you're only here about the TV thing, Ellen,' Bobby said, then sculled half of his rum. 'I know you think we're stupid, but we're not, you know. You just want to use Dad. We know that. Just look at ya.'

Cate's alarm had risen to vibration level—it was hard for Elle not to start shaking just sitting next to her.

'The TV "thing" is only one reason I'm here,' Elle said as calmly as she could manage. 'I wanted to see Dad.'

'You never have before.' The Bundy was gone. Elle was torn between wanting Cate out of the way at the bar and not wanting her brother to get fighting drunk. Or more fighting drunk than he already was.

'Bobby, I don't really want to talk about this now, but I'm happy to sort you and Kai out for any inconvenience this is causing you. Why don't we discuss it tomorrow, in town?'

'Sort what out?'

'Well, if you and Kai need to go away for a couple of days, you're going to need some cash to do it, right?'

'Where are we going? And why the fuck would we be going now, when Dad needs us?'

'Just for forty-eight hours, Bobby. I'd love to catch up with you and Kai properly, of course, but with everything that's going on, I think it would be better for us to do it after the TV interview, right?'

Bobby was looking right at Elle. His hulking presence dominated the table, next to the two tiny women. 'So you're rich now, are ya?'

'We do okay, my husband and I,' she said. 'Well enough to be able to help family out when we need to.'

Cate's eyes were huge in her head. She was clutching her purse in her lap, as if the scary man might run off with it.

Something seemed to click for Bobby, and he relaxed. 'Alright then.' His shoulders dropped, and he slumped a little in his seat. He smiled. He'd always had a lovely smile, Elle thought. Sometimes she saw it on Freddie. 'Wanna have another drink with me?'

'Cate's got to go back up to the motel—haven't you, Cate? But I'll stay for one.' Elle looked at her assistant, who couldn't get off her seat fast enough.

'Yes, of course, I do, and lovely to meet you, Bobby. Elle, I'll, um, see you later...'

As the young woman hurried out the door, Bobby stared after her. 'Who the fuck is that? And what's up her arse?'

'She works for me,' said Elle, reaching into her wallet for some notes, and passing them to her brother.

'Is that right?' Bobby raised his eyebrows, gave a little nod.

He's impressed, thought Elle.

'I'll have a vodka and soda,' she said. Just one. 'And we can work out some family business, hey?'

Bobby had just reached the bar when the pub door opened and another young woman walked in. Her all-black outfit and the fringe halfway up her forehead couldn't have shouted 'out-of-towner' any louder than a sign around her neck. She had a laptop case under her arm. As she looked around, Elle scooted off her stool and sped over to the bar. 'Bobby. We're leaving. I'll buy you a drink in the top pub.'

***

'Great,' Adrian said, head in his hands at the kitchen bench. 'So now we're paying off your brothers, as well as your dad.'

'They're pretty cheap, babe, to be honest. No one here's getting rich.'

'The idea, Elle, behind all of this shit is that *we* are getting rich, remember? Not spending all our money on your family dramas.'

Elle looked up at her husband. How dare he talk to her like that? He was clearly on the edge of losing it. 'Adrian! Are you okay?'

'I am, babe. I'm just... worried. So what happened with the TV crew?'

***

Agility. That was one of the key skills you needed to survive in a disrupted universe. The rules for almost everything were being rewritten, so why not be one of the people rewriting them, rather than one of the people moaning about what they used to be?

Elle was explaining this to Cate, who was about to head off in the Toyota back to Swan Hill to track down some smart clothes, and a hair and make-up person they could trust.

'But the *Sunday Evening* crew will bring wardrobe with them,' Cate protested. She looked a little green. The night before, Elle had texted her and ordered her back to the main pub to stay up drinking with Bette, the *SE* researcher, while Elle and Bobby's 'family catch-up' at the top pub had gone longer than planned.

Now it was the day before the interview and plans had changed.

'I know they will, Cate, but I need someone *before* that. My brother used to date this make-up artist, says she's a sweetheart. And can you get into Lowes while you're there, please, and grab a couple of the nicest men's shirts you can find? XLs, please.'

'So I'm driving this make-up girl back. A stranger?' Cate looked stricken at the thought of having to talk to someone she didn't know.

'You'll survive, Cate. Put some music on.'

'It's just not... what I was expecting.'

'Well, no, me neither,' said Elle. 'But that's what we've got. So. Agility!'

Elle had to head over to Pam's house. This time, she would make it in the door. This time, she had a plan. Her armour was in place. She was ready.

Seeing her father was still a shock. He wasn't an old man—not much older than Adrian, really, but he could have been from a completely different generation. Partly that was the illness, of course, which had diminished him, stripping the flesh from his bones and trapping him in an armchair. His hair was mostly gone, his teeth were brown and uneven. His T-shirt hung off him. His skin was yellowing, papery where Elle kissed him on the head. 'So, Dad, I'm here. What do you think?'

'You look gorgeous, love,' he said. He was smiling at her, something she didn't remember much from childhood. 'You're a sight for sore eyes.'

'Thanks, Dad.' Elle sat on one of the mismatched armchairs across from his. The TV was on mute. As requested, the boys weren't in the house. Pam was making tea in the kitchen. Elle's father lit a cigarette.

'Should you be doing that, Dad?' she asked gently.

'Bit late now to be honest, love,' he said, pulling hard.

'So I've been thinking about what to do with this TV thing, now I know you're so ill, Dad. You really should have told me, you know.'

'I wanted to tell you myself. Face to face. Of course, Pam always knows best—'

'You bet!' Pam called from the kitchen.

Elle nodded. 'I know, Dad. I know—and, look, now I do know, it's obvious you're not up to the cameras. I'm going to cancel that interview. Don't need to put you through that.'

'But love,' he wheezed, 'I thought it was important to you?'

'It is. But so are you, even though I'm not good at showing it.' Elle put her hand on his knee. 'And anyway, the boys have offered to help me.'

'Your brothers? But—'

'Dad, let it be, it's done. Let's just have a cup of tea and enjoy seeing each other, hey?'

'Tell me about these grandsons of mine, Ellen. Show me some pictures.'

Elle had allowed exactly twenty minutes for this catch-up. Then she was meeting Bobby at one of his mate's houses in town, along with Kai (Bobby had been tasked with filling him in). Bette the researcher would meet the three of them at the house. It was a perfect location. Humble but clean. Modest but respectable. Its back deck would have the perfect light in the afternoon for a TV interview that signalled 'Aussie outback'—and the perfect view, from one angle, of an old-fashioned iron windmill.

Elle knew all this because she'd met Bobby there first thing that morning, to check out the place and iron out a few more details.

The next day, she would be sitting in that house, flanked by her brothers wearing their new, respectable shirts, their neck tattoos disguised with industrial-strength foundation. The three of them would be talking to the camera about how it had felt to be brought up poor by a proud father in country Australia.

About their beloved mum and how she had never wanted to leave them.

And about their heroic dad, who had raised them single-handedly before losing his own battle with cancer just a few months before.

They were orphans now.

***

'And is that what you said in the interview?' asked Adrian.

'Yes, it went off without a hitch. We kept Bette busy from the day she got there until the cameras turned on.'

'So you're going to be telling Australia that your dad is dead?'

'Yes. Already have.'

'But, Elle...' Adrian looked astounded. 'Why?'

'It was so messy, Adrian. There was no way Dad was up to that interview. And I knew it would really confuse the #cancerwife narrative to have another family member dying of cancer.'

'I didn't think I was *dying*—'

'You know what I mean. Suffering,' Elle couldn't see why Adrian wasn't congratulating her on her quick-thinking. 'It was tricky, babe. Like, why wouldn't I have raised it before now, you know? A bit weird. A bit off-putting.'

'A bit off-putting? Jesus, Elle. What did your dad think of this? Of having to pretend that he's dead?'

'Oh, he doesn't know.' Elle went and put her arms around Adrian's neck, stood on her tip-toes to kiss him just below his ear. 'He doesn't leave that house. He won't watch the interview. He was just happy to see me, I think. We had a good chat.'

'And Pam?' Adrian pulled away, just a little.

'Oh, I told her. The boys and I sat her down, made a new deal. She was fine with it, really—she's not the type for a media fuss.'

'And the money? How many people are we paying off now?'

'Well, I just transferred the money from my dad's account to the boys' account. Gave a bit to Pam, too, of course.'

'All that money you gave to your dad, you just took it back?'

'Not *all* of it.' Elle looked up at Adrian, smiled. '*Most* of it. I'm not a monster, you know.'

CHAPTER TWENTY-THREE

ABI

'That is a high-risk strategy,' Abi told Zoe, guiltily shoving the plastic pie wrapper into the side compartment of the car. 'I mean, she's basically faked your father's death.'

Abi had picked Zoe up at the train station and was driving her back to Daylesford. Zoe was moving in—and she was sharing.

'Her whole life is a high-risk strategy,' Zoe said through a mouthful of pie and chips in the passenger seat. Abi could tell this kid was going to be a bad dietary influence on her macrobiotic household.

'But that seems particularly crazy. She needed the whole family's buy-in. What happens—and I don't mean to be insensitive—but what happens when your dad does... pass away?'

'Who's looking at what happens in a little shitty town in the middle of nowhere? It's hardly going to make the nightly news.'

'Wow.' Abi, despite herself, was impressed by Elle's nerve. She had seriously underestimated her ex-husband's hot wife. 'And I thought she was just a pretty face.'

Zoe laughed out loud. 'Oh, that's funny. But anyway, she didn't get the whole family's buy-in. She didn't ask me. Or Liam.'

'There are *more* of you?'

'One more. Liam, the oldest. Haven't seen him for years, but if—wherever the fuck he is—he flicks on the TV in a couple of Sundays and hears that Dad is dead, he might just turn up somewhere.'

'God, it's like a soap opera. And I thought my life was complicated.'

***

Grace had finally agreed to Zoe coming to stay under one condition—no more drama.

'I know you guys think you're Woodward and Bernstein,' she said, 'uncovering the truth and everything, but just keep a lid on it. This doesn't have to be a big deal. Find out if Adrian's okay, talk to him about it, move on. No more trolling, no more inciting your followers. That's not the way to win.'

Sometimes, Grace's inner school teacher reared her head and roared.

'We're probably more like Nancy Drew and the Hardy Boys,' Abi said with a laugh, hugging Grace. 'Thank you. You know, you'll like Zoe. She's got a lot of guts. Came from absolutely nothing. She has the kind of initiative and drive I'd love our kids to end up with.'

'Be careful, baby.' Grace hugged Abi back. 'You sound kind of normal—suburban, even.'

'That's me. Just a normal, suburban hippie these days,' Abi said into Grace's hair.

***

Zoe's room was just a space in the podshed with a pull-out bed, a little desk, a TV. But she seemed beyond grateful, telling Abi that she loved the energy of the farm, the kids running around, the chickens, the space. 'So this is what living in the country is like if you're not broke,' she said, exclaiming over the plumbed-in outdoor bath, the veggie patch, the wood-fire oven, the daybed that was in exactly the right spot for stargazing.

Grace gave Zoe the house rules. 'No smoking around the kids. No drinking at all, ever. No bitching. No music videos. No negativity. No gluten.'

'We feel more strongly about gluten than crack cocaine around here,' Abi whispered to her.

'Good to know,' Zoe said, grinning.

She was full of ideas about how Abi could extend the appeal of The Green Diva.

'I know we've only got a few more weeks to go, but I reckon there's a case for a big follower push to the end. We need some relatable posts, some great images. And you need to lay off the crazy. Just a little.'

'Crazy, me?' Abi chuckled. 'Surely fucking not.'

'Your followers are passionate, which is a big plus. But the flipside to that adoration is the army of people who hate you.'

'Well, I have trolls... There are armies of people who hate me?'

'There are whole Facebook groups dedicated only to hating you, Abi. Elle and Leisel have those too, but neither of them has a record of being so... combative. It makes the Blog-ahh people itchy.'

'Well, fuck them.'

'NOT the attitude, Abi. Let's give the people something they can relate to.'

'Like...?'

'Like pie.'

Abi's first Zoe-sanctioned Facebook post got more than ten thousand Likes:

It's hard to be holy.

Forgive me, GDs, for I have sinned. Today I ate a meat pie—from a SERVICE STATION. Yes, one of those pies that has an expiry date somewhere in the next, next century. One of those pies chock-full of mystery meat and gristle that would be inedible if it wasn't all doused in that goopy, fatty, salty gravy.

That's not all. It had TOMATO SAUCE ON IT. Yes, that fake red slop that's got more sugar in it than fairy floss.

I don't know about the rest of you, but since you're on this page, I'm going to hazard a guess you understand where I'm coming from—I don't usually eat processed foods, sugary foods, fake foods. I don't usually eat food that hasn't come from the paddock or the veggie patch. Food whose ingredients are just a list of numbers and letters and a collection of euphemisms. Food that could live on a servo shelf for two years without growing a single culture is not a normal part of my diet.

Usually, I would look right through that pie and not even consider it food.

But today, I was tired, I was hungry, I was a little bit emotional and I stopped at the servo at exactly the moment those emotions collided. So I bought the damn pie, and I ate it in the car like a fugitive shovelling down the first bread roll they've seen in a week.

You know what? It was GLORIOUS.

I try to live a mindful life, to eat mindfully, and act mindfully and parent mindfully, but seriously, some days, it's TOO FUCKING HARD and you just want to eat the damn pie.

So, forgive me, my beautiful GDs, and if you have a food sin you'd like to get off your chest, go for it right here.

Remember, there are no 'bad' foods, only bad people.

JOKING.

Never apologise for being imperfect. #eatthedamnpie

It was accompanied by a picture of the pie—complete with tomato sauce pool—that Zoe had selflessly recreated with a pie of her own.

Abi's followers erupted, some with laughter:

I was meant to have cauliflower rice for dinner, again. Sod it. I went the hot chips. #humanafterall

Life's too short not to #eatthedamnpie @greendiva, just go for it

One meat pie does not a traitor make #eatthedamnpie

Some with shock:

I thought this was a genuine macrobiotic community. That you could even consider eating that processed mush is horrific. #notfood #donoteatthedamnpie

Do I need to tell you that you just ate camel muscle and sheep tendons? #disgrace

And some were just incredulous that this was a thing:

When a blogger goes viral for eating a pie, things are out of hand. #eatthedamnpie

Meet Abi Black, the woman who's gone viral for eating a damn pie. #hilarious

'See?' said Zoe. 'The people are responding to you being less than the untouchable Green Diva. Let's build on that. Advertisers might like it, too.'

Zoe also started posting pleasing shots of the farm on Instagram.

'Don't make me look like some rustic picture-perfect fuckwit,' Abi warned. 'That's too far for me.'

'Impossible,' Zoe said. 'This place is a mess. But it's an *aspirational* mess.'

Scheduled to run: Faceless snaps of Otto and Sol feeding the chickens at sunset. Silhouette of Abi in the outside bath against a starry sky. Wildflowers in a jam jar next to the podcast sound-recording panel in the shed.

'Wildflowers in a fucking jam jar?' Abi asked, eyebrows raised.

'Trust me,' said Zoe.

Likes were up. The trolls were quiet. Grace's drama-meter was resting.

Alex and Arden were also delighted to have Zoe on the farm, not least because they sensed that she might have some dirt on their stepmother.

Abi overheard some of their questions:

'So what was Elle like a teenager?'

'Are those really her boobs?'

'Does she secretly hate our dad?'

'No comment, girls,' was Zoe's standard answer, in light of Grace's 'no negativity' rule, and she distracted them with YouTube eyeliner tutorials.

***

When they got a chance, Abi and Zoe hung out in the podshed, plotting how to find out for sure what was going on with Adrian's health.

'I should just confront him,' Abi suggested. 'I don't know

if he could lie to my face, even after everything. I could always tell when he was lying.'

'Um, wasn't he sleeping with my sister under your nose for months?' Zoe had a way of cutting to the chase.

'Well, yes. But, you know, I wasn't really paying attention.'

Finally, they decided on a two-fold strategy: a good old-fashioned stake-out, and an attempt to flip a source closer to the heart of the story.

Zoe's theory about Adrian being perfectly healthy had started with Cate.

'I was still in Thalwyn when Elle came to town,' Zoe told Abi. 'She thought I'd gone, but I stayed with an old mate. And I kept an ear out for what was happening at the motel.'

'Jesus, this whole thing is like deep throat. You were spying on your sister?'

'Isn't deep throat a porno? Well, you know what, when we spoke on the phone, I just knew she was up to something. And I thought that when she found out about Dad, there was a chance she might be upset and call me, and... well, I wanted to be close by.'

'But that never happened.'

'No. I went over to see Dad and Pam on the day she'd visited, and Pam told me that she'd told Elle about the cancer and she'd just driven away. Not even said hello to Dad or the boys.'

'Well, she could have been upset. It must be a lot, coming back to your family home for the first time in ten years, and then finding that out.'

'Whose fucking side are you on?'

'You're right, what's wrong with me? What a bitch.' Abi grinned. A part of her—a part much bigger than she'd like to admit—was thoroughly enjoying all this drama. Grace could see it in her: that was why she hadn't joined in this plotting session.

'Anyway, like I've said before, Pam's house is not our

family home. We don't have a family home. We're just...
wherever we are.'

'Okay, okay.'

'So Elle and this girl Cate had rooms at the motel. I was
talking to my friend Deb about it—her family runs the place.
Cate didn't leave the motel unless she was with Elle. I was
watching Elle's social accounts, and you could see the Adrian
posts rolling up, as if it was happening that minute, but neither
of them was anywhere near Melbourne or Adrian.'

'I hope that's not your only evidence, Zoe, because even I
know about scheduling posts to roll-out whenever.' Abi took
a gulp of the new-batch kombucha. 'At least, I do now.'

'Look, I know you'll think this is flimsy but seriously, it's
an instinct I have. And you have it, too. Watching the way
she's carrying on. The way she dealt with all that family shit,
so cold. Even I was surprised by that. The Adrian story is the
one she wants to tell, but there's something really dodgy about
it. Anyway, I spoke to Cate.'

'Oh, god, I wish I had popcorn,' Abi said. 'This is better
than a movie.'

'That poor kid. She's fucking talented, but Elle is treating
her like shit, and it's only a matter of time before she kicks
her out. Elle doesn't like anyone getting too close, and this
girl, well, she knows too much.'

'You spoke to her. GO ON.'

'Can I smoke here? The kids are in bed, right?'

'You can smoke outside. In here, and Grace would kill
us both.'

'She's so fierce, Grace, I love her.'

'Me too. GO ON.'

The two women wrapped rugs from the bed around
themselves and headed out to sit on op-shop chairs beside
the shed.

'So the only time Cate did leave without Elle was on the
first night. Barmaid texted to tell me that Elle had basically
dumped her in the pub to hang out with this other girl—the TV

researcher. Elle and Bobby had gone off together, so I went and had a couple with Cate and her mate. She had no idea who I was, so I just got chatting to her.'

'And?'

'Look, she was cagey. Mostly she wanted to ask me about living in such a "shit hole"—which was, you know, lovely...'

'She didn't recognise you? You do look like your sister.'

'No, she didn't. She was a bit pissed, and very nervous about being "in the middle of nowhere", as she kept saying. I let it be known that I followed Elle online—local girl done good and all that—and how sad I was about Adrian. And after I mentioned it a couple of times, Cate started giggling, saying things like "I suppose so..."'

'Where was the TV woman? Elle's judgement about leaving Cate with her wasn't the smartest, was it?'

'In and out of the front, smoking, on her phone. And look, she might have had Elle rattled, but she was just a researcher, there to plot out interview locations and shit. She wasn't investigating, unfortunately. But Cate, with the giggles, and the eye rolls... It's just—it's just not true. Elle has made all this up to win the Blog-ahhs. That's it.'

Again, Abi felt the truth of this, but it still shocked her. 'The thing that's so wild about that, Zoe, is how Adrian could do it. The boys might be none the wiser, but what he's putting the girls through... Why would he do that? Why the fuck would he do that?'

Zoe blew out a big plume of smoke. 'Same reason. To win the Blog-ahhs. Make money.'

Abi considered this. She remembered that phone call with Adrian, weeks ago. 'If that's it, that's just fucking amazing.'

'Amazingly fucked.' Zoe stubbed her cigarette out, waved the smoke away, cautiously palmed the butt. 'Anyway, I was happy to keep all that in the family until this shit went down with Dad. Now, I think she deserves public humiliation.'

And the women went back inside the shed to make a plan.

***

That night, Abi went up to bed to find Grace still awake, pretending to read, worrying.

'What's up?' Abi climbed in next to her, snuggled up close.

'You and Zoe and this thing with Elle and Adrian—I know why you're doing it, but I hate that our lives have been hijacked by this... poison.'

'Grace. We've been through this. He's my daughters' father. His wife is trying to win the award by living a great big, fat lie. Zoe and I are just trying to set things right.'

'How? How are you going to do that in a way that doesn't blow our lives sky-high?' Grace rolled over to face Abi, their faces level.

'I don't know yet. But we're going to Melbourne in a couple of days. I have interviews about the awards, and Adrian's meant to have chemo. Zoe and I will try to get to the bottom of it all.'

'And then what? Will we forget about this award, get on with our lives?'

'God no, Gracey.' Abi rolled onto her back, exhaling in a frustrated huff. 'In two weeks, we're all going to Sydney and we're going to win the award. It could change our lives.'

'I don't want our lives to change,' said Grace. 'Except back to how they were.'

'Bad luck, beautiful.' Abi turned to look into Grace's eyes. 'That ship has sailed.'

CHAPTER TWENTY-FOUR

KRISTEN

Kristen Worther had never seen such bright lights.

'I don't think I'll be able to see,' she said to the young woman who was attaching her microphone in the makeshift studio. 'Those lights are blinding.'

'You won't be looking at them,' the girl said, squeezing her arm. 'You'll get used to it.'

Everyone was being so nice. Why?

Kristen's psych, Mel, was getting them both coffee. She had personally advised Kristen not to do this interview about the attack, but professionally it wasn't her place to step in. She'd come to provide support. 'It could be dangerous for your recovery,' she'd said. 'This kind of confrontation is going to be very triggering for you.'

'But it will be good for my sentencing,' Kristen had told her. 'And that's more important. I need to be out for my kids.'

Kristen's kids, Ruby and Tom, were living with her ex, Dalton. She could see with complete clarity now what she couldn't see on the night she'd followed Leisel home from work: her kids were all that mattered. Showing them that their mum loved them was more important than silencing that roaring anger inside her head.

Dalton had brought them to see her twice since that night, but he'd had to stay in the room at all times, and so had Mel, and so had the kids' psych. Until then, Kristen had never realised what a privilege being in a room on your own with your children was. To think she'd spent all that time trying to escape them. Hiding in the bathroom with her phone. Yelling at them to get to their room.

Never again. When all this was over, she would never leave them alone. If Dalton and the psychs would let her, that was.

Kristen sat down on the beige sofa, in front of a huge piece of pink paper that hung from the wall. On it was the logo of The Jasmine Foundation — a charity, she'd been told, that helped women who had suffered violence at the hands of another. Kristen was that other, she knew. She was the baddie today.

Mel brought the coffees over, passed one into Kristen's shaking hand and sat next to her. 'I think Leisel's coming out. Now, are you absolutely certain about this? You do not need to do this — you know that, right?'

Kristen nodded.

She had met Leisel yesterday. Well, she'd met her that night, but not really. Not really.

They had met yesterday, at these offices. Kristen thought they belonged to the video people. The offices were busy, full of young people walking quickly, looking at their phones, earbuds in. Some of them stared at her — they must have been the ones who knew who she was, because otherwise these young people wouldn't look at her. She wouldn't be interesting to them.

Mel had predicted that Kristen would like Leisel when she met her properly. 'People aren't who you think they are from the outside,' she'd told her. 'People are just like you, mostly. Try to find a way to see that.'

And she'd been right — Leisel had been nice. It was hard for Kristen to imagine why Leisel would be kind to her, smile at her, shake her hand.

'You have to know,' Kristen had said to her, 'I don't understand who I was six weeks ago. I need you to know, I wasn't myself. I hadn't been myself for months. Not since...'

Not since Tom and Ruby had gone to live with their dad. Not since she'd had that miscarriage, another one. Lost that baby boy who was going to make everything better. The one she was going to raise right.

At least, that was what she'd thought six weeks ago.

Leisel had been lovely to her. She'd told her she was 'working on forgiveness'. And Kristen had said, 'Me, too.' Leisel had looked at her a bit strangely then, but Kristen hadn't meant forgiving Leisel, she'd meant forgiving herself. And Dalton.

And the universe.

Now Mel was talking calmly to her. 'Okay. Remember, you can choose to stop this at any time. You have a signal for Leisel, and if she hears you use it, she will gesture for the cameras to stop. No one will know, there won't be a fuss. Are you sure you're ready?'

'Yes. I'm ready.' As Kristen watched Leisel coming towards her, smiling, holding a cup of tea, she felt the room settle down—people were beginning to leave.

'Hi, Kristen,' Leisel said. 'How are you feeling?'

It was so weird, Kristen thought, how for months she'd looked at Leisel's face and hated her. In the flesh, Leisel was tall and strong-looking with thick, shiny brown hair. She had wrinkles around her eyes, faded freckles and a huge open grin when she chose to use it.

More than once, in the Facebook groups of haters that Kristen used to marinate in, she'd typed:

Old horse face is whingeing again. Doesn't that ungrateful bitch realise how ugly she is? While we're at it, she needs to give up on selfies. She's way too old.

And in a direct message to Leisel, she'd typed:

> I'm so sick of seeing your old, ugly face. Feeling so
> sorry for yourself when you have EVERYTHING.
> EVERYTHING. Take your self-pity and smash
> yourself over the head with it, you ungrateful bitch.

Now Kristen tried to smile up at Leisel. 'I'm okay, thank
you. I think I'm ready.'

Mel didn't move when Leisel sat down, meaning she was
balancing awkwardly on the edge of the couch. 'It's okay,
Mel, you can go,' Kristen said, 'I'll be able to see you.'

'You will. I'll be right behind the camera,' said Mel. She
turned to Leisel. 'Remember, please—'

'No specifics, I know,' Leisel said, arranging herself
more comfortably on the lounge now that Mel was standing.
'I wouldn't want to do anything to jeopardise Kristen's
rehabilitation, or her chances with her kids.'

Kristen found herself trying to make a joke. 'It will be a
boring chat then, right!' She immediately regretted it.

'I'll explain all that,' Leisel said to her, smiling. 'We are
here to talk about "trolling".' She used finger quotes, little
wiggly worms in the air. 'Why people do it. How they can stop
doing it. We won't talk about the details of the case.'

The room was emptying. A handful of people took up
spots behind the camera: a journalist scribbling notes, Mel
and a woman Kristen recognised as Leisel's psychologist.
Bella, from the police liaison office, was there too. A woman
operated the camera. A woman wielded the microphones. Some
other young woman was looking closely at a phone. So many
women, thought Kristen.

'That's it, closed set!' shouted the woman who had two
camera stands going: one for her giant phone, one for a real
camera. A door closed loudly, as if to illustrate the point. It
got very quiet.

'Remember, Kristen, it's just you and me,' Leisel said. 'In

this conversation, it's just you and me. Remember what to say if you want this thing to stop?'

Kristen nodded. 'I'm saying that I want a drink of water.'

'We'd better have a drink of water, then.' Leisel motioned at the bottle by Kristen's chair. 'So we can get it out of shot.'

Kristen took a drink, but her mouth still felt dry. The kids, she told herself. Just think of the kids.

'Okay, let's go.'

To Kristen, Leisel looked less relaxed than she had yesterday, when Kristen had been surprised by how comfortable she seemed around her. Much edgier today.

Kristen couldn't help but look at Leisel's arm for signs of the wound that she'd inflicted. Leisel was wearing long sleeves, and she didn't seem to be wincing. It must be healing, thought Kristen.

The camerawoman pushed some buttons and mouthed 'Yes'.

Leisel started talking. Kristen couldn't focus on all of it, but Leisel was explaining who they both were. She was explaining why they were doing this: 'We want to make a statement about online bullying and harassment. We want to understand why people lose themselves online the way they do. And we want to move on with our lives...'

She sounds so polished, Kristen thought as she watched Leisel.

Mel had helped Kristen get dressed that day—as in, picking out her clothes: things weren't so bad that she needed help getting dressed. 'Calming colours,' Mel had said. 'This rose dress is perfect.' It was her 'good' dress. A birthday present from Dalton, when things were good. He always had such great taste. The dress went with her hair, brought out the red under the brown.

Leisel turned to her. It felt sudden, but perhaps she'd just zoned out a little.

'Hello, Kristen,' Leisel said. 'Thank you so much for coming here today and agreeing to do this. It can't be easy.'

'N-no...' Kristen stuttered. 'It's not easy.'

'I'm going to ask you some questions,' Leisel continued. 'And we might have some from the people watching us on Facebook, too.'

'Okay.'

Leisel had told Kristen what her first question would be. 'Do you spend a lot of time online, Kristen?'

'I did, Leisel.' My kids, she thought. My kids. 'I used to spend a lot of time on social media. I'm trying to give it up. For obvious reasons.'

'And do you remember, when you started using it, did it make you feel good or bad?'

'At first, I loved it. I was one of those mums who put up lots of pictures of my children, all the silly little things they did. I loved it when I was happy. And then, a lot of things started to go wrong for me. My marriage broke down. I had to find a second job. I developed some... personal issues. In the space of a year, a lot changed.'

'And how did you cope?'

'I don't think I did cope, Leisel. That's part of what's brought me here. I think for some people, when things get bad and they sort of spiral, then there's some stuff on the internet that fuels that.'

'What do you mean?'

'Well, I can't talk much about my kids in this interview, but when they were around and I was busy, it wasn't too bad. When they went to their dad's, though, and I had time... I was lonely and I was miserable and I would sit on Facebook for hours and hours, looking at everyone else's lives. They all seemed so great, so shiny. And mine, well, mine felt hopeless.'

'But you are aware of the fact that people only put their "highlights reel" on Facebook, yes? You know that everyone else's life isn't really perfect, don't you?'

'I do. I do now.' Kristen swallowed. Looked up at Mel, who nodded at her. 'And there was probably a bit of me that did then, too. But it's hard to tell yourself that when you just feel like you are the only one who doesn't have highlights to share. Like, I know there are shitty bits to everyone's life—but at the time, I used to think, What would I put up here? That bit where I got abused at work by a drunk? The bit where my kids' beds are empty? I became obsessive, and I got some kind of pleasure, some kind of... charge, out of following certain people whose lives seemed so perfect, and just... hating them. It sounds crazy.' Kristen gazed down at her hands. 'It was crazy.'

While she spoke, Kristen had mainly been looking away from Leisel, but every time she glanced back, Leisel was staring right into her eyes. It was unnerving.

'When did you start commenting?'

Kristen sighed. 'As I say, there was nothing very good going on in my life. For lots of reasons, I found that I... had time on my hands. And so I created a profile for the person that I kind of wanted to be, I suppose. I called it The Contented Mum, because it was almost the opposite of what was happening in my life, but it was everything that I wanted to be happening, if that makes sense—'

'It does.'

'And I was obsessed with my children, and what sort of mother I was or I wasn't. Was I really the worst mother in the world? One who had deserved to lose my kids? That kind of thing. I would come home from work and look for, on purpose, these mummy blogs—like yours. And I would read and read, and drink sometimes. And get angrier and angrier.'

Leisel blushed when she asked the next question. 'What was it about "mummy blogs" that made you so angry? About my blog?'

'For me, what was hard at the time was the complaining. And I realise—I know, because I've been a normal mum, I was one for years—that of course you do a lot of complaining. It's hard raising kids. But for me, then, I would have given anything to be a normal mum again. I had suffered miscarriages—'

'I have written about miscarriage. Did you know that?'

'I'd read that, yes. I don't know why.' Kristen coughed a little. 'I couldn't find any sympathy for anyone else then. I just couldn't. I don't know why.' She paused.

'Sorry, go on...'

'One of the things that I'm understanding now, through the counselling I'm doing, is that what I was trying to do— lashing out at the bloggers who seemed to have everything when I had nothing—was a very destructive behaviour. For me, for everyone.'

'Did you enjoy it? Writing mean things, getting a reaction?'

Mel looked distressed, so Kristen raised a hand to show it was okay. 'Yes. Sometimes. I think "enjoy" is the wrong word, but I got a kick out of it. Out of saying something horrible to someone, anyone, and seeing others join in. Or seeing the target get upset. It feels terrible to me now to say this. But I felt I had no power at all, and this behaviour made me feel a bit less helpless.'

'Now, we can't talk about the details of what happened... between us. But Kristen, can I ask, broadly, about online abuse crossing over into real life? When did that start for you?'

The police liaison officer, Bella, was shaking her head.

'I don't think a lot of people do that,' Kristen started. Paused. My kids, she thought. She remembered the conversation she'd had with Bella and Mel about this very question. 'For me, it was one bad choice after another at that time, Leisel. I can see this now—but then, it felt like all these things were happening *to* me. I had a very brief new relationship. It went badly wrong. Then I found out I was pregnant, and I... I lost the baby. A baby boy. That's when I allowed my obsession to overtake my life. I didn't do much during that time other than sit online at home. And then I started... doing other things. It gave me a little bit of comfort to strike out. Not a good idea.'

Kristen wondered how this was playing on the internet. She knew she didn't look dangerous. Everyone always told her, 'You look so young'—she was a little, skinny thing. The people watching probably wondered how she could have attacked Leisel at all. Leisel was so much bigger, stronger.

She looked up at Leisel. 'Are you afraid of me?' she asked.

Leisel looked shocked. There was movement behind the camera as people began to flap.

'I was,' Leisel said, gathering herself. 'I was.'

'But not now? You don't think I'm a scary person?'

'I think you're a person who's had a lot of bad luck, Kristen.'

'It's not all bad luck,' she corrected. 'I did a lot of stupid things. But I just want everyone watching to know—I'm not a danger to you. I'm not a danger to my kids. I'm getting help. I'm getting my head straight. I would *never* do what I did that night again. I don't even know why I did it. I just... really fucking hated you right then...' She ran out of breath.

My kids.

'But I know now, I didn't hate you. I hated myself. What I'd become. And seeing all of that out there—but it wasn't *out there*. It was in my house, in my phone, all this stuff that I couldn't have. To me it looked like all these people had no idea what they had. How lucky they were. I just... lost it.'

Everything went silent for a moment. Then Leisel reached across the couch, held Kristen's hand and said, 'I think I need a drink of water.'

CHAPTER TWENTY-FIVE

LEISEL

Now that she was by herself, bedtime really sucked. Leisel didn't know why she'd ever complained that Mark didn't do enough during The Returns, the endless stroking and patting and fetching of urgently needed glasses of water that dragged on before the children eventually slept.

It had been a huge day. A very strange day, and now the reality of solo bedtime loomed. Leisel wasn't sure how to process what had happened with Kristen, or the reaction to it. And she didn't have time to try. Her phone was still buzzing in her pocket. She was home and trying to get a fussy three-year-old to eat his shop-bought lasagna. And to get Maggie to say something to her — anything.

What lay ahead, if the past few nights were anything to go by, was not going to be an improvement on this dinnertime battleground. Rich was crying for his daddy every night in at least three shifts before he'd pass out into a deep sleep, and Maggie was being as well-behaved as a six-year-old could possibly be, clearly unwilling to make any waves at all, which Leisel found even more distressing.

She wanted Mark and Harri to come home. She missed

them both so much that her insides ached. But something was stopping her from calling Mark, even when Rich was wailing, 'I want my daddddeeeee!' at 3 a.m.

'Daddy will be back soon,' was her line. 'He and Harri have just gone to visit with Uncle Dan.'

***

On the morning after Mark left, she had called him. She'd managed the double drop-off, then raced into the office at 9.05 and collapsed into her chair. Seeing no sign of Zac, she grabbed her phone and went to the bathroom.

Mark picked up. She'd been sure he wouldn't.

'Mark.'

'Leisel.' He hardly ever called her Leisel.

'Come home.'

'Rough morning?'

'That's not fair. What are you doing? It's ridiculous.'

'I'm not doing anything. I just need some space, and I'm taking it.'

'And Harri?'

'You couldn't manage all three of them, not with work.'

That was true.

'Is she okay?'

'Yes. She's asking for you. We'll see you soon.'

'Mark, please don't—'

'Leisel!' Zac was yelling... into the ladies' toilets?

Jesus Christ. Suddenly, Leisel realised that she was a grown woman hiding from her boss in the bathroom, begging her husband to bring her baby home. Clearly she was at the top of her game.

'I have to go,' she said. 'Please, just come home.'

'Leisel, I need to clear some stuff up.'

'Just... come home.'

'Leeeeeisel!' Zac again.

'And kiss Harri for me.'

The whole exchange made her cringe. But in the days since, she'd also got angry. Organising the Kristen interview had been insanely stressful. Zac wasn't letting up on her at work. The Blog-ahhs were a week away. And Mark was choosing *now* to throw his tantrum?

Fuck him. She was the one bringing home the bacon, so she was the one who would decide how it was earned. He could take his holier-than-thou bullshit to his brother's and stay there.

But it was hard for Leisel to maintain the rage when her baby was gone, and a weeping three-year-old and silent six-year-old were glued to her side.

***

Midway through another plea for Rich to let something pass his lips, Leisel heard a knock at the flat door. She got up from her knees and went to look through the peephole, her newly installed chain lock in place.

When she saw who was there, she couldn't get it off fast enough.

'Grace!'

She stood back and took in the sight of her little sister, standing right there on her Sydney doorstep. Miles from the farm. With — Leisel peered down the hall, left and right — apparently no children in tow. And definitely no Abi.

'Grace!' She hugged her hard. The way Grace hugged her back made her think that she wasn't the only one on a real winning streak.

'Can I come in?'

'Well, of course, but what are you doing here? I didn't think you and Abi would be up here until the awards.'

'I just needed to get away, come say hi to you. I figure we probably have a lot to talk about. I saw your Facebook Live today on the way up, you crazy woman.'

Rich came barrelling around the corner, straight into

Grace's legs. 'Auntie Grace!' he yelled. Then, 'I thought you were Daddy.'

'Daddy?' Grace raised an eyebrow in Leisel's direction, who shrugged. 'I'm way better than Daddy. I have gifts!' Grace produced a beaten-up leather duffle bag that Leisel was sure she'd packed to go on Guides camp when they were teenagers.

Of course, Auntie Grace's gifts were a bar of hand-milled soap for Maggie and some roughly hewn fingerless mittens for Rich, but the kids exclaimed appropriately. Oh, the glorious age where they just like getting anything new, thought Leisel.

'I've got a mobile for Harri,' Grace said, looking around.

'She and Mark are... away.'

'Oh.' Grace gave Leisel a hard look, but then said only, 'Let me help you get these kids in the bath, hey?'

***

That was one of the bravest things I've ever seen. #forgivenessproject

This is a deeply irresponsible stunt. The woman is clearly unwell. #forgivenessproject

I hope both of you are getting the help you need. #forgivenessproject

I'm sorry, but getting divorced doesn't mean you can go around stabbing people. She should be in jail. #forgivenessproject

Leisel and Grace were sitting at the kitchen table. The kids were finally down, and they were scrolling through the thousands of comments about Leisel's Kristen interview.

'It was hard to watch, Lee,' said Grace, helping herself to

a corn chip and hommus. 'I can't imagine what it was like to actually do that interview.'

'It was confronting. It was... complicated. Look, I don't know.' Leisel shook her head, took a sip of wine. 'I've almost forgotten why I wanted to do it. But seriously... that poor fucking woman.'

'I admire your generosity in saying that,' Grace said. 'But there must have been something in this for her.'

'Oh yeah. I've said I won't pursue the charges. I mean, it's assault, so she has to be charged, but without a cooperating victim, she'll get a better outcome. No question.'

'So the mystery only remains, what was in it for you, then? Putting yourself through all that again?'

'I don't know.' Leisel reached for a chip.

'The numbers look pretty good.' Grace motioned to the laptop they'd just been looking at. 'Engagement will be huge. Picked up everywhere, I'd imagine. That wouldn't be why, would it?'

'You sound like Mark.'

'If I've got the right idea about what's going on around here, I think I might *be* Mark,' said Grace, sipping her green tea. 'This is all coming between you, right? Where is he?'

'At his brother's.'

'With Harri?'

'With Harri.'

'Is he okay?'

'Yes, I think so. He just needs some "room to think".'

'Sounds familiar.'

'Abi?'

'I needed to get away from that insanity for a minute, Lee. Things have become really... dramatic.'

'Not your favourite scene.'

'Hell no.' Grace took another chip, looked at Leisel. 'Does Mark feel like I do? Like this blog stuff is getting too big? Is that what it is?'

'Well, yes, that's a large part of what it is. I'm sick of

carrying all the earning pressure, he's sick of me moaning about him and the kids on the internet—'

'Ha!'

'Grace. I know you're on the other team but, for me, I feel like this is a chance to change our lives! And I want that.'

'That's exactly what Abi says to me. I told her that I don't want our lives to change.'

'And that—' Leisel took another slug of pinot gris '—is exactly what Mark says to me.'

CHAPTER TWENTY-SIX

ELLE

Adrian was eating too much. And working too much.

'How is Adrian? He looks well, considering, poor man.' That was the teacher at Teddy's preschool, when Elle arrived to collect him on Tuesday.

Elle lowered her sunglasses and stared at the woman. Did she know something?

'Yes,' Elle said, 'he's coping really well, but it's tough.'

The preschool teacher, who—working, as she did, at a $250-a-day centre—surely knew better than to pry into the parents' lives, smiled and nodded and gave Teddy a gentle shove towards his mother. 'Well, we're all thinking of him. Teddy was great today. His French is coming on really well, *n'est-ce pas*, Teddy?'

'*Oui*, Mademoiselle Sondra,' three-year-old Teddy replied, taking his mum's outstretched hand.

'Well, that's great, isn't it.' Elle put her sunnies back on. 'He didn't nap today, did he? It's such a pain for us if he sleeps when he's here. We really like him to be tired for bedtime.'

'No, of course not, Mrs Campbell, we kept him up while the others were napping, like you asked. We've got some Baby Sudoku puzzles in just for him.'

'Good. Well, we're off. Say bye, Teddy.'

'Oh!' the teacher called after her. 'And I was sorry to hear about your dad!'

Back in the car, Teddy was telling Elle about how, when the other kids were sleeping, he'd put spiky Lego pieces under his enemies' pillows — but Elle was barely listening as she checked her phone for more messages.

The text she'd received that morning while she was stretching after her workout was still sitting in her inbox.

I know you're lying about Adrian's cancer.

It was from a number she didn't recognise.

She'd stared at it for two minutes and then replied: *Who is this? I will report this heartless harassment to the police.*

No reply.

It had put Elle on edge all day. She'd had a photoshoot for Abbott's and a conference call with the Blog-ahhs PR people (who were flying everyone up to Sydney on Thursday for press), and now, when she got Teddy home, she had a styling session with the boys. She needed a good run of their fashion shots to get them through until they were all back from Sydney next week. Post Blog-ahhs and pre-new life.

'Mum,' Teddy said from the back seat, 'I don't want to do clothes today.'

'You have to, darling. You and Freddie will get iPad time straight after. I promise.'

'I HATE CLOTHES!' Teddy shouted, kicking his feet against the white leather seats beneath his booster. 'I HATE STUPID CLOTHES!'

This was not what Elle needed. 'Teddy. STOP. You are giving Mummy a headache and making her feel sad.'

'I don't care. I HATE DUMB, *DUMB*, STUPID CLOTHES!'

This carried on through the short drive home until Elle was basically dragging him up the path to the glass-and-white house, hoping this wasn't a day that the *Daily Trail* paps were outside. She thought that she'd seen a strange car out here yesterday.

'Take him,' she said to Cate when she got in the door, and she pushed a kicking and squirming Teddy towards the young woman. 'I can't handle any tantrums right now. Get him and Freddie ready any way you can.'

Cate put her arms around Teddy tightly, and he started to quiet down. It was going to take a few minutes.

Elle went into the kitchen, closed the door, turned towards the bench and found Freddie, standing on a stool, drawing on the ironbark benchtop with a marker. 'Are you fucking kidding me?' Elle lifted him off the stool and put him on the floor. 'Cate!'

Teddy's wails had subsided. Cate opened the kitchen door, the sniffling boy still in her arms.

'These boys are completely out of control today,' Elle said. 'I don't know what you're telling them about discipline, but they have no fucking idea. My kids are not brats. Do you hear me? My kids are *not brats*.'

Freddie started kicking his mother's lycra-clad leg with his socked foot. 'No yelling at Cate, Mummy!' he shouted.

'Elle, they're not brats, they're just having a bad day—aren't you, boys?' Cate reached out a hand to Freddie. He took it.

Elle looked at Cate standing in the kitchen doorway, one of Elle's son's sucking his thumb on her hip, the other dangling from her hand and giving Elle what could only be described as the stink eye.

She exhaled. 'Cate. Please take the boys upstairs and lay out some clothes for the next few days. Then I'd like to talk to you back here.'

Cate and the boys retreated.

***

Two days ago, Elle's *Sunday Evening* episode had aired. On Sunday afternoon, she'd written:

255

My Stylish Mummas,

Tonight, I'm really honoured to be featuring on a special episode of Sunday Evening about bloggers. If you watch it—or record it, because it is slap-bang in the middle of kiddie bedtime for most of us!—you're going to learn some things about me and my life that you might not have known before.

My A asked not to appear on the show—and I respected his wishes, of course, as I always do. He is struggling with his treatment right now, feeling a little bit vain (men!) about the way he looks (gorgeous to me, of course!) and he just needs to focus on drawing strength from family and getting well.

But what you will get a good look at is our beautiful home (eeek! oh how I scrubbed it before the cameras came!), and our beautiful boys, who had the best day with the film crew here.

You'll also see the town where I grew up. I haven't shared this with you before, SMs, but my family suffered the loss of my father a few months ago, and what you will see tonight are siblings struggling to come to terms with a life without parents. Until now, we have kept this great loss private, which I'm sure you will understand, but tonight, we pay tribute to the man who made us.

You'll also see the house where we grew up, poor but happy, you'll hear some words about our beautiful mum, God rest her soul, and you'll witness the spirit of the outback, which is what gives me strength every day to face everything that the world can throw at all of us. #cancerwife

I'd love to share all this with you if you will sit down with me and watch tonight. I know many of you out there are going through much more difficult struggles of your own, and maybe by getting a little window into my world, you'll know that anything is possible.

Remember, we put our brave faces on every day, SMs. Stay strong, shine brightly and let's share a night on the lounge tonight.

#loveandlight

Elle x

And they had watched.

They saw Elle making raw kale and lemon juices for a perfectly behaved Teddy and Freddie in her immaculate kitchen. They got a peek into Elle's dressing-room: actually two adjoining mirrored rooms, one for day and evening clothes, one for active wear.

And then, of course, they travelled with her to Thalwyn. Her brothers came across remarkably well, she thought, considering how nervous they had been. They said very little, but they looked suitably serious beside Elle, throwing in the odd word.

When the interviewer asked them, 'What was it like to lose your mother at such a young age?' Kai replied, 'Pretty shithouse, really.' And although Elle had cringed at the time, on TV it played as endearing honesty.

When the interviewer asked, 'Do you sometimes look at your glamorous sister and wonder where she came from?' Bobby answered, 'You bet we do. She wasn't such a looker when she was a kid!' It came across as authentic pride.

And when they were all asked about their father, and Elle said, 'It's a loss we feel every day. He was such an enormously important part of our lives, not just as kids but as adults, too. He was the first person I would call with any problem, and we talked all the time. I miss that,' neither of the boys laughed or even smirked. They just looked at their hands.

Then the camera followed her around Thalwyn on her own, as she looked at buildings wistfully, like the old school and the corner shop where she'd had her first job, saying things such as, 'It's hard to leave a town like this — the community is like nowhere else. It's in your blood.'

All in all, the episode had played pretty well, Elle thought. Her followers agreed.

My heart breaks for your beautiful family, @ stylishmumma You have such a lot on your plate. Praying for you.

Your brothers are bogan babes, @stylishmumma. Where do we get us one of those?

What a special lady you are, @stylishmumma, to come from nothing and be where you are. Hats off.

Afterwards, she spoke to Bobby on the phone. 'You alright?' she asked. 'Think you'll get any grief for it?'

'No, mate,' Bobby said. She could tell he'd had a couple. 'Pretty shitty reception for Channel 8 up here, and no one's seen the old man in months. She'll be right.'

'Okay. Just remember, any drama at all, call me.'

'Got it, boss.'

Being reunited with her shitbag brothers wasn't as bad as she'd thought.

Elle had been working on Adrian ever since she'd got back from Thalwyn, and once he was reassured her family treachery had come pretty cheap, he mellowed about Elle's decision kill off her dad. Sitting beside him watching the show, Elle was pleased to see Adrian was back on board, proud of his clever wife.

So Elle had spent Monday breathing easy, going through the motions of another fake chemo session.

But now, there was the text message.

***

Elle called Adrian.

'What's up, baby?'

'I want you to come home. You're too sick to work.'

'Actually, I'm in the middle of a merger meeting. I'll be home about seven.'

'No. I'm serious, Adrian. You need to say you're struggling, that you need a lie-down. You're not convincing enough. You're not thin enough, not pale enough... Look, someone's on to us.'

'What?'

Elle heard Adrian shift from a room full of people into a quiet space. The soft closing of a door.

'Adrian. We can't talk about this now. Someone's on to us, and I need you to come home.'

A pause, a sigh. 'Do we need to speak to anyone?'

'I'm about to speak to someone, but we don't know what we're dealing with yet. Just come.'

'Okay, okay. I'll be there as soon as I can.' He hung up.

Cate came back into the kitchen. 'Those boys,' she said. 'Just one of those days! They've calmed down now, I've put them on the iPads while we prep the shoot. Are you okay?' She walked over to the benchtop, examined Freddie's handiwork. 'That'll come up. We'll just have to tell Ena to use that special cleaner, I'll make a note—'

'Cate.' Elle stepped in front of her, put out a glossy white-nailed finger, lifted Cate's chin so she was looking into Elle's eyes. Cate seemed startled.

'Cate. Who have you been talking to?'

'Um... what do you mean?'

Elle pressed harder on Cate's chin. 'You know what I mean. Who have you been talking to?'

'About what?' Cate asked, shaking her head loose.

Elle put her hands on Cate's shoulders. 'About Adrian. Who have you been talking to about Adrian?'

CHAPTER TWENTY-SEVEN

ABI

'Who do I have to fuck around here to get a chai soy latte?'

Abi was waiting to go on talkback radio in Melbourne. In the week leading up to the Blog-ahhs, she was on the promotional trail. She and Zoe were sitting in the radio station reception, poring over their phones and feeling jubilant.

Abi overheard the intern hiss to the receptionist, 'Who *is* that?'

'It's that really scary mummy blogger,' the receptionist whispered back. That made Abi's heart sing.

She was texting Arden. Her being up and down from the farm a lot lately had left the girls a little... untethered. They were still worrying about their dad, spending a lot of time at home with an increasingly stressed-out Grace, and now Arden was telling her that Grace wasn't home either.

SHE GN TO SYD. The text read. *BOYS WITH EDIE. JENELLE IS STAYING.* 😫

Jenelle was a former student of Grace's who sometimes babysat the kids—a nineteen-year-old hippie chick who was always trying to get Alex and Arden to plait her hair and chant. She called it 'mane meditation'.

Arden was not a fan. *I DNT NEED A BABYSITTER. CAN I JST GO TO DAN'S?*

NOPE, Abi replied. *STAY WITH YOUR SISTER. I'LL CALL YOU AFTER THIS INTERVIEW.*

'Where the fuck is Grace?' she said out loud.

'What?' Zoe pulled out one of her headphones. She'd been raving to Abi about this investigative journalism podcast she was listening to, going deep on conspiracy and cover-up.

'The girls are home alone as of last night.'

Abi called Grace. Grace's phone rang out. 'Very weird. I think I'm in trouble.'

Where are you? she texted. ♥♥♥♥♥

***

Abi and Zoe's hotel was very close to Elle and Adrian's Brighton glass-house. They'd spent the previous afternoon playing at being private investigators, and their amateur efforts were paying off. Abi couldn't remember when she'd had more fun.

They'd sat outside the house in a hire-car and borrowed hats — Abi had Otto's school baseball cap — and watched as, at lunchtime, Adrian drove up in his Porsche and went inside. He looked terrible. His expensive work suits were hanging off him, his hair was gone, and he was an odd colour. As soon as Abi saw him, she decided they must be wrong.

Then she re-read Elle's morning Instagram post, which said:

It's chemo day #cancerwife 😔🖤

The picture was of her hand on a thin male hand, presumably Adrian's, and it was sepia-toned.

'Corny as all shit,' Abi said, waving her phone around. 'Who puts a sad-face emoji on a cancer post? I mean, seriously?'

'My sister does,' said Zoe, sinking deeper in the car seat.

About half an hour after Adrian came home, he and Elle emerged holding hands. Adrian had changed into... 'Is that a tracksuit?' Abi asked. 'Are you fucking kidding me?'

'It's a fancy tracksuit,' said Zoe. 'I think it's like Hilfiger or something. Anyway, you want the guy to wear a three-piece suit to chemo?'

'You mean, to fake chemo?'

Abi couldn't believe she agreed to it, but they followed Elle's Range Rover through the city. 'We're staying at a distance of two cars,' said Zoe. 'Google says it's the most effective interval for surveillance.'

'Can you believe this? Follow that car! We are idiots.' Abi was tempted to eat a doughnut, just to add to her sense of being in a bad cop movie, but things really had been getting out of hand on the processed food front lately.

Elle and Adrian drove to exactly where anyone would have expected them to go to—the cancer centre—and went into the underground car park.

Abi and Zoe debated what to do, then decided against following them in. 'Too risky,' said Zoe. 'But it doesn't really prove anything, that they're at a hospital.'

'Well, come on,' Abi said grudgingly, 'if it walks like a duck and quacks like a duck... He has no hair, looks a hundred years old and they're at a cancer hospital.'

'I know my sister. I say we go back to the house.'

And that was how Abi—a grown woman with two almost-teenage daughters and two stepsons—found herself standing at the gate to the glass-and-white mansion, pressing the intercom.

'Hello?' a young woman answered.

'We have a delivery for Elle Campbell,' said Zoe. 'Can you sign?'

'Hold on. I'll buzz you in.'

Just like that, Abi and Zoe were granted access to Elle and Adrian's world.

Poor Cate looked stricken as she threw open the door and saw that the two people standing there were not the parcel guys. She went to slam it, but Zoe had presumably looked up door-stopping on YouTube — she stuck out her foot and hand, holding it firm.

'There's a panic button!' Cate said. 'I'll call the police.'

'I'm Elle's sister,' Zoe said, arm and foot still extended. It didn't look comfortable.

'And I'm Adrian's ex-wife,' said Abi. 'We just want to stand here for one second and talk to you about something.'

Zoe got straight to it while her arm still had the strength to hold the door — Cate was pushing back hard and showed no sign that she would run for the panic button.

'We know Adrian doesn't have cancer,' Zoe said loudly.

The look on the young girl's face told Abi what she needed to know.

'The kids are in the house,' was all Cate said.

'We're not going to hurt anyone.' Abi peered past Cate to see inside, where she'd never been. Was that a teardrop chandelier? 'Just tell us yes or no about Adrian. Nothing else. We'll do the rest.'

'I can't...' But Cate had stopped pushing on the door. Her shoulders slumped. She looked defeated. 'I really can't.'

'Cate, love,' Abi said, in what she hoped was a motherly tone, 'Adrian and I have two daughters. They think he might be dying. Can you imagine what that's like for them?'

Zoe sighed, pulling her hat a little further down over her eyes.

'I know you,' Cate suddenly said to her. 'From that terrible town.'

'Hey,' said Zoe, 'I *grew up* there.'

'Just tell us, Cate. Is Adrian really sick?' Abi said.

'I signed an NDA.'

'A what now?' Zoe really had watched a lot of movies, thought Abi.

'A non-disclosure agreement. I can't tell you anything — I'd get in huge trouble. I just, I just... help with the social media, babysit the boys.'

'That's not a yes, though, is it?' said Abi. 'To the question of whether Adrian has cancer. That's not a yes.'

'CAAAATE!' screamed a little boy, and then an impossibly cute child in a ridiculous skinny-jeans-bow-tie combo popped into view. He was familiar to Abi from Instagram—one of Adrian's astonishingly beautiful sons. He stared at them, looked at Cate. 'What you doing?'

'That's not a yes, is it?' Abi asked Cate again.

She shook her head. And Zoe took her hand off the door. Pulled her foot back.

Cate bent down to the little boy. 'Nothing, Freddie, everything's fine.' She straightened, looked at Abi and Zoe, and shook her head again. Then she closed the door. That was that.

Abi met Zoe's eyes. There was a beat. Then Abi felt a huge grin spread across her face. 'We're excellent at this! Legends!'

'And your husband doesn't have cancer,' said Zoe.

'Ex-husband. No. He doesn't. Seriously, what an absolute prick.'

'And my sister. What an idiot.'

'I wonder where they really are when they're meant to be at the cancer centre...' Abi started.

They both almost ran to the car.

***

At the radio station, Abi and Zoe still felt like giddy teenagers. They hadn't told anyone what they'd found out—not yet. But thirty minutes earlier, they'd sent their first 'deep throat' text to Elle from an old Nokia that Zoe had bought at Cash Converters.

'It's called a burner phone,' Zoe had explained to Abi. 'We want to keep her guessing.'

'I watched *The Wire*, I know what it is,' Abi had assured her.

The DJ was ready for Abi. He was Dave Ellis, a thirty-something comedian, and this was his morning talkback show. Abi was there to chat about the Blog-ahhs, about trolls and Shannon Smart, and all the usual things she'd been interviewed about lately.

'Remember,' Zoe said to her before she walked into the sound-proof room, 'dial down the crazy, just a little.'

Abi laughed.

Dave gave his spiel as soon as she sat down. 'Today I have with me one of the nominees for the prestigious Parenting Blogger of the Year Award at this Sunday's Blog-ahh event in Sydney. Daylesford's very own Abi Black blogs as The Green Diva with more than eighty thousand followers. Very impressive, Abi. How do you do that?'

'Hi, Dave,' Abi said, then gave her usual intro. 'Well, I have a voice that some parents really want to hear more of — a voice outside the mainstream. I'm telling people to throw the rule book out when it comes to raising your kids, to go with your gut, and people really respond to that. There's not enough authenticity out there.'

'Sure, but not everyone likes it. Am I right that you cop your fair share of abuse online, Abi?'

'Well, yes, we all do, Dave. It seems a woman with an opinion is always going to be a bit too scary for some guys. I like to think of them as guys with tiny — '

'Woah! I can see why they call you the most dangerous mummy blogger, Abi.' Dave laughed a big, radio laugh. 'Well, well, aren't you a firecracker? How do you deal with the trolls? Didn't one of the other nominees for this award get attacked recently?'

'Yes, they did, Dave. That was Leisel Adams, a blogger out of Sydney, and someone I know a little bit. It was terrible what happened to Leisel, but she's just been tremendously brave — if not a little bit foolish — with what she did, talking to her troll on camera. I think that's just wild. I like to keep my trolls at arm's-length.'

'Good, good. Well, we have some callers for you today, Abi, a few people who want to talk to you about the things you say online. Are you ready?'

'Ready as anything, Dave. I have the confidence of a mediocre white man.'

'Oh, that's hilarious.' The DJ glared at Abi.

'Yes, Dave, it is.' Obviously, a bit close to the bone.

'Our first caller is Adele from Dandenong. Adele? You're on with Abi, The Green Diva.'

'Hi, Abi, I have a question about nappies—'

'Oh, here we go,' Dave interrupted. 'Mothers talking nappies on the call-in show, who would have thought it?'

'Dave, you really are a dickhead,' Abi said, knowing the producer would get to the censor-beep. She did.

'Woah, woah, she bites again! Living up to your reputation there, Abi. Come on, Adele, tell us about nappies.' Dave couldn't have looked less impressed with his guest.

'Well, I want to use cloth nappies because they're better for the environment, but washing them is just the worst job in the world. And the thing is, my partner, well, he's the one who's absolutely insistent that we should use them and that disposables are the devil's work, but he's not the one up to his armpits in, you know... That's me.'

'Oh, Adele, Adele.' Abi was shaking her head.

'So, what do I do? Can I use disposables sometimes? Am I really killing the planet with my laziness?'

Dave raised his eyebrows at Abi. 'So, Abi, is Adele killing the planet?'

'Yes, absolutely. Our environmental catastrophes are all your fault, Adele, it's all on your shoulders... No, no, truly, Adele, I'll tell you what your problem is—and it isn't the nappies. It's your beep-head husband. Look, disposables are not great, they do end up in landfill, and they are responsible for millions of tonnes of waste each year. But seriously? Looking after babies is hard. And babies crap a lot. And if you are the one who is wiping the arses, you should be the one who gets to choose the nappies. Buy the greenest disposables you can, and tell your husband that if he doesn't like it, he's on poo duty from here on in.'

'Abi, I like your style,' Dave said, looking over her shoulder at his producer. 'Adele, are you happy with that?'

Adele was still laughing. 'Oh yes, that's great.'

'Our next caller is Samantha from Ballarat. Samantha, what do you want to say to The Green Diva?'

'I want to tell her that she's a dangerous monster.'

The atmosphere in the studio changed instantly. Dave actually smiled, leaning in to the microphone, as Abi stiffened.

'Those are strong words, Samantha,' he said. 'Do you think you could keep things civil while you explain?'

'I am very happy to keep things civil, Dave, but people need to know that the lies that woman spreads are very dangerous. She kills babies.'

'You don't kill babies, do you, Abi? I mean, I know you're pretty scary, but you're not actually a witch, right?'

Abi could sense where this was going well before dickhead Dave, who clearly still thought this was all a hilarious gag. She opened her mouth to speak, but Samantha got there first, her voice breaking. 'My beautiful baby daughter Lucy died of whooping cough nine months ago. She was too little to be vaccinated. And I know that it's because of people like you, Abi, who tell parents that vaccines are dangerous, who have convinced so many vulnerable idiots to believe you. My baby should still be here. Lots of babies should still be here. You are a dangerous, evil woman—'

The producer cut her off, and Dave jumped right in. 'Samantha, we have stopped you there. Not because we don't respect your opinion, but things were just getting a little too heated, which is completely understandable. Abi, I have to ask you the question that Samantha wanted to ask you: do you tell people not to vaccinate their children?'

'No, I don't,' said Abi, but her voice was small. 'I am not in the business of telling parents what to do.'

'But... and my producer is handing me some notes on this now—' Dave was looking at his screen '—don't you give a platform to anti-vaccination voices, the so-called anti-vaxxers? Didn't you support that movie *Spiked*, for example, that was banned recently?'

Abi looked up to see if Zoe was on the other side of the glass panel. She wasn't, just a desk of serious-faced producers. Abi thought about Grace: *Is that really what you believe, Abi?* She thought about Shannon Smart, and Stephen from the Keen Clean Green brigade, and all the crunchy mamas she'd had on her podcasts.

'Yes, Dave, I have done that,' she said.

There was a muffled noise, and she glanced up again to see Zoe on the other side of the glass now—she'd pushed her way into the producers' pod. She was at the studio window, looking stricken.

'I have done that before. I'm doing a lot of soul-searching about it at the moment, to be honest.'

Dave raised his eyebrows. 'Anything else you'd like to say about that, Abi?'

'I'd like to say how sorry I am for Samantha, and for any parent who has lost a child. I am a mother. My heart breaks for her. Samantha, I'm very sorry about your beautiful little Lucy.'

CHAPTER TWENTY-EIGHT

Breakfast!

'Holy shit, they're all wearing white. What do I do?'

Leisel heard Samira, the Blog-ahhs' publicity assistant, hissing into her phone, and it made her smile.

Leisel was sitting in hair and make-up at Channel 8 studios, once more appreciating the skill of the professionals turning her into a fresh-faced 32-year-old.

One of the biggest moments of the Blog-ahh publicity schedule was about to happen: Leisel, Abi and Elle were about to appear on *Breakfast!*, the highest-rating morning show in the country.

'All white!' Leisel stage-whispered to the make-up artist who was colouring in her eye-bags. 'It's a disaster.'

'Actually, it kind of is,' she replied with a look that said: Don't patronise us, lady.

Two chairs over, Abi Black was telling everyone, loudly, that she didn't want to 'look like someone I'm not'.

Leisel watched Samira run off to solve the terrible wardrobe dilemma, with one eye on the monitor that showed the studio downstairs.

The floor was being set up for the three women to sit

side by side across a desk from Simon Hedley, the host of *Breakfast!* It was the spot on the show when the blokey Simon asked three female commentators what they thought about various issues in the news cycle. It was called 'She Says', and Leisel had it on good authority that it was Simon's least favourite part of the morning.

The night before, Claire had told her, 'He'll be saying to himself, "Mummy bloggers? Are you effing kidding me?" He'll be all, "I guess today's not Walkleys day, right?"'

Given the all-clear by make-up, Leisel smiled and waved at Abi, then headed up to the green room, where she went back to what she'd been doing all morning: trying to reach Mark on his mobile.

On the third try, he finally picked up.

'Mark,' she said, 'you have to answer my calls. Whatever's going on with us, you have our daughter with you. You *have* to answer my calls.'

'Sure, Lee.' Mark sounded groggy. 'What's up?'

'I'm about to go on TV.'

'Again? Okay.'

'With Abi. And Elle.'

'Oh shit, okay.'

'Will you watch? I need someone honest to tell me how I do.'

'Really, me?' The fog in Mark's voice was beginning to clear.

'Yes, you. You are my husband. Your opinion matters to me.' Even if you are my husband still sleeping at your brother's.

'Wow.' Mark laughed—a croaky kind of laugh. 'That's new.'

'Are you sure you're okay? Where's Harri? Are you coming over later?'

'She's right here. She's watching *Peppa Pig* and destroying Dan's DVD collection.'

'He's so '90s, your brother.'

'Yup.'

They'd slipped into their usual banter, so easy and comfortable between them, but then Leisel remembered why she had called.

'So, you coming over later?' she asked again.

'Yes. Harri and I will be there.'

'You might stay?' Leisel asked, turning her back on the green room.

'Leisel, I... Let's talk about it later.' He sounded distracted again.

'Okay.'

'And Lee... good luck.'

'Thank you.' She hung up, feeling better. She turned around—and there was Elle.

She looked exactly like she did on Instagram, if a little shorter. Immaculate in a tight white dress, sky-high heels and a bright smile.

Leisel glanced down at her white smock top and dark jeans, and gave a little shrug.

'Hi,' she said. 'I'm Leisel.'

***

Elle had been watching the traffic helicopter take off, jiggling her phone in her hand, when Leisel introduced herself.

'Is your arm better?' Elle asked her, gesturing towards Leisel's peasant sleeve.

'Yes, thanks, it's almost back to normal. How's your husband?'

'He's doing well, thanks.' Elle thought about the text she'd got that morning. Same number: *You need to come clean before we tell the world.*

It had been four days. One message every day.

Adrian was barely sleeping. At first he'd said that they needed to pull the plug on the whole thing. But Elle had convinced him otherwise. 'What do we tell people? That we were mistaken? That you don't have cancer after all? You'd look like a complete idiot.'

She knew that Cate was hiding something, but the girl insisted she wasn't.

I just need to keep her onside until the Blog-ahhs, Elle had decided, *and then she's gone.* In fact, if Elle could just hold off any of this shit breaking until she had that award in her hand, she could handle it. After all, medical records were private: no one could prove a thing.

She looked around the green room, knowing that at any minute, Abi would walk in.

'Just checking on my boys,' she said to Leisel, and fished her phone out of her giant bag.

Are you on your way to the airport? she texted to Adrian. *Remember to look terrible.*

He texted back straight away: *Not coming.*

Elle sighed so loudly that Leisel turned around. *YOU'RE COMING*, she replied. *Don't be weak. We need a united front.*

No answer.

Samira walked into the green room, followed by a wardrobe assistant carrying a blue jacket. Elle watched as they walked over to Leisel.

'Leisel,' Samira said, in the sort of calm tone that expects to meet resistance, 'do you mind wearing a jacket onscreen today? It's just, all three of you ladies are in white...'

'It's not great TV,' added the wardrobe lady.

Leisel glanced at her flouncy top. Glanced at the expensive-looking jacket. 'Sure,' she said. 'Can I try it on?'

'Of course,' said Samira. 'Ten minutes till we call you.'

What a push-over, thought Elle. *I knew I didn't need to worry about you.*

***

Abi was staring at herself in the bathroom mirror. Who was that person with the smooth hair and the pink lips? It didn't look much like her. She went into the toilet stall, grabbed some paper, came back and started dabbing at her mouth, her eyes.

Then she checked the other stalls and called Zoe, asking, 'How are you going down there?'

'I'm alright. None of the cancer centre receptionists will talk to me, but I'm still trying. How about you? Have you seen her yet?'

'Not yet,' said Abi. 'I'm about to go in there. Did she reply to this morning's message?'

'Nope.' Zoe changed the subject. 'What about you, big week, hey? How's Grace?'

'She's barely talking to me, but she's around. You guys are flying up tomorrow together, right?'

'Yep.'

'Okay. Look, I've had an idea. About what to do tomorrow if we get nowhere with our evidence. I won't tell you yet, but I know what to do.'

'High-risk strategy?'

'It's time. Anyway, I've got to go.'

'Kiss my sister for me?'

'That's funny. Talk later.'

Abi hung up. Sent Grace a quick text: *Thinking of you and the kids. Love you xxx*

And then she pushed open the bathroom door, into the green room.

'Well, hi, Elle! Hi, Leisel. Don't you look great in that jacket!'

***

Simon Hedley didn't glance up from his notes as the three women took their seats. He waited for them to be settled in before he finally raised his head. 'So, mummy bloggers, hey?' he said, with a leery smile in Elle's direction. 'Where do you ladies find the time?'

They looked at him in silence, as the wardrobe assistant fussed around their stools, straightening their shirts, smoothing errant hairs.

'My wife's flat out between drop-off and coffee and yoga,' he said, beaming. Simon Hedley was Australia's best mate, apparently. A truly top bloke. 'Nice to have a hobby, though, right?'

Abi, of course, was the first to say anything. 'How's your hobby working out for you, Simon? Must be exhausting, being a TV presenter and an idiot at the same time.'

'Like rubbing your tummy and patting your head,' added Leisel, and the two women smiled at each other.

Elle rolled her eyes.

Samira, who stood watching from behind the cameras, started audibly deep-breathing.

'Ouch,' said Simon. 'I see. Bloggers or bitches was it, ladies?' And he pulled out his most dazzling, top-bloke smile.

The countdown started, and the intro rolled up on the autocue.

'We are doing something a bit different on "*She Says*" this morning,' Simon boomed. 'This weekend, digital media experts from all over the world are coming to Sydney for the biggest-ever awards celebrating online writing. The winners of the Blog-ahhs will walk away not only with hefty cash prizes, but also the opportunity for serious investment to turn their blogs into big business. I have THREE of those bloggers in for "She Says" today, those nominated for the Best Parenting Blog. Meet the mummy bloggers Elle Campbell, Leisel Adams and Abi Black. Welcome to *Breakfast!*, ladies.'

The women all nodded, tumbling over one another with their hellos.

Hair and teeth, thought Elle, shaking her head.

Keep the back of the jacket under your bum, thought Leisel.

Try not to say anything that might get you killed, thought Abi.

'Now, as I understand it, ladies, you are all what they call "mummy bloggers", but you all write for very different audiences, am I right?' Simon looked to Elle.

'Yes, Simon, that's right,' she said. And stopped.

Genius, thought Abi.

'So you'll all have very different opinions on today's "She Says" topics, which is exactly the way we like it. Are you ready, ladies?'

'We sure are,' said Leisel. Remember to smile, she told herself.

'Okay. Let's go. So, today, a primary school in South Australia is in the headlines for emailing parents, asking them to keep their phones in their bags at school pick-up. The email, and I quote, says, "Your children want to see your faces. They want to know you're happy to see them. No phones are to be visible on school grounds." Extraordinary. Elle, do you think the school was within its rights to do this?'

Elle leant in, her smile on high beam. 'Yes, Simon, I do. There's nothing sadder than children thinking their parents would rather look at their phone than their own child's face. I understand the school's frustration.' Elle gave a slight giggle and shook her hair a little. 'I love my phone as much as the next girl, but I try to make sure it's away whenever my children are around. They need to know that they come first. Not Facebook.'

'Ha, interesting. Leisel?'

'Well, look, I disagree. I think parents, and particularly working parents, are busy people trying to fit more and more into their lives. We'd all love to be 100 per cent present with our children, but that moment waiting for them to come out of the gate might be the only one when we can make that doctor's appointment or return our sister's text message, or check the calendar to see what time ballet starts. It seems very patronising to me that a school is trying to tell parents how to behave. Back off!'

'Great answer, Leisel. What about you, Abi?'

'Okay, Simon, this is a completely bullshit topic,' Abi began, sending a ripple through the studio. Elle and Leisel's heads turned towards Abi at the same moment.

'Language, Abi!' Simon looked momentarily panicked. 'Sorry, everyone.'

'Sorry, *mate*. But it is. What one judgemental principal does with one stupid little private school in Adelaide is not exactly a serious issue facing the world, is it? If my kids went to that school—and thank god they don't—I'd be walking around the playground with my phone glued to my forehead. It is none of their business how a parent relates to their child at that moment or any other. This kind of topic is just designed to make women feel guilty no matter what they do. And the right answer to that is, "Stuff you."' Abi ended with a fist-bang on the desk, and then remembered to smile.

'Okay,' Simon pushed on. 'Well, ladies, I'm a bit worried about this next topic after that, although it is about politics. The Federal Member for Finbar made waves this week when he mounted a campaign to get paid maternity leave dumped altogether, because—he argues—it encourages women to work when their children are small. Mr Boorman says, and again I quote: "There was a time when women resigned from their paid jobs to take up another job, and that job title was Mum. Our society would be a lot better off with fewer broken families, obese children and less unemployment among young men, if we returned to considering motherhood as vocation and a duty." I'm nervous, but Abi, I'm going to you first on this one.'

'Well, Simon.' Abi could sense the energy lingering from her last answer. She was beginning to enjoy herself. 'There's no question that the honourable Member for Finbar is an idiot of epic proportions, but he has one thing right—'

'He does?' asked Leisel, in a high-pitched voice.

'Yes, he does. We have convinced people—men and women—that the only purpose they serve is being a corporate wage slave. That their only value is in earning money for someone else. That the only way to be productive is to be slugging away in an office all day, and that's clearly nonsense.' Abi was remembering not to swear, even as she felt the anxiety fizz in the air all around her. 'Rushing mothers back to their corporate wage slavery as quickly as possible isn't serving women any better than it was when they were locked out of the work force.'

'That's rubbish, Abi,' Leisel said. 'The vast majority of mothers in Australia work and they have to. Paid maternity leave allows them a little more breathing room than they would otherwise have to settle into parenthood and take care of their baby. Mr Boorman is directly attacking mothers and women in general by suggesting that they don't value motherhood if they are returning to paid work after giving birth. He's a dinosaur.'

'Dinosaur?' Simon asked. 'Really? Elle, you've been quiet on this, what are your thoughts?'

'Simon, in my opinion, these two women to my left are perfect examples of those who have alienated men like Mr Boorman.' Elle had realised she needed to get in this game—it was time to turn it up. 'Shouty and aggressive. It's not the way to get your point across. I'm sure you'd agree, Simon.' She directed her most dazzling smile his way.

'I wasn't being shouty—' Leisel started.

'But what do you think of the point, Elle?' Simon cut across Leisel, smiling back at Elle.

'If you can manage not to work when your children are small, you should choose not to,' said Elle, flicking her hair over her shoulder. 'Children need their mothers. It's not fashionable to say so, but they do. The happiest mothers are the ones who have embraced their role, their homes and their husbands, who aren't pulled in a million directions, who aren't frazzled all the time—'

'So you think women shouldn't work?' Leisel was trying very hard to keep her voice calm.

'I come from a poor background,' said Elle. 'I understand

the economic realities better than most—' she shot a look at Abi '—and I'm saying that if they can afford not to work, mothers should spend some time at home.'

Abi leant forward to stare at Elle. 'Can *you* afford not to work?'

'Let's not get personal here.' Simon had the look of a man who was losing control.

'At the moment,' Elle said, 'I am fortunate enough that yes, I can afford to be at home with my boys.'

'But you're not at home, are you?' Abi fired back. 'You're here, working. As you are every time you're writing a blog post, or posting on Instagram, or cutting a deal with a sponsor...'

'It's hardly the same thing as leaving them for hours at a time to go into an office every day,' Elle said, somehow managing to stay serene.

Leisel, whose face was red even through the TV make-up, opened her mouth.

'Let's move on,' said Simon. 'There's one more topic— hopefully we can find some common ground on this one.' Simon looked like he wished it was 10 a.m. and he was on the golf course hitting his way into a four-hour Friday lunch. 'A nurse in the US is claiming that she's invented a program that can teach a baby to sleep through the night from just six days old. She's been offered a six-figure advance by a publisher in anticipation of a landslide of interest from mums desperate to get tiny babies to sleep. Previously, according to the research—and it's not like I'd know, ladies!—it's been thought you can't sleep-train a child until they're six months old. Detractors are calling this child abuse. What do we think? Leisel?'

Leisel had regained her composure. She took a breath. 'New mothers are very vulnerable to anything that makes them feel in control. And at risk of sounding *shouty*, I would say that it's not helpful to either them or their babies to give them false hope.'

'Did your babies sleep through the night, Leisel?'

She could hear the chirping of a producer in Simon's earpiece—she knew he was being encouraged to stir up an argument.

'Nope. Never. Still don't. We just muddle our way through. And, you know, some weeks are better than others. Some nights are better than others. It's not like that for everyone, but I would just suggest taking these kinds of promises with a pinch of salt.'

'Thank you, very reasonable. Elle?'

'Well, Simon—' Elle sat a little taller in her seat '—my children have slept through the night from six weeks old. I know, I know, ladies, don't hate me. I strongly believe that if your baby feels loved and secure, and you follow a calming routine from an early age, any baby can sleep. I think—and Leisel, I hope you're not offended by this—'

'You weren't worried about that before.'

'—I think that *lazy* parents can't put in the effort required to get their children into a happy night-time routine. It takes discipline and effort, I really believe that. And my boys have been excellent sleepers as a result.'

Simon's earpiece buzzed again—probably one more instruction to stir the pot. 'Leisel? You want to respond to that?'

She suddenly felt exhausted to her bones. She wasn't sure if she could reply without crying, and she didn't want to be a grown woman crying on national TV. She shook her head and, as she did, she felt a hand on her knee. It was Abi.

'Simon,' Abi said, in a loud, authoritative voice, 'I think the less time we spend on silly topics that only divide women, the better, don't you? I mean, really, you have three mothers on the panel, so you think you have to ask us about babies and schoolyards and controlled crying to stir up some kind of catfight?'

'You three women are mummy bloggers—did you expect us to ask you about peace in the Middle East?' Simon's patience had apparently run out.

'Why the hell not?' Abi asked. Elle laughed delicately. Leisel swallowed hard.

Simon wrapped it up. 'That's all we have time for. After the break, Dom is going to show us how to cook the perfect rib-eye for a Sunday barbecue. Be right back.'

A producer rushed over. 'That was awesome! You guys should be on every week!'

'If they are, I'm not,' said Simon Hedley, pulling out his earpiece and stomping away from the desk while signalling madly to the control room.

Leisel turned to Elle and said, 'What was that? You just attacked me on national television. *Lazy? Aggressive?* Seriously, who ARE you?'

'You know exactly who I am, Leisel,' said Elle, slipping off her stool with an elegant shimmy.

'Yes,' said Abi. 'And so do I.'

CHAPTER TWENTY-NINE

LEISEL

'Thank everything that's over.' Leisel kicked her front door closed, dropped her armful of tiny backpacks and fell into the living-room armchair.

Maggie came over and curled up on her knee. 'What's the matter, Mum?'

'Nothing, darling. I just feel like I've been at war for months. I don't think I'm cut out for it.'

Maggie curled up tighter. 'Well, I love you.'

'I love you, too, my girl.' Leisel kissed her on the head, wrapping her into a hug.

Rich came barrelling over, waving a Lego rocket. 'MUM! Look what I made!'

'That's great, Rich.'

Leisel felt absolutely empty. Drained dry. As if this morning's TV slot hadn't been dramatic enough, she'd endured a photoshoot with Abi and Elle for Sunday's awards. Elle and Abi refused to speak to each other. Leisel, still bruised from the onscreen combat, had tried to play her natural role of peacemaker, but her heart wasn't in it.

'See you all Sunday,' she'd called half-heartedly as they'd left each other at Channel 8.

'Can't wait,' said Elle, and it had taken Leisel a minute to identify her tone: contempt.

The headlines had started instantly:

MUMMY BLOGGERS IN *BREAKFAST!* WAR

CATFIGHT! BITCHY BLOGGERS LEAVE SIMON SPEECHLESS

'LAZY, SHOUTY' MOTHERS DO WOMEN NO FAVOURS, SAYS BLOGGER

And there were endless tweets and DMs and comments on the cheery post that Leisel had put up before the show, with a shot the publicist had taken of the three of them in the green room.

About to have Breakfast! with these two amazing women.

That had been overly optimistic.

After the shoot, Leisel had to go to the office, where everyone had seen *Breakfast!* and wanted a full debrief, mostly about what Elle Campbell looked like in the flesh. Then she'd had to pivot to meetings with Zac and various editors and clients until four-thirty, when she'd had to excuse herself and leave under her boss's furious gaze to make the pick-up times for Rich and Maggie.

And then she'd fallen in the door to the flat with the kids and felt what was waiting: the silence. No one was there. No Mark to tell about her awful day, no Harri to cuddle and sniff and tease. Just her and two hungry kids and a godawful mess from the morning.

'Is Daddy coming?' asked Maggie, from Leisel's knee.

Leisel squeezed her tighter. 'I think so, sweetie.'

Mark had called her after the show, but she hadn't picked up. He'd sent a worried text, *Are you ok? I thought you were great.* But she hadn't replied.

What was he trying to do? How did he think this was okay, disappearing on them like this?

'Mum?'

'What, Mags?'

'I was meant to go to the dentist today. Daddy said it was Friday, after school.'

'Oh.' Leisel's stomach plummeted, and internally she began to shape this story into a post:

> There is no worse feeling in the world than the one when you feel like you've let down your child, the person who needs you most in the world. A knife entering your flesh is nothing in comparison. My heart is twisting...

And then she stopped herself from mentally composing such melodramatic tosh, and said to Maggie, 'I am so sorry, Mags. I hate letting you down. I really am sorry. But it's okay, the dentist isn't going anywhere. We will make another appointment and I will take you, I promise.'

'I don't care if I don't go,' Maggie said. 'Dentists are weird.'

'It's important, Mags, and I'll come in with you.'

Rich crawled up on Leisel's knee, too, almost spiking her with his Lego rocket. She held one of her children in each arm. Closed her eyes.

I am so lucky, she thought. I am so fucking lucky.

A key was in the door, but the chain was on. 'Hello, anyone home?'

'Daddy!' In a second, Maggie and Rich jumped off Leisel's knee and were at the door. 'Mum, it's Daddy. It's Daddy! Let him in.'

Leisel rested her head back on the top of the armchair

and smiled. Then she jumped up, too, rushing to get her baby in her arms.

***

Mark had taken care of stories and bathtime, while Leisel had cleaned up and put some spaghetti on.

They were back in the kitchen, sitting together at the table. The Returns were finished, the house was quiet. Mark and Leisel were looking at each other over drippy red pasta.

Leisel's anger at Mark was mixing with relief at seeing him back at home.

'I missed you so fucking much,' she said suddenly.

'You did?' said Mark, smiling at her. 'What I do, or who I am?'

'What a stupid question.' Leisel stuffed some spaghetti into her mouth. 'What you do, of course,' she said through a mess of gluten and cheese. 'I'm the world's worst housewife.'

'I want you to stop that,' Mark said softly, seriously.

'Stop what? Talking with my mouth full?'

'Talking about how shit you are all the time. Online, in real life, whatever. It's bullshit.'

She stared at him. He seemed tired—rumpled and handsome, like he always did to her, but the circles under his eyes were deeper, his face more drawn.

'I'm so angry with you for leaving,' she said. 'I have to tell you that.'

'That's fair enough. But I wasn't really leaving. I just needed to stop being angry with *you*. Living in the middle of all that tension is...' He paused and looked down.

'Are you okay?' she asked. 'Have you been okay, while you've been at Dan's? Have you been going to Meetings?'

He looked up. 'Are you asking me if I've been using?'

'Well...' Leisel didn't want to say yes. But she meant yes.

'I haven't been using, Lee. I would never... Well, I'm not

supposed to ever say never. I mean, I would never, *never*, with Harri with me. You can always trust that, whatever happens.'

'Whatever happens? What's going to happen?' Leisel felt her little bubble of happiness, the one that had blocked out some of the day's anxiety, shrinking.

'I'm just tired, Lee. Sleeping on the couch. Looking after Harri.' He put his hand on hers. 'Missing you and Maggie and Rich.'

Leisel's bubble started to reinflate.

'Okay. So where are we? I feel like a teenager, asking you where this is going. But I'm a 43-year-old woman, and you're my husband.' She smiled into the spaghetti. 'It's getting kind of embarrassing.'

'I'm home. We're home.'

Here we go, thought Leisel. 'I have to tell you that I'm not going to give up the blog,' she said. 'I know you have your issues with it, and that I sound like a wanker when I say this, but... It's so important to me. And not just me. I feel like it actually does something useful in the world. Also, the truth is, I love it.'

'You do sound like a bit of a wanker when you say that.' He smiled back. 'But seriously, I don't want you to give up anything. Especially not anything that makes you happy. I was freaked out by the attack, and worried about our kids—but you know, I've figured out it's not about the blog. I've realised it's something else that's been really getting to me.'

'Is it my work? That I'm never home? That I'm a shit wife?'

'It's that.' Mark pointed a fork at her. 'It's that right there. You're always so critical of everything. You. Our home. Our family. Sometimes I feel like we're not good enough.'

'Well, come on, Mark. Things have been pretty crazy around here the past few years, yes?'

He stood up. Leisel wasn't sure where he was going—out of the room or to the kettle. But then he came over to her side of the table, leant on it, looked down at her. 'They have been crazy, Lee, but they've also been the happiest of my life. Seriously. What's so awful about our life?'

'Well, let's see.' She half-smiled before she started the list. 'The fact we live in a shoebox. The fact that I am stressed out of my mind. And tired. And a terrible mother.'

'A terrible mother? Are you fucking kidding me?'

'Come on, Mark. I'm hardly mother of the year—'

'I used to score from a woman who had four kids, about twenty minutes' drive from where we're standing right now.'

Leisel went quiet, stared at the table.

'She used her kids as couriers, Lee. From when they were tiny babies. Little wraps of powder hidden in their pockets, in their pram. She'd forget to feed them for days when things got a bit hectic. We used to lie around her house, and they'd be playing in our ashtrays, and we barely even noticed them. *SHE* was a terrible mother.'

'Well, she had problems—'

'Bullshit, Leisel. Don't make excuses for things you don't understand.'

'It's hard for me to argue with you when you bring up that part of your life.'

'Why are you trying to mount an argument that you are a terrible mother? You are an excellent mother. You love your kids to bits and you work fucking hard to provide for them. What's so terrible? They are loved and safe and have two parents who are obsessed with them. Just... stop.'

Leisel looked at him. I know the post I want to write right now, she thought. It's the post no one wants to read:

> I love my husband. He thinks I'm amazing. I love the me that he sees. My kids are spectacular. My life is full and fulfilling.

Leisel knew that was a thought best kept to herself.
Mark pulled Leisel out of her chair and kissed her in the

kitchen. Two forty-something parents, kissing against the kitchen table. Look at us, thought Leisel. We are still here.

'And I'm really glad you got the chain on the door,' he said, when he stopped kissing her for a moment. 'That was a sensible thing to do.'

'How long have we got until one of the kids gets into our bed?' asked Leisel.

Mark glanced at an imaginary watch on his wrist. 'About fifty minutes.'

'Let's go.' And Leisel took Mark's hand.

CHAPTER THIRTY

ABI

My Dear Green Divas,

There are some things I need to tell you.

It's been a wild few months on the farm. You've been along for a lot of that ride, so I won't revisit it, but anyone who says life in the country is dull has never been to a gay farmhouse with 24 chickens, four children, two dogs, a podcast shed and one massive ego in residence.

Tomorrow, I'll find out if our blog The Green Diva has won the Parenting Blog of the Year at these big fancy blogging awards, the Blog-ahhs. Grace and I will be in Sydney town, all dressed up in our finest cheesecloth* and rubbing shoulders with all the great and good of the 'digital community'.

For the last few months, the outcome of tomorrow night has been preoccupying me above all things. The stakes are high, you see. The rewards are money, influence, connections. These are all things that every day, I rant and rage against.

Every day, I say that's the kind of bullshit that

us GDs just don't need, that it's all part of some fucking conspiracy to keep us all buzzing away like worker bees, when really we should be heads up, smelling the roses, planting our own shit and watching it grow.

So I don't think I'm overstating much to say that I've lost my way these last few weeks. Let's face it, the Blog-ahhs nominated The Green Diva community because we are a strong and formidable force, but we are way too dangerous to actually win. So why have I been chasing after it like a kelpie with the sniff of a ewe? Because I have bullshitting myself about what matters.

It's time for a reckoning. A re-set, as the 'digital community' would say. I've got some things to tell you. You ready, GDs?

*We will not be wearing cheesecloth, you fools.

Thing 1. I am a proud gay woman.

Sometimes on GD I gloss over the fact that I share my life with one remarkable woman, Grace Adams. She is a mother, a lover, a friend, a teacher, a nurturer of all things. And she is the reason why when my life exploded five years ago, I was not smashed to smithereens, but rose like a slightly battered phoenix.

My marriage was not a bad one. Not really. But for years I was denying who I really was, in so many ways.

If you ever get the chance to be who you really are, GDs, grab it with both hands and run. I was too cowardly to make that choice and I will always regret that. But when it was made for me, I was smart enough to know that I had been handed a gift. The wrapping was a bit soiled, it was tied up with a pretty shitty bow, but it was a gift, all the same.

My life has been immeasurably better for it. And, I believe, so have the lives of my daughters.

Their possibilities have opened like fucking lotuses. Divorce doesn't have to be an ending.

Okay...

Thing 2. I really have been a dangerous cunt. I have worn that moniker like a badge of honour. Some of you might even have the T-shirt. But it's all smoke and mirrors, sisters.

I believe in choice. I believe that if you want to let your kids run around naked in the woods all day and that Naplan is the devil and gluten is worse, all power to you.

But my belief in choice has a hard limit—a ceiling, and here it is: I believe in vaccination. My daughters are fully vaccinated. I am fully vaccinated. Grace's boys are fully vaccinated. We all have fluoride in our water and our toothpaste. Our medicine cabinet is overflowing with the product of Big-Pharma.

Yes, I believe in choice, but I also believe in science. I believe in keeping babies safe. Your babies, the babies down the road, the babies three towns over, the babies three continents over.

If I am ashamed of something, I am ashamed of the fact I have cloaked that belief to personally benefit from a nonsense stereotype. That when Samantha Garner calls me and tells me her daughter is dead and that people like me have blood on my hands, deep down I know she's right.

Do you know why there isn't a credible scientist in the world who thinks there's a link between autism and vaccinations? Because there isn't one. That's not what I believe, it's what I know.

So I don't want to be one of the crazy internet voices on this issue anymore. I know this one of my three things is going to piss off a large section of my followers, but if that's what you're here for, you can leave now, because from here on in, I'm going to be using my voice to challenge the anti-vaxxers in our beautiful community.

To quote my father, who is a bit of a dickhead but very smart, there are no simple answers to complex questions.

And lastly:

Thing 3. My ex-husband is a man called Adrian Campbell. We were together for 16 years and married for 12. We have two completely incredible daughters together.

Adrian is now married to Elle Campbell, who you might know as The Stylish Mumma. He is a decent man, a good father, a dutiful son, a maker-of-money.

But here's the thing: He does not have cancer.

Throw the lawyers at us if you like, Elle, but he does not.

I know I am wading into a fight that is not my own here, but there are two reasons why this is my business: My daughters are terrified that their father is dying. And, this level of deceit is bad for all of us. All of us.

I admitted, earlier, that I have lost my head in the pursuit of this award, but Adrian and Elle have gone farther than that—they have lost their souls.

I am not asking you to attack them, GDs. In fact, I would rather you didn't.

Taking pleasure from seeing others under siege online is not something I'm particularly proud of.

So I am not asking you to chase them down, but simply that the truth does. Adrian, you are not sick. Or at least not in the way that you are telling the world. Stop punishing your daughters and say so.

Those are my three things, GDs, my big bang, my mea-culpa. If you are furious with me and decide to leave our little felt-lined community, I understand. Or, at least, I will pretend to understand. I don't know what the future holds for Grace and me and our little family, but I know what it doesn't hold: It doesn't hold lies.

Go forth, be awe-inspiring.

Your QGD, Abi. x

It was six o'clock on the Saturday night before the Blog-ahhs, and Abi pushed publish.

CHAPTER THIRTY-ONE

ELLE

Elle was at the ensuite mirror in her hotel room when her phone chimed.

It was Zoe.

YOU NEED TO LOOK AT ABI BLACK'S BLOG, NOW.

As soon as Elle had read those words, her phone starting ringing and beeping and vibrating. Every notification at the same time. The thing was going to explode.

She dropped her phone on the dresser and backed away from it.

Then someone started banging at the door. 'ELLE! ELLE! OPEN IT NOW!'

Adrian's voice. He'd come.

When she pulled it open, he practically fell into the room. 'My phone,' he said. 'It's blowing up. Something's going on.' And then he heard hers.

Elle went to her phone, flicked it to silent and walked over to the bathroom, placing it inside. She put her hand out for Adrian's phone, then did the same with it: silent, in the bathroom, door closed.

She sat down on the bed. She'd been getting ready for

dinner with the Blog-ahh heads from San Francisco. They were going to Spice Temple. She was wearing a white silk kimono dress. It was going to be a beautiful night.

'What's happened?' Adrian asked as he sat next to her. His face was grey, he was sweating. She thought she could smell whisky on his breath — from the plane?

'You weren't up to this,' she said quietly. 'You're falling apart.'

'What has happened?' he asked again.

'Abi. Zoe. Cate — '

'Abi?' Adrian lay back on the bed, his feet still on the floor. He was in a suit. His hand-luggage wheelie case was on the floor. 'Zoe? What?'

'When we look at our phones,' Elle said, 'we will find a blog post by Abi accusing us of making up your cancer.'

'But... I haven't seen Abi. I've barely seen the girls.'

'It doesn't matter. She's been talking to someone who *has* seen you.' Suddenly, Elle realised there was a loose end. 'Are the boys home with Cate?'

'No. When I told her I'd decided to go to Sydney after all, she said she wouldn't be able to look after the boys, that she had to go to her mother's. So they're with my mum for the night.'

Elle lay back on the bed, too. She took Adrian's hand, and they just lay there, phones silent behind the closed bathroom door.

***

On Elle and Adrian's wedding day, they had lain together on a hotel bed like this in the morning before the ceremony.

As per tradition, Elle had spent the night away from the townhouse they'd shared for just a few months. The wedding was going to be tiny. Just a few of Elle's gym friends, a few of Adrian's old rowing buddies. His mother, begrudgingly. Alex and Arden.

Elle had asked the girls if they wanted to be her bridesmaids, and she was secretly relieved when they'd said no. Relieved and insulted in equal measure. It would have made a neat story to have his daughters publicly bless their union, but it was better for the photographs if they didn't. Too bohemian by far.

That morning, Elle was getting ready at the Langham, her hair and make-up people arriving any moment, when there was a banging on the door.

Adrian. He was flushed, sweaty. He was wearing his suit.

'Elle, I can't. I just can't. I want to, but it's too soon. Everything has happened so fast. I'm worried about the girls, my parents, what they're going to think at work...'

Elle took his hand, walked him inside and gently pushed him down on the bed.

'You're being silly, babe,' she whispered in his ear, lying next to him. 'You're a man who knows what he wants. You want this. You can't let what everyone else thinks stop you from getting what you want, can you?'

'But... we're already together. My divorce came through three weeks ago. It's just too fast.'

'When we fell in love,' Elle whispered, 'that first night, in the shower. What did you tell me?'

She could see that he was thinking about that moment— that she was getting through to him. 'I told you,' said Adrian, 'I told you, I thought with a woman like you, I could do absolutely anything, that I felt invincible.'

'Well then, why are you suddenly doubting that?' Elle began undoing Adrian's belt. 'Why are you letting that fear in? You need to focus on one thing: us. We can do anything together.'

It wasn't the most conventional pre-wedding ritual, but it worked for them.

Afterwards, they lay on the hotel bed, holding hands, feet on the floor.

'It's only us,' she said. 'Shut out everyone else. They don't know who you are. I do.'

'Adrian, we can fix this,' Elle said now.

'How? How can we possibly fix this?'

'We need to focus. I am focused—now it's your turn.'

A knock on the door. 'Elle, we need to talk. It's Samira, and it's kind of urgent.' The Blog-ahhs publicity assistant sounded terrified.

'Give me five minutes, Samira darling,' Elle called back. 'I'll come and find you then.'

'Okay... I'll, I'll wait in the conference room.' The girl padded away.

Adrian looked sick. Really sick. His eyes were closed, his brow was sweaty. He looked like he was willing himself somewhere else.

Elle started whispering in his ear. 'It's just a rumour, Adrian. At this point, it's just a rumour. It's Saturday night, so it will be a slow pick-up. As soon as possible, we will issue a denial. There is no evidence. Medical records are sealed. Yes, everyone will be talking about this tomorrow, but no one will be able to prove anything before the awards.'

Adrian's eyes opened. He turned his head and met her gaze. 'We can't go to the awards tomorrow, Elle. Are you fucking crazy?'

'Yes, we can.' She stood up. 'In fact, you know what else we can do? We can go to dinner with the San Francisco people, once you get cleaned up. Everything as normal. You are ill, but you are not dying. You will smile and shake hands, you will look strong and serious—like you are. You will push your food around your plate. No one is going to accuse you of lying to your face. I will be sad but smiling while I tell whoever's listening that this ongoing hostility between me and Abi stretches back to me and you getting together, and that it's unfortunate, misplaced jealousy.'

'You could... do that?'

'Adrian—' she bent over him '—for us, I can do anything. We can do anything.'

He jumped off the bed, pushed her out of the way, ran to the bathroom and threw up in the toilet.

CHAPTER THIRTY-TWO

The Blog-ahhs

'Oh shit, it's Shannon Smart.' Abi tried to duck behind Grace as they walked towards the neon-lit entrance.

'Babe, she's *hosting the awards*,' said Grace. 'She'll be here all night. Besides, I think your chance of flying under the radar is minimal.'

On the way in, all nominees had to walk up the Blog-ahhs' idea of a red carpet—a Scrabble-board floor with light-up letters—and then pose for pictures against a huge media wall that spelled out 'Blog-ahh' in tiny photos of all the nominees.

Thanks to the tabloid excitement surrounding the 'mummy bloggers', tonight's ceremony—usually only interesting to industry—had attracted a swarm of young reporters, all craning to see who would arrive next. Waiting, Abi thought, for Elle.

'I can't decide if the Blog-ahh people will be loving or hating all this attention you've brought them,' Grace said to Abi as they posed for a picture.

'You don't have to guess, I know,' said Abi. '*Hating*. I've had my telling off. I think they're scrambling for a new winner, don't you?'

'ABI!' called a young man who was waving a smartphone across the media barricade. 'Can you elaborate on your shocking accusation that Elle and Adrian Campbell are trying to win this award by faking his serious illness?'

'I've said everything I'm going to say on that subject,' Abi said calmly. 'It's up to you guys now.'

Samira appeared at Abi's side, looking like she was out of her depth. 'Nice answer, Abi,' she said. 'The Heads are very keen that we don't pour any more fuel on this fire. Your guests are at your table, by the way. We got the last-minute tickets.'

'Thank you, Samira, you have been a little star through all of this.' Abi gave her a grin and a one-armed hug.

Samira almost smiled back.

***

'I don't have to walk up that thing, do I?' At the sight of the neon carpet, Mark tried to pull his hand free of Leisel's. 'Are you serious?'

'Come *on*, this is my moment.' She yanked his hand. 'You wouldn't want to ruin it for me, would you?'

'No. No, I wouldn't.' Mark visibly checked himself and ran his hand through his hair. 'Let's do it.'

My husband looks really fucking handsome in his wedding suit, Leisel thought as he stopped in front of the cameras and grabbed her firmly around the waist.

'Was that a *pout*?' she had to ask him, laughing, as they walked away.

'Hey, you wanted me to pose. I posed.'

'LEISEL!!!' a young reporter was yelling. 'How's your arm? What do you think of the controversy around Abi Black and Elle Campbell? Do you have any comment on the fake cancer scandal?'

'Is that what we're calling it now?' Mark whispered in Leisel's ear.

'I don't have any comment on that, thank you for asking,'

Leisel said to the reporter. 'And my arm's fine.' I used to be you, she thought, looking at the young man. I had to bring something, anything, back to the newsroom to lay at the editor's feet. 'But,' she added, 'I'll give you a quote about something else if you need it.'

'What about Elle Campbell calling you a lazy mother on a national TV show on Friday? That's got to sting, right?' the young man asked, wagging his phone at her.

Actually, I was never you, Leisel realised.

'Lazy mothers are like glitter-shitting unicorns,' she said to him. 'They don't exist.' Then she turned to Mark. 'Come on, I'll shout you a free fizzy water.'

***

Adrian was having trouble getting out of the car.

'Darling, this is the last thing I am going to ask you to do.' Elle spoke slowly and calmly, the way she talked to Freddie when she wanted him to put on some pants. 'This is the last thing we have to do. After tonight, we will go to ground. We will regroup. We will get professional help. There are people who can help crisis-manage us out of this. You cannot let Abi beat us. Just get out of the car. Smile. You don't have to say a word.'

'Abi? All this wasn't Abi's idea,' Adrian hissed at her through his teeth. 'It was *yours*. I can't go to war with her for telling the truth. She is the mother of my daughters.'

'And I am the mother of your sons,' said Elle. 'Pull yourself together, and let's see this through.'

Last night, Adrian had let Elle talk him down. He had done what she'd asked. They had gone to dinner at Spice Temple, and Adrian had followed the script. He had maintained a dignified distance from conversation, moved food around his plate and retired early, as someone with a serious illness might. And then, this morning, Elle had disappeared for a meeting with the directors of the awards.

She had returned to their room smiling. 'It's fine, darling, they don't believe any of this. They're on our side. I think I'm their *favourite*.'

Sitting in the car now, Adrian felt like he was back on the floor of that shower in the Balwyn house, five years ago. He couldn't breathe, the lights of the casino outside were blurring, his heart was smashing in his chest.

'Adrian,' Elle said, 'come on. One last thing. For *us*.'

Fuck it. Get it together, Adrian told himself. This was your choice. All of it. Get it done.

He shook his head, took a deep breath and pushed the car door open.

***

'ELLE, ELLE!' The cry went up as soon as Elle and Adrian stepped onto the flashing Blog-ahh Carpet. With just a couple of tiny edits, thought Elle, this moment would be perfect. If only I didn't know what they were going to ask me.

'Elle, does your husband really have cancer?'

'Adrian, are you really suffering from lymphoma?'

'Elle, do you have a message for Abi Black?'

Elle pivoted left and right for the cameras. She looked immaculate in her white lace dress. Back at the hotel, she'd shared getting-ready Instagram posts with her people, each including the hashtags #businessasusual and #hatersgonnahate, and the responses had been suitably gushy.

Perfection. #babe

Looking flawless is the best revenge #eyebrowgoals

The jewels! Slay, sister #stylishmumma

It was true that Elle's phone had been under siege all day, but after her meeting with the Blog-ahh directors this morning, she was feeling calm.

Adrian, standing next to her, gaunt and grey in his Tom Ford tux, whispered, 'You don't seriously think you might still *win*, do you?'

'Darling, you'd be amazed,' she replied. 'Let's go over to the reporters—can you lead the way?' He looked at her, eyes wide open. And did as he was asked.

'We've been advised by our lawyers not to comment any further,' Elle said into the many phones pointed her way, as Adrian stood, silent, behind her. 'We won't be making any statements about Abi Black's outrageous claims. We don't want to cause any further distress to any of the children involved. Thank you.'

'Come on,' Adrian said under his breath, tugging her away. 'Let's get this over with.'

Samira appeared from the crowd. 'Elle, Adrian. We've changed the seating plan in light of the... developments, as discussed. Let me show you where you are.'

***

'Where are the Bay Area overlords?' hissed Grace, as she and Abi looked around the cavernous ballroom for the Parenting bloggers' table.

The room glimmered under a million fairy lights. Large round tables were set for dinner, surrounded by waiters with white napkins over their arms, juggling their reds and whites. Extroverts were milling and laughing with people they used to work with, introverts were finding their seats early and sticking to them.

'There.' Abi pointed to an oblong table near the stage at the front of the room. A woman and three men were trying to take their seats but kept being interrupted by guest after guest, desperate for a brush with greatness. 'They want to kiss the ring,' Abi said. 'I've already tasted it—it's bitter.'

Like Elle, Abi had attended a meeting with the Americans this morning. They were deeply unimpressed by the grenade she'd thrown into tonight's proceedings, and they had made it clear that if they could have disqualified her, they would have.

'But that wouldn't be very good optics for us at this point,' the woman, Patty Semple, had told Abi, knitting her eyebrows together in concern. 'So we're just going to let things play out. We would, however, appreciate you not setting off any more bombs.'

They're about to be disappointed, Abi had thought. But what she'd said was, 'So you're perfectly happy to have a lying sociopath as one of your guests of honour tonight?'

'That's the kind of unfortunate outburst we'd appreciate you keeping to yourself,' Patty had said. And that was the end of the conversation.

'Oh well, baby, at least we got to stay in a swanky hotel and kick off our farm boots,' Abi said to Grace.

'I like this new you,' said Grace, swirling her sequinned skirt. 'You seem lighter.'

Abi found their table on the seating plan. 'Samira's right, they're already here.'

***

'Oh my god, she *didn't*.' Elle saw the Parenting bloggers' table at the same moment that Abi sat down. And she saw that sitting in the seats previously reserved for her and Adrian were her sister, Zoe, and next to her, Cate.

'What?' Adrian followed Elle's line of sight. 'Jesus. What are they doing here?'

'Abi invited them, obviously. So much for not being at war.'

Samira was trying to steer Elle and Adrian to their new table. 'Is there something wrong?'

'Those people, at the Parenting table,' Elle hissed at her, 'how did they get tickets?'

'Oh, Abi asked me for a couple of extras late yesterday. I knew we were juggling the tables, so I said it was fine.'

Samira suddenly seemed panicked. 'Did you want extras? Oh, I should have asked you.'

'You are an idiot,' Elle said to Samira, who looked like she'd been slapped.

'Elle.' Adrian touched her arm. 'Come on, it's not her fault. Let's just sit—it's about to start.'

***

Mark was looking at the awards' program. 'So before we get to Parenting, we have to sit through Fashion, Tech, Beauty, Food...'

'Interiors, Travel, Health,' Grace added from where she sat, in between Abi and Leisel.

'So good to see you, Gracey,' Leisel said to Grace, squeezing her hand. 'You seem a lot happier than last time, despite the fact that your missus is—' and Leisel lowered her voice to a whisper '—a complete fire starter.'

'I know.' Grace smiled. 'She's fucking fearless.'

'Stop talking about me, I can hear you,' said Abi. 'Anyway, Leisel, I am almost 100 per cent certain that you are going to win this thing tonight, and you should meet some of the people who helped make that happen—'

'Oh, come on.' Leisel threw back a mouthful of champagne. 'I don't think we can assume anything.'

'Ha. I think we can. This is Zoe, she is Elle Campbell's sister, and my genius full-time content-producer-slash-social-media manager.'

'*Really*?' Leisel almost spat out her wine.

'Really. And this is Cate Bajkowski. Cate is a brilliant social media brain and is looking for a new gig. Any fabulous ideas?'

Leisel laughed. 'Far out, Abi, you are a piece of work. Let's talk, Cate.'

The girl beamed.

Zoe was looking nervous, as if she could feel the heat of Elle's fury from across the room.

'Don't worry, Zoe,' Mark offered. 'She'd have to leap about six tables to throttle you.'

'I bet she could,' Zoe said, glancing over at the door. 'Have you seen her glutes?'

***

For Adrian, the awards, once they started, seemed to go at an unbearably slow crawl. Plates were cleared, glasses were refilled, victory speeches were made, tables leapt up screaming, others groaned and plunged heads into hands. He and Elle had been put on a table with the Interior bloggers, and they all wanted to talk to his wife, to admire her jewellery, to shower her with compliments about the glass-and-white house.

To him, they just shot nervous, sympathetic glances and offered to refill his water glass before the waiter got there, just in case Adrian was too weak.

His eyes had only met Abi's once, and she'd made a thumb-and-little-finger phone gesture at him and mouthed 'Call your girls'. He'd looked away.

He knew Elle was seething, but she seemed remarkably serene on the surface, chatting about benchtop details and on-trend tiles.

And then, finally, it was time.

***

Shannon Smart was clapping the Best Travel Bloggers offstage and receiving a new set of envelopes. She was straightening her dress and stepping up to the microphone.

'The night's final award is one of the most highly contested of this whole campaign. Partly because Parenting is such a huge segment of the blogging market, and partly because of the—' Shannon paused, raised an eyebrow at the crowd '—colourful nature of many of the personalities involved. I don't think there's anyone here who doesn't know what I'm talking about, and believe me—' she paused again, for effect '—I have encountered some of this colour first-hand.'

'*Fuck you*,' muttered Abi. Grace squeezed her hand.

'But it's a serious business: the winner of tonight's Blog-ahh for Best Parenting Blog will receive a $500,000 cash injection, plus the chance to sit down this week with some of the world's biggest tech investors at the Blog-ahh conference and pitch their vision for taking their brands global.'

Leisel's hands were sweaty. Elle was straightening in her seat.

'The nominees for Best Parenting Blog of 2017, are Abi Black, The Green Diva...'

Abi's face appeared on the huge screen behind Shannon Smart's head and then broke into tiny pixels that rearranged themselves into a page from her blog, spinning away into nothingness.

'Seems about right,' Abi whispered to Grace.

'...Elle Campbell, The Stylish Mumma...'

Among the cheers were a few audible boos, mostly from Abi.

'...and Leisel Adams, The Working Mum.'

Mark stood up as he clapped for Leisel, her smiling photo dissolving into mini-Facebook Like symbols on the screen.

'I'm going to throw up,' she said, pulling on Mark's suit sleeve for him to sit down.

'And the winner is...' Shannon Smart seemed to open the envelope a millimetre at a time, pull the card out in slow motion, and look it over three times before she read the contents out loud. 'Elle Campbell, The Stylish Mumma!'

Hundreds of people breathed in at once. There was a tiny pause before the first few claps rang out, breaking into hoots, and then hundreds of mobile phones lit up as everyone took to Twitter at exactly the same time.

Adrian looked at Elle. She looked at him. She didn't seem even a little bit surprised, he thought—her mouth was pulled tight, but she was smiling. She stood up slowly, bending to kiss him on the head. 'I'm sorry, darling,' she whispered in his ear as she pushed back her chair. The Interior bloggers at the table were standing and clapping, stomping and whooping. He heard Abi shouting something in the background while he watched Elle walk slowly up to the stage. Every noise felt like a blow to his head.

'Sorry?' Adrian said, to no one.

Elle lifted her hem as she walked up the three steps to the microphone, where Shannon Smart was standing with the award: a great, big, glittering glass iPhone on a silver stand.

'Oh!' Elle took the award from Shannon, kissed her on the cheek. Shannon whispered something in her ear, and Elle turned to the mic. 'Oh,' she said again. 'I can't believe this.'

'NO ONE CAN BELIEVE THIS!' Abi yelled from her seat and was immediately shushed by an usher. Zoe was crying and getting out of her seat. Cate's head was in her hands. Leisel was laughing, Mark rubbing her back.

'I can't believe this,' Elle repeated, smiling, looking at the award in her hand. 'Because it's an extraordinary act of kindness, this decision.'

Then she stopped smiling. Her smooth face settled into as serious an expression as her fillers would allow, and she took a meaningful pause, gazing around the crowd and breathing through pursed lips in a way that suggested she was building up the courage for a revelation.

'There's something I need to tell you. It's something I told the wonderful Heads from Blog-ahh—Patty, Abe and Ivan— this morning, something that I was sure would mean there was no chance I would be lucky enough to stand up here tonight.'

Adrian began to feel dizzy. All eyes were turned in his direction. His vision was getting shimmery around the corners. He grabbed a glass of water, his hand shaking, and took a gulp.

'You might have heard,' Elle went on, 'you might have heard some rumours about my husband and me, these past few days. Anyone who follows The Stylish Mumma—and thank you, all of you—knows that these past couple of months have been extremely difficult. I have been helping my husband, Adrian, through cancer treatment.'

Is it possible for air to be heavy? thought Adrian. He undid his top button, pulling at his tie.

'Or, at least, I thought I was.'

This time, the collective gasp was more like a shriek. Elle paused, letting her words sink in.

'It's true, what you have read. My husband, Adrian Campbell, does not have cancer. He is perfectly well... physically, at least. These past couple of months, I too have been the victim of his conspiracy, as have my followers. As have—' Elle cast down her eyes '—my two little boys, who have been worrying about their daddy every day.'

Nothing was making sense to Adrian. What was she saying?

'You see, it has only become clear in these past few days that Adrian Campbell has been pretending to have an illness in order to win fame and influence—and to stop me from leaving him. Any woman who has found herself in an emotionally abusive marriage will understand that a desperate man will do anything to keep you under his control. Adrian's always been an ambitious, driven person, and I genuinely think that he believed this conspiracy was going to help him, and he didn't care who he hurt along the way.'

Adrian found himself standing up, knocking over his chair. 'It's not true,' he said quietly, and then louder, 'It's not true!'

But it was like being in a dream where you shouted at the top of your lungs and no one could hear you. An usher was suddenly taking his arm. The whole room was turned towards him, phones in the air, recording the whole thing. 'It's not true!' he yelled as another usher came, and the two men pulled him away from the table, towards the door.

'I want to thank the wonderful people from ATGT and the Blog-ahhs,' Elle was saying. 'They could easily have changed the outcome of tonight's awards under the circumstances, but they have decided to support me, to stick by me in this difficult moment. And I am so grateful they chose to do that. I know that my followers are, too.' Elle held her award up high, as actors do on televised award shows. 'This is for them. We will keep going, we will keep smiling. We will keep shining. Thank you all!'

The cheers were still deafening as Elle stepped back from the microphone and hugged a weepy Shannon Smart.

The crowd's applause and chatter drowned out Adrian's shouts from outside the auditorium. 'It's not true!'

***

For a glorious moment, Elle looked out on a room of approval and respect. She had won. The award was hers, the money was hers, the moment was hers. She had created this, and it was just the beginning.

But something was happening at the Blog-ahh table in the front, where the Heads whom Elle had met with ought to have been standing, beaming, applauding her win. They had been so full of understanding for a woman fooled by an ambitious man.

Now a uniformed man was bending over their table, talking to Patty Semple. The other Heads were on their phones.

The crowd's eyes had shifted from Elle—they were looking at the scurrying ushers, the flustered officials. They were turning to the doors at the back of the room.

Elle was still at the microphone, where seconds seemed to pass like minutes. None of this movement made any sense to her. Only this morning, she had explained to Patty that she was the victim here, not the villain, and the Heads had agreed to stick to their original decision. They had known the attention their decision would attract.

At the side of the stage, Samira, the young publicity assistant, was crying into her phone. 'What?' Elle said, to the room. 'What?'

All eyes shifted back to her. And suddenly, Patty was up and walking the few steps to the stage, a young woman by her side. Patty smiled as she approached Elle, a smile that didn't reach her eyes.

'What?' Elle asked again before instinctively stepping back, holding the award to her chest.

'I'm going to need to take that,' Patty said in a steady voice. She pulled the award from Elle with both hands. 'Elle, we have a problem here.'

As if the room had suddenly come into sharp focus, Elle saw clearly that the young woman with Patty was Zoe.

'What? What is it?' Elle shouted now. 'What's she doing?'

'This young woman has something to say.' Patty gave Zoe a gentle push towards the microphone. The babble of confusion seemed to pause.

'Hello.' Zoe's voice was quiet. 'My name is Zoe Wright, and I'm not a blogger. I don't belong here. I know this has been a crazy evening, everyone. But there's something I have just told the officials, something that I think is important for you all to know. And there's someone I need you to meet...' Zoe motioned to the back of the auditorium, and hundreds of head swivelled. 'Abi, could you bring them in?'

The back doors opened, and Abi ushered in a tall man who was pushing a wheelchair. In the chair was a frail, older man, wearing a suit, clean-shaven, with an uncertain expression. The man pushing the chair was familiar to Elle: he had a strong look about his face, familiar milky colouring, freckles across a flat nose.

'The older man is my dad,' Zoe said, as Abi walked with the two men over to their table, all eyes on them. 'And Elle Campbell's dad. His name is Bill Wright. Some of you might have seen my sister, Elle, on the television just a week ago, telling the world that she doesn't have a dad. That he died a few months ago. But that's not true. Our dad is alive. He is not well, he's fighting hard, but he is here.

'All of you lovely people who got all dressed up to come out here tonight, you need to know that this woman up here, Elle Campbell, is not a real person. She has created an avatar for you to follow, and that avatar is a liar. That monster lies and hurts other people as it takes what it wants. Elle Campbell has pretended that my father is dead, has pretended that her husband has cancer—and, right now, she is pretending to have earned that award. She has not.'

'Thank you, Zoe,' Patty said, putting a gentle hand on Zoe's arm and stepping in front of the mic. 'That's enough. I need to try to get tonight's proceedings back on track.'

An uneasy giggle went up around the room. Elle was still on stage. She was frozen, unable to look away from the man in wheelchair, who was smiling at the crowd, appearing for all the world like a proud father who hadn't got the joke.

Zoe, on her way offstage, said quietly to Elle, 'That's Liam. Our brother, remember? I don't think you've paid him anything.'

'I don't need to tell you that this is completely unprecedented,' Patty told the room. 'When the Blog-ahhs decided to have an event in Australia to honour your vibrant blogging community, we could never have imagined that it would be quite this—'

'Colourful,' Shannon Smart chipped in. She was back in host mode, taking the award from Patty.

'Thank you, Shannon, "colourful" is one word for it. But it seems, when it comes to this very important Parenting category, that we made a mistake. The Blog-ahhs stand for authenticity. As an organisation passionate about user influence, we do not, in any way, condone lying, bullying or cheating your way to more followers, engagement and glory.

Tonight, we got this wrong. And I hope we can go some way to putting it right before the night is over.'

Patty turned to where Elle was still standing and said, 'Goodnight, Mrs Campbell.' Two security guards appeared, one gently taking her arm.

Elle hadn't taken her eyes off her brother and her father since the doors opened—two terrible ghosts who had floated into her perfect moment. Her dad, she could see, was trying to make eye contact with her, all the way across the room. What could he possibly want to communicate to her?

The crowd cheered as she was guided offstage.

***

Over at the Parenting table, Leisel had her head buried in Mark's shoulder. 'This is remarkable,' he said to her. 'I had no idea it would be this exciting.'

'Oh, shut up,' she said. 'I can't watch that poor woman get walked out of here.'

'Poor woman?' Mark leant over to Liam and Bill Wright, extending a hand. 'Hello, fellas, quite an entrance there. Lovely to meet you.'

Liam reached out and shook Mark's hand. 'Pleasure,' he said simply, then went back to adjusting his dad's chair, pouring him a water.

Leisel looked at Abi. 'You really are remarkable,' she said. 'We so need to be friends.'

Abi smiled back. 'We're family, Leisel. More than friends.' In that moment, Abi was feeling so generous she even dashed off a text to her mother. *Tell the Doctor we're all on for dinner next week. And I mean all.*

'So, we are going to try to put this right,' Patty Semple announced. 'Tonight's award for excellence in Parenting blogging will go to the category's rightful runner-up, a woman whose frank writing has built a loyal army of followers who find solace and strength in her and one another. It has also put her in considerable danger, and if this award was for bravery as well as blogging, it would be totally appropriate.'

'Oh my god,' Leisel said, pulling at Mark's sleeve. 'I really am going to throw up.'

'No, Lee, you're going to win,' he said.

'It gives me great pleasure to present this award to Leisel Adams, champion of working mums everywhere. Leisel, up you come.'

The room erupted in applause one more time, foot-stamps and hollers and whooping rising from all corners, as Leisel stood and hugged Mark. She went to embrace her sister, but suddenly, in that crazy moment, Grace was gone. The only people left at their table were the Wrights, who were deep in conversation, and Cate, who smiled and gave her a double thumbs-up as she turned for the stage.

Up there, lights in her eyes, Leisel looked at the award and felt it heavy in her hand. She thought about the $500,000 prize. She thought about the text she would send to Zac in the morning: *Taking a break. Think you'll manage without me.*

She gazed out at a room of people who were all now heads-down, typing madly into their phones. And she said, 'I wasn't meant to win this tonight, I know that. The woman who everyone wanted to win was the one we all thought we wanted to be: the beautiful woman with the perfect house, the handsome husband, the photogenic kids.

'Most of us suspected that woman didn't exist. I'm not talking about Elle Campbell, I'm talking about the illusion of that perfect wife, mother, friend. She only exists on your Instagram feed, filtered and facetuned and hashtagged. We wanted her to win tonight, didn't we? Until we realised just how empty that image is.'

Leisel took a big breath. She looked at Shannon Smart—who seemed like she needed a good lie-down—and then out at the table, at Mark who was grinning at her.

'Influence is a currency we trade in now,' Leisel went on, finding the speech she'd allowed herself to recite in her head a hundred times. 'And influence is everything. We talk about the influences we want around our children, our workplaces, our planet. But in this world, we only care how much of it you've got, not what you do with it. So I...'

Here we go, thought Leisel, it's my Oprah moment.

'I want all of us to consider the kind of influence that counts. The kinds of opinions worth listening to. The stories that we share to lift us, not drive us to make dangerous decisions to hate ourselves, or hurt someone, or lie, or pretend we are someone we are not. From here on, let's focus on our real lives, not the illusions.

'So I'm dedicating this award to the people who raise my roof and mess up my table, and to the children who crowd our bed every fucking night.

'Thank you, I love you. Good night.'

The audience lifted their heads long enough to cheer.

***

The video of the moment Elle's dead dad was wheeled into the awards was already on YouTube. Fifty thousand views in four minutes.

Outside the auditorium, past the neon carpet, down the escalator and in the chilly night air, Abi, Grace and Adrian were sitting on a step under the close eye of security guards. Grace's head was on Abi's shoulder, Abi's hand was on Adrian's.

He looked like a shell of the man she'd lived with, married, raised kids with, divorced. He looked like a ghost.

'I can't believe I didn't see that coming,' he said, after a long time of saying nothing. 'I just can't believe that after everything, I thought I was the person she wouldn't throw under the bus.'

'Oh, shush,' said Abi, knocking him gently with her knee. 'What's so special about you?'

'Are you coming home with us?' Grace asked Adrian, who now looked as if he had just woken up from a very long sleep, groggy and disoriented. 'Abi and I think the girls would like that.'

'We've got a spare room,' Abi said. 'Zoe's in the shed, but there's still space for another one. The more the fucking merrier, really.'

'Yes,' Adrian said. 'Yes, I'd like that. While I work out —'

'What's next, I know,' Abi said. 'The boys need their dad.'

***

Five minutes away, Elle was walking across the Pyrmont Bridge. Her gown was whipping around her in the cold wind. The water was black underneath her. She was crying.

And she was typing into her phone.

> You won't be seeing me for a while, SMs. It's time for me to step away.
> You're going to be hearing a lot of stories about me in the next little while. Some of them will be true. Some of them won't. But never forget, SMs, bitter people will try to hold you back. Hold you down and keep you small. It doesn't matter where you come from, online you can be absolutely anyone. You can be as big as you want. You can be free of all that's weighing you down. You can get revenge on the people who've tried to stop you. Whatever you do, SMs, be bold.
> When you see me again, I will have evolved past these petty haters once more. There is no way they will beat me. Kiss my boys for me. I'll be back.
> No excuses.

Elle hit publish. And kept on walking.

Acknowledgements

This book would have stayed lodged in my head if it weren't for two women. One of them is my immensely talented colleague and friend Monique Bowley. Over cheap noodles in an uninspiring food court, I told her that I thought a story behind the women telling stories could be spun into something interesting. She told me to stop talking and to go home and write a synopsis. I did, because Monique is six-foot-two and scary when she's excited. Lucy Ormonde, who I spent almost three years working alongside and for whom I have enormous respect, was the one who convinced me it was more than an idea, but maybe a book that someone might want to publish and other people might want to read. To Lucy and Monz, the people who say women don't support other women just haven't met you yet.

Then there's my boss, Mia Freedman, who has been an extraordinary cheerleader for me during this process. These are cheesy words for a woman who loves words, but Mia inspires me — and many others — to be better, to push harder, to back myself. I hear her words in my head whenever I know I'm selling myself short.

The tribe of girlfriends who listened to my ideas, entertained my children, read drafts and told me straight all deserve thanks: Penny Kaleta (another constant inspiration),

Karen Graham, Miranda Herron, Angie McMenamin, Sally Godfrey, Mel Ware, Sam Marshall and Rebecca Rodwell. There's a man in there, my friend Mark Brandon, who told me to stop worrying about what others thought and just enjoy writing something people will enjoy reading. It's unlikely Mark remembers saying that, but he did.

To wise advisors: Jackie Lunn, Andrew Daddo, Caroline Overington, Rebecca Sparrow. To Jamila Rizvi who schooled me on how it feels to be at the centre of a social media storm and Elissa Ratliff who taught me the mysterious ways of small-town life.

To the clever and generous Mamamia team who allowed me the space to write this: Kylie Rogers, Bec Jacobs, Gemma Garkut, Laura Brodnik, Briony Benjamin and again, Monique — all of their work lives were made a little bit harder in the process. Thank you.

Thank you to Claire Kingston, my publisher at Allen & Unwin, who understood this book immediately. And to Kate Goldsworthy, who edited it, and was the first person who'd never met me to read it. Thank you for your enthusiasm, and for your deep hatred of Elle. I'm sure the feeling's mutual.

And to my family. My parents Jeff and Judith Wainwright travelled across the world and took on extra grandparent duties so I could spend last Summer writing. I don't tell them often enough how jammy I am to always have their support at my back. Same for my brother Tom, his partner Emilie and their kids Lila, Louie, Poppy and Henry. I can feel them willing us on all the way from Manchester. And to my beloved Lindsay Frankel, the funniest person on the planet and the one I've been making up stories with since we were 11.

And so to my small people, Matilda and Billy. They will never read this book because it has lots of rude words in it, so they'll just have to trust me when I tell them that it was worth all those afternoons I couldn't play with them, pick them up from somewhere or, you know, feed them. Lucky for M&B, there's Brent McKean, who is every inch the capable parent.

Without Brent, nothing works. At home, in my head or in our lives. I love you.

And lastly to the parents who do share their lives online: It's a gift. There was a time when mothers had to shut up and smile. Now, telling the stories that allow other women to feel just a little more normal, more connected and understood is no small thing. 'Mummy bloggers' or not, the lives of countless women around the world are little less isolating because of you.

Thank you.

Holly Wainwright

If you enjoyed what you read, don't keep it a secret.

Review the book online and tell anyone who will listen.

Thanks for your support spreading the word about Legend Press!

Follow us on Twitter
@legend_press

Follow us on Instagram
@legendpress